T0012621

BY MADELEINE ROUX

Allison Hewitt Is Trapped

Sadie Walker Is Stranded

Salvaged

Reclaimed

The Book of Living Secrets

The Proposition

Dungeons & Dragons: Dungeon Academy: No Humans Allowed!

World of Warcraft: Shadowlands: Shadows Rising

Critical Role: The Mighty Nein: The Nine Eyes of Lucien

THE HOUSE OF FURIES

House of Furies

Court of Shadows

Tomb of Ancients

ASYLUM

Asylum

The Scarlets

Sanctum

The Bone Artists

Catacomb

The Warden

Escape from Asylum

THE MIGHTY NEIN
THE NINE EYES
OF LUCIEN

THE MIGHTY NEIN

THE NINE EYES OF LUCIEN

MADELEINE ROUX

RANDOM HOUSE WORLDS
NEW YORK

Critical Role: The Mighty Nein—The Nine Eyes of Lucien
is a work of fiction. Names, places, characters, and incidents either
are the product of the author's imagination or are used fictitiously.
Any resemblance to actual persons, living or dead, events,
or locales is entirely coincidental.

2023 Random House Worlds Trade Paperback Edition

Published in the United States by Random House Worlds,
an imprint of Random House, a division of
Penguin Random House LLC, New York.

RANDOM HOUSE is a registered trademark, and
RANDOM HOUSE WORLDS and colophon are trademarks of
Penguin Random House LLC.

Originally published in hardcover in the United States
by Del Rey, an imprint of Random House, a division of
Penguin Random House LLC, in 2022.

LIBRARY OF CONGRESS CATALOGING-IN-PUBLICATION DATA
Names: Roux, Madeleine, author.
Title: The Mighty Nein : the nine eyes of Lucien / Madeleine Roux.
Other titles: Nine eyes of Lucien | Critical role (Television program)
Description: New York: Del Rey, 2022 | Series: Critical role
Identifiers: LCCN 2022040014 (print) | LCCN 2022040015 (ebook) |
ISBN 9780593496732 (hardcover; acid-free paper) |
ISBN 9780593496749 (ebook)
Subjects: LCGFT: Fantasy fiction. | Novels.
Classification: LCC PS3618.O87235 M54 2022 (print) |
LCC PS3618.O87235 (ebook) | DDC 813/.6—dc23/eng/20220919
LC record available at https://lccn.loc.gov/2022040014
LC ebook record available at https://lccn.loc.gov/2022040015

Trade paperback ISBN 978-0-593-49675-6

Printed in the United States of America on acid-free paper

randomhousebooks.com

2 4 6 8 9 7 5 3

Book design by Alexis Capitini

For Trevor,
who took the journey with me,
Gods help him.

There is no more wisdom in order than in chaos.
—Unknown

THE MIGHTY NEIN
THE NINE EYES
OF LUCIEN

CHAPTER 1

Shadycreek Run
822 PD

Lucien shoved open the cellar door and tumbled out into the sunlight. His stomach gurgled a desperate tune (priority one) and as he lifted his arms to stretch, he noted how light his pockets felt (priority two). Some enterprising so-and-so had left a twig crossed over a thistle in the dirt just outside the stone lip of the cellar. Crouching for a better look, Lucien discovered ten slapdash marks under the twig and thistle. Ten coppers. To a boy of twelve squatting in a cave-cold cellar belonging to a retired madame, that was a lot of coin.

Priorities one and two, he smirked, were quickly getting sorted.

These little signs appeared outside the door from time to time, and only when someone on Clover Street had a job for an itinerant, broke, morally unbothered freelancer. Check, check, and check. Lucien swept up the pile of rubbish, inspected it, and discovered the stick had been dipped in mauve paint. That meant someone from the Mardoons was offering the work, and they tended to be good for whatever coin was promised. A beggar couldn't be a chooser in Shadycreek Run, so Lucien stuffed the twig and thistle in his pocket and locked the cellar door behind him. He didn't pocket the key, but instead tossed it to himself idly and whistled a made-up song while he swung around to the front side of the townhouse.

Viewed from the street proper, Auntie Mama's two-story shack listed drunkenly to the right, nearly leaning on the shoulder of the also precariously crooked building beside it. Auntie Mama's place always reminded him of a teakettle—squat, tapered toward the "foundation," and with a single tower that jutted out to the east like a spigot. Jammed between two swillholes of competingly ill repute, the stoop smelled alternately of piss and vomit.

A stiff, threatening wind blew down the lane, rattling the entire ramshackle block. That gust ran straight through Lucien's threadbare coat, slicing like a cutpurse's knife.

Auntie Mama was outside the door, not waiting for him, but sweeping a few stray leaves into a corner where the detritus would accumulate, a mushy bed for whatever wandering stray dog favored her that day. She named the mutts after jewels—Jet, Emerald, Diamond—never remembering which dog was which, but jangling her beringed fingers through the mangy, flea-ridden fur of the strays as if they were the king's own spaniels. The sun was well out, but the collective Shadycreek hangover meant only a handful of productive citizens wandered around—a half-elf baker dusted in flour, a pair of working girls half asleep on their feet after an all-night shift, a knock-kneed dwarf leaning against the back door of a tavern, pipe in one hand, chewed turkey leg in the other, the smell of which started an agonizing call-and-response between the food and Lucien's ravenous stomach.

He hung from the porch banister and sighed, watching the turkey disappear down the lane, waiting for Auntie Mama to notice him. It didn't take long. He felt her broom poke at his behind and he spun, laughing.

"Another mutt darkens my door," she mumbled. A skinny, aimless orphan was no rare sight in the Run, though Lucien's combination of lavender skin, crimson eyes, curling horns, and deep-purple hair was indeed striking. To Lucien's young eyes, Auntie Mama seemed impossibly old, which meant she had lived around fifty summers. *If I live to be that old,* he often thought, *I'll be cramming my face with cold fruit in a hot bath, not raking leaves for strays.* It was an easy thought to think, and it comforted him. Auntie Mama was a comfort in her own way, one of the only recurring roles in the rotating cast of characters that paraded through Lucien's days.

"No breakfast today, mutt," Auntie Mama added. Her voice rattled out, hoarse from decades of the pipe. "My girl's coming to town. You need to find a new place to stay."

"You're breaking my heart," Lucien murmured, dragging down his lip into an exaggerated pout. He relinquished the key to her cellar with a dramatic bow. "Not even a crumb for your favorite?"

Auntie Mama's face was hardly more than a pile of increasingly wide wrinkles, a few spikes of eyebrow and chin hair, and rouged lips, but she could still pull a cheeky smile.

"Favorite! Ha! Favorite . . ." She muttered something unintelligible and puttered back toward the door. Every morning she wore the same layers of brown-and-green housecoat, belted, and floppy felt slippers that ended in points. Her graying human hair was full of bits of rags to make curls. When Auntie Mama opened the door to the house, the scent of stale perfume and last night's roast rushed out.

"Favorites. Favorites will get you nowhere. 'Sides Brevyn. Oh, Brevyn, wasting away in the valley. Poor, poor Brevyn . . ."

Lucien settled back against the banister, waiting. He knew that if he just hung around long enough, Auntie Mama would cave and toss him a crust of bread or a bit of cheese and roll. It had been like this ever since she first found him hiding in her cellar. She had forgotten to lock it up one night, and a sudden northern blizzard had forced a desperate Lucien to grab whatever shelter he could find. His nightmares had given him away. Through the floors she heard him screaming in his sleep, and discovered him curled up in the cellar, skin and bone, shivering so violently he could have been seizing.

Auntie Mama had done nothing to address the mold in the cellar that ran thick and furred as carpets around the edges of the stonework, but she had brought him a mug of rose tea and a few tatty blankets, and barked out a cold, *This better not be an every-night sort of arrangement.* Then she'd hobbled away, and that was Shadycreek kindness.

Over time, Lucien realized that if he made himself scarce, didn't overstay his welcome, and occasionally ran errands for the old woman, she would allow him to use the cellar whenever the weather turned nasty. She even allowed him the key sometimes. They never spoke overmuch, and Lucien didn't know a thing about her beyond what he could glean from the rumors around town and the portraits hanging in her front room. Many of those battered frames were empty, but one held a round, pink face, bright with promise. Brevyn, he decided, her daughter. The favorite.

"Psst."

Lucien wasn't startled by much, but Cree Deeproots had a way of sneaking up on him. The catfolk's yellow eyes sparkled with mischief, which was a bad sign if you were rich and a good sign if you were Lucien. Cree's black fur was shining that morning, as it normally was, though her paws and face were somewhat mussed. She wore a well-used leather duster with the sleeves rolled up, and a knitted shawl that matched her eyes was bundled around her neck. They were the same age, though Cree had started her life on the streets a few years before Lucien had.

"Fair morning to ye, Cree," Lucien said, bowing. Cree merely rolled her shining eyes. Her expression changed, however, the moment he pulled the thistle and twig out of his pocket. "Shall we take a jaunt over to the Thirsty Grotto this morning? Looks like there's work to be done."

"How many hash marks?" she asked, ears twitching.

"Ten."

"Not enough to tempt me," Cree said with a shrug. Lucien was about to point out that they could hardly afford to turn their noses up at ten coppers when the sly girl thrust out her hand, revealing her palm and the acorn, flecked with gold dust, within. Lucien felt his own eyes grow wide.

"I'll be damned," he whispered. He wetted his lips, hungry in a different way. "Where'd you find that, then?"

"Champ slipped it into my pocket last night at the Lady."

The haze of greed that had descended at the sight of the acorn briefly lifted. By *the Lady,* Cree in fact meant the Landlocked Lady, a popular brothel in the Run that was fine, expensive, and not particularly amenable to street orphans.

"What the blazes were you doing there?" Lucien asked, tearing his eyes away from the acorn.

"Picking pockets," Cree answered lightly. "Champ said a few regulars were stiffing on their bills, wanted me to make sure they were paid in full, as it were."

"Cushy gig."

"Bathe more often and he might let you have a chance at it," Cree told him in a purr.

It was Lucien's turn to roll his eyes. "Well, Your Highness, why come to me if you've struck it rich? That job will set you up for the year."

An acorn like that paid an entire gold coin. Lucien shifted uneasily. The pay was always commensurate with the danger, and he had never tackled anything that offered more than a handful of coppers, a silver at the most. But even as the scant purple hairs on his neck prickled with consequence, he felt an answering pang from his gut. Auntie Mama's kindness could end any day, and then where would he be? His toes seemed to stay in a state of semipermanent frostbite, always tingling, always warning of one night too many stuck in the cold. There was a time in his childhood when he knew the dignity of warmth, family, home— and while the taste of it lingered bitter in his mouth, it was at least a taste of *something.*

He heard the woman's puttering steps returning from the bowels of the dilapidated house, bringing with her another gust of perfumed wind and incoherent mumbling.

"All I can spare today, child, with my girl arriving so soon," said Auntie Mama. When Lucien turned to face her, her trembling hand offered a pale scone, crumbling before his eyes like some ancient relic.

"Cheers," he replied, slapping on a smile.

"If you're coming with, half of that is mine," added Cree, reaching for the scone as soon as it was in Lucien's grasp.

"Eh? Shoo! Off you go, shoo!" Auntie Mama grabbed her broom, wagging it at the pair. Within the townhouse, a raucous chorus of barking and snarling began, Auntie Mama's legion of tiny dogs sensing their master's distress. "Stay out of mischief, child! And be back before sunset, or there will be no key for you."

"Not a cat person, as it turns out." Lucien chuckled, bouncing down the stairs, Cree already several steps ahead. Auntie Mama hurled a few more warnings after him, but he didn't heed them.

The barking went on and on until they were well down the lane. "I hate when you're rude," replied Cree. "It suits you too well."

"Oh now, I can be charming." Lucien snapped the meager breakfast in half and gave Cree her share.

At that, she grinned, and licked a bit of scone from her fingers. "Charming like the grippe."

"Can your folk come down with that?"

"Well, you're here with me, so."

Lucien snorted, finishing his piece of the sandy, stale scone in two big bites. He couldn't be flapped, which Cree knew from only their short acquaintance. It was why he enjoyed passing his time and working jobs with her so much. Other Shadycreek kids had an ego, but not Cree. She could banter and bullshit with the best of them, but keep her trap shut, too, when the need arose. Lucien was less successful at biting his tongue, and begrudged that he was quicker, slyer, and better looking than the tight-fisted Mardoon thugs doling out errands. He couldn't stand their dead-eyed, condescending looks, or the way they constantly smirked at the urchins begging them for scraps.

Cree seemed to have no such compunctions. He wouldn't call her shameless, exactly, but everything rolled off her in an effortless way he admired and somewhat coveted.

"Why me?" Lucien suddenly asked.

"Why you what, hell-squirt?"

"Why bring me in on this?" He nodded toward the acorn, which Cree swiftly stuffed in the pocket of her leather coat. She was leading them, he noted, away from the square and toward the outskirts that bled into the thickly treed, thickly cursed Savalirwood.

"Why go halfsies on such a big opportunity?"

"Sixty–forty," Cree corrected, eyes trained on the road ahead.

"Right. Whatever. Still?"

Cree's narrow shoulders bunched into a troubled shrug. She paused, the dense shadow of the forest draping over them like a bracing nighttime fog. Her yellow eyes swept the tree line before she glanced up at the taller Lucien. "For one, I don't have the skills for the job."

"And second?"

Cree hesitated, "Because you have the glint, and I was taught that if you stumble upon a fellow with the glint, you follow and follow close. Wherever they go, fate comes fast on their heels."

CHAPTER 2

"Explain this . . . glint."

Cree dashed, almost sheepishly, ahead of him and into the Savalirwood. She followed a narrow dirt path that began between two ominously silent, identical shacks and then, several yards into the forest proper, forked. They traveled the left-leading tine, and the ashen purple trees, twisted and strangely plump, grew closer and closer, crowding the path. It was clear to Lucien that Cree knew exactly where she was headed, and that whatever information was necessary for this job had already been acquired.

For now, he wanted to know what this mysterious power was that Cree saw in him.

"Not all can see the glint," Cree told him, quietly, glancing from side to side as if the very trees were eavesdropping. She always spoke in a purring, low voice, but now she wouldn't go above a whisper. The sun vanished the moment the canopy enveloped them. It was impossible to tell if an actual storm was moving in or if the forest had simply swallowed them whole. He peered between branches and bunches of bruise-colored leaves, finding that a low, steely sky and mist had descended, winter's cold omens. "But in my family, we can. Comes from my mother's side. She could always see a light around folk, a shine that meant they were different."

"How do you mean 'different'?" Lucien asked. He, too, kept his voice down.

"It's just as likely to be a blessing as a curse, but . . ." Cree trailed off, searching for something in the recesses of memory. "How did Mother put it? Yes. *Yes*. Bristling with destiny. Ravens collect shiny things, right?"

"So I've been told."

Cree nodded sagely. "And it is said that the Matron of Ravens herself will notice a glimmer, a glint." She made an odd gesture with her hand, a sign of warding, perhaps. "Yes, the Matron will notice a shimmer."

Bristling with destiny. That was true. Cree couldn't know it, but in Lucien's heart it was true. He fished around in his own mind for what to share and what to keep close. The benefit of running wild on the streets of Shadycreek Run meant owing loyalty to nothing and no one.

Lucien bargained with himself while following the dark-furred cat-folk deeper into the twisting snarl of the wood.

"You could be right," he finally murmured.

"I know I am," Cree replied. "But go on."

He chewed his lip and thrust his hands into his pockets, finding the trusty hole in the left one and worrying it with his thumb. "It might be I have a sister, Aldreda. She went off on her own and found a life for herself in Rexxentrum. She still sends word now and then, and one day she's coming back for me. She'll be swimming in gold. I know it, I feel it. She wasn't born that beautiful for nothing."

Her letters always began, "My sweet brother." Lucien didn't know if he felt sweet, but he had always endeavored to protect Aldreda, whose aimless, dreamy nature (the foreordination of the youngest sibling and only daughter) often left her at the mercy of others. The others, in this case, had been their parents. Lucien had done what he could to shield Aldreda and himself, and it was a point of pride for him that his younger sister had escaped the cutthroat speed of the Run for a better life out west. They were only a year apart, but she always seemed so much younger. He could still remember her huge, round, red eyes as she waved goodbye, sitting off the back of a merchant's wagon, the last of their money sewn into the waistband of her skirt. The silk merchants that agreed to take her had promised she would find work in a manor house quickly, and it would only be a matter of time before she caught the eye of some rich, young nobleman in need of a pretty mistress or wife.

They had both chosen a hard way. But Lucien never doubted her. He couldn't. So, it didn't surprise him when her letters trickled in, confirming that she was cleaning house for a jeweler in Rexxentrum. The hours were long and tedious, but she had a roof over her head.

"When the time is right," Lucien added confidently. "Aldreda will send for me. I just have to keep my head down, stay alive, and be patient."

"For how long?"

"However long it takes, Cree."

"Waiting doesn't seem your style," Cree pointed out. "Why not make your own fortune and join her?"

"I might just do that, eh? With you and this glint of mine, I might just do it."

Cree turned to him and frowned. They had reached another fork, this one deep enough in the forest that it felt like they had walked into a cold, dank cave. "It can be a blessing *or* a curse, mind."

"With this face?" Lucien threw back his head and laughed. "It's quite obviously a blessing."

"This way," Cree said, pointing and ignoring him. "Not far now."

"What does this job entail anyway?"

"Champ had it from Seneca who had it from Rufus Mardoon himself," said Cree, who paused a moment before choosing a path this time. She moved as if a pack of corrupted wolves nipped at her heels, racing with ears back and head down along the narrowing path. A passel of crows landed above them on a swooping branch, nine pairs of ink-black eyes marking their progress. Cree made the same strange gesture as before, a quick fluttering of her hand over her heart, her thumb and forefinger pinched together, then began to walk even faster. "Bunch of hired Jagentoth muscle ambushed a caravan—"

"Let me guess, it was a caravan belonging to Rufus Mardoon?"

"Got it in one. Lord Anselm Mardoon already sent some boys hunting, and they turned up every member of the crew that did it, but Lady Sulia had all their tongues ripped out. They were useless. All but one."

"Shit," Lucien muttered. He didn't like the way that "all but one" dangled in the air between them.

"Jagentoth justice," Cree said. "One poor bastard escaped with her tongue intact, but she might as well have swallowed it for all the good it's doing her. Mardoon wants to know where his things are, and we're to extract that information." She hesitated, then pulled back her shoulders, seeming to drown in the fabric of the oversized coat. "I might have . . .

oversold our experience. A bit. Somewhat. But we can do it, right? We can do it."

Lucien almost blurted out a confused, *Us?* but kept it to himself. *Yes, us. Why not us?* He might by facts alone be a boy, but in truth there were no children on the streets of Shadycreek Run. Innocence was a luxury afforded to none, and so came these rare opportunities—and the coin and stink that came with them, even if his belly felt a little wobbly at the thought. The crows above cawed after them, and Lucien chose to take it as a rallying cry.

Onward, onward, onward. And why not? According to Cree, he had the glint, and as she suggested, perhaps it was his time to start making something of himself, lest the burden of riches and greatness fall all on the shoulders of his younger sister. But pressing onward in the Savalir-wood was easier thought than accomplished; only a fool ventured deeper than necessary. The northern reaches of Shadycreek Run bled into the forest, keeping those shallow pockets relatively safe for travelers, but the mitigating effect of civilization only went so far, and Lucien felt a steady, dark encroachment as they walked. He felt hunched and hunted, aware now of every creak of wood, sigh of wind, and birdcall. A whistling, strangled squawk sounded from down the path, and then another. Lucien glanced over his shoulder, but there was little more to see than shadows.

He had not ventured this deep into the Savalirwood for a long while, and he shuddered at the memories.

Cree pointed to an almost invisible marker along the path, a series of stone cairns stacked with intention, three piles of three.

"Should be the next bend," she murmured.

"Good," Lucien replied. "I'd rather not go any deeper."

The gurgling pained bird noise came again, this time much closer, then the forest fell abruptly silent. Lucien liked that less. He wondered if other forests in other places felt like this: alive, but not because of an abundance of animals and plants, but because something ancient and knowing and indescribable ran through root and leaf. The pungent smell of rot and wet settled over everything, and it would gradually infiltrate the body, breathed in, working on a person from the inside out.

Lucien shook his head and pulled his thin coat tighter across his chest.

Fortunately, as Cree promised, they took a hard right turn around a cluster of squat, dense trees and nearly stumbled over a body. The young dwarf woman was bound at the ankles and arms with rope, her hands behind her back and shackled. A chain hung from her manacles, looped several times around a sturdy tree and locked in place. She must have been left in the forest for a day or more, caked in dirt and leaves, her eyes huge and hungry. The prisoner went still at the sight of them, huddling behind a trunk.

"Water," she wheezed. Her brown skin was cracked and dry, black braids hanging lank and limp over her shoulders. Her dark-navy leathers and fur-lined cloak struck Lucien as oddly flash for a mere bandit. "Please . . . water . . ."

"Oh, we can discuss water, food, freedom, all manner of things," Cree told her gently, crouching. The woman shied away. "After you talk."

"W-Waste of time," the dwarf stammered, coughing. She tried to spit but couldn't muster the moisture.

"I don't want to hurt you," said Cree.

"Yes, you do."

Cree sighed and glanced up at Lucien. "We just want to know where you hid the coffer. Those things don't belong to you, mm? Just tell us, Danya. That is your name, yes? Danya?"

The captive glanced away from them with her jaw firmly set.

"Maybe you should stay out here a few more days," Cree muttered. "That will soften you up."

"I won't be out here another hour," she bit back, defiant. "And you'll be dead."

Chuckling and snorting, Cree stood, nudging Lucien in the ribs. "Hear that? This useless sack of potatoes is going to kill us! Are you quaking in your boots yet?"

"Shut up." Lucien sliced his hand through the air, aware of a distant rushing growing closer. Bushes rattling. Leaves fluttering. Boots. Too many boots pounding the dirt path, and the softest clank of metal on metal, the sound of chain mail jangling as soldiers ran.

Cree heard it, too, her ears flattening against her skull as she took Lucien by the forearm and yanked him toward the opposite side of the road and into the cover of brush. The curious birdsong ripped through the forest again, and the woman on the ground answered it, mimicking the call.

"Too many of them," Cree breathed, already springing to her feet and hurling herself into the shadows. But the road behind them was filling up with bodies and Lucien heard the dwarf laughing at their expense.

"Just there, they dove into the trees," she was telling her rescuers.

"Cooked," Cree called to him frantically. "We're cooked!"

And they were if they didn't act quickly. Two scrawny street kids wouldn't last long against half a dozen armed smugglers hell-bent on revenging their tongueless and captive compatriots. An idea, birthed from pure desperation, gripped him, and though sense and reason rebelled, wild panic took hold. Catching up to Cree, he spoke between gasps for breath, directing her north, farther into the untamed snarl of the Savalirwood.

"I know somewhere we can go, somewhere they would be fools to follow."

CHAPTER 3

Lucien knew he had taken them in the "right" direction when the ground beneath their feet became pocked with inky-black mushrooms. It was "right" in that it was the place Lucien had decided to take them, but it was not the sort of place anyone thinking clearly would want to go. He heard Cree's breathing grow more ragged as they continued their brutal pace, dodging tree and bush and boulder.

No matter how fast they ran, the bandits behind them gained.

"Where . . ." Cree managed to say. "How much farther?"

Lucien himself couldn't say until he saw the trees thinning ahead, and then came the soft trickle of water, hints that they were approaching the clearing. Gentler, sweeter birdsong and that babbling, running water promised an oasis, but Lucien knew better.

"Not out in the open," Cree cried, following anyway. "Shit! *Shit*, they'll see us . . ."

"Trust me," Lucien replied.

This was an unbelievably stupid idea, he realized, but now they were too close to reasonably turn back. He had cast this die; it was already rolling. The mushrooms sprang back under their feet, completely overtaking the moss and grass. Every broken cap released an oddly sweet scent into the air, cloying and seductive as a noblewoman's smear of ambergris. They broke through the wood and into the clearing, where a dark-red cottage sat perfectly centered in the open, ringed by a narrow waterway that disappeared north into the Savalirwood.

There was no time to explain why or how Lucien knew of the cottage's location, and he was not convinced he would want to give Cree an explanation. He might have to, eventually, but only after they survived this ambush.

Part of him hoped the cottage would be empty. Discovering that the witch had vanished and the place had been deserted might prove a pleasant enough final thought as the bandits slit their throats. But a mocking little voice in his head told him that was pure fantasy. Whoever the witch was, she was as vital to the forest as sap and sunlight. The woods sprouted, began, and then she was there—that was how he had always seen it in his mind.

They leapt the brook and Lucien hurried to the door. He felt a ripple of disgust pull at his stomach as he lifted his hand to knock. The bandits would know where they were hiding, but that suited Lucien just fine. What did not suit him was the flood of memories that threatened to leave him sprawled in the dirt.

The door handle, just as he remembered, was shaped like a stretched, smiling face.

His knuckles had barely grazed the wood when the door snapped open, and his knees nearly buckled as her face emerged from the cool, crisp darkness of the house.

"What an unexpected surprise," said the woman. She had not aged a single day since Lucien had seen her years ago. She stood a head taller than them both, agelessly beautiful, with a prominent, refined nose and a long, graceful neck. Her icy-blond ringlets were gathered up around the crown of her head, circling the gray horns that swept back from her forehead. *Wolfsbane is lovely to behold, too,* he thought. Cree's head snapped back and forth between her and the way they had come, back and forth, as she no doubt counted the seconds until they were caught. If the witch sensed their obvious urgency, she did not show it. "Normally I only greet visitors who have an appointment. But for *you*"—her fiercely blue eyes brightened as she looked at Lucien—"I could be moved to make a rare exception."

Peace. Calm. The witch exuded a natural serenity, from her smooth folded hands to the open, casual tilt of her hips. She wore a beaded black robe, the only ornament upon her a large and attention-grabbing amulet that hung low on her chest. It was shaped like a wide face, gold, with two exaggerated silver needles stabbed diagonally through the head.

"I . . ." Lucien struggled for the right words. He wanted to run or vomit, he couldn't decide. He settled for a mush of words that made his already warm cheeks blossom with heat. "Please let us in, Azrahari. We're being hunted and I, well, I could think of nowhere else to go in the forest."

"I'm not surprised you remembered the way."

"*Please,*" Lucien pleaded, then softer: "You owe me."

Her plumed eyelashes fluttered. She seemed almost . . . offended. "Why, of course you can come in, dear child. What do I call your friend?"

"Nothing," Lucien replied quickly, before Cree could speak. "You don't need to know her name."

"A touch rude, but I'll allow it. Make yourselves at home."

We won't do that, either.

The witch Azrahari stepped gracefully to the side, though not so far away that she didn't crowd them as they crossed the threshold. Intentional, of course; everything she did was intentional. Lucien pinned his eyes to the clean, swept floor and the single black, crocheted rug in the middle of the room. No sunlight penetrated the curtains, but a smoky glow emanated from a firepit. A grate over that pit held a collection of iron tools—shears, a hammer, tongs, and a collection of unsettlingly large needles. An image of her amulet flashed in front of his eyes.

None of it had changed, not the witch and not her environs. It was all how he remembered, and Lucien swiftly dragged Cree to one of the windows, where they knelt. His stomach lurched. It felt as if he had tilted headlong into a memory, plunging from present to past. He remembered the exact temperature of the cottage, the hickory tang to the woodsmoke, the medicinal scent of bark tannin, the eerie quiet punctuated by an occasional, jarring pop from the fire . . .

Azrahari remained at the door, given no chance to close it before the clearing was full. The bandits had brought Danya along, and she slurped greedily from a waterskin at the back of the pack while a collection of half-elves, humans, and dwarves sidled up to the front door of the cottage, dressed head-to-foot in red leather and bits of black fur.

"Look at their cloaks. The leathers. They're from The Red Debt," Lucien whispered. His mouth had gone sandy dry.

Cree shifted nervously. "Lucien, she's but one woman . . ."

"No. She's nothing like that."

"But if she sells us out . . ."

Lucien did not know what the witch was or where her allegiances lay, yet he felt confident she could not only survive far more than a handful of mercenaries, but would protect him. *She owes me that much.*

If she did fall or turn them over, though, no merciful fate awaited them. It was known in the Run that The Red Debt were not-so-discreetly funded by the Jagentoths, their coffers dripping in wealth, their hands dripping with blood. They had no qualms with public executions, and while their revenge was not elaborate or poetic, it trended toward final. Two complete nobodies like Cree and Lucien would be an afterthought, two tallies at the bottom of the daily death column. It was best one kept up with the ever-shifting rivalries, loyalties, and squabbles of the families controlling the Run, lest one find oneself on the wrong side of a feud. Lucien kept his distance from the Jagentoths, preferring the marginally more civilized methods of the Mardoons, who, when squinted at over a great distance, could almost seem enlightened.

But these were The Red Debt. They collected. Cree and Lucien would be stripped to their bones and tossed in a ditch if Lucien had miscalculated.

"A pair of guests and a gaggle of strangers on my doorstep," the witch purred. "What a lively day, and me unprepared, with nary a teacake in the oven."

"*Lucien,*" Cree hissed, warning. He noticed her craning her neck, searching for another exit.

"Hush up," he replied, pulling her back below the windowsill. "And keep your eyes down."

"I'll look where I please."

"There are things here you do not want to see," Lucien promised her. "Trust me."

"Why should I? You've led us straight into a trap."

Lucien took her by the wrist and squeezed. Cree stilled, and they both listened to the half dozen Red Debt thugs outside shifting and creaking in their splattered scarlet leathers. Carefully, gradually, Lucien inched back up to look through the barely open curtain, giving them a limited view of their pursuers on the stoop.

"Those two guests." One of the mercenaries grunted, a tall, bearded human with a vast, daring array of facial piercings. "We'll be having them now. Hand them over, peaceful-like, and we won't trouble you a jot longer, miss."

"Manners, how quaint." Azrahari stared, unruffled. "I'm afraid that what is within my house is mine. You will leave, I think, and take nothing but your lives with you. Consider this my generosity."

The man showed her a sparkling-sharp kukri lashed to his belt. "No, you see, that don't work for me. I'm a taker by nature, miss, a *collector,* and I don't fancy leaving here empty-handed. I'm not prone to generosity, never have been, so I'll take your life as well if that's what's required."

"What an unfortunate impasse we've arrived at," she said, puffing out a lavish sigh. "Before you resort to murder and mayhem, may I offer a bribe?"

The bearded mercenary snorted. "You can certainly try."

"Well, splendid. Then if you will just feast your eyes on this amulet of mine. Yes, very good, take a long, hard look at it. Consider its worth. Silver and gold. Consider the price it might fetch. Look. Look *harder.*" The witch Azrahari lifted the necklace for them, cradling it with both palms.

It was a magnificent piece, weighty, nearly spanning both of her hands, with the roughness and patina of a true relic.

"Wait—" Danya tried to intervene, but the mercenaries had already gathered closer for a glimpse at the witch's amulet.

Lucien assumed she might hypnotize the mercenaries, stun them, allow Cree and Lucien a chance to slip out a window unnoticed for a head start. But it was nothing so simple or so innocent. Instead, the instant she had their attention on the necklace, she whispered a single, guttural word that Lucien had never heard before, though his attention quickly snapped from the strange sound to its immediate effect. The Red Debt fools who had taken that good, long look at the amulet went still, and then shivered. Lucien watched as the bearded one's mouth fell wide open, releasing a strangled groan, and then his clothes and skin dropped to the ground, empty. Whatever bones, guts, and spirits had been within the six killers vanished, leaving nothing but loose, deflated piles of flesh, cloaks, leather, and armor.

Danya froze in place, gaping in horror before twisting, falling, and losing the meager contents of her stomach all over the nearest patch of bushes.

Cree shot to her feet, backing away from the window. She covered her mouth with both hands, eyes reeling. Slowly, Lucien stood, sick, reaching for Cree. But it was too late. She had spun, and looked, and beheld the dark recesses of the cottage. She had noticed the high shelves running along every wall, and along those shelves the many puppets sitting propped up, lifeless now but not always so. They were too realistic, too ghoulish, to be stitched from yarn and fabric and beads.

"What is this place?" Cree whispered, flashing fangs as she tried and failed to tear her eyes away from the rows and rows of large, still puppets.

Lucien was given no chance to answer. The witch swept back inside the cottage, dragging a limp and bleary-eyed Danya with her. She tossed the girl on the floor and stood over her, smirking, stroking the top edge of her amulet with one thumb.

"Bracing, I know," Azrahari cooed. "The hollowing is not for the faint of heart."

"Tell us," Lucien said, moving on shaky legs to Danya. "Where did you bury the goods?"

The sooner she talked, the sooner they could leave.

"P-Please," she begged, shielding herself from the witch and the amulet. "Please don't do to me what you did to them . . ."

Azrahari thumped her toes on the floor impatiently. "This young man asked you a question."

"Switchback C-Cave," Danya squeaked. "There's a pile of rocks outside. Disturbed earth. You w-won't miss it."

That was enough for Cree. She fled, hurtling over the collapsed dwarf, racing out the door and past the carnage. Lucien heard her soft footfalls retreating into the forest. He hazarded one last glance at the witch, sidling toward the exit. Maybe it should have occurred to him sooner that she might not let him leave.

"Know this: I owe you nothing now," she told him, all traces of civility and gentility erased from her tone. "You destroyed one of my finest creations, child. Do not find yourself in this part of the Savalirwood again, Lucien Tavelle. Consider that warning my generosity."

He nodded, once. Lucien paused at the door, throwing a glance over his shoulder at Danya. Pity for her flared in his heart, but it was her or him, and he was damned sure his destiny lay elsewhere. He wouldn't let his luck run out and wind up a pile of empty skin in a witch's dark hovel. "What will you do with her?"

"Little fool." The witch smiled and tilted her head to one side. "You already know."

CHAPTER 4

"The hollowing? *The hollowing?*"

Cree had not stopped repeating those two words for the better part of their journey to Switchback Cave. Storming well ahead of Lucien, she finally changed it up, tossing her hands in the air and muttering, "Did you know that was going to happen? I swear on my mother's grave, Lucien, if you knew . . ."

"I didn't know," he insisted. "I knew she was dangerous, but I had no idea she could turn spines to jelly with her necklace."

"Can you imagine? Just . . . ceasing to be like that? Becoming some fleshy sack?" She fake-gagged and then real-gagged, detouring into a stand of blackberry bushes to dry-heave. When she was finished, she stood and wiped her mouth with her sleeve, groaning. "I can't stop seeing it."

"I'm sorry, Cree," he said, falling into step with her on the path. The way to Switchback Cave wasn't a secret; it was a popular spot for smugglers moving weapons, hooch, and other various contraband. The Mardoons must have gotten their hands on the ambushers before they could relocate the goods to a less obvious location.

Up ahead, the shadowy path curved, the trees thinning as the road sloped toward a tunnel system etched into a low range of hills, a ridge so low it wasn't even visible above the canopy. Discarded bits of arms and armor, charred, bloodstained, and torn, warned of what went on in those caves. Lucien dodged ahead, wary, but they were alone, and a tumble of rocks to the right of the unwelcoming cave's entrance caught his eye immediately.

Cree hung back as he went to dig about in the ground near the rocks. He could feel her keen yellow eyes boring into his skull.

"That woman," she began, suspicious, drawing out the second word. "How do you know her?"

"I have a past, too, Cree. We all do. I don't press you about yours." Lucien's fingernails scraped the top of something hard. Crouching there over the shallow mound of dirt reminded him of fresh winter snowfalls when he and dozens of others would scamper out at dawn, poking the new white drifts to see if any drunks had fallen, frozen, and died there, easy pockets for picking. He brushed more of the dirt away from what he was becoming increasingly sure was a coffer, and flinched as, out of the corner of one eye, he watched Cree bend to snatch up a discarded and half-blunted dagger.

Cree adopted a low stance and made sure to keep the old, charred weapon between them.

"There's nothing like that woman in my past," she hissed.

"Do you really plan to use that dagger on me?" Lucien asked. "Feels like such a damned cliché for you to turn on me like this what with the treasure now ours for the taking."

She wrinkled her nose but kept the blade thrust in his direction. "Tell me. Why would that woman owe you a favor?"

"Because she—" Lucien spat, the rest of it lodged in his throat. *Because she ruined my life and forced me to ruin others'.* "If I say it true, will you drop that bloody dagger and let us be as we were? This was your job, remember? *Your* gold."

"Hmph. It depends on what you say."

Lucien busied himself with the pile of dirt. It was easier than looking Cree in the eye. "I had a family, and more than just a sister. We were happy, too, for a moment, traveling and performing, songs and dances, mummery, and the like. My parents looked after the music, and we children would put on little plays. Little to others, I suppose, but grand to us. Yes, grand." He shook his head and shrugged. The box beneath the earth was exposed now, the latch still in place but unlocked. "But my folk owed the Jagentoths coin, and lots of it. My older brother paid the price for it with his life. But Mum and Da . . . They couldn't—

wouldn't—let him go. He was always their favorite. Easily the best performer of the three of us, always knew his lines, early to rise, eager for chores. He was the best of us, and the Jagentoths took that all away. My parents kept his body in the snow until they decided what to do with it. So . . ." Lucien's eyes fixed on the road behind Cree. "So."

Cree's ears twitched straight up. "Those puppets in her house—"

"We called him Sock Brother, Aldreda and I," Lucien said, hoarse. "That thing wasn't our real kin, even if it made Mum and Da smile again."

Cree hung her head and sniffed. "That sounds like your family owe her a favor, not the other way 'round."

He bristled. "That's all you can say?"

She shrugged.

"We *did* owe her. Mum and Da did, I mean, but I was the one who paid that blood price." *I'm not surprised you remember the way.* His stomach lurched. "I'd . . . lure folk out to her cottage. Da would hand me a little paper slip, and whoever it said, I'd convince them to come along, get them near her cottage, then she would charm them into gazing at her amulet. You saw what happens after that."

"I . . . oh." Cree shuddered and pressed her knuckles hard against her mouth. Her eyes flashed at him, suspicion overtaking her nausea. "But you said you didn't kn—"

Lucien barreled on, "Mum said it was a fair trade, because I had my brother back after all, didn't I? But it wasn't him, and they wanted me to pretend like a cursed sack of skin was a living, breathing person. 'Now kiss your brother good night,' Mum would say." He mimicked her forcefully cheery voice and grimaced. "And if we didn't kiss and hug and make the big fuss they wanted, there were consequences. *We* were punished for seeing what they couldn't. After a while I couldn't let it go on, couldn't look at myself or live with myself, so I burned down the caravan with all three of them inside, took my sister, and that was that."

With his fingertips he dusted off the lid of the coffer until it was relatively clean. "No more little songs. No more farces." He raised his eyes to Cree's and held them there. "Satisfied?"

"No," said Cree, dropping the dagger. "Shattered."

Lucien nodded, somehow relieved. "I'd prefer we not speak of it again."

"You have my word," Cree replied, coming to join him near the box.

She nudged it gently with her clawed foot. "You saved my hide back there, so this reward we'll split fifty–fifty."

He managed a wry smile. "That's fair."

Lucien reached for the latch and flicked it open, feeling a sudden, terrible heat shoot against his hands. Treasure. Easily spotted. No lock.

Booby-trapped.

He took the full blast of it in the face and jerked away from the coffer, falling—limp and poisoned—flat on his back in the dirt.

CHAPTER 5

829 PD

"You're not distracted like the others."

Lucien shifted his eyes in the mirror, discovering Karem Ferentus observing him from the doorway. Karem was the strangest adult Lucien had ever met. He lived with a permanent smile, and even when he was angry at his learners, that grin never wavered. Nothing and no one seemed to bother Karem. It was something Lucien admired, but it frightened him, too. Lucien couldn't list a single adult in his life that hadn't, at some point, let him down completely, abandoned him, or turned out to be a know-nothing fraud, and he kept waiting for the day Karem would true-colors his way out of Lucien's regard.

"This place is practically a monastery," Lucien replied with a shrug. His leg bounced restlessly under the vanity table. He was nineteen on the verge of twenty, and shrugging was the gesture that came most naturally now. "What would there be to distract me?"

Karem shouldered his way deeper into the chamber. It was low-ceilinged, made of soft white stone and mortar, and held a chill like the bowels of a forgotten church. Bronze sconces glowed from the pillars and arches, igniting Karem's deep-brown skin as he came closer. And smiled.

Cree and Brevyn had tucked themselves under Karem Ferentus's welcoming wing without hesitation and accepted all that came with it: the training, the lessons, the lectures, the chores . . . It had taken Lucien longer to accept the yoke of a ghostslayer learner. He often joked to the others that Karem and the other senior members of the Orders made initiation so boring to repel the thrill-seekers. It certainly *sounded* sexy and mysterious, the Claret Orders, ancient blood-magic-wielding warriors that culled the lands of monsters and undead, but the reality was anything but glamorous.

The tedium, he decided, was the real test, not the final trial of the Hunter's Bane. From the moment they arrived (vouched for by Brevyn), his schedule had remained largely the same: wake just after dawn, bring in water from the central well (redolent with moss and worms), kneel in the Sanguine Chapel for daily recitations (As blood flows through and invigorates the body, so faith flows through and invigorates the soul. Ever remember this: Thy blood and thy faith are one in the same. Spill not thy blood nor that of another heedlessly, but do not hesitate to spill either when the cause is just), then wedge himself between Cree and Brevyn on a bench in the mess and eat black bread softened in bone broth under a suspended glass chalice holding the commingled, vile mixture of their blood. As soon as they'd passed the Hunter's Bane trial, a measure of their blood had been taken and added to the chalice.

They were brothers and sisters forever, or for as long as that nasty thing hung in the mess.

They wore nondescript garb and they led nondescript lives—young, burgeoning members of Orders that must exist in secret. Ancient conflicts had pushed the Orders—of Ghostslayer, Lycan, Mutant, and Profane Soul alike—into near extinction, and now Elias de Corvo, Karem Ferentus, Director Alasterre de Vitrevos, and others maintained the Orders under a banner of joined silence.

Within that mind-numbing day-to-day, Lucien was largely concerned with his own problems, but not so much so that he missed the way Karem's eyes became veiled when they fell on him. *Disappointment* was perhaps too harsh a word to assign, but Lucien had resisted Karem's fatherly overtures; his own parents had failed him, and eventually Auntie Mama had turned them out, afraid of the trouble they would bring to her home. In the end, she had shunned even her own daughter, all over a few freelance jobs gone awry.

Lucien had only just moved from the cellar to the main house when a man broke in during the dead of night, held a knife to Auntie Mama's throat, and demanded to know where his wife had gone. The wife, it turned out, had left town under the cover of darkness, the escape master-minded and carried out by he, Cree, and Brevyn, and she may have absconded with most of the man's valuables. A tiny fraction of those valuables had ended up in their possession as payment, sure, and that tiny fraction was quickly spent on dice and drink. Unfortunately, given the knife incident, Auntie Mama was not interested in digesting these crucial mitigating facts:

1. The man (Gundobal Gorbus) was a violent drunk.
2. His wife (Everleen Gorbus) had repeatedly tried to leave, only to be chained up in her home.
3. Auntie Mama knew and liked Everleen.
4. His name was Gundobal Fucking Gorbus.

If Lucien had been a better predictor of Gundobal's behavior, he would've kept a few coppers for a rainy-day fund and made the journey from Shadycreek Run to the Marrow Valley with considerably more than lint in his pockets. Auntie Mama gave them a pittance for the road and watched them go while hugging her whimpering dogs. Even the mutts, Jet and Emerald, seemed to sense the unfairness of it all, for the trio were young, foolhardy, and just trying to survive. But Auntie Mama wouldn't budge, and so they fled. Brevyn had saved enough coin to buy them passage on a merchant convoy, and she promised them a better living in the south, down in the Marrow Valley where she had spent a summer apprenticed to Karem Ferentus.

We're all of us caught in patterns, Lucien thought to himself. Brevyn had been sent away to escape the inevitable life of crime that awaited her in the Run, only to wind up snared in another cycle, this time in the underground halls of the Claret Orders.

"Your friend Cree enjoys the garden, I think," Karem was saying in his steady, sonorous voice. "And Brevyn busies herself drilling the new learners. But you . . . you . . ."

"I have a black thumb," replied Lucien. He stopped himself from shrugging again. "And I've never been fond of children. How are their little hands always so disgusting?"

Karem laughed. He hovered just over Lucien's shoulder, homing in on what Lucien himself had been fretting over in the mirror.

"How did you get that mark?" he asked, running his finger along the ridge of his own left cheekbone. It was just the place Lucien wore a thin, barely noticeable scar.

"A job went sideways," Lucien replied. "Brevyn took care of the other scars. She left this one for me to fix, a little incentive to follow her here and dedicate myself to the Orders."

"A lot has gone sideways for you, hasn't it?"

"Right now, I'm alive and eating, and nobody is actively trying to murder me. I'd call that a win."

Karem nodded, his amber eyes still keenly trained on Lucien's scar. He placed one hand on his hip while his other sleeve dangled loose—the ghostslayer had lost his left arm from the elbow down during an ill-fated hunt years ago. An undead ghoul had reared up out of a mud-filled gully and torn the appendage away. It was a story Karem had told them all over supper in the mess hall at least six times.

"That scar might be better work for Cree," Karem finally said. "She's become quite the capable blood healer."

"Yes, she has," Lucien responded, a little tartly. His gaze shifted to find Karem's in the mirror. "Which is why I can't understand you and Elias constantly underestimating her. She survived the Hunter's Bane, didn't she? She's ready for a contract. A real one."

Karem's smile didn't falter. "Curious. She hasn't expressed as much to me."

"She's not here to become a gardener."

"There is more to this life than simply hunting, Lucien. The taro feeds the hunter that protects the villagers that make the linens that clothe the hunters, and on and on. If we spent every waking moment hunting monstrosities, there wouldn't be any of us left." Lucien's bouncing knee jostled the vanity table. The mirror sitting on it tipped, and Karem reached over Lucien's shoulder with his right hand, catching it before it could fall and shatter. "These ruins can be a home, but a home requires more than ice and magic and fury, my young friend. You have a handle on your magic, but that doesn't mean you have nothing left to learn." Then he chuckled to himself. "Ah, to be young and hungry again, and filled with terrible impatience."

Lucien looked down at his hands where they were bundled in his lap. He wanted to know gratitude, and perhaps even patience, but instead he found himself bored. He hadn't expected the life of a monster hunter to involve so much fetching water and saying prayers.

Letting go of the mirror's edge, Karem touched a single finger to a stack of letters on the vanity table.

"I see now," he said softly. "Maybe home is elsewhere?"

"Not really," Lucien lied.

Karem nodded and, off Lucien's cold expression, turned and strode back to the doorway. There he paused and told him: "I doubt you're interested in my opinion, but I think the scar suits you, Lucien. Consider keeping it."

He wouldn't. When Karem was gone and Lucien was alone again, he reached for a small knife in the vanity drawer and flicked the blade across his chest. Blood welled, and so did Lucien's magic. He gathered the blood on his finger before it could drip down to stain his shirt, a flicker of light passing from the crimson smudge to his face. His skin warmed at the touch of blood and magic, and the scar faded somewhat but did not fully heal. He hissed as a droplet of the blood slid free of his finger, splattering on top of the letter stack.

Cursing, he fumbled for a handkerchief and tried to wipe off the mark, but he only succeeded in rubbing the stain deeper into the parchment.

He shouldn't have left them out anyway, as they were the closest thing to treasure that he owned. A tavern keeper in Berleben had agreed to accept correspondence for him, so long as Lucien handed over a few coppers each month. His sister Aldreda wrote when she could, and Lucien wrote when he remembered to. No, that wasn't quite right. He wrote when he felt there was something meaningful to say, and more and more he found that well running dry.

Aldreda begged him to come to her in Rexxentrum, promising him a place to live and work, even if the accommodations were nothing special. In fact, she wrote, she had grown very close to the family she kept house for, particularly after the lady of the family took ill and died. Aldreda had become indispensable, and clearly, she felt being needed would confer greater standing. Every letter, she made the same promises with the same darling conviction, a conviction Lucien wanted desperately to share. Aldreda's luck was rising, but he was stuck in place. He wasn't making a fortune for himself with the Claret Orders, though they fed, housed, and trained him. Eventually, when he was more proficient, the hunting contracts would come, or so the directors promised. Villages could hire them to run off whatever horrifying creature terrorized their town, a dangerous living, but a living, nonetheless.

Inevitably, that coin would be split three ways, and then the Orders would take a cut, and where would that leave him?

And how would sweet Aldreda enjoy living side by side with a monster hunter? Lucien had been intentionally vague about his current pursuits, only assuring his sister that he had escaped the Run and traveled with friends to a village near Berleben, where he hoped to educate and raise himself up. The last letter he had sent to her, roughly six months earlier, included the sentiments: "Everything is much improved here. I have true friendship, warm meals, and much-needed guidance. I've changed for the better, Aldreda, and I cannot wait for you to see the man I am becoming."

It was true. Ish. True if one squinted, perhaps. He was becoming a ghoul-killer, a wielder of blood magic, drawing his own life force and transforming it into deadly shards of ice. Aldreda deserved the truth, but he didn't want to give it to her until he could write, with unvarnished prose, that he had amassed the kind of coin that would furnish a comfortable existence, and a comfortable existence on their own terms.

But he couldn't say that, not yet, and so she wrote, all the time, begging and pleading with him, and Lucien let the letters heap higher on his vanity table in plain sight, the guilt washing over him whenever he chanced to look upon them.

Deep in the rabbit warrens of the ruins, a gong sounded. Supper. Another titillating mouthful of soggy vegetables and broth. Lucien forced himself to stand and leave behind the communal dorm, turning the corner and finding Brevyn Oakbender swaggering down the corridor. She didn't so much walk as charge, arriving like a battering ram wherever she went. His old friend lived up to her father's name, tall and sturdy, muscled from nose to toes, more architecture than physiognomy. She wore a sleeveless ivory tunic, open at the neck, the top buttons undone to show off the large, colorful butterfly inked across her clavicles.

She took one look at him and snorted. "Why is there blood on your chest? Practicing?"

Lucien batted away her searching fingers, which were trying to pry his shirt farther open. "I wanted to see to this last scar, but I'm a hopeless healer. You or Cree will have to do it."

"You've really committed to the deep vee," she teased, flicking the wide-open edge of his white shirt. "Stealing my look, are you? You're always copying me, Tavelle."

He fell in step with her as they walked toward the mess. "Never underestimate the persuasive power of a billowy blouse, Brev."

"Oh, it's persuading me, all right—persuading me that you're a horrid prat."

"Horrid, *handsome* prat, though."

"Regrettably true." Brevyn thumped him on the back. "Karem came whirling through the mess like a hurricane, grabbed Cree, and took her to his office."

Lucien frowned. "Oh?"

"Did you say something to him?" Brevyn asked, devilishly, annoyingly good at reading even his coolest looks. "I know you've been banging on about Cree getting her first contract, so don't try to deny it."

"Gods, that was quick," he muttered.

"She'll thank you for it."

"Not if it goes sideways."

"It won't," Brevyn assured him. "We'll be there with her."

"Just us, you think?" Lucien asked. His mind flashed to his own first contract, handed out to him by Karem and overseen by him, too. Lucien, Cree, Brevyn, and Karem had trekked north to the Silberquel foothills, following reports of undead activity.

"Karem might tag along, this being her first and all."

"Annoying."

"Why are you always so sour with him? He's only looking out for us."

"We're not children anymore, Brev. We don't need his supervision."

She fell silent, chewing that over. At the end of the corridor, they turned right and descended to an even lower level of the warrens. The mess, deeply scooped out of the bowels of the ruin, held the pervasive, wet chill of a cistern. A roaring hearth at the far end did little to cut through the cold damp. Aboveground, the smoke churned out from a disguising crofter's cottage, where a sympathetic shepherd maintained the illusion that there was nothing more than empty, picked-clean ruins above and below.

The benches snugged up tight to the two long feasting tables were already crammed with learners, apprentices, and senior members. The directors of the Orders, when present, dined at their own table apart from the rest. Brevyn led them to where Cree usually sat studying her claws, waiting for prayer to begin. A smallish halfling sat next to Cree's empty place; they were a curly-headed blood warlock with shifty eyes. Brevyn was friendly with just about everyone in the ruins, and Lucien had heard her call the halfling Otis. Otis was sometimes he, sometimes she, and sometimes they, according to Brevyn, with no real preference.

As soon as Brevyn and Lucien were seated, the double doors near the hearth burst open and three figures stormed in—a hulking, bald half-giant with face tattoos flanked by two elf women, one of them brown-skinned and covered in piercings, the other with long, flowing black hair. Lucien had seen them around, but like he and Cree, that trio kept to themselves.

"This is unbelievable," the half-giant roared, the floor shaking as he came to stand near the tables.

"Hardly," muttered the pierced elf. "I told you they would muzzle us. You never listen."

From those same double doors, a human woman glided out. Sarenne de Chastain. She crossed her arms over her black leather cuirass and jutted one hip to the side.

"You will control yourselves and end this outburst immediately," said de Chastain.

"End *this,*" the black-haired elf squeaked, showing de Chastain a juvenile, rude gesture.

De Chastain simply rolled her eyes. "Disperse. Elias will hear your complaints tomorrow."

"Sure, sure." The half-giant led the others out the way Lucien had come in. As they went, he heard the man add in an undertone, "Giving that soft paws a contract over us. Fucking idiots."

"Begin the prayer," de Chastain snapped, going to stand at the head of the tables. A senior member near her began the litany, but Lucien didn't join in. Instead, he bowed his head and watched de Chastain. Sarenne was white as a snowdrop, with delicately pointed half-elven ears. That was the beginning and end of her delicacy—she was otherwise severe, with beaky, sharp features, stark ivory hair (done up in a tumult of braids), and hunting black eyes. It was said that the first time she transformed into her wolf form, it took nine men to subdue her. More than half walked away from that encounter missing ears, fingers, and pride.

She was not a permanent fixture in the Oltu Ruins; rather she was on loan from the Order of the Lycan headquarters based in the Cyrengreen Forest. De Chastain was the sort of woman that, Lucien felt confident, would put his head on a spike if she knew he was even internally referring to her as *on loan.*

She didn't like him, and the feeling was mutual.

De Chastain's black gaze ate him up, and she sneered, mouthing only the word: *Pray.* Without breaking eye contact, Lucien joined in with the others. "Spill not thy blood nor that of another heedlessly, but do not hesitate to spill either when the cause is just . . ."

CHAPTER 6

Lucien watched the fog dissipate through the trees of the Savalirwood, the twisted, corrupted trunks growing brighter with each passing moment. The strange branches reaching through the mist shook, bloodstained fingers sifting through cloud. His legs stretched out in front of him, poking out of the opening to their tent, an ugly worm of mistrust slithering through his belly.

Cree had gone off to relieve herself, but now she appeared through the fog, her long, ragged duster brushing the tops of overgrown weeds desperately clinging to rotten soil. She stopped as soon as she saw his tight-lipped expression. Rubbing at her nose, Cree shuffled up to the dwindling fire and kicked dirt over the coals. Somewhere in the forest surrounding them, Sarenne stood watch. Brevyn had asked repeatedly to join them for Cree's first contract monster hunt, but Karem needed her in Oltu, and so Sarenne was assigned to be their third.

She tolerated minimal chatter on the road. From the ruins, they followed the Eisfus River southeast, then crossed at the Jamberlain Bridge to meet the Gravelway Path cutting north, taking them by and by to the Glory Run Road. De Chastain confiscated the small flask Lucien had packed, dumping out the whiskey in the Eisfus and tossing the container into a thicket of thorny bushes.

"This is not a pleasant picnic, Tavelle," de Chastain had snarled as she discarded his property. "You and Deeproots will need clear heads for this hunt."

Nothing with you is pleasant, he thought, as de Chastain stalked away and back to her mount. She paused before swinging up into the saddle, her head canting toward him as if she could hear his very thoughts. The intimidation worked on Cree, who was uncharacteristically silent and jumpy as they joined the flow of caravans and travelers on the Glory Run. It wasn't until they reached the gates outside Shadycreek Run that Lucien began to grow suspicious of this contract. When they bypassed the untold numbers of thieves, murderers, and monsters hiding among the topsy-turvy taverns and turrets of the town, his suspicion blossomed and stung, dogged as a migraine.

Lucien picked at a thread on his trousers, though his gaze remained fixed on Cree.

"Show me the contract," he said.

Cree's ears swung back. "You've always trusted me before."

"And I still do. Show it to me, then. Let's have it."

"Sarenne told me not to share it with you. She didn't want you along for this hunt in the first place. You're here because I refused to go without you."

"Fuck Sarenne," Lucien muttered. She probably heard it. He didn't care. *Fuck her.* "It's you and me, Cree. It's always been you and me and it always will be, yeah?" Cree flinched and looked away. Lucien's lip curled. It was the fog or the nearness of the damned, freakish woods that turned his mood so fast, or so he told himself. "If this is what I think it is, and you take the kill, I'll never forgive you."

At that, Cree's eyes snapped to him, burning. "You don't mean that."

"It's her, isn't it? The witch. The hollower."

Cree's guilty hesitation told him everything. But he wanted the words, too. "I'm sorry, Lucien. It's the contract they gave me."

"Bullshit," he spat. He stood and shoved his coat back, resting his hands low on his back. "This is de Corvo and Ferentus and de Chastain and all the rest testing me."

"I swear it isn't—"

"Why are you so bloody mystified by them? They're not gods, Cree, they're just hunters!"

Cree froze. Slowly, she reached into the satchel on her belt and withdrew a folded piece of parchment with a broken black wax seal. She offered it to Lucien, and when he reached for the contract, slapped his hand with it. "This may surprise you, but not everything is about you. It's my contract and I'm going to execute it."

He ripped open the paper, his vision glazing red when he glimpsed the name Azrahari.

"You know what she did to my family," he said in a deadly whisper. Tears were coming, and he loathed it.

"You'll be there with me," Cree insisted.

"It's not the same. You kept this from me! You lied."

"Because I knew you would react this way."

"Give me the kill," he hissed. "Let me keep the contract."

Cree dropped her face into her hands, claws digging into the fur of her forehead.

"My brother, Cree. *My brother.*"

"I know." Her voice was muffled and watery, and Lucien gave one final push.

"It's you and me. There will be other contracts, and I'll be there for them. Whatever comes to me next you can have it, Cree, I swear it. I swear it. Please, just give me this one thing." Lucien spread the paper across his chest, hands trembling.

Cree sagged. "Just . . . just put it away before Sarenne sees you, all right? She fucking scares me."

He did as she asked, shoving the paper hastily into his pocket as a bloom of vicious warmth grew in his chest. The contract was his.

"WE PAUSE HERE," SARENNE ANNOUNCED, halting a few paces in front of them and crouching as the trees thinned, a clearing just ahead. They had left the horses back at their meager camp. Lucien heard running water, and smelled the odd perfume of the fungi that grew around the witch's cottage. Dressed all in black, with slashes through her cloak, Sarenne crept silently among the wildflowers and mushrooms. Thick clumps of bleeding heart flowers grew, their heart-shaped blossoms ebony, the eerie little drip emanating from them yellow, almost gold. Lucien stooped to pick one of the flowers, and as soon as he held it up to the light, the blossom withered and turned to dust. He used to come back to his family's caravan with his trousers covered in that dust, the mark of a boy who had lured another unsuspecting victim to a gruesome end.

"Will you transform for the hunt?" Cree whispered, a shake in her voice.

Sarenne smiled at them over her shoulder, showing her teeth. "Pray I do not need to."

She drew her sword, a beautifully enameled rapier, the basket hilt chased in red stones.

"The witch is a hollower," Sarenne was saying. Her smooth, beautiful face was impassive, as if she were discussing the weather or a new tavern in town. "Whatever she says, whatever she tells you to do, resist. She will have the better of us unless we perform a clean ambush."

I know what she is.

Lucien said nothing. Again, he had the strange sense that Sarenne had somehow intuited his thoughts. She glared at him, then shook her head.

"I will draw her out with a call from the northern side of the clearing, Cree will have her chance to strike, and Lucien will assist, but only if the witch proves too powerful." Cree said nothing of their true plan, and so Sarenne lifted her rapier and touched the hilt to her forehead. "Hunt well, hunt clean."

Then she disappeared, vanishing among the trees as she snaked around the perimeter of the clearing. The brook grew louder and more talkative as he and Cree crawled their way west, through the thinning line of trees, waiting in the cool, concealing darkness of the forest for Sarenne's next move. Beside him, Cree shuddered.

"I didn't think I would be this afraid," she murmured.

"Neither did I."

Lucien knew better than anyone what Azrahari was capable of, and though his blood simmered with rage and yearned to be spilled for the magic that would end her, he worried that it would not be enough. In his mind, the witch loomed as permanent and primordial as the forest itself, not a being that had chosen to put down her small red cottage there and perform her horrible spells, but a thing that had always been and would always be.

From the northern edge of the clearing came a soft cry. It grew in intensity until it sounded exactly like an infant whimpering and shrieking.

"How is she doing that?" Cree asked. "It's uncanny."

It didn't matter how, it only mattered that it worked. A moment later, the door of the cottage squeaked open. Lucien reached for the daggers holstered at his belt, his hands numb. Azrahari emerged, the fingers of her right hand curled and tucked under her chin. She turned a complete circle, searching for the sound of the crying child. Carefully, she drifted a few steps down the path leading from the entrance. Cree shifted, but Lucien shook his head. The door closed behind her on its own, and that was the moment to pounce.

Elias and Karem had drilled the movements into him for two years, and now they sprang from him with ease. He sliced the dagger blades in an X across his bared chest, blood coating the steel, a pale-blue light surging from his fingers and leaping to the weapons. White frost crackled across the dagger blades, and Lucien moved into the clearing. The bushes near Sarenne rustled, keeping the witch's attention for one last crucial instant. When Azrahari turned, blue eyes wide, hands fumbling for the amulet, Lucien was already upon her.

She made a strangled, curious sound, then tried to thrust the amulet toward his face. His right dagger lashed out, severing the amulet's chain and four of her fingers. Ice gathered on the bloodied stumps. Her mouth dropped open in horror. She could no doubt see Cree sliding into the clearing behind him and hear Sarenne approaching from her left flank.

"My beautiful boy," the witch murmured. The amulet dropped uselessly to the ground and rolled away. She began falling to her knees, reaching for Lucien's face as tears sped down her cheeks. "I had hoped to make you mine one day. What a perfect specimen you would have made. Oh, how you would have been merry with laughter and dance . . ."

"Fight." He growled, slicing with his other dagger, lopping off her left hand at the wrist.

She sighed and fell, and shook her head, her curling blond hair spreading out on the grass at his feet. When he looked closer, her face was heavily lined, as if the intervening years had rapidly aged her. She was still beautiful, but now she was old. Her legs jerked weakly as she grinned up at him, staring as if he were a friend long missed.

"Fight, damn you!" Lucien screamed.

Sarenne appeared at his side swiftly, little more than a furious black-and-white blur. "This is not how we hunt. Cree—come, end her. Though she be a monster, suffering is not our aim."

Lucien ignored her and dropped to his knees, breathing hard. Shards of frost crackled up his forearms to his elbows, searingly cold, and then he plunged the icy daggers into the witch's chest, skewering her to the ground. He leaned close, listening carefully for her dying gurgle.

"You'll make no more puppets of men," he whispered, so close he could smell the liniment and perfume on her papery skin. "The hells await you, witch, their fires too gentle a kiss."

Azrahari managed a laugh and rolled her eyes. The witch looked away from him as her life bled away.

Lucien blinked, waiting . . . waiting. There had to be more. She was more dangerous than this. If all along her demise only required a dagger to the heart, then why had he let it go on so long? A parade of faces whipped by, and Lucien abruptly had to know, had to see. Before he went, he palmed her fallen amulet, slipping it into his pocket. He stood, leaving his daggers in the witch's chest, just in case, and—dulled to what Cree and Sarenne said to him—he raced to the cottage and threw open the door.

There he saw the parade of faces again, now lifeless and stretched, and attached to bodies both human and wood and felt. He recognized those he had led to her clutches, the rapists, the thieves, the murderers . . . they all grinned back. Lucien strode on shaking legs to the open fire in the middle of the room, grabbed an iron poker, and began churning life into the coals, then scattered them, bright and burning, across the carpets and wooden floor. The smoke began to rise, and Lucien stumbled back out to face Cree and Sarenne.

Cree stood by the body, still vigilant, but Sarenne came to him at the cottage door. She looked past him, into the main room, her eyes sweeping the walls. After glancing over her shoulder at the dead witch, she said, "I didn't know this was personal."

"Well. It's over now."

"Is it?" Sarenne tsked softly. Lucien tried to continue back toward the forest's edge, but Sarenne put up her hand, holding him there. Her tone lowered and hardened until it was velvet-wrapped steel.

"This was Cree's contract."

"She gave it to me."

"She doesn't have the authority to do that."

"Take it up with her," he muttered, exhausted, and wanting to be away from the now burning cottage. He pushed against Sarenne's hand, but she held fast.

"No, boy, I'm taking it up with you," she whispered. Sarenne inched to the right, making damned sure she was in his way, and that he had no choice but to gaze into her black eyes. "Listen carefully to me now: Elias and Karem might fall for your act, but I see you. I *see* you. I've trained pompous little imps like you before, and like them, a pompous little imp you will remain unless you disabuse yourself of certain things. You are not great, Lucien Tavelle, not yet, and while your friends might have you convinced that you are special, being special and being great are two different things. By the Matron, if only you accepted tutelage, if you welcomed humility, you might just come to understand the difference."

Lucien iced over, schooling his face into a confounding mask. Even if she had handily cut a hole and slid right under his skin, Lucien refused to give her the satisfaction of his outrage.

"I don't want your tutelage," he said, and shouldered her out of the way.

Sarenne let him go with a sigh. "Does it feel empty?" she called as he went to collect his daggers.

"No," he replied, with forced cheer. He winked at Cree, who stared at him with worried eyes. "It feels wonderful."

In the pit of his stomach, he knew it felt like nothing.

CHAPTER 7

Rexxentrum
831 PD

The ale at the Clever Copper Inn went down smoothly enough but left a moldy aftertaste. A curious raft of scum floated atop every mug of it, the beer full-bodied yet somehow watered down. Lucien could only conclude that whatever well water they were using to cheapen the brew was as flavorful as the ale itself.

He choked down another gulp.

The Clever Copper hovered where two twisty roads kissed, avenues that ultimately led to nowhere. Not an unusual sight in the Tangles, a messy conundrum of an old town running southwest alongside Rexxentrum's Shimmer Ward. Even after receiving detailed instructions on how to locate the Clever Copper, it had taken Cree and him two hours to find the place, looping and backtracking, consulting a map that may as well have been drawn with a drunken, shaking fist. It didn't help that the only indication they had found the right place was a faded, weather-blasted sign swinging crookedly in a dark doorway.

It read: THE LEVE   PER INN.

They had filled in the blanks and ducked inside, grateful to escape the cold and expecting the suspected front to be empty, as most fronts were, but instead the tavern was doing brisk business. Bad Sign The First.

Their third, Brevyn, had promised to meet them there. So far, she was a no-show. Bad Sign The Second.

Of course, she could just be lost. Or someone might have stumbled across the same intel and detained her.

Whatever the case, Lucien tried to remain coolheaded. He contemplated the halfway point of his third disgusting pint, listening with a dull yet dutiful smile to the halfling joining them. Endless prattle. Endless prattle that he needed to pay close attention to, or so Brevyn had instructed him. She had never steered him wrong before and had saved his life too many times to reasonably keep score. Now that they were on their own and relatively free from the watchful eyes of Karem and Sarenne, he leaned on Brevyn's gut even more.

Repeat after me, Brevyn had said, staring down into his face before he and Cree left for the Clever Copper. *Thirty-five gold.*

Thirty-five gold. He had felt like a child but did it anyway. The clucking reminded him a little of Sarenne, but Brevyn was eminently less punchable.

That's all you can spend, yeah? Keep that in the forefront of your mind, Lu, and you'll do just fine.

Brevyn usually handled the talking on this sort of job, but not this time. This was Lucien's chance to spearhead a contract. He hadn't been given the chance in months, and Lucien felt this one falling flat on its face in slow motion. This was a different sort of contract than they were used to—Lucien had already grown bored of hunting monsters for the Orders, and specifically he had grown tired of that killjoy Sarenne breathing down his neck. Brevyn had taken to arranging different kinds of jobs for them, inching them further and further away from the monastic hunting ideals of the Orders. He could also feel Cree's bright eyes burning into the side of his face as he listened to another of the halfling's anecdotes. His name was Musty Deg, and he lived up to it, communicating in a series of weird, wet little burps that only sometimes resembled full sentences.

"We don't see many infernals around here." Musty Deg was burping. "Or catkind, come to think of it."

"Catfolk," Cree gently corrected.

"That's what—*hic*—I said." Deg had been in the middle of filling them in on the history of the Clever Copper Inn, a pedigree quite noticeably riddled with gaps and inconsistencies, a plot so full of holes it wouldn't even have made it to the unscrupulous troubadour stages of Shadycreek Run. But that made perfect sense, because this place was bullshit and Lucien knew it, Cree knew it, Brevyn knew it, and their employers knew it. They were drinking in a box of a building sitting on top of a gold mine. Not literal gold, unfortunately, but books, which were glittering temptations to a certain set of clienteles. That was good enough for Lucien, Cree, and Brevyn.

"Humans mostly wander by," Deg continued. He gestured to the full room around them. Lucien noted that the crowd primarily comprised humans. "But of an evening we prefer it quiet. There's a little girl comes around and strums her lute for a few coppers, and our people like that. We don't usually go in for this, you know . . ." He gestured again. "Not so gredari—gregory—"

Gregarious, Lucien thought with a silent snarl.

"Lively?" Lucien supplied with a smile.

"Noisy," finished Deg. He tapped the sides of his face. "Sensitive ears, I've got. Passed down from my mother."

"Ah. And what a luminous creature she must have been."

Deg grimaced. "No, no, was a crusty old stump, that woman."

"Well! Then those good looks are all due to your father."

"Crustier and stumpier, my pop was," said the halfling. "Never seen a fellow—*hic*—so carious with gout."

"Oh," Lucien murmured. "Enchanting."

Cree kicked him under the table.

Lucien kept his smile in place; he had already concluded that the halfling hated the din. The fellow jumped and winced whenever a patron laughed too raucously, or a mug hit the floor, or the front door slammed shut from hand or wind. Musty Deg's burping was not his only nervous habit, as his red hands had been picked to bits, his nails jagged and bleeding. Deg's left heel bounced constantly, rasping against the leg of his chair. Not the demeanor of a typical tavern owner on a busy night.

Deg also seemed to want to project an air of dejected poverty; his clothes were dirty and dull, and his greenish hair was snarled over the sensitive ears that were too big for his head, lending him a childlike visage. But while the velvet on his collar was drab, it was of good quality, and the gold pin on the breast of his black leather armor was new. Lucien also saw six tiny rings glinting in the tavern keeper's right nostril.

Deg had money, and it wasn't flowing from the inn's profits. The care and intention he put into his appearance was not at all reflected in his establishment; Lucien had seen more tastefully decorated outhouses.

No, Deg and his partner were not prepared for the influx of visitors that night, and he had overheard the barmaid complaining that this was more people in one evening than the whole of the previous month. He was chronically nervous or touchy, but given the circumstances and what Lucien knew, it was likely both.

Lucien could go on. He also had plenty of feelings about the nondescript gnome sitting beside Deg, but she was holding her tongue. And so he softened his gaze, realizing his piercing red eyes were probably giving him away. He was an observer, a sharp one, and the tendency had only grown stronger recently. Maybe he had always been doing this. Maybe it protected him. He read a stranger before they could read him, and he offered what he wanted them to see. The rest of his cards? The true ones? Those remained tight to the vest. Cree and Cree alone knew a handful of his secrets, and he intended to keep it that way.

"Speaking of humans," he heard Cree say in a delighted purr.

The door blasted open, rattling on ancient hinges, and Deg leapt out of his seat again, swearing. In swaggered Brevyn, who collected interested eyes wherever she went, and this time it was no different. He watched as most of the tables lurched under the weight of palms as patrons twisted in their seats, angling for a look. Lucien suspected that the glances in that inn on that particular evening were due to reasons beyond her commanding presence.

Sizing up the competition.

Brevyn looked luminous that evening, lights dancing in her dark-brown eyes, no doubt because she would get to use her fists for a beatdown, and soon. Lucien never considered himself ordinary, but Brevyn had a way of making even him feel like a potted plant in the corner. He had taken to wearing more billowy, open blouses and sleek, black coats, inspiring Brevyn to constantly tease him about entering a room "nipples first."

Brevyn herself cultivated a particular kind of look, and it worked for her. And he *liked* that about her. Brevyn spotted them at once, and with deliberate nonchalance took her time arriving at the table. As soon as she had lowered herself into the empty chair to Lucien's left, the halfling's jaw unhinged.

"*This* is your promised antiquities expert?" Musty Deg snorted.

Unseen, Brevyn's hand clamped down on his thigh. Lucien bit the inside of his cheek.

Brevyn nodded and shrugged, unbothered. "Looks can be deceiving."

"You have a pretty face," the halfling across from him burbled, pointing at Brevyn's nose. That finger moved from hers, to Cree's, then finally to Lucien's. "You all do. Pah. I don't—*hic*—trust pretty faces."

Lucien raised a brow. Cree sat up straighter. It felt like they had been going in wet burping circles for hours now and this was the first interesting thing the halfling had said all evening. Well, besides the gout thing. Lucien watched the fur on Cree's forearms stand on end. To his left, Brevyn shifted in her seat. One of them was going to die or get maimed that night, he could just feel it.

Thirty-five gold, thirty-five gold . . . He just had to keep remembering that. It was his responsibility to keep this whole job from going south in a hurry.

"Now, now," Lucien said softly, opening his palms on top of the sticky table. "We can obviously reach an understanding tonight, my friends. We've shared such pleasant conversation, passed the time well, have we not?"

"I'm not—*hic*—your friend," said Musty Deg.

"Nor am I." The gnome sitting at Deg's side spoke at last. She had a far simpler, gentler appearance than the halfling, which almost certainly meant she was the dangerous one.

"We need not be friends," Lucien pointed out. "Only business associates."

"Deg told you the moment you sat down the whole lot goes for fifty. He wants fifty. You are not willing to meet his demands, you have wasted our time with blather, and thus our business is concluded."

Now the gnome, Sundry Daly, started doing *all* the talking. Interesting. Despite her words, Lucien knew they were getting somewhere. Time spent reluctantly with Sarenne de Chastain had taught him the value in almost painful vigilance. The steely glint in Sundry's brown eyes told him there was a dagger pointed at him below the table. That was fine. To make sure they knew it, Lucien leaned back in his chair and sighed as if to say: *Get comfortable, the night is young.*

"Fifty is a joke." Brevyn grunted. "We both know it's insulting."

Lucien nudged her lightly with his knee. Brevyn was many things, but good at ceding control was not one of them. This was his night, his ship to steer safely into port. She could knock skulls, thread streams of blood magic with dizzying sophistication, negotiate a standoff, and drink most of the city under the table—all qualities he admired—but for once, she was supposed to ease off the reins and let him have a go. She went quiet, leaning forward, silent but not relaxed.

Deg was all posture, he decided, not even a blunt instrument, a clumsy one. The brains? Those belonged to Sundry. Lucien fixed his eyes on the gnome, grinning.

"Fifty *is* a joke."

"And yet nobody is laughing," Sundry pointed out, clucking her tongue. She started to push her chair back, and Lucien felt the whole room shift. Indeed, one of them was going to die that night; he just had to make damned sure it was Deg or Sundry, not his people. Sundry must have felt the change in the air—the charge—and carefully sat back down. Cree and Lucien had accumulated a row of empty ale mugs, and the lone wretch left to tend the whole of the tavern finally returned. She swiveled exhausted, drooping eyes toward them, not bothering with a smile, though they had tipped well every round. It was understandable. The tavern chatter was loud and getting louder as the crowd swelled and the liquor flowed. The woman scooped their mugs onto a tray, a quill and single piece of parchment poking out of her stained apron.

Now was the time. Deg and Sundry weren't budging. Lucien wasn't parting with more than thirty-five of their employer's gold coins. If they were savvy, the crates would be theirs for thirty, and those extra five coins would fatten his pockets, to be split among he, Cree, and Brev. Not a bad profit for a night's work, so long as they made it out unscathed.

"Do ye mind?" Lucien winked at the tavern girl, smoothly stealing the pen and parchment from her pocket. He conspicuously left a few jangling coins behind.

She shrugged and lumbered away with their empty mugs. "Do as you like. Everyone does."

"What's this now?" burped Musty Deg, pushing himself up on the table to get a better view as Lucien tapped the end of the pen on his tongue and then started scribbling. Over Lucien's bent head, he felt Cree and Brevyn share a quick glance.

Now was the time.

"We just need to land on the same page, so to speak." Lucien folded the paper lightly, so as not to smudge the ink, and pushed the parchment across the table.

It was Sundry Daly who intercepted it, reading the message with widening gray eyes.

"All of them?" she whispered. Now her eyes flitted around the room. "Surely not."

"I'm afraid so," said Lucien with a shrug.

Sundry showed the parchment to Deg, the blood draining swiftly from his face. The gnome pressed her lips together tightly, wiggled her nose, and gave Lucien a single nod.

"Say more words."

"As you like," Lucien whispered silkily. He rested his elbows on the table, keeping a keen eye on the room around them as he leaned in to say, "Thirty-five was more than fair, but now the price is thirty, friends. No budging. Agree to it, and we may just get you out of here alive, too."

Brevyn placed her closed fist on the table, and that seemed to be enough to convince Musty Deg and Sundry Daly. Lucien felt Cree's eyes searching his face, imploring. He knew, implicitly, the question. Could the three of them, capable though they may be, really clear out an entire tavern of mercenaries?

"Twenty-eight if we both survive!" Deg burp-blurted.

"Half now, half when we're finished," Lucien replied. "Under the table where you can feel it. Nothing stupid and nothing coy."

Brevyn squeezed her fist, scarred knuckles popping above the din. Cree reached into the pack on the floor between them, extricating a small sack of coins. He heard the quiet clink as she counted out the right amount, then slid the satchel under the table. A moment later, Deg and Sundry exchanged a look, then the gnome briefly crossed her arms over her chest. Lucien only realized she had smoothly palmed a key when it was peeking out from under her fingers on the table between them.

"There's a trapdoor under the flour sacks in the kitchen," she whispered, barely moving her mouth. "That will get you inside."

"Cree, take these two upstairs, please." Lucien slipped the key into his coat pocket.

Her ears flattened, then perked. "Are . . . Are you certain?"

"Lu and I can handle this," Brevyn assured her, already getting up.

Lucien was confident, too, but perhaps not in the constant, all-consuming way Brevyn was at any given moment.

"Wouldn't hurt to duck your head in," he told Cree as the catfolk ushered Musty Deg and Sundry Daly toward the stairs a few paces from the inn door.

The whole place was as fragrant and cheap as the ale it served. The first floor contained only two visible rooms—the combined kitchen and pantry in the back, and the large, open serving and eating area where they had been haggling. The main room had about a dozen or so tables scattered randomly, with equally random numbers of mismatched chairs. Three wrought-iron chandeliers hung from the ceiling. Deg and Sundry clearly had an affinity for hunting, or knew someone who did, as many different stuffed and preserved heads decorated the walls. Lucien had tried not to look at them throughout the evening, perturbed by their ghoulish, moldering appearance.

The kitchen was partially hidden behind the single bar counter. The cellar they needed would be back there, but it was pointless to approach when he could already hear blades being unsheathed.

"Is it walking into a trap if you know the bloodbath is coming?" Lucien mused, taking a quick head count.

"Ha! You're just lucky I arrived when I did," Brevyn replied. "No chance you could crack this many skulls without me."

"My dear, why would I want to?"

She drew a sharp, gold hairpin from her mess of yellow-blond hair. The long waves tumbled free as she drew the pointed edge of the pin down her forearm. Blood seeped through the wound, then sprayed into a mist, drawn in two streams toward her fists. Hard, black stone rippling with molten fire formed around her hands—hands that immediately started swinging. A mercenary at the table behind them crumpled in a heap before he even knew the battle had begun.

Lucien took the high ground, stepping from his own chair onto the tavern table before leaping onto the counter. Mugs and pewter plates scattered. He flicked a dagger out of his belt, one formerly concealed by his long, oiled coat. He nicked the skin of his middle chest, elemental power rising from his veins, manipulated, and pulled to his blade, giving the weapon a crackling sheen of ice.

The floorboards and rafters shook as the mercenaries filling the inn flung back their cloaks and coats to reveal their own arsenals. Lucien watched the barmaid dive behind the counter, cowering under his feet. Brevyn didn't waste an instant, grabbing the table they had just vacated, lifting it high over her head and grunting, throwing it across the room and pinning a flailing dwarf underneath. Eight of the remaining ten mercenaries turned their attention on Brevyn, rightly assessing her as the larger threat. But Lucien was not without fangs. A dwarf and a halfling in mottled, tawny cloaks and pale leather armor dove toward the counter.

The dwarf swung her heavy pike, trying to sweep Lucien's legs. He nimbly danced down the length of the counter, tossing his dagger into the air, catching it by the pointed tip, and then hurling it with deadly speed at the dwarf's dominant hand, shards of ice following. The blade and shards struck true, then were drawn back by a gust of Lucien's magic and dispatched again to slice across the halfling's throat.

The pike clattered to the floor, an arterial spray hitting the wounded dwarf as she flailed for her weapon, disarmed. Through the blood, Lucien saw a shape like a black shadow slide down the stairs.

Brevyn had taken up another table, using this one to shield herself from the onslaught of blows aimed her way. She used it like a battering ram, shoving hard against the bodies piled up on the other side—but the tide pushed back, trapping Brevyn against the far wall. Lucien hopped down from the bar counter, kicking the injured dwarf hard in the head and knocking her out. He then scooped up the now limp and increasingly lifeless halfling, heaving him up into the air over the crowd of advancing mercenaries.

Cree, flattened against the wall near the door, saw her opportunity at once. She raised her arms, catching the halfling, not with her hands but with a spell. The halfling stopped in midair, suspended above his comrades, the gash across his neck weeping freely. That blood supplied Cree what she needed, power surging through her hands, a dark miasma emanating from her palms, the spell gradually encircling the mercenaries, binding them, holding them.

Those closest to Cree noticed first, crying out and struggling against the magic. It was the perfect distraction for Brevyn. She dropped the shield table and swung mightily with her molten-rock-encrusted fists. The mercenaries were surrounded, and while one or two managed to land a blow on her, it was nothing a bit of Cree's magic couldn't cure later.

More chaos, more blood. More blood, more power.

Only a moment later the fray was violent enough to give Cree another massive surge, the floor slippery with blood, allowing her to plunge the whole mess of scrabbling, fighting, gnashing thugs into a deep, instant sleep.

Bodies thudded to the floor, a sudden, terrible silence descending on the inn.

A cup rolled away toward the door. The barmaid, shaking, poked her head up above the counter. She had taken a pewter plate, holding it with both trembling hands to protect her face.

"Is . . . Is it over?"

Nobody answered her. Brevyn kicked aside a few useless limbs blocking her way, tearing off the bottom bit of her tunic to wrap around a cut on her upper arm. Lucien, Cree, and Brevyn wordlessly marched toward the back room, Lucien producing the key for the cellar from his coat pocket. As they passed, he flicked the barmaid one last tip.

CHAPTER 8

"How long will they be like that?" Musty Deg asked, huddled near the door. Brevyn handed him a small sack of coins, this one with the rest of their payment.

"Long enough for you to leave this place," Cree replied, nodding toward the still-slumbering pile of mercenaries cluttering up the inn's main room.

Lucien doffed an invisible cap and gave Deg the key to his cellar. At least Deg had stopped burping. Beside him, Sundry Daly surveyed the damage, unmoved, apparently, by the carnage. The barmaid had already fled. Lucien wandered over to the nearest mercenary, an elf flat on his back, with his bloodied cape spread beneath him as he slept, bound by Cree's spell. A strange charm hung around his neck, and Lucien took it in hand, plucking it leather-thong-and-all from the elf's neck.

He held it up to the light. The gold had been worked into the shape of a triangle, with three blue gems at each point.

"The Knowing Mentor," he murmured.

"Take it," Brevyn told him. "She'll want to see it."

"Who?" demanded Sundry, shaking herself out of contemplative silence. "You never mentioned who wanted our books, or why."

Cree slid past Brevyn, holding the door for her.

"You're right," Brevyn said, hoisting the crate in her arms a little higher. "I never did."

Lucien followed her out, and Cree lingered only a moment longer. "I would not tarry here; the spell will soon lift. I recommend somewhere far from here, and perhaps new names."

When they were outside in the cool, bracing night, Lucien added, "Surely he's not attached to *Musty Deg*. I'd be clamoring for a change."

"The heart wants what it wants." Brevyn chuckled, leading them around the corner and into a narrow alley. A cart waited there, along with an impatient, stamping mule.

"And this heart wants another drink, a proper one without pond scum," Lucien replied. He snorted, pointing at the shabby little cart. "Is that what took you so long?"

"Volunteering to carry the crate, are we? Dare you to try. Weighs a bloody ton." Brevyn carefully placed the wooden box into the back of the cart, grimacing as it brushed her injured arm. "Assholes put up more of a fight than I expected."

Lucien and Cree hopped into the back with the crate while Brevyn took the driver's bench, hauling up the reins.

"They went down in five minutes flat," said Lucien, laughing.

"Not a record for me by any means," replied Brevyn.

"Drinks, then?" Lucien settled down next to the crate, resting his back against it. As soon as he touched the wood, he felt a shiver run up his spine. Whatever books were inside were not ordinary. That perhaps went without saying, since they were such a pain to acquire, but still, it shocked him that they seemed to release a noticeable, troubling aura. "The Drinking Druid? The Hilt and Pommel? No, no, let me think . . . The Whistling Teakettler, a finer mead you won't find in the whole of Rexxentrum."

"Too many prying eyes at the Teakettler," Cree muttered. "Karem knows folk there. I'd rather our activities not get back to the ruins."

"I suppose discretion is preferable at the moment. But that mead . . ."

"The Dusty Carriage?" suggested Cree. "I like their silk pillows."

"You thirsty louts can stop bickering," Brevyn called over her shoulder. "We're heading straight back to the Academy grounds. I'm not risking this cargo a moment longer. You can drink yourselves stupid after we make good on the delivery."

"Ah yes, the boring and tragically responsible thing to do." Lucien sighed. "Perhaps it's for the best, mm? Even concealed I can feel the malice in those tomes. What do you reckon they say?"

"Nothing good," Brevyn said, her tone taking a darker turn. "And that makes them valuable."

Valuable, indeed. At least the Shimmer Ward, with its high golden walls and vast academic gardens, was only a stone's throw from the Tangles. Their benefactor had not sent them far, but she had sent them urgently. While he would have preferred a post-battle swig, a seven-gold profit sparkled on the horizon. He had no intention of spending it wisely, of course, which made its potential that much more enticing.

And there was another reward waiting for him. One the others knew nothing about. Gold was nice, but information could be even better.

Lucien tucked his knuckles under his chin and gazed up at the stars, breathing deep. He preferred city air; he had been sucking it down since he was a babe. Rexxentrum bore little resemblance to Shadycreek Run, but it was a vast improvement over their lodgings in the Marrow Valley. The swamps had made everything stink like sulfur, gnats and mosquitoes swarmed in bloodsucking clouds, the incessant croaks of fire toads kept him awake all hours of the night. For four years he had lived in what Elias called "easy country." It was a place of wounds and patched-over sorrows, war scarring the lands and the hearts and minds that occupied them. Those years in the Marrow Valley had been plenty for Lucien, and if it weren't for daily study and distractions, the Oltu Ruins might have driven him mad in the space of a month.

The Orders had given him power and training and the chance to destroy the witch Azrahari, but mistrust had been brewing among the low-level hunters. Contracts were becoming rarer, boredom was setting in. He was never going to make a living that way.

Lucien's eyes drifted downward and fixed on the back of Brevyn's head. She had swept up her long hair again, the pin still stained with a mercenary's blood.

The mule click-clacked over the cobbles, the cart winding along the uneven road, swerving right onto a wider thoroughfare that ran along the high walls of the Shimmer Ward. Slender towers appeared over its edge, gleaming with light from within, beckoning like lovers' fingers.

"When we reach the Academy, let me do the talking," said Brevyn. She swiveled and noticed him staring at her with half-lidded, unfocused eyes. "Are you listening?"

"I'm admiring and listening, lass."

Cree made a soft gagging sound.

"Deg and Sundry were small-time," Brevyn continued, rolling the shoulder on her injured arm. "This is . . . just keep your mouths shut unless she addresses you."

"Fine. I've nothing to say to her," Cree promised.

Lucien watched Cree as she said it, noticing an odd twitch in her left ear. He wondered if, like him, Cree had gone quietly to their employer and asked for something on the side. It almost eased the knot in his belly to think that he wasn't the only one keeping secrets from friends.

The cart jerked forward, rounded a corner, and even under the dimming drape of night the Shimmer Ward unfolded before them like a jeweler's wares spread across a green velvet cushion. The Soltryce Academy, their destination, rose like a crystalline spike from the center of a maze of lower yet no-less-impressive buildings and gardens. The hacked cobbles of the Tangles gave way to smooth, gray paving stones, an imposing arch separating the old town from the sparkling wink of the Academy grounds. Fireflies flashed in the hedges and message-carrying ravens soared overhead, the cut of their wings against the wind like whispers in the night.

Lucien sat up straighter. It was a sight to take even the most jaded boy's breath away.

At that late hour, the slumbering ward lay almost empty, though a few individuals wandered the paths and gardens, paying little attention to the bedraggled cart and bedraggled trio trundling toward the central plaza, and the broad avenue that led toward the Academy's main hall.

Dismounting, he wondered what they must have looked like to the scholars and students that paused and watched them pass, each of them splashed with blood and armed, Brevyn carrying a conspicuously large crate.

"Don't we just fit right in," he heard Brevyn mutter as they entered a soaring, arched antechamber. The purpose of the place announced itself immediately: A rotating gyroscope of bright metals whirred in the room just beyond, a circular rotunda whose walls were lined with the portraits of, he assumed, great thinkers who had walked those hallowed halls. A lone, robed elf swept the black-and-gold-tiled floor. His eyes wandered to them across the lonely expanse, noticed the crate in Brevyn's arms, and visibly widened.

Lucien saw there the light of intent curiosity, no different from the shine in a greedy tyrant's eyes.

Brevyn led the way, slowed not even a little by her burden. They veered left out of the rotunda and up a series of climbing, swirling staircases. The sounds of hushed learning reached them from the arches of long corridors, study proceeding at all hours of the day. They reached the third-floor landing and turned again, this time down the narrower, quieter hall that led to their benefactor's private offices. The walls muffled their steps, draped in dark, somber velvets. An open door along the way showed a modest study crowded with bookcases and a desk strewn with maps.

Lucien tried to imagine himself there as a lad, all wild purple hair and spiraled horns, kneeling on the study chair, huddled over the map, skinny elbows digging into unknown, unseen territories. The image never fully formed in his mind, vanishing in a blink. His chest throbbed from where he had cut himself for the blood his spells required.

A moment later he stood on the deep, plush carpeting of the Archmage of Antiquity's well-appointed apartment. He had been there briefly once before, and nothing had changed except for the quantity of books stacked on her desk. An imposing hearth beside an equally imposing desk spat sparks as the archmage placed another log on the fire. She moved only when she had to, seeming to float toward them in her emerald-green robes trimmed in dazzling jewels. A half-elven woman of somewhat advanced age, she wore her short brown hair twisting behind her pointed ears, and favored a severe, dark lacquer painted over her lips.

The crate thudded onto the floor between them. He, Cree, and Brevyn stood in a row and waited while the archmage carefully leaned down and opened the lid on the box.

A spasm ran through the room, an ancient chill, like the long-held breath of some forgotten titan.

"Just the one shipment?" asked Vess DeRogna. She folded her hands and stared down into the box.

"The others didn't have the marking on the outside you described," Brevyn replied. She shifted a little from foot to foot. Only two people seemed to make Brevyn this uneasy: Vess DeRogna and Sarenne de Chastain.

"There were others there looking for the same thing," she added.

Lucien plucked the triangular necklace from his pocket and offered it to the archmage.

"Indeed," DeRogna murmured. She tilted the charm toward her, examining it. "I warned you there might be friendly competition."

Brevyn nodded. "We weren't so friendly with them."

"That's quite all right. These little spats are expected, and you were hardly locked in battle with scholars of note. They sent mercenaries, I imagine, and not very expensive ones at that."

"No trouble for us," Brevyn assured her.

"Is that so?" DeRogna's pale-gray eyes moved from the charm to the bound wound on Brevyn's arm. "It appears they were a little trouble."

"No. None at all."

Vess DeRogna gave them a chilly smile. "I must admit, I was somewhat skeptical when Elias mentioned you, but it seems your work continues to impress. Contract work for the Orders drying up is bad for him, but good for me." She returned to her desk, collecting a black velvet sack, then presented the little bag to Brevyn. Lucien recognized the beautiful music of coins within. "There will likely come a time when I need your assistance again. I trust you will remain in the city?"

"As long as the coins flow," Brevyn replied, accepting the payment with a courteous tilt of her head. A piece of yellow hair swung free, and she brushed it aside impatiently.

"Of course you are aware of my affiliation with the Cerberus Assembly." DeRogna gave them a tight smile, peering under the lid of the crate before letting it fall shut. "These trifles continue to trickle in from northern digs, and though they are of varying fascination, the Assembly has deemed it necessary to control their presence," DeRogna said with a light shrug. What Lucien knew of the Assembly could fit neatly in a thimble. He knew they were mages, powerful ones at that, and deeply entrenched in Dwendalian politics. "Meddlers like the Cobalt Soul will continue to seek these trifles as well, and we, of course, will continue to disappoint them." Her arresting eyes appraised them each in turn, and Lucien thought nothing of it until she looked at him. There, her gaze lingered. A prickle of heat along the nape of his neck encouraged him to disengage, but he couldn't, holding her eye long after it felt appropriate. Her smile changed, widening before dissipating altogether.

"If that will be all, my lady . . ." Brevyn quietly interrupted.

"You may go," she said, dismissing Cree and Brevyn with a flick of her fingers, as if dislodging an errant fly. "But you . . ." Her eyes settled on Lucien. "You stay."

Brevyn's jaw hung open. "But he—"

"Don't make me repeat myself."

"Yes, certainly, Archmage."

Cree tugged lightly on Brevyn's shirt, and then the two of them slipped around the open door, Brevyn's mouth dragging along the floor. Lucien's and Brevyn's gazes locked fleetingly. The haunt in her eyes, Lucien realized with a jolt, was one of mistrust.

She need not fear his betrayal, only his abandonment. And, well, that might sting, it was true, but Lucien felt certain she would recover. Brevyn was resilient, one of her many respectable qualities. She also possessed a hair trigger of a temper.

Lucien wasn't sure he would even be there to see the coming rage.

After the door closed, Vess DeRogna opened her folded hands to him. "Now, I believe it is time we discussed our private arrangement."

CHAPTER 9

"There's no need for the theatrics, Archmage. I could have come back another day," said Lucien. He paced, drifting away from the crate of old books, then changing his mind. It felt stranger to have his back to the tomes, as if the lifeless pages might somehow conspire against him.

"You could have," DeRogna agreed, passing him and approaching a low side table near the hearth. She bent and withdrew a folded and sealed parchment. "But that would be a waste of my time. Do not mistake my willingness to meet with you at this late hour as availability. Only your usefulness and the value of this find justify my attention. Here, boy, is the other portion of your payment. Let us have it settled, and quickly."

Lucien bowed his head. Asking her for it in the first place had been a risk and a kick to his pride. Elias and the other senior members of the Orders had not responded well to his need for independence. But Lucien, Cree, and Brevyn had proved themselves capable hunters, and competent enough to take work outside the Orders' purview. Reluctantly, Elias had made introductions. DeRogna wanted relics, Lucien and his friends had the willingness and means to acquire them, and DeRogna's vaunted hands would not be publicly sullied in the process.

"So you know where she is?" Lucien asked, anxious to grab the parchment and go.

"I think you will be pleased."

The paper was warm when DeRogna handed it over. Lucien burned to tear open the seal and see what the archmage's spies had found, but instead he forced himself to slip his reward into his pocket. Lucien pulled his coat closed as their business concluded, and thanked her as she dismissed him with a wave. DeRogna moved away from him, her green robes spread out along the floor as she crouched to inspect the crate, a slight shimmer emanating from her hands as she lifted the top book out of the box with a spell. It hovered there between them, bound in mottled black leather, cracked purple script running along the spine.

Lucien meant to be gone already. He felt the warmth of the study wrap around him like a heavy blanket. His eyes drooped as the book drew on him, a soft, invisible hook grabbing him by the throat and taking hold. A meaningless whisper chased through his mind, the language unknown to him, but the voice rich with promises. He took a small step forward, almost tumbling against the crate. The spell broke, the book tumbled back into its box with its mates, and DeRogna stood, clearing her throat.

"Shit, I . . ." Lucien rubbed his jaw. Vess DeRogna put up her hand, silencing him.

A glow like fairy lights twinkled in her pale eyes as she studied him. "What I haven't sorted out yet is if you're a seeker or a follower."

"Gold leads and I follow," he replied, bowing.

"Perhaps." DeRogna crossed the distance between them and took him hard by the chin. "There's a quality to your eyes I know well. You sense the power in these books, don't you?"

Lucien snorted. "I thought they were mere trifles."

"To the untrained, uncurious eye, they are just that. Relics. Dust and ash from an obliterated past. Pre-Calamity antiquities that might make a nice paperweight or wither on the shelves of a fool. They could be that, or they could turn the tide of wars, shatter empires, and decide the course of history." She let go of his chin, smirking. "How did you fall in with Elias and his blood hunters?"

"Brevyn trained under him, she recommended me, and I was willing to spend my days in a swamp slicing open my own veins and listening to Elias bark orders." Lucien shrugged. "What can I say? It was better than scrimping and begging and thieving in the Run. The Claret Orders were a place to land. Maybe not a permanent place or a soft one, but a place nonetheless."

"Elias has no patience for imbeciles. Sarenne even less."

"I tend to agree," he said with a laugh.

DeRogna sketched a wide circle back to the hearth, the fire casting impossible, imposing shadows as she glided by and tented her long fingers. She was a rich, insufferable windbag but undeniably skilled at making it look good. She took a decanter from among the tidy stacks of books and scrolls on her desk and poured herself a small measure of garnet-colored wine. Sipping, she stared into the fire.

"Wherever that scrap of paper takes you, I suggest you not go far. I meant what I said earlier—I could use someone like you. I think you might be wasted on the Orders."

Lucien's brow shot up. Like him? Not like Brevyn or Cree? He pulled his shoulders back and rested his palms on his hips. There were times to fold and times to bluff. "Cunning? Thoughtful? Unbearably good looking?"

"Bold." She laughed. "And more than a little reckless."

With that, she nodded, and Lucien shuffled to the door.

"Your work for me has been sufficient," Vess DeRogna called after him. "There will be more, and there will be better."

"What did she want with you, then?" Brevyn asked. She and Cree waited for him beside the cart. Cree had lit a small cigarillo, puffing on it idly, though her eyes bored into him as he conjured a fib.

"Now, now, don't be jealous," Lucien replied with a wink. "Think she's soft on me. Just wanted to flirt a little and feel alive again, can't begrudge the old cudgel that . . ."

"Uh-huh. Right. Vess DeRogna isn't 'soft' on anyone, Lu." Brevyn rolled her eyes and hopped into the driver's bench, startling the mule. "Sew that mouth shut, I won't pry."

"But you want to," Cree added. The catfolk shared her cigarillo with Lucien as they climbed into the cart.

"Let a man have his secrets. I've precious little else."

"You've gold enough now in your pocket to do plenty of things. Plenty of *daft* things, knowing you," Brevyn pointed out—rather harshly, in Lucien's opinion. A shower of coins fell on them as she emptied the velvet satchel over their heads. "Cut it fair, Cree," she said. "I trust you."

"Ouch!" Lucien chuckled, rolling onto his side. "To the bone with that one!"

"Says the man keeping secrets." Brevyn whistled and brought the mule into a trot.

Lucien took the handful of coins Cree pushed his way, scooping them into the same pocket holding the real prize of the job. Giddy bubbles filled his stomach when he put the coins there and felt the brush of the parchment. What felt like ages of waiting, and he would finally have his answers. When his sister's letters dried up earlier that year, Lucien had begun to worry. After arriving in Rexxentrum, he found her last known address a dead end. She had stopped writing and moved on.

That was his fault, he knew; the length between his own letters had gone so long that it must have seemed like he had given up on their promise of being a family one day.

"You can drop me at the gates," he announced. The giddiness ebbed, and in its place came sober determination. "I'll grab a rickshaw where I'm going."

"And where, pray tell, is that?" Brevyn snorted.

"I'll meet you both at the Shattered Lance," he said, watching the gates as they neared. "Won't be long, and if I am, you'll be too soused to care."

"Oh!" cooed Cree. "The Shattered Lance, hadn't thought of that one."

The thought of cold ale and warm hearths didn't move Brevyn, however, who spat off the side of the cart. "You're just leaving us? *Now?* After that job?"

"'Tis only an errand, lass, I'm not leaving."

But he was just leaving them. Then. After that job. He leapt from the cart before Brevyn brought it to a complete stop, squinting into the murky darkness of the Tangles, the shadows little dispersed by the grimy lanterns dotting the roadside.

"The Shattered Lance!" Cree waved as the cart rattled on. The end of her cigarillo flared in the darkness. "First round is mine!"

Lucien felt a stab of remorse as he wandered down the lane, listening for the sound of hooves and wheels, hoping his destination wasn't far. The guilt didn't last long, vanishing the instant he took the parchment from DeRogna out of his pocket and broke the seal. He waited until he couldn't hear Brevyn's cart any longer and unfolded the paper to read. Skimming the formalities, his pulse quickened.

The woman in question has been located, though not as Aldreda Tavelle. She has taken the name of her husband, Panvel Seriblo, a silversmith of some renown, owner of The Center Stone, located in the Court of Colors. It appears the family lives at his place of business.

The address followed, pointing Lucien toward the northeastern quadrant of the Court of Colors. The Court wasn't terribly far, just southwest of where he stood, eyes wide, heart racing, hands increasingly sweaty. He wouldn't remember stumbling through the streets searching desperately for a rickshaw, nor would he remember the bumpy, nauseating ride from the gates of the Shimmer Ward, through the twisty-turny maze of the Tangles to the Court of Colors. He couldn't remember if he tipped the driver or if he just spilled out of the rickshaw and onto the cobbles, clutching the parchment as if it were the very talisman of immortality itself.

She's here, she's here, she's here . . .

A juggler in a tricolored jerkin tossed pins into the air next to a small stage not far from where the rickshaw dropped him. A fountain bubbled quietly in the plaza, circled by blue, pink, and yellow buildings of polished stone, pennants flying from their balconies, flags snapping in the steady night wind. He picked his way around the plaza, searching the front of each building for the right words. The Center Stone. Leave it to his beautiful little sister to wind up living among silver and gems. She would fit right in.

What a gift that his gamble with DeRogna had paid off, and what a boon that he went to Aldreda not impoverished, not useless, but with a few gold coins in his coat and powerful blood magic at his beck and call. This was what he had been waiting for, a chance to prove himself to her. They had so much life to do over, so much history to rewrite, and Brevyn and Cree—mercenaries, when one boiled it down—had no place in this new, pristine, so-earned life.

Lucien steeled himself. He drifted to a sweaty halt near the juggler and the small wooden stage. A curly-headed child brushed by him in a hurry, rushing to get a better view of the stage. Lucien patted his pockets, making sure the kid hadn't fleeced him, but his coins were all there. A few drunks had gathered to lean against one another and pretend to watch the show, waiting until they were coherent enough to return to worrying husbands and wives. Lucien swallowed a gulp of disgust as a few handmade puppets bobbled into view. A thin glaze of tears filmed his eyes as he thought of how luminous Aldreda had been on the stage when their family performed. Just a tiny bit of a thing, but she could sing and dance, and twirl for minutes on end without getting dizzy.

He didn't want to remember Sock Brother, but he was there in the memory, too, stiff and ever-smiling, eyes like twinkling jet beads, looming over Aldreda with his leathery head loose and bobbing, the smell of new shoes following him wherever he went. His bones were so brittle they sang like castanets as he twirled beneath the fabric pavilion, for they could never perform in the rain. When Sock Brother got wet, his hair began to shed . . .

Lucien's stomach tightened at the sight of the puppets, but he couldn't turn away.

"Behold! Behold!" one puppeteer shrieked from behind his blind. The pointy-hatted crier puppet on his hand shook back and forth. "Now stop and witness a grand tale, a tale for all times and all folk, and heed well its lesson lest ye repeat the errors of the past!"

A painted castle on a rickety board rose behind the crier puppet, and three more characters appeared—a knight in all black, a golden king with a curly beard, and a maiden in white. From behind the puppet stage, a tinny horn sounded. *Ba-badabaa-bup-bup-bup-bapa-baaaah!* One of the drunks in front of him knelt and heaved. Another drunk laughed. A sliver of moon came out from behind the clouds, bathing the plaza in pearls.

"Look upon your end, King Daldred!" thundered the black knight. "Your lands are surrounded, your castle besieged. Send out your lady love, strike her down before my armies. Her blood for your freedom!"

The puppet king collapsed, squished inward by the hand performing him. A patchwork peasant of felt and yarn poked up from behind the blind, flopping around pitifully and wailing. "Not the queen! Not the queen! For our king loves her beyond measure, and she is vanity itself. The kingdom for one soul, and the price never to be paid!"

The drunk on the ground composed himself and wobbled to his feet, hissing at the stage. "Ah'vsheen this one afor. Boo! Boooo!" He was hushed by the woman beside him, who took two leaping steps away to avoid the reek of his vomit.

Why are you hesitating? Go to Aldreda, go!

His feet felt as if they were stuck in a bear trap. Lucien knew this tragedy well, had performed it himself with his family when they still greeted each other with smiles, when his brother was still alive. They always made Lucien play the invader knight, Taeleron the Cleaver. The story originated in the Menagerie Coast but had gone through so many iterations and retellings that on modern stages it took on fantastical proportions. Lucien had no doubt that there had once been a lord or chief called Daldred whose love made a tremendous sacrifice, but the tale had become so fantastically warped over time, it was beyond recognition.

He found himself mouthing along with the black knight's lines.

"Send her out! Send her out!" the knight roared. "And bring a headsman's axe!"

The maiden puppet of Queen Andica mimed combing her long, raven hair with her blobby hands. Lucien watched as the puppets dropped down behind the fabric barrier one by one, until only the queen was left. She sang a melancholy song, an ode to her own beauty, her lovely long hair, her perfect heart-shaped face, and her lean, strong limbs. A tiny hook with a paper moon hanging from a string appeared beside her. Night had fallen over her kingdom, and she fled the castle, leaving the safety of the walls and parapets behind.

The little doll shook and then went still, and she raised her arms to the paper moon, calling, "They think me vain. They hate me, they hate me. Hate me not. Doubt me not."

Queen Andica plunged a knife into her own chest, bleeding red yarn. Lucien turned away just as King Daldred returned to sing his own song of lamentation. "I am the King of Nothing! King of Woe!"

He had always thought it was too much, that the fable ought to end with Andica's unexpected choice. Even in cloth and yarn it captured a perfect sadness. Lucien couldn't help but grin morosely as he remembered Aldreda taking his side. It was her favorite part to play.

"Lucien is right!" she would shout at their parents, stamping a tiny, impetuous foot in their caravan. Her upturned nose would scrunch as they ignored her and continued darning the family costumes. "The king is such a whining baby. It should really end with her, she's the interesting one."

"And you know better, child? I don't think so," their father would say, laughing at her suggestions. "These things are the way they are, no use changing them. Your mother agrees with me, and so does your brother." He meant Sock Brother, of course. Lucien's opinions were never requested.

"Father knows best," came Brother's wooden reply.

The Center Stone was located only several paces off the main plaza, down a lantern-brightened alley to the right of the puppet stage. He left a few coppers for the performers, remembering what it was to play to a belligerent, cheap audience, and to feel the cutting rejection of total strangers. Hands in his pockets, pulse only marginally steadier, he passed beneath the rows of colored bunting hanging between storefronts, walking by a closed shop advertising leather goods, a butcher's stand, and a boarded-up pub. Then came The Center Stone, notable in that it was the lone white building of the row. A dark-blue curtain protected the wares in the window, but a light was still on behind it.

Lucien took the four short steps up to the door to the right of the display windows. The hours were neatly painted on an oval, rough-edged wooden sign that hung from the door latch. An invisible hand reached in and squeezed his heart. He knew the handwriting at once.

This changes everything or nothing, he thought, stricken. He hoped for everything. He hoped, even if it meant abandoning a way of life he had come to accept. As he lifted his hand to knock, he saw a fresh, healing cut on his forearm from the earlier battle.

He grimaced and knocked anyway.

CHAPTER 10

A child answered the door, a human boy with a stranger's face. Perhaps this was the wrong place. The boy stared up at Lucien with a finger crooked in the corner of his mouth. There was a gasp and harried footsteps, and then light poured over them from an inner door opening wide.

"Dawnfather's grace, what are you doing, Kyvir? You're never to answer the door without me!" A beautiful young infernal appeared, her black hair draped over one magenta shoulder in a neat plait. Horns speared through the braids. She cradled a sleeping, swaddled infant in her arms.

"Aldreda? Who would that be at this hour? Aldreda?!" a deep, male voice boomed from upstairs.

"I've handled it, darling!" she called back. "About the door, Kyvir . . ."

"But . . . But he looks like you, Aldreda."

"Go up to bed, Kyvir."

"Aldreda—"

"Bed, I said. Now. Do not make me say it again."

Lucien froze—his mother's voice from his sister's lips. At last, she looked at him, really looked at him, and Aldreda pursed her lips and nodded toward the warm interior of the shop.

"Well?" she asked. "What are you waiting for? Come in."

Lucien watched the little human boy scamper up the stairs and throw looks back down from every other step. He gave a friendly wave and a half smile, then slid around the door and joined his grown sister in the foyer. She wore a simple black kirtle with puffed sleeves, a dark-purple belt looped at the waist. Aldreda led Lucien away from the draft and around a corner, into a main room with a high ceiling and raw wooden crossbeams. Long, narrow tables held empty cushions for jewelry, their impressions still visible in the velvet. Across from those tables, toward the back of the room, Lucien spied a worn desk strewn with papers, quills, and an abacus. She went at once and tried futilely to tidy it.

"You caught me in the middle of some figures," she muttered, a bright sheen on her forehead. Her breath rattled the candle beside her abacus.

"Will you not hug me, sister?"

"Marii will cry if I put her down." But she came toward him and let Lucien wrap them both in an embrace. It didn't last long. Aldreda pulled away, placing the counting table between them again. She studied him closely. "I had given up on ever seeing you again."

Lucien heard someone walking around above them and hunched. "Well, here I am."

"Here you are."

"I've pictured this so many times." He laughed sadly and ran both hands through his hair. "But life is never like dreams, is it?"

Aldreda was still a young woman, but he noticed puckering around her lips, lines at the corners of her eyes and across her forehead. He also took stock of the quality of her frock, the clean, perfect blanket around her babe, and the shop around them—signifiers of comfort, if not obvious wealth. He thought of the heavy gold coins in his coat pocket and what he had done to earn them. What had she done for all of this?

"You're already a mother?" So young. *So* young.

"And why not?" Aldreda sniffed. "Kyvir is not mine, fever took his mother two winters ago. After she was gone, it just seemed like the natural thing. Panvel and I—my husband, I mean—Gods, there is so much you don't know."

Lucien tried not to let his temper flare. "So much you haven't told me?"

"How could I?" Aldreda wilted, gesturing helplessly to the walls around them. "You stopped returning my letters, and I was half convinced you were dead and gone. I can see it in your eyes, Lucien, you cannot lie to me, you never could. You think I've lived a soft life here, an easy one, but I can assure you there is always suffering you cannot see!"

Her voice rose as she spoke, before she flinched, holding the infant closer to her breast.

"Sister—"

"There is always a cost. Always."

"I know that well," he said. "I didn't write because I had nothing to offer you. It wasn't for lack of love, sister, but for shame."

Aldreda bounced the baby, looking away. "What are you now anyway? A thief? A mercenary?"

"It doesn't matter what I did, it got me here, didn't it?" He took one of the fat, gold coins out of his pocket and showed it to her, then let it disappear up his sleeve, an old trick from an old life. "I do all right, and with the two of us there's no telling how far we might go."

Something was wrong. Aldreda flinched again and closed her eyes tightly.

He took a single step toward her. "You don't have to suffer, Aldreda. I'm here."

Aldreda barked out an exasperated laugh. "And what can you do for me? For us? You've been ignoring me for years, and at first it hurt, but then I came to realize it could be for the best. I could forget our family, leave the nightmares behind, make something good of my own."

"I've taken care of all that," he insisted. An image of the witch, his daggers stabbed into her chest, flashed before him. "I went to the cottage and I destroyed it, and the woman who ruined our lives."

"Our parents made the decision, not her."

"They're gone, too." She turned away from him. His brow furrowed as he put up his hands in easy surrender. "Dreda, I—"

"I didn't think it would be like this," she whispered fiercely into her baby's covered head. "In my heart I fretted, but I refused to believe." Aldreda studied him once more. "I thought there might be room for you here, that you would join Panvel and me, learn a trade, make an honest life, but I don't recognize you anymore. Who knows what kind of danger you've brought to our doorstep just by coming!"

"No! I haven't endangered you," Lucien insisted. "I wouldn't."

"Then what were you doing in Berleben, Lucien. Tell me."

He knew the truth would frighten her. Turning, he stalked to the windows and stared through the crack in the curtains. Moonlight shifted across the cobblestone street. Gooseflesh rippled down his arms. He felt a pull to that glow, but he stuffed the impulse down.

"I can't tell you everything. I wish I could, but it just wouldn't help either of us," Lucien replied softly. Members of the Orders were hunted by imperial soldiers. There was a reason he couldn't have her letters sent to the Oltu Ruins. "But the people I ran with won't come looking for me." Cree and Brevyn would, of course, but that he could explain away. Old friends. Legitimate business associates. "Please . . ." Lucien turned back to face her, pressing his palms together tightly. "I've left the Run behind me, destroyed what was there to haunt us, and come to you with enough gold for us to start over."

"Start over?" she blurted. She glanced down at the infant in her arms in disbelief. "I worked my hands raw for this family. I scrubbed their floors and their toilets, looked after their boy, cleaned their puke and their shit, and now I am the lady of the house. I've already started over, brother, at the very bottom, and I was lucky enough to land here. It isn't perfect, but it's safe and it's mine. What you're offering is . . . impossible. You can't even tell me what you are now or what you've become!"

A tremor ran through his hands. It was only a trick of the mind, but as she spoke, he heard the disapproving sneer of Sarenne de Chastain. Aldreda was his younger sister. He wouldn't be chided.

Have patience with her. City life has gone to her head.

"Of course you would have your family, I would never ask you to abandon—"

"It's too late, Lucien. It's too late. Maybe years ago, I don't know . . . I can't think properly. Just looking at you stirs up such evil feelings in me. It isn't fair, I know, but it's true. I look at you and I smell smoke, I hear distant screams, I see again our brother's face leering, bloated with unnatural life." Aldreda shivered and leaned against the doorway, nearly collapsing to her knees. Lucien leapt forward to support her, but she shied away, gathered herself, and stood.

Have patience.

"I should have written, Dreda. I didn't mean to frighten you."

She nodded. "I thought you were gone. I thought you were dead. I grieved you."

"I'm alive and here," said Lucien, gently. "I came to be with you, and shame on me, but I only came when I was enough to support you, you see? I waited and worked until I was enough. I didn't want to come to you begging with open, empty hands. I wanted to give you everything you deserve."

Everything we deserve.

Her shoulders slumped. Carefully, she drew back the blanket on the infant's face, revealing a round pink face, a dusting of fine black hair, and two little nubs of horns on the babe's forehead. Lucien's chest caved inward. He reached for the baby's head, grazing his thumb across the petal-soft skin. As he did, Aldreda saw the fresh marks on his chest and recoiled.

"How? How can we be a family again?" she asked. "I don't even know you."

"But you will know me. You could."

"No," she murmured, a veil falling across her bright eyes. "I already have a family, someone who can support me, someone who is enough."

Aldreda shook her head and pulled the covering over her child, turning away as if to shield the babe from him. The lines around her eyes tightened, and she sidled past him, her gaze wary as if he might be diseased or dangerous. Her chin tilted upward, and she walked slowly to the entryway, then nodded toward the door.

"Let us at least meet from time to time," he said, shuffling past her with the bent neck of a defeated man. "We don't have to start a new life, but we could at least *try* to get to know each other, start over as—"

"No, I don't think so. I've already started over, Lucien, I can't do it again. I started over with a family that loves me, that would never leave me out in the cold or . . . or hurt me." Aldreda closed the door firmly as she said, "I have everyone I need."

CHAPTER 11

Lucien wandered the plaza for what felt like days. By the time he returned to the room he had rented above a seamster's shop, dawn's pale hem fluttered across the horizon. In the distance, the spires of Castle Ungebroch reached dark fingers toward that wan light, and a cold, clear day dawned in the Tangles. He dragged iron-heavy feet up the rickety stairs on the outside of the shop and shouldered open the door.

It wasn't until he was inside that he realized it had been unlocked.

If this was an ambush, then he was already dead and welcomed it.

Instead of knives, he was hit with the smell of frying oatcakes. It was a two-room dwelling, musty with age and the previous renter's mysterious predilections. The only windows faced the slender avenue below, just beside a door out to the balcony that was home to a concerning number of pigeons and a single bold cockerel. A few straw-filled pallets had been tossed under the windows, a circular table at the center home to a collection of cards, dice, daggers, and scandalous leaflets. There was a new, polished leather case on the table now, and Cree and a halfling lay, drunk and snoring, on one of the rough mattresses.

A shape moved near the balcony door, and Lucien jerked his head up. It was only Brevyn, ducking inside with a grim expression. Her shirt was missing, a tight, blue band of fabric tied around her chest, her baggy trousers slung low across her hips. She looked beautiful, but Lucien was too soul-tired to act on it.

Brevyn wandered to the cramped fireplace against the left wall of the apartment. She picked up a fork, crouched, and poked at the cakes wiggling in frying lard on the skillet. "How was your errand? Find what you were looking for in the Court of Colors?"

Lucien frowned, puzzled. Then he snorted, realizing the curly-haired halfling draped halfway over Cree's legs looked familiar. The "child" that bumped into him near the puppet stage. He now recognized Otis, the halfling he had trained with in the Orders' ruins.

"You had me followed?"

Brevyn shrugged. "You'll do the same when you have a crew to look after. That time might be approaching fast, mm?"

She nudged the skillet off the coals, retrieved a wooden platter from the cupboard beside the hearth, and fished out the cakes. They met at the circular table, and Lucien's stomach roared at the sight of food. Brevyn sat with a grunt and poured cider from a pitcher lost among the mess of the table.

"What makes you say that?" Lucien asked. He reached for a cake without asking and licked his fingers after it was eaten.

"You're leaving us." Brevyn didn't touch the food, but sipped her cider and watched him over the rim of the mug.

Lucien hung his head and shook it. "She's my sister, Brev. I had to try. It turns out I've been dead to her for years, and perhaps it is best I stay that way."

She pushed a mug of cider toward him. In the corner, Cree croak-snorted and flopped onto her side, then giggled in her sleep. "Do you remember after we left Auntie Mama in the Run and I said I needed to clear up some business with Ophelia Mardoon before we left?"

Lucien nodded.

"I did fuck-all with Ophelia Mardoon. I sat down in the forest and cried until I vomited, and then I cleaned myself up and we packed our things. Never in a hundred thousand years did I think my own mother would turn her back on me, but here we are."

"Here we are," he echoed. "Thanks for nothing, Gundobal Gorbus." His sister's words returned with a jolt to his brain. *There is always suffering you cannot see.* Lucien reached for Brevyn's hand and, after a moment, she let him take it. "I'm not leaving you all."

"Good."

"But I do need to leave the city. I don't belong here."

Brevyn's hand curled up in his. "So where will you go?"

Lucien didn't need to think about it. "Back to Shadycreek Run. That's where I belong, with the scum and the mercs and the creeps in their hidey-holes. I'm a criminal, eh? And that's where criminals belong."

"There are criminals aplenty in Rexxentrum, Lu," Brevyn reminded him with a crooked grin.

"Aye, but not like there are in the Run. There we can be kings and queens and whatever else we want. We don't need the Claret Orders or DeRogna or anyone else to raise us up and make us. We can be our own makers."

Brevyn's eyes widened. Cree suddenly sat up, stretching her long, lean limbs over her head before climbing unsteadily to her feet and tripping over to them. She leaned heavily on one of the chairbacks. "Would you two keep it down? *Fuck.*"

"My apologies." Lucien chuckled. "What the hell happened to you?"

"The Shattered Lance happened to us," Cree grumbled, rubbing at bloodshot eyes. The fur of her face was ale-spattered and a little matted. "And we happened to it. It was strongly suggested that we leave."

"And that halfling you were wearing as a skirt a minute ago?" he asked.

"Who?" Cree's brow turned down, then she glanced over her back. "Oh, Otis?"

"He hates de Chastain almost as much as you," Brevyn answered.

"Then he has excellent taste."

She shrugged. "Mm. I had a feeling you two would get on."

Cree stumbled away toward the curtain separating them from the second room of the apartment. Lucien lifted a brow. "And we can trust him?"

"More or less," said Brevyn.

"Brilliant. He's in my rooms, you know."

"*Our* rooms," Brevyn replied stiffly, but there was a mischievous shine in her eyes.

"Paid for with my coin."

"*Our* coin," she said. "What? You already said it, Lucien. Rexxentrum isn't right for us. We can make something bigger in the north, and you can't do it alone. If you're going to leave the Orders behind and start something new, then you'll need our help."

"Sounds like just the thing," Cree slurred, grabbing the curtain over the door for balance. "This whole city smells like piss."

"Just the parts we tend to hang around," Lucien murmured.

"See? I'm in. Cree is in. Bet you a copper Otis will be in, too, once he sleeps the night off."

"Lucien has the glint, I'd follow him anywhere," Cree concluded. "Now if you two will excuse me, I am going to be fighting for my bloody life over a bucket for the next six hours."

Lucien leaned back in his chair, the weight of exhaustion settling over his chest as he nested his head in his hands. Possibilities gave him the jitters; there'd be no sleeping for a while.

"You've got that look." Brevyn sighed. "That look like you don't know which way is up."

"It's all fine to talk of grand things," he replied. "Doing them is something else."

"A member of the Cerberus Assembly just filled our pockets with gold, there's raw, raging magic at our fingertips, and we have the hearts of gryphons. What more could we need?"

"Ha! And I thought I was the one with vision." He chuckled.

"Lucien, if you doubt us then we've already failed." She stood and placed a hand on the lacquered case he had noticed earlier among the junk. "Here, maybe this will help."

Brevyn flipped the silver latches on the case and pushed, the heavy lid thudding on the table between them. A few coppers fell to the ground. Lucien didn't bother to fetch them, spellbound by the prize inside the box.

"Grand enough to make all that talk feel real?" she asked softly.

Lucien met her gaze, and the weight on his chest lessened a little. Running his hands over the hard, enameled scabbards, he enjoyed the thrill that ran up his spine.

"Brev, they're beautiful."

"Scimitars seemed good," she replied. "Go on, pick them up. Let's see how they look."

"You really shouldn't have," said Lucien, but the moment he took the matching, blackened scimitars in hand, felt their weight and their balance, he knew they were just right. Just him. "Scratch that, you absolutely should have."

Brevyn slouched and watched him, resting her hands on her stomach. "Think of them like a graduation gift. You did well last night, you earned those."

"What about you?" he asked, sliding the holstered scimitars into either side of his belt and turning, letting her admire him. "Where are your shiny new toys?"

"Oh, you know me. Don't need weapons, I got these." She held up a hand and twinkled her callused fingers. Lucien rounded the table and took that hand by the wrist, dropping a warm, slow kiss on each knuckle. The familiarity of her skin and the rhythm of her pulse banished any lingering exhaustion. He craved her, craved the touch of another who wanted him in return.

"Thank you," he murmured. "I can always count on you to bring me back around."

"Bollocks. You know what you are," Brevyn assured him. She rolled her eyes and yanked her hand back, never one for the mushy shit.

"Do you reckon?" He sighed and crouched, resting his chin on one forearm. "Thought I did, but finding my sister made everything tilt. I felt . . . wiped clean. Blank. Just a child again, shivering and naked and stupid."

Brevyn shook her head. "If she can't see you clearly that's not your fault. She lacks imagination. Vision. You've got that in spades. You've only been in the city a few months and you've already outgrown it."

"Maybe. I'm not so sure. That feels too easy."

"No. *No.* It's a bright day, Lucien," she said, standing and stretching. "You're only seeing the shadows cast by the trees. Look up, there's plenty of sunlight. Now . . ." She yanked him to his feet and turned him bodily toward the door while he dissolved into laughter. "Speaking of shivering and naked, there's a nubile elf somewhere who can't wait to climb into bed with us."

CHAPTER 12

The broad avenue carving north through Shadycreek Run was choked with mud, jumbled cobbles threatening to snap an ankle or horse's leg over one misstep. A sloppy drizzle fell, chunky raindrops half freezing on their descent, a heavy-bottomed gray sky shutting out whatever thin succor sunlight might have offered. They rode carefully up the gauntlet of huddled beggars, outstretched hands bristling from every direction like sodden spikes on a bulwark.

"Mum always said there are four seasons in the Run," Otis groused to his right, seated on a spotted white horse with one eye. "Winter, Wet Winter, Bit of Spring, and Pigshit."

On the other side of Lucien, Cree receded into her leather hood. The fur along her nose was ridged with water droplets. "And which one is this?"

"Guess."

"Auntie Mama can put up with us for one night," said Brevyn, her eyes bright with determination. Yet her broad shoulders shifted nervously under her cloak. It didn't fill Lucien with confidence. Brevyn eased her mount ahead, though she maintained a leery pace. "She'll take pity when she sees the state of us."

Lucien wasn't so sure. Auntie Mama had never answered a single one of Brevyn's letters sent from their outpost in the Marrow Valley or in Rexxentrum, but they had spent their last coppers on the journey, and he wasn't keen to pull focus before they found their feet. There was more than just the Mardoons and Jagentoths to consider; the Trebains and Uttolots could get mixed up in ugly shit, too, as none of the main families making up the Tribes trucked in purely wholesome business. The Run had a way of punishing even the savviest rogue. There were no laws, but there were plenty of unspoken, understood rules.

Someone might think they were encroaching on claimed territory if they didn't play their cards in the right order. Even so, Lucien decided it was wise to form a backup plan then and there. Their journey from Rexxentrum had been marred by misadventure. At first, the easy country surrounding the city provided a forgiving route; the Glory Run Road was ever crowded with merchants and travelers, adventure-seekers, and pilgrims. But as they left behind the lush green of the Pearlbow Wilderness surrounding the city and reached the foothills outside Nogvurot, their troubles began. Otis drank from a rotted river without boiling the canteen first, and emptied her guts, pale and sickly, for days in a Nogvurot inn. It was a stay they could little afford, and the healer they hired came even dearer. It was no ailment for Cree's magic, and so they had pooled their coins to keep the halfling alive. Lucien had tried not to let bitterness take him—Otis Brunkel had so far proved an amiable enough companion, and came out of the same fires of the Orders that had forged him, Cree, and Brevyn, which mattered. Otis sang songs of Trostenwald when the sun was out on travel days, and hardly whimpered a complaint when the gut rot wrung her dry.

Otis was tough, and they would need tough where they were going.

Their troubles only worsened when Cree botched a cheater's hand of cards in the inn's tavern, drawing the ire of a handful of Righteous Brand soldiers. Nogvurot was crawling with the empire's finest in silver and crimson, and the four of them were forced to flee the inn that very night, making camp in a snarl of wilderness north of the outskirts. It was enough to shake the heat, but spending a few nights pinched between the outstretched fingers of the Dunrock Mountains nearly finished Otis off for good.

They rallied, gods be merciful, and the company continued east, swinging north to pay their toll to the enforcing Uttolot family in the mountain break at the Quannah Breach. Otis, recovering day by day, had made a rude gesture at the Crownsguard fools warning travelers that the way north was dangerous and riddled with thieves.

"We *are* the thieves, genius." Otis had grunted as they passed across the bridge.

The rain shifted in Shadycreek Run, a sudden cold sheet drenching them as the wind pressed from the mountains. They urged their tired horses with tired feet, and Lucien's mind spun in place, trying to think them out of the plight of light pockets. Otis lifted a finger in the air and sniffed. "Aye. Definitely Bit of Spring coming on Pigshit."

The brown hovels of South Clover gradually gave way to the browner hovels of North Clover. The downpour redoubled, sending even beggars fleeing for the meager shelter of shop overhangs and the forest's edge. Lucien felt confident he could navigate the muddy streets while blindfolded, but he let Brevyn pull ahead. Their horses slopped through the muck, rain drummed on their hoods, and Lucien shifted in the saddle to ease the strain on his protesting legs and back. When just the three of them had left for the Marrow Valley those years ago, he remembered the path being dry. Their horses seemed to fly over the roads. The wind was everywhere and wild, filled with the scent of hay and grass, and it had all felt like a grand escape, like they were pulling one over on life. This, he thought with a grimace, felt like a funeral march.

Hardly the grand beginning of the grand vision he had pictured, but every criminal enterprise began with a single step.

A muddy one, in this case.

Lucien eased his horse up to the hitching post a few houses down from Auntie Mama's crooked, cozy home. The smell of the woodsmoke mixed with dung and the purpled leaves of the Savalirwood was achingly familiar. He didn't know if it was the scent of home, but it was the closest thing to it, and it filled him up with an ease that soothed his leaping mind.

Otis and Brevyn slid into the mud first, rearranging their hoods and cloaks and adjusting their belts before squelching up to the front steps. Cree followed, grumbling about the state of her boots. They mustered on the porch, finding reprieve at last from the onslaught of weather. Lucien went to the edge of the porch and reached his bare hand out over the banister, cupping his palm and watching the raindrops collect.

"Here goes nothing." Brevyn sighed, pounding a heavy hand on the front door.

It rattled, then swung inward with a high, shrieking screech.

"That can't be good," he heard Otis murmur.

Cree shook off her hood, her ears flat with alarm. She sidled up to Brevyn, pushing her back flat against the outside of the house, then peering into the darkness. For a moment, Cree simply sniffed and stared.

"Not a soul about," she finally whispered. "Been that way for some time."

"How is that possible?" Brevyn drew herself up to her full height, and if Lucien knew her, then she was preparing to bull-rush right in. He lunged forward and grabbed her wrist, holding her fast.

"It could be a trap," he told her fiercely. "Head not heart, Brev."

"Head not heart," she replied. With a small, sad frown, she backed up and let Cree slip nimbly into the house first. Otis went after her, melting into the shadows in a sly crouch.

"She might have moved elsewhere," Lucien pointed out quietly. "Could have had trouble getting a letter to the ruins or Rexxentrum."

"No. Not her. Not this house. She is this house." And then, almost silently, "Was."

Lucien's fingertips grazed her shoulder, but Brevyn shuddered.

"Bring a torch," he heard Cree call from inside. "The place is empty."

Lucien dug for a dry torch in his pack, shaking one out from the very bottom. He unwrapped the linen covering it and fished out a flint, striking it and carrying the flaring, spitting fire into the dark antechamber. A faint odor of dog remained, as well as a thick coating of dust and the portraits on the wall he had glimpsed when he was younger. Most of them were broken or askew now. The door wheezed shut behind them, loose on its hinges.

They stood in one large room, with a smaller corridor and kitchen visible on the right edge of the far wall. On the left, a narrow staircase led up to a second floor, a floor that bowed over them severely, giving the impression the place might collapse at any moment. Debris swirled in the hearth, kicked up by the wind outside. Lucien moved to the fireplace and tossed the torch inside, watching the light spread and rise. Some of the boards were loose on the walls, as if they had been pried open and searched. Looters, Lucien concluded, all but expected in the Run.

Brevyn paced a wide circle through the dust.

"You looked upstairs? You looked in the kitchen? What about the cellar? We haven't gone to the cellar yet . . ."

"Brev, I doubt very much that your ancient mother is hiding out in the cellar. It doesn't look like anyone has been here for years." Lucien went to the table and chairs near the fire and kicked out a seat, then dropped down into it. "Someone in the neighborhood can tell us what happened in the morning. We should all dry out and get some rest."

"If someone hurt her, by the gods I swear I'll rip them in half," Brevyn hissed, still pacing.

"Try to calm yourself, we don't know that she's hurt. We—" Lucien snapped to his feet, freezing. His eyes flew instinctively to Cree. A raised brow was inquiry enough. She nodded and flipped up her sleeve, using a claw to slice a thin line up her wrist. Lucien drew his scimitars, the black blades reflecting a flash of the firelight as he readied himself for intruders.

The door exploded into a hail of sawdust and shards. Brevyn burst past him, kicking the table out of the way with a roar. She cracked her fists together and took a swing at the first thing that came through the door. It happened to be the jaw of an elven woman, who flew across the room, slamming into the nearest wall and taking a portrait down with her. The elf wasn't alone. Another elven woman and someone the size of a cave troll hurried in behind her, shaking the house, more frames dancing off the walls and breaking as the paintings clattered to the floor.

Lucien had only an instant to realize it wasn't a troll coming at them after all, but a half-giant man wielding a long, studded hammer. He ducked as the heavy iron end swung toward him, slashing with both scimitars on the way down. The half-giant was more agile than he looked, using the momentum of his hammer swing to jump backward and away from Lucien's blades. A crossbow bolt loosed by Otis sang over Lucien's right shoulder, thunking into the half-giant's thick armor. The stranger grunted and broke off the feathered end, more annoyed than anything else.

Pale wisps of Cree's magic intercepted the second elven woman, binding her before she could lash out with a strange and elegant rapier. She screamed and twisted, but the magical bonds held. Lucien stayed low, rolling toward Brevyn in the corner. Another crossbow bolt shot across the room, grazing the half-giant's ear.

"Clear out of here, rats!" the half-giant thundered, hefting his maul again.

"This house is ours!" Brevyn wrestled the fallen elf up from the floor, wrapping both hands around the woman's head and squeezing.

The half-giant smirked. "My hammer says otherwise."

"We've been eyeing this dump for weeks," the other woman caught in Cree's magic spat out. "It's ours to claim, we found it first!"

"Drop your weapons or I pop her head like a grape!" Brevyn shouted. The elf under her thrashed. "Shit, shit, shit, she means it! *Agh!*"

The half-giant either didn't hear or didn't care, stumbling toward Brevyn, raising the hammer high over his head to strike. Lucien dashed forward to defend her, but hesitated, watching as the half-giant went still, his black eyes landing on something over Brevyn's shoulder, something that gave him pause. Lucien risked a glance in that same direction, finding that she was squeezing the life out of the elf right beside a portrait of herself, only younger and less tattooed.

"Fuck me," the half-giant muttered. "Don't I know you?"

"Know me?" Brevyn replied, breathless. "Hang on, your tattoos . . . your hammer. You came up in the Orders. Profane Soul?"

"Ghostslayer." The hammer lowered and Brevyn, carefully, eased up on the dazed elf. Well, the big man wasn't polite, but at least they were trained by the same folk. Standing, Brevyn kicked the elf in the back, sending her sprawling toward the half-giant. He caught her lightly around the waist before she could tumble back out the door. Cree loosened her magical grip on the other elf, who sagged against the bonds and then shook them free. A wild tousle of black hair fell down her back, brushing the round shield strapped there.

"We washed out," the half-giant told them. "Never enough contracts, and I personally like to eat."

"So much," the black-haired elf chimed in. "He eats so much."

"Heh." The half-giant gestured to the others with him. "Weapons down, then. We're brothers and sisters all."

"This one I've seen before." The bald elf sniffed suspiciously. Her eyes swept keenly over Brevyn. "Is it you in those paintings?" she asked, gesturing to the frames hanging crookedly on the walls and littering the floor.

"Brevyn Oakbender is my name," she said. Stooping, she took one of the fallen portraits near the stairs and brushed away some of the debris, then showed it to the intruders, pointing to each figure in turn. "That's me. Those are my brothers, Narath and Vik. That is my mother, Chidra the Blue Rose, and that is my father, Lazak Oakbender, the Dark Forge." She gave the strangers a cold smile. "He was a half-giant like you."

"I know of the Dark Forge, though he was but legend on the coast," the half-giant replied, as awestruck as a stoic stone of a man could be. From the glitter in his eyes, Lucien gathered that there was a deep measure of respect there.

The black-haired elf woman wasn't so moved. Her voice was softer than Lucien expected, almost girlish. Singsong. "Brothers and sisters or not, Zoran, it could be some craftiness. Tell me, Brevyn Oakbender, this house has not seen a spark of life for two years. Why do you return here now?"

"Two years . . ." Lucien whispered, shocked, then recovered. "Brevyn—"

Otis and Cree gathered behind them, the halfling still cradling their crossbow close.

"'Tis none of your business why I've returned," Brevyn said through clenched teeth, glaring down at the far shorter elf. "This is my family home, mine to claim, and I do not look kindly on trespassers."

"No harm meant by the trespass," the other elven woman, the one Brevyn had nearly squish-decapitated, cut in. She had brown skin and a gleaming, shaved head with a plethora of runic tattoos running in lines over the smooth dome, the designs disappearing into the front of her jerkin past her neck. Both of her eyebrows were pierced with three tiny rings, and three more studs pierced her lower lip. "The house was for the taking, we thought you lot were Tribe thugs come to finish the job."

"Job?" Lucien blurted. "What job?"

The bald elf furrowed her brow. "That old woman what lived here was smuggling for the Mardoons. Mark the walls, brother. Why do you reckon they're stripped?"

"Looters," he replied. "That's obvious."

"Obvious, is it? Oh. Then why did they march the old lady out in chains?" asked the elf.

"Who?" Brevyn asked in a deadly whisper. "Who marched her out in chains?"

"Reese Jagentoth," the black-haired elf replied. "He dragged her to the plaza just there," she said, pointing, "and killed her for all to see."

CHAPTER 13

"We can't go toe-to-toe with Reese Jagentoth, Brevyn, even if the bastard deserves it," Lucien said, hugging a cup of bad wine to his chest. The fire blazed, fed with wood from the broken table Brevyn had kicked apart. "Even if he deserves the worst of what we can give him."

They had managed to find a single untouched bottle of wine in the kitchen pantry. Warmed, it was almost tolerable. Brevyn didn't touch her drink or say anything, her hand clasped on the mantel tight enough to make it splinter, her eyes fixed on the flames as if they might hint at answers.

Otis sat perched midway up the open staircase, crossbow near, keen eyes constantly trained on their "guests." For now, Lucien saw no reason to distrust the half-giant and his two elven friends—they had information, information he desperately wanted. Their shared time in the Orders demanded, at least for the moment, a wary truce. Auntie Mama had been the only person to show him even a glimpse of kindness as an orphaned boy, and publicly disgracing her was out of line, even for the Run. But what could they do?

Lucien lingered near the hearth; Cree crouched in the window near the front door keeping watch.

"We've hardly six coppers to scrape together," Lucien reminded

Brevyn quietly, a little ashamed to admit as much in front of the others. "Otis is still recovering. It's an unbearable insult, but what can we do?"

"We can collect Reese Jagentoth's head and stuff it, and I can forever use it as a footstool." Brevyn closed her eyes, inhaling deeply.

Lucien sighed. "Brev, darling, be reasonable."

"Be my *friend*," she whispered, hoarse, turning her attention away from the fire to stare at him. He knew well the pain in her brown eyes. And he knew an appeal when he saw one.

Lucien brushed her shoulder and then took his wine across the room. What was left in the bottle was being shared among the intruders. Cree had offered it to them, perhaps hoping it was enough to keep them pacified while Brevyn collected herself.

"I'm afraid we can't afford to buy your information or your silence," Lucien told them with a shrug. "This is, well, a little awkward. A little precarious . . ."

"You don't say," the black-haired elf muttered.

Brevyn turned to watch them, and Lucien began his next suggestion slowly, watching her reaction as he dropped each word, gauging whether he was going to survive the night or end up bent into a horseshoe. "But we do have something you want," Lucien began. "This place, shelter, what is it worth to you?"

Brevyn's eyes snapped open, and for an instant he was sure her fist was going to come soaring across the room, but instead she simply frowned, her lips slightly parted.

The half-giant scratched the back of his bald head. Like the elf, his scalp was lined with patterns, four red stripes arcing over his head and bleeding down across his eyes. "What did you have in mind?"

"We are *not* working with them." The black-haired elf grunted, elbowing the half-giant in the stomach.

"Sleep in the storm, then, you pissant."

"We could take them."

"Bloody shits, Tyffial, we already tried. And besides, they're brothers and sisters of the Ord—"

"Attacking Reese in the open is suicide," the bald elf interjected, stepping in front of her less amenable compatriot. "But there are . . . other ways."

Lucien exchanged a glance with Brevyn. She gave a single nod.

"We're listening," he replied. "But first I'll have your names."

"Briyakar Jurrell, commonly called Jurrell," the bald elf introduced herself, sweeping them an elaborate bow. "The pretty little naysayer behind me is Tyffial Wase, and the big boy is Zoran Kluthidol."

"You can call me Lucien," he said, skipping the ludicrous bow. "Brevyn you've already met, and the catfolk there is Cree Deeproots—"

"Otis Brunkel," rasped the halfling from the stairs.

"That is all very civilized, yes, yes, good," Jurrell replied, breaking away from the others to hold court near the hall leading to the kitchen. There was a manner in her speech and gestures that suggested she had spent many years away from the Run, perhaps in the proper cities, among more refined folk. "But let us now discuss less civilized things and, as it just so happens, one of my favorite pastimes."

"Windbaggery?" Tyffial murmured, rolling her hazel eyes.

"The redistribution of ill-gotten goods," said Jurrell, unruffled.

Over Lucien's shoulder, the half-giant, Zoran, barked out a single laugh. "We gonna steal from those Jagentoth cunts? Excellent."

"We may not be able to execute perfect justice, but we might at least acquire the woman's remains and whatever was buried with her. If she was sly enough to smuggle for the Mardoons then a secret or two might have gone with her to the grave."

"You're a grave robber?" Otis snarled, her hand tightening on the crossbow. "That's low."

"It might be, my dear, it might be, but the dead complain a lot less than the living. Besides, the expertise of a *low* grave robber like myself is precisely what you need just now."

"And in exchange?" Brevyn asked. The firelight hollowed out her cheeks, and she looked gaunt, as if the last hour had aged her a decade.

Jurrell seemed to consult the others only with her eyes. "We claim the upper floors of this lovely home to do with as we please. If you inhabit the lower floors, then that is your choice."

"That," said Cree from the doorway, her tail swishing thoughtfully, "would require a proper truce."

For a long, tense moment, nobody spoke. Lucien looked at Brevyn, who in turn looked at Otis, who waited until Cree turned to consider them, and then the cycle started again.

"Betray us," Brevyn told them, "and there will be consequences."

Jurrell gave them a broad smile. Her teeth had been filed to points. "Likewise."

Within hours, Lucien discerned that Tyffial Wase was the least enthusiastic adopter of the temporary peace. She kept a hand on the elaborate, twisting hilt of her rapier, worrying the edge of her glove while she stood protectively behind Jurrell. They mustered in the middle of the main room while the wind rattled the door, sparks flying from the hearth with each blasting gust. The storm outside worsened, rain turning to hail that drummed angrily on the roof.

Jurrell borrowed a small pot of ink from Lucien's pack and used the linen wrap he had discarded from the torch to draw a rudimentary map.

"How do you know the Jagentoth grounds so well?" asked Otis, picking their teeth as they stood behind Lucien.

She chuckled to herself and continued drawing out her map. "If there is something more than a thief, then that is what I am. There is no way shut to me, no treasure unreachable, no coffer unpilferable . . ."

Looming over her, Tyffial cleared her throat.

"To be concise, I am wanted by imperial decree. Even Queen Duvia Dwendal herself could not escape my touch."

"She posed as her handmaiden and filched a royal jewel," Tyffial explained.

"Aye," grunted Zoran. "And she never shuts up about it."

"If you're going to steal, steal for a cause," Jurrell demurred.

"And what cause would that be?" asked Lucien.

She gave him a razor-sharp, gap-toothed smile and lifted the hem of her shirt, showing where she had pierced an immense jewel into her navel. A royal one. "Self-improvement."

Lucien snorted. "I could turn you in right now for a fat bounty."

"Ah, but our truce! Besides, I could drop dead tomorrow, the sky could fall, you could turn into a purple slug and dance the saraband," Jurrell replied with a breezy shrug. "I don't like to overthink things. Who needs a boring life when I can have this one?"

"The plan?" Brevyn prompted, crossing her arms over her chest impatiently and swaying. They encircled the map, Brevyn standing with her back to the fire, the light burning bright around her edges.

"This is the Promontory, and this is Betrayer's Row," Jurrell explained. "They keep the bodies of their enemies here, with signs warning of what they did to earn that fate."

Brevyn growled.

"Or did not earn! As the case may be!" she hurried to correct. "Their compound begins here and continues northeast into the forest. The north and south entrances are too dangerous to attempt, but a small stream exits the walls here, for drainage. Over the years, the water has cut deeper into the hillside, allowing some enterprising folk to slip through."

"What about patrols?" asked Otis.

"Thin, and thinner in this storm. They rely on the nearby boar warrens to dissuade trespassers."

"Boars?" Cree asked. "How scary could a few pigs be?"

"Very," said Brevyn. "But I'd worry more about Jagentoth steel."

Jurrell drew a sort of bridge with several pillars and boxy shapes on top, then four stick figures with pointed helmets. "As I was saying, this is Betrayer's Row. The main entrance is above from the Jagentoth Compound and the Promontory, but the crypt itself is accessible from the ground. I've never seen more than four fellows standing guard, but they will have to be considered. Removing the contents of a tomb will make too much noise, and the graves are near one another, so no chance you rob something without alerting the guards."

"'Considered,'" Lucien echoed. "Considered meaning killed?"

"Not a problem," Brevyn quickly added. "Go on, then."

The elf grinned, perhaps eager for bloodshed. "I recommend that two of us distract the patrol, leading them deeper into the forest before shaking them. With the proper tools, it will only take one person to open the tomb. The rest? Well . . . Their job is obvious."

"And we have those proper tools?" asked Otis.

"Please!" Jurrell threw her hands up, batting her lashes.

"All right, all right, we get it, you're a professional," Otis muttered, exasperated.

"So professional, in fact, that I will hardly leave a mark on the grave," Jurrell replied. "The Jagentoths will never bother to check every tomb, but I'll break open another one as a decoy. No extra charge."

"We're not paying you," Lucien reminded her.

"You really should be."

Brevyn knelt and took one last look at the map, running her eyes over it carefully, no doubt committing it all to memory. "So when do we do this? Now? With the cover of the storm?"

Jurrell again consulted the others with a curious glance. The half-giant Zoran stood and knocked the bottom of his maul against the floor. "Now."

That sparked consensus, and Lucien watched Jurrell roll up the map and carry it out onto the porch, where she waited with Tyffial and Zoran. He noticed packs they had dropped outside the door, which they then hefted as they talked in low voices among themselves. Cree slipped by to spy on them without being asked, molding herself against the wall in the doorway, her ears bent with focus.

"I need to, well, find something . . . something to carry her home in, and her things," Brevyn muttered, suddenly jittery. She shook out her hands and then disappeared into the kitchen. She returned soon with a large, faded flour sack. Holding it taut, she stared down at the thing as if she had never seen one before and couldn't fathom its use. Lucien went to her, not knowing what to say to someone who was about to carry their dead mother home in a wretched little bag. It crumpled as her hands drooped.

"Every time I lose someone it's like a door or a window shutting in a house. One by one," she said, snapping the sack taut again, "it all goes dark." Then she raised her head and her brown eyes darkened. "Let's go. Time to set things right."

CHAPTER 14

Lucien sheltered under a flat shelf of stone balanced on the pillar wedged against his left shoulder. The rain pelted his unprotected side, and he slicked water from his forehead, squinting into the murky distance, breathing hard as Brevyn ambushed the guard facing him. In the driving tumult, it was impossible to see even five feet away, but now the way was safer, and he rushed forward, reaching the fallen guard just as Brevyn brought her boot down hard on his head, cracking whatever was concealed by a now dented helmet.

In the distance, he heard the distinct, squealing shriek of an irritated wild boar.

"So much for just pigs," he muttered, hoping Cree and Otis were up to the task of luring away both a ferocious beast and a patrol of Jagentoth shitlords.

"Behind you!" Brevyn knocked him to the side, a blue-and-gray-clad man surging from around a pillar.

The first swing of his broadsword deflected off Brevyn's gauntlets, sparks flashing through the downpour, and it was enough to knock her off balance. Lucien dove forward, scimitars slicing, the blades skimming the guard's chain mail. He saw the fear-bright shine in the man's eyes, but he was trained and ready, and brought his broadsword back around, this time to take off Lucien's head. A figure danced behind the man, plate armor pinging with the driving raindrops, her tongue just a strange pink smudge in the darkness before the elf Tyffial ran the edge of her rapier along her tongue, the blood sending a twisting ebony swirl down the sword.

Blood dribbled ghoulishly down her chin as she took the man's shoulder and then drove the rapier through his back, straight through until it sprang from his chest. It was always a thrill to watch a mutant blood hunter in action.

"That's the last of them," Tyffial announced. Her high, reedy voice was even more out of place when her face was covered in blood. The magic along her sword diminished and she wiped the blade clean, then motioned for Jurrell to come forward and begin her work.

Another squeal from the boar reverberated off the stones.

"Go help Cree and Otis," Brevyn instructed, following Jurrell through the maze of stone pillars. The elf went ahead, craning up to read the inscriptions on plaques secured to the bottom slats closing the tombs.

"Are you certain?" Lucien asked, glancing at the damp sack in her hands.

"I'm certain. Go."

It didn't take him long to backtrack the way they had come—up the overflowing stream, under the crumbling wall, and then up the adjoining river—tracking the havoc in the muddy trails and the sound of a charging boar. He discovered four bodies along the way, some of them viciously gored, others prickly with crossbow bolts. Two blurry shapes raced toward him through the sluicing rain, and before he could protest, Otis and Cree came screaming through the trees, hooking him around the elbows and catapulting him backward.

"Boar!" shrieked Otis. "The biggest fucking pig you've ever seen!"

"Should we not kill it?" Lucien cried, gaining his feet. But Otis and Cree didn't stop, and he tumbled and turned, struggling to keep up, his boots sliding helplessly across the slick surface of the river trail.

"No, no, leave it!" Cree called. She had the easiest go of it by far, the claws of her feet digging deep into the ground as she pelted back toward the shallower ford they had crossed near the broken wall of Betrayer's Row. "Better to let the Jagentoths think their guards were mauled!"

"The crossbow bolts somewhat dispute that!" Lucien growled. It didn't matter, Cree and Otis weren't stopping, and he soon understood why, feeling the ground tremble and quake as the boar gained ground behind them.

Otis blind-fired, swearing as their crossbow jammed.

"You'll just piss it off more!" Cree paused at the slope leading down to the river ford. "Do we wait for the others?"

Lucien hesitated, then heard the deafening crack of a tree splintering as the beast slammed into it in pursuit of them. "Definitely not! Gods, what do you suppose that thing *eats*?"

"Us, if we don't beat feet," Otis replied and hurled themself into the water. Lucien and Cree hurried in after, helping the far smaller Otis navigate to the other side. Soaked from head to foot, they disappeared into the tree line not far from the river's edge, the boar trotting to sniff the footprints that bled into the water. Lucien had never seen a creature so large in his entire life. The beast took a moment to snuffle and taste the air, and then lose interest in the hunt. Its stained tusks were daggersharp, orange fur studded with burrs and leaves, a wide scar running across its snout. Turning a wide circle, it thundered back down the path, nosing a fallen Jagentoth soldier beneath a shattered pine.

It was a long, wet, shivery journey back to the crooked house overlooking a flooded plaza in North Clover. Lucien left his destroyed boots by the door, and wordlessly they all stripped to their small clothes, hanging their coats and shirts and trousers by the fire to dry while they waited for the others to return. The draft near the door kept Lucien from pacing there, but he couldn't sit still until he knew Brevyn had retrieved what she wanted.

Zoran, Tyffial, Jurrell, and Brevyn trundled up the stairs an hour later, dreary, bedraggled, but alive. Cree had poked around upstairs and found a pile of moth-eaten, dirty blankets; she and Otis shared one by the fire, and Lucien met Brevyn at the door wrapped in a patchwork monstrosity that barely reached his upper thigh.

"Did you . . . Are you . . ." He searched her face, then noted the bag cradled against her chest. Without removing her boots, she tracked water and mud through the main room and to the stairs. She was gone for a long while, so long that Lucien drifted off against a chair while Zoran and Jurrell ventured out to find food and wine.

When the half-giant and elf turned up with a crate of supplies, Lucien grabbed a hunk of brown bread and an earthen jar of ale, taking them upstairs and letting his tread fall heavy on each step. He didn't want to take Brevyn by surprise. When he reached the upper landing, he heard her voice call from deeper within the adjoined rooms.

"Come through, I won't take your head off."

Lucien found her sitting with her knees tucked up against a child's bed. It looked comically tiny beside her muscular bulk. She, too, had stripped to her underthings and huddled under a scrap of blanket. When he drew near enough, he noticed the flour sack on another child's bed across from her; it was laid flat, like an altar cloth, with bones carefully arranged. One of Auntie Mama's tattered brown-and-green housecoats was neatly folded beside the remains, though a seam was visibly torn.

"The old bat sewed her will into her sleeve." Brevyn snorted. "She was clever, I'll give you that. Mean, but clever. She's left the house to me, along with instructions on where to find 'certain assets of interest.' "

"Then we're not only fabulous but fabulously wealthy, too?" Lucien asked, sliding down next to her. She took the brown bread and bit off a massive piece.

"Who knows? It might just be her wine collection, or a list of every prostitute in town," said Brevyn. "But aye, let's hope for riches beyond imagining." After swallowing the bread and a swig of ale, she rested her head on his shoulder. "You never speak about your own kin," Brevyn prodded gently. "Only your sister, but surely—"

"I don't speak of them for a reason," he said. His upper lip curled without him wanting it to. It occurred to him then that he couldn't conjure an image of his brother before his defilement. There was only the reek of leather and smoke, a crooked silhouette slumped against the foot of the bed. After the witch hollowed him, his brother never slept. Lucien would come awake at night and see his jet-black eyes gleaming in the shadows, eyes that ever found him in the darkness. "They met a bad end, and they are better remembered how they were, before broken hearts made more broken things."

"She killed my father, I know she did." Brevyn sighed. "He used to take me with him to the forge across town and tell me stories for hours, all the fables of his folk, and the stories of his youth . . . I loved him like nothing else, but I know he beat her black and blue when we weren't looking. One day she slipped poison into his porridge and that was it, he keeled over into the forge and burned to cinders. I remember thinking it smelled like breakfast. Couldn't stomach bacon for years . . ." Brevyn shook her head, narrowing her eyes at the pile of bones across from her. "She never cried, even when we were sent away, but then she was free to collect her dogs and her girls and make a small fortune fleecing all the men she hated in town."

Brevyn lifted the ale jar and drank to her mother, then put her head down on his shoulder again.

"This is going to cause trouble, Lu. The Jagentoths are stupid but they're not *that* stupid."

"So it will," he said, wondering when the real storm would come for them.

CHAPTER 15

For a while, it felt like the storm might miss them completely. The season changed, and when the new year dawned, Lucien began to convince himself that they had gotten away with the Auntie Mama heist entirely.

The families warred all the time, and their little gambit might have gone unnoticed, lost in the bloody shuffle. He expected Zoran, Jurrell, and Tyffial to fuck off back to the Orders to sniff around for more contracts, but they stayed, and strangely, he didn't hate it. Jurrell began arranging a few simple contracts for the whole crew. She had a knack for tracking down clients comfortable with both-ways anonymity. Brevyn and Zoran played bodyguard for an anxious disaster of a halfling who needed some debts collected; Jurrell and Otis oversaw a tense property exchange just outside the town gates. Then the real jewel fell in their laps: Cree, Lucien, and Tyffial managed to push through the dense fog surrounding the northern ruins of Molaesmyr, hired by a wealthy collector and entrepreneur in South Clover looking for a few relics to decorate his brothel. After that impressive feat, the work came even steadier, which alternately delighted and terrified Lucien—sooner or later, important folk, Reese Jagentoth included, would note their presence, and connect the dots on who had assaulted Betrayer's Row.

The day arrived long after collective anxiety had faded to camaraderie and complacency. That morning, Tyffial had been playing her lute beside the staircase, strumming a sour note as a brick came hurtling over the porch and through a window.

Not long after, the house was surrounded, and an arrow buried itself in the door. They gathered on the first floor, staying low to avoid the next round of projectiles. Another brick joined the first, breaking and scattering dust across the floor, debris skidding to a stop against Lucien's boot. They had just begun to patch the place up, but the Jagentoths had come for their pound of flesh.

"Don't suppose they're willing to negotiate . . ." Lucien winced, listening to a torch flare to life just outside the door. "Right."

"Come out, come out, you thieving fucks!"

Jurrell gasped and closed her eyes tightly. "That's Reese Jagentoth. I'd know his sniveling snot-faced whine anywhere."

"I suppose we can take comfort knowing they sent their best," Otis added. They crawled to the row of packs lined up against the wall beside the foyer. Sliding the crossbow out of their bag, they rejoined the group, silently cocking the weapon and priming a bolt with a practiced, fluid motion.

"Think that bolt could have his name on it?" Brevyn whispered, hazarding a peek above the window ledge. She dropped down, cursing, an arrow zipping over her head, close enough to take off a lock of yellow hair. Cree slithered along the dust-strewn floor to the kitchen corridor but returned with dire news.

"No way out," she told them, pursing her lips. "We make our stand here."

A communal search for weapons was swiftly interrupted by the all-too-specific, dry *whoosh* of fire taking to ready wood. It was a sound he was hauntingly familiar with, and conjured a dry scream that he stifled with a grimace.

"Burn in the Nine Hells, you wretched sods! Let all know! Let all witness what happens to those who steal from Reese Jagentoth!" His laughter could be heard just above the spreading crackle of the fire. Smoke poured in through the windows overlooking the porch, a hail of arrows not far behind.

"Any grand ideas?" Cree hissed, protecting her head with both hands.

"What about the upstairs?" Tyffial squeaked, then coughed. "Could try and pick a few of them off and make a jump for it."

Thick, black gouts filled the room, Lucien's eyes watering as he pulled his shirt up to cover his mouth and nose. The blaze spread eagerly, two days of dry weather working to Reese's advantage, bright-orange tongues licking up the walls, curling paint into snapping, bubbling sores. Otis tried to suggest something, but Lucien couldn't hear it over the roar of the fire and the ragged, painful coughing . . .

The front door hinges creaked. Lucien fell on his side, peering around the corner to watch as the gush of air sent the fire screaming across the front porch. Coughing, laughing, jeering, it was all he could hear as his eyes burned and the smoke filled his lungs. It came on so unfairly fast, no time to think or react, just the sear of hot air as he struggled to breathe.

A weird, icy gust fluttered across his cheek. *I'm dying,* he thought, *I'm going mad.* But then the blast came again, colder, and sweeter than the first. He heard muffled voices as the flames seemed to freeze in place, then recede unnaturally, as if sucked back into the instigating torch, life flowing in reverse. Then came a distinct click-clack of heeled boots, and he blinked his blurry eyes to find someone standing just outside the open door. She was indeed wearing high boots, shiny and black, a floating hem of green silk brushing the tops of her toes.

It was the last person Lucien expected to see on the door of their burning house. It was the half-elven Archmage of Antiquity and member of the Cerberus Assembly. The smoke drifted above them like a haze, and Lucien didn't dare raise his head for fear of taking an arrow to the eyeball. Vess DeRogna assessed him with a quizzical smile, holding a clean, ivory handkerchief to her nose as the smoke dissipated out the open door and broken windows.

"I've bargained for your lives," she said coolly, as if it were the simplest thing in the world. "The least you could do is rise to greet me."

LUCIEN ESCORTED VESS DEROGNA UPSTAIRS, summoned with a single finger flick to follow her. The others watched, frozen, in dumbstruck awe as they went by, no more bricks or flames or arrows coming for their demise. Once upstairs, she perused the rearranged and repurposed furniture, casually testing the fabric on a bedspread as she wandered by. At the very end of the vaulted, attic-style rooms, she sat primly on a narrow child's bed, opening a triangular window and breathing in a fresh rush of cold air.

"Don't look a gift horse in the mouth, and so on, I know," he said slowly, standing with his hands tucked behind his coat. "But what are you doing here?"

Vess waved him off. "Reese is a thug, and like all thugs his demands are simple. I paid for him to ignore the insult and reminded him that this putrid little hive is only allowed to exist because nobody in the civilized world gives a damn about it. But they could give a damn. They could." She cast her gaze around the room. "Which child's bed is yours, Lucien?"

"None of them," he muttered, prickled. "I sleep downstairs."

"Ah, you and that catfolk curl up on a mat by the fire, do you? Practically quaint. But surely you're not to play out the life of a housecat forever, mm? When last we met, I spied a hunger in your eye that I understand."

Lucien rocked on his heels. He could hear the others stirring downstairs, disembodied murmurs snaking their way up the stairs. Like them, he was curious how and why they had been rescued.

"Currently interested in seeing to the hunger in my belly and not much else," he told her. "Could you be here to help with that?"

"Clever man," DeRogna replied, propping one leg on the other and resting her hands on her knee. "Now that you no longer take work for the Orders, do you have a name? This . . . This collective of yours?"

"We do," Lucien bluffed. He racked his brain, stumbling, then his mind snagged on the very first thing they had accomplished together. It seemed accurate enough. "The Tombtakers."

"Menacing," she remarked. "I approve. Should I be speaking with all of you, or have you put yourself in charge?"

Lucien hesitated, but only for a moment. Brevyn had always been the stronger of them, but she was growing more distant, almost as if her childhood home were absorbing her back into it. She hadn't been the same since Auntie Mama's remains were rescued. "You can speak to me," he said.

"Well then, I wish to hire these 'Tombtakers' for a particularly dangerous undertaking. A journey, an expedition, if you will, to a Calamity ruin far, far to the north. There will be plenty of reward in it for you, and a bonus should we acquire the precise antiquities I'm looking for. Secrecy in this matter is not valued, it is required."

Lucien waited for more, a buzz of warning and elation tingling in his palms.

"Aeor," said DeRogna. "Do you know of it?"

"Not well," he replied. "But I will."

"That's precisely the kind of brash confidence you're going to need on this journey." DeRogna chuckled.

"Why us?"

"Despite my own vast capabilities, this is not a task one can perform alone. I'm certain you've heard the saying: Should you want something done correctly, do it yourself."

Lucien smirked. "Or in this case: Should you want something done correctly, hire a team of deadly mercenaries to do it for you."

"Yes, well." She sighed. "I'm not paying you for your cheek."

"You haven't paid me for anything yet," Lucien reminded her. "And the cheek is on the house."

From within her voluminous, heavy cloak she produced a black satchel, bloated with coin. She flung it casually on the floor near his feet.

"That's a mere quarter of what I'm offering," she said. "That should give you an idea of the seriousness of this work. There will be no room for error. I need a competent team to escort me to the ruins, one willing to endure dangerous climes and even more treacherous wreckage. It is unlikely that relics of this value will wait for us in the open and unprotected. If the freezing temperatures and ice storms do not kill us, the local wildlife will be keen to finish the job."

That nervous thrill chased through his hands again, but he tested the weight of the coin sack with his boot and knew an unmissable offer when one landed on the floor at his feet.

"Sounds perfect, Your Worship," he said with a wink. "When do we begin?"

CHAPTER 16

Lucien thought he knew what cold was, but as he stood shivering behind a stone outcropping on the ice fields of Foren, he realized the cold he was accustomed to in the Run was basically a lark. This was air with teeth and claws, it hurt on the way down, it made his eyeballs feel as if they might shatter at any moment. White speckles gathered on his eyelashes as another fresh kiss of snow began to fall. He briefly considered pissing down his own leg just to feel something warm.

A blushing dawn spread across the near dunes and the far, jagged mountains. Every mile traveled north from the ferry landing at Balenpost felt like an extraordinary accomplishment. Archmage Vess DeRogna had outfitted them well when they reached Palebank Village, doling out thick woolens, velvet-soft suede coats, and tiny enchanted fire rocks that could be held and rolled around between the palms or deposited in a pocket to bring a flare of heat to an otherwise freezing environment. She had taken the liberty of teleporting their strange band of misfits from Shadycreek Run to the village, briefed them efficiently on the challenges of the weather, and then equipped them. The next morning, they had taken the crossing, gliding on a massive ferry with a handful of fishermen and two grizzled dwarves who Lucien assumed were headed for the ruins at Aeor, too. The cold didn't seem to bother those two old boulders, the ice decorating their beards as natural as beads or rings. The crossing took nearly eight days, and that, he was told, was a lucky voyage. Zoran took the opportunity to broaden his knowledge of shanties, making eventual friends with the ferry captain. Most frosty eves ended with Zoran drunkenly singing his favorite shanty of the Menagerie Coast, "Big Treasure's Banty Rooster," the lyrics of which were so blue that DeRogna excused herself whenever the chanting began.

It was on that ferry, with the wind cutting like a frozen blade from the west, that Lucien saw the gravity of what they had agreed to setting in. He had seen it most plainly on Cree's face. She spent the better part of the ferry ride sitting with her back to one of their equipment crates, her yellow agate eyes blank, almost unblinking. This was a far cry from picking pockets and cheating at cards.

Balenpost had served as a temporary balm. DeRogna was unshaken no matter what, but the others seemed to come alive when they could at least sit by a fire until their cheeks were warm. There was ale to soothe anxieties, and soldiers manning the fort there to pass the time. Travelers and traders coming through told stories of ice dragons and yetis, strange lights in the sky at night that looked like glowing ribbons of green and blue. But the relative ease of Balenpost was quickly abandoned.

Lucien decided he would always remember the first step he took outside the gates of the fort city. There was a certain magic to feeling on the cusp of something big, but also a sickly dread that settled in his gut like a stone in a pool.

And days later, gazing ahead and considering the last leg of their journey to Aeor, the ripples of that settling stone could still be felt. Shadycreek Run was not a warm, easy place. If the assholes running it didn't drive one out, the weather often did instead. The wet and gray could be relentless, but the stark, mean brutality of Eiselcross and the island of Foren astonished him.

He felt Cree brush up against him. She kept her arms crossed over her stomach, her mittened paws stuffed under her armpits.

"Do you feel that?" Lucien asked her. His breath swirled out in silver curlicues.

"I c-can't feel a fucking thing," Cree muttered, teeth chattering. She pulled the fire stone out of her coat pocket and rubbed it fiercely between her mittens.

"A wall," Lucien continued, sketching his hand broadly across the horizon. "It's like there's a wall there. A presence. I'm going to have to push through it to go on."

"You?" Cree snorted. "Not us?"

"Look at me," he said, suddenly panicked. Cree did as he asked, her yellow eyes painfully bright against the snow. "Do you still see it?"

"What?"

"The glint. Is it still upon me? You told me once I was lucky, am I still?"

Cree snorted softly. "Yes, Lucien, you still have it."

"You'll tell me when it fades?"

She nodded.

Lucien's pulse still raced, and he shook his head. "I can't explain it. It's the damnedest thing."

"This whole debacle is the damnedest thing," Cree replied crossly. "What amount of g-gold is worth this?"

"It made your eyes dance lively enough back in the Run."

"No point turning back now," said Cree. "Are those the ruins in the distance there? Or just more mountains?"

"Aeor," he told her. "We're close."

"Mm, any thoughts on how we're going to c-cross the river of lava between us and it?"

"That's for DeRogna to solve, I think. She's had plenty of tricks up her sleeve so far."

"Aye," Cree whispered, turning away to trundle back to camp. "That's what I'm afraid of."

Lucien twisted to watch her retreat to the others. Zoran and Brevyn had trekked in huge wooden frames on their backs, enough to support heavy packs loaded with supplies. Every stop to camp required setting up a tented structure, the outside hung with insulating furs and pelts. Vess DeRogna demanded her own private tent apart from the others, and would retire at once in the evenings, leaving them to drink and bullshit until the ale took the edge off the cold. A pit would be dug for fire, the smoke and flames keeping predators at bay. Even so, they split the watch. They chose rocky, sheltered areas to break the wind, and positioned the tent to capture maximum early-morning sunlight.

Just such light shone off the hard shell of icy ground, sloped planes of ivory stretching as far as the eye could see. Vess DeRogna had not yet emerged from her private accommodations. But tea was on, and Jurrell cooked a pot of porridge, flavorless but hearty enough to fill the belly for a hard march and warm enough to be tempting. Lucien's boots crunched across the snow, breaking the crust of ice floating on top of it. He picked a tumbled boulder near Cree and sat down, luxuriating in the welcome gleam of the firepit. Otis sat on his other side, back to the firepit, crossbow on their lap and at the ready as they stared out across the ice fields.

"What do you suppose she does in there all night?" Tyffial asked. Her long ebony hair had been braided and looped over her ears, a scarf wrapped completely around her head and tucked into her shimmery sealskin coat.

"Sleep," Zoran grunted. He seemed to tolerate the cold best, or maybe he just spoke so little that his complaints were never lodged. Even he kept his tattooed, bald head covered with a dark, fur-lined hood.

"That's boring." Jurrell sighed, offering Tyffial a wooden bowl of porridge. "Why are you so bloody boring?"

"What?" Zoran shrugged. "It's what I think."

"Your thoughts are boring."

"Do vampires sleep?" Otis joked, smirking.

"I think she reads," Brevyn offered. She sat across the fire from Lucien, huddling under a blue, knit shawl.

"Why?" Zoran frowned at Jurrell. "What do you think about that's so damned clever?"

"All sorts of things," Jurrell told him lightly. "Like, why are there no dogkin?"

Cree spat up her drink while the others raged with laughter. "Why *are* there elves? They're nothing but a pain in my ass!"

Jurrell howled. "Dogkin! Imagine it! They'd be as plum dumb and loyal as Zoran!"

"Hounds are quite smart, actually," Zoran huffed.

"Friends like these, eh?" Cree said to him.

"I don't do friends, though I suppose you lot could be worse."

"Pah." Cree ducked her head and dug at the snow with the toe of her boot. The laughter died down, and a moment later Cree lifted her snout and murmured, "I think she schemes a way to leave us all in this crumbling ruin. Then she wouldn't have to share the spoils with anyone, would she?"

They all fell silent. Lucien heard the toggles click on DeRogna's tent, and a moment later she stood in puffy layers of patterned green wool, somehow elegant despite the number of robes keeping her warm. A large, old book was tucked beneath her right arm. She appraised them with a single sweep of her eyes and smirked.

"That's quite a theory, Deeproots, but I would never make it back to Rexxentrum alive that way," DeRogna said. She glided to the edge of their circle and gave a single sniff. "Teleportation is wildly unsteady this close to the fallen city, otherwise we could have skipped all this unpleasantness. It is in my best interest to see you all safely back to Balenpost. After that, your fates are your own to manage. Is there tea?"

Nobody moved to serve her. Lucien grumbled wordlessly and fished a cup out of the supply bag tossed near the fire. A gritty inch of tea remained in the pot they had boiled. He dumped it into the cup and hopped up to deliver it to DeRogna.

She took a dainty sip and swallowed a gag, then forced a smile.

"How gracious. Thank you."

"Speaking of unpleasantness," Lucien prompted. "How do you plan to cross the river of lava between us and the ruins?"

"All will be explained in time," she said.

It was perhaps the eighteenth time she had said that phrase during the journey. Zoran groaned, and Tyffial silenced him with a slap to the shoulder. None of them liked DeRogna, Lucien didn't have to guess about that, but they still needed to stay on her good side until the rest of the coin landed in their coffers. It was enough gold to set them up nicely—they could furnish new weapons and armor, eat, drink, and even afford a new hideout if Brevyn ever managed to let go of the smoldering ruin that her family home had become.

The stakes were too high to let DeRogna's snotty attitude cloud judgments. Lucien was reminded of traveling with de Chastain and her constant disdain. He really had to find a way to avoid such people in the future, he thought.

Lucien had just taken his porridge bowl in hand when the archmage's teacup landed in the snow near his feet. She drew in a deep, bracing breath and then smacked her lips.

"Well! No dawdling. Shall we begin our day?"

She marched back to her tent to retrieve something while the Tombtakers shared a chain of rolled eyes. Lucien saw Brevyn's hands curl into menacing fists. DeRogna was terribly strange, almost deliberately unpleasant, and aloof, he thought. She never seemed to eat, refused to socialize, and didn't make a peep in her tent. Brevyn probably had the right of it—she was studying and reading. Planning.

The dread in his stomach ached, and he glanced at Cree. Maybe she wasn't wrong to be paranoid, and to mistrust DeRogna's intentions. It wouldn't hurt to keep a close eye on her in the ruins, and make sure she really needed them for the return trip as much as she claimed. All the cutthroats and smugglers and mercenaries in Shadycreek Run were not so dangerous as a woman like Vess DeRogna, who did not need a crackle of lightning or a fireball at her fingertips to exude an aura of absolute, deadly power.

Brevyn nudged his knee with her boot, looming. "Help me break down camp?"

"Sure," Lucien muttered. "Of course."

But his eyes had strayed back to DeRogna's tent, and he listened, hard, realizing she was making sounds in there, the first he had detected on the entire trek. She was humming to herself, making a merry little tune.

Lucien struggled to hear his own thoughts over the roar of the molten lava carving a bright scar through the snowy fields. Just on the other side, high mountains flaring east hugged a darker, sinking heap to the west.

Aeor, the city that once blazed in the sky.

"The River Inferno," Vess DeRogna called over the surge of the lava. "It cuts straight down the island, dividing east and west, and keeping us from our goal. But no impediment is uncrossable. It is here that the river is narrowest, just shy of a mile." She began to walk slowly toward the edge of the blazing-hot river, visible waves of heat rising from the surface. Lucien was grateful for the reprieve, his face actually beginning to sweat, though he was loath to consider what bravery it would require to successfully cross.

"Observe," said the archmage, withdrawing her bare hands from her voluminous, layered sleeves.

"Maybe we'll get lucky and she'll just walk in," Cree muttered under her breath.

"Gold melts, too," Lucien replied. "We need only tolerate her awhile longer, Cree. Chin up."

"She hates us, Lucien, can't you see it in her eyes?" Cree asked. She turned toward him, yellow eyes pleading. "The disdain? The disgust? We're beneath her."

"We're nothing of the sort, Cree, not so long as she needs us."

"And after that?"

"This place is a graveyard; it's making you paranoid."

Cree spat onto the crust of snow. That crust gradually sloped, giving way to a rugged swath of volcanic stone running alongside the River Inferno. The others crowded near Lucien to watch DeRogna as she processed to the shimmering edge of the river. She raised her hands high above her head, and the air around them snapped, the scent of ozone, clean and pungent, descended. The thin island of clouds above them swelled, and then a driving, directed snow began to fall. At first, the flakes swirled and dissipated as they reached the lava, but more and more gathered, forming an unnatural, resilient sheet of ice, a bridge that stretched from their side of the divide to the other.

"Quickly!" DeRogna yelled, her voice uncharacteristically strained. "Such magic draws the attention of elementals and defending against them would only cost us more time. Hurry now! Across!"

Zoran coughed out a laugh. "Not likely."

Brevyn turned to Lucien, who was not at all eager to try his luck on the magical ice bridge. "She's deranged. She can't mean for us to walk on that!"

"What are you fools waiting for?" DeRogna almost shrieked.

Lucien cleared his throat, pulling back his shoulders and screwing up his courage. He felt Brevyn's hand close over his forearm, stalling him, but he shook her off and started toward the river.

"To go forth," he said softly. "That is the mandate of the soul."

"Who said that?" Brevyn asked.

Lucien smirked. It didn't shock him. He was always quoting bits and pieces of plays and tales, the performances of his childhood forever imprinted on his heart.

"I did. Come on then, go with me, Tombtakers, there's glory and adventure to be found in those ruins, a whole abandoned city of wonders to explore, and all the gold that comes after."

Zoran snorted, then shrugged and adjusted the weighty pack on his back as he fell into step beside Lucien. "S'pose it's better than freezing to death. Lava's a quick way to go."

"Sure, that's the spirit." Lucien chuckled.

"It'll hold me, but the rest of you might be fucked," Otis said, shrugging.

Lucien took the lead. He passed DeRogna at the banks of the molten river, and his daring dipped as the real heat of the lava blasted against his face. Yet the ice bridge held, thin as it was, treacherous as it seemed, so he placed one boot on the edge of it and pushed, testing its strength. His foot did not immediately melt off, and so he closed his eyes and ventured forward, finding that the magical strip of snow and ice held.

Immediately, it began to crackle under his weight.

That was enough to send him trotting along, not running outright, for he didn't trust himself not to slip. Cree and Otis came next, hot on his heels, nearly tripping him in their eagerness to be across, then Jurrell and Tyffial, who seemed to handle it deftly, agile on their feet. Zoran and Brevyn brought up the rear, with the unenviable task of balancing their nightmarish packs while navigating the narrow, crackling bridge. DeRogna crossed last, her arms still lifted above her head, eyes narrowed in concentration as she continued to cast the spell. Behind her, the ice began to disappear, hissing as it melted into the lava. They had a long way to go, for even a mile taken briskly took some minutes. Worse, out of the corner of his eye, to the east, Lucien spied a growing turbulence in the lava. It bubbled and rose, shapeless globs of seething red and orange forming into the rough outline of arms.

Lucien threw caution aside, picking up his stride, skidding across the last few feet of the bridge, leaping to safety on the rocks. Gasping for breath, he spun and motioned for the others to hurry.

"Elementals!" he shouted. "They've spotted us!"

Through the rising steam, halfway across the bridge, he saw DeRogna's head snap in his direction. Pockets of flame seeped through the shiny white surface of the bridge; the cracks deepened, steam hissing through the widening gaps. Zoran dodged awkwardly around a split that opened up, stumbling, and dropping to one knee. Brevyn swiveled back to aid him, scooping one arm under his shoulder and hauling him back to his feet. The erupting body of fire given life broke the surface of the lava completely, arms wide, as if stretching after a prolonged slumber. It charged toward the ice bridge, head low like a battering ram, gaining speed, Vess DeRogna in its immediate path.

Lucien grabbed a pile of rocks from a broken boulder near his feet, and began hurling stones at the thing, trying to distract it. Cree joined in just as Jurrell and Tyffial landed safely at their side. Scrambling, Otis loaded their crossbow and fired a bolt that burst into flames on impact with the elemental.

But their distraction worked, the elemental veering slightly to the right, though it had drawn near enough to the bridge to eat away at its edge, dissolving precious turf. More and more rocks were thrown, but the elemental remained fixated on the bridge, rearing back, lava dripping from its arms as it prepared to bring them crashing down.

Vess DeRogna paused, pivoting to face the elemental, all but nose-to-nose with the creature as she summoned another vestige of power, her right hand lashing out, a burst of energy exploding from her palm. The surface of the shield, colorful as a dripping rainbow, warped as it collided with the elemental, stunning it just long enough to allow Brevyn and Zoran to arrive ruffled but safe on the other side. The interruption in concentration left DeRogna's bridge in pieces. She leapt from patch to patch, the ice splintering under her foot after each light step. Lucien dropped his handful of stones and met her at the final gap, where the snow had disappeared for a full three feet.

Without a word, she hurled herself across the chasm, the edges of her robes igniting as Lucien and Zoran leaned out over the lava and pulled her to safety.

The elemental threw itself onto the bridge, breaching across it like a whale, a fountain of lava spitting into the air as it melted back into the flow of the river and was gone. DeRogna stamped out her own smoldering clothes, hurrying out onto the snow and leaving a trail of ashes. She did not rouse them with a speech or thank them, simply continued marching off in the direction of the mountains to the north.

"Still think she means to kill us?" Lucien asked Cree breathlessly as they gathered their wits and left the lava churning behind them.

"And if it were you or I behind her?" asked Cree, shivering.

Lucien didn't have an answer to that. He was spared fumbling around for a response by Jurrell, who streamed past them, hooting and shrieking, pounding her fist into a snowbank. She laughed and laughed, then slapped herself across the face. "Conquering a bloody river of *fire*. That will put hair on your fucking chest!"

Ahead of them, Vess DeRogna vented a low, cynical laugh. Dusk fell around them, though the river of lava provided a steady, red light, even as they drifted onward through the snow. "If danger is what you crave, elf, that was only the beginning."

CHAPTER 17

Aeor.

Lucien had been privy to a restricted number of DeRogna's maps and books regarding the subject, and he had expected to see a dazzling, broken city, but the fields before them were little more than craters, deep depressions with spires of ice and snow. He imagined what might lie beneath—a vast maze of pale and cracked towers, shattered, colorful windows, parapets tumbling over one another like a pile of sticks dropped by a childlike god. For now, it looked simply like a low-lying town blanketed in acres of thick snow.

"What lies beneath," he heard himself say. The others gazed on with him, perhaps likewise lost in their imaginations, except Zoran, who had taken one look at the place and wandered off to take a piss.

The ice fields north of the River Inferno sloped away, gradually at first, then sharply, the craterous city of Aeor burrowing into the base of the mountains, creating its own depressions and tunnels.

"We'll make our descent, then camp for the evening," said the archmage. Her eyes were brighter, clearer, now that they were close to the crash site. He saw the stark-white snow reflected there. "The depression made by the city should provide a break from the wind."

"Is it safe?" asked Cree, peering carefully over the precipice, the last sloping edge before the crater began in earnest. Brevyn pretended to give her a playful shove, and Cree hissed.

"Nowhere in these ice fields are we truly safe, Deeproots," said DeRogna, motioning imperiously to Zoran, who had just returned from taking a leak. "We can at least enjoy a brief respite from the cold before we try our chances in Aeor. We shall enter from a northwestern tunnel, come."

DeRogna stood back and supervised while Zoran and Brevyn spearheaded the effort to drive stakes deep, through the crust of ice and snow, into the frozen ground feet below. It was no easy task, but within two hours they had secured lines down into the sunken basin. They tied spikes to their boots and took up the ropes, lowering themselves inch by inch to the piled drifts of snow half a mile beneath them.

When they reached the ground, Lucien untied the spikes from his boots and let them hang limp from his fingers, drawn again by the topography of the snow-covered ruins. Though he could see little, he sensed a powerful presence below.

Brevyn and Zoran had finished descending. Their ropes could not be retrieved, secured as they were from above, and so they were burned, lest ill-intentioned adventurers follow. They had packed plenty of replacements. Setting up and tearing down the camp had become routine after a week's march from Balenpost. The same roles fell to the same folk—Zoran and Brevyn hammered the shelters together, Cree and Lucien covered the frames of those shelters with skins and furs, then arranged the interior for their communal tent (DeRogna insisted on doing her own), Tyffial and Jurrell dug the firepit and sorted out the meal, and Otis kept watch.

Despite the near miss on the ice bridge, the Tombtakers were in high spirits. The trek was over—at least the *exposed to the cold, elements, and lava rivers* part—and the windless quiet of the crater made for a welcome change. Lucien slurped down his salted porridge, choked on a bit of cured fish, and half listened to another of Tyffial and Jurrell's tales. This one covered their washing out of the Righteous Brand, abandoning the army to study the mysteries of hemocraft with the Claret Orders. It didn't surprise Lucien one bit that they had all fallen in together—practitioners of their shunned arts tended to move in one small circle.

It did, however, make him pause to consider what Cree had always claimed, that he was somehow set apart. The glint. If there was anything to it, maybe that was the secret force that had collected them. *Water seeks its own level.* Maybe blood did as well.

In the dark, only their fire and the strange, effervescent blue orbs in the city competed with the blanket of stars overhead. Jurrell had just finished explaining how the first time she attempted to draw her own blood for use in magic, she nearly bled to death by accident, when Vess DeRogna appeared, dressed in somber black wool chased with leafy-green embroidery. She stayed on the fringe, her toes just touching the outer ring of firelight, and waited until they noticed her presence and grew silent.

"A word," she proclaimed, nodding once at Lucien.

The others groaned as if he were being summoned by a headmaster for pushing someone down during lessons. Lucien smirked along with their jeers, following DeRogna to her tent with a blanket draped loosely over his shoulders. She had already disappeared into the shelter when he reached the toggled flap. When he drew back the strip of hide, he was not expecting to find himself in a veritable palace. It was no crude tent at all inside but a lofty tower, the walls glass and iron, vines and plants tumbling from the high crossbeams. He almost couldn't see the very top of the ceiling, as everywhere there were black birdcages, some empty, others hosting ravens, pigeons, and exotic feathered creatures he had never clapped eyes on before.

"Not a terribly complicated spell, all told," DeRogna said, as if that served as an explanation. She led him to a small tea table set in the very center of the tower. Tucked away behind that, he noticed a modest wooden bower, also bright with greenery, where a canopied bed with white linens waited, looking an awful lot more comfortable than the straw-stuffed tick he had been using, usually under Zoran's foot and Cree's armpit.

"It never occurred to you to share?" Lucien asked with a snort. Even so, he took the warm, inviting cup of tea she offered him. It was lightly scented with lavender, and he tasted blackberry honey the moment he took a sip.

"The Aviary is a private place," she replied, pouring her own cup of tea from a spotless porcelain pot. "You should be honored; it has played host to only a handful of visitors."

"Why all the birds?" he asked. As he did, a raven resettled in a cage above them, a puff of black feathers floating down to the table. DeRogna flicked them away.

"I enjoy birds. Even the humble pigeon can recognize and remember a face. They are surprising creatures, silent observers that meld into their surroundings; rarely perceived but ever vigilant. They are messengers and entertainers, builders, pollinators, predators, and far-travelers." She smiled faintly at the birds populating her hideaway, seemingly immune to the constant noise they made. Lucien had no idea how she slept with all the racket. "But I did not invite you here to speak of such things."

He paced idly, warm under his blanket, and sipped his tea. "This must be about the ruins . . ."

"It is. Now that we are close to the city, I thought it imperative to restate certain terms of our arrangement. Here," she said, taking a tarnished, ugly ring out of her pocket and handing it to him. It looked like junk, with a misshapen face worked into the metal. "Students at the Academy call them babblers, but I call it a Whisper Ring. Keep it close. It will allow us to communicate should we become separated in the ruins. And there will of course be distractions within that might influence a person to stray. I need you to guarantee that I remain your absolute priority."

Lucien nodded, annoyed. "Aye. That was the deal, we get you safely in and out of the ruins."

"Yes, but deals have a way of changing when sudden opportunities abound. The wonders of Aeor are many and, more important, the temptations are many. Our mission—my mission—must not be endangered because one of your friends gets greedy eyes. I expect you will want to keep a few treasures of your own from the ruins, and that I can abide, so long as they are of no real magical value." He was about to respond, but she swiftly continued, "Tell me of Molaesmyr. Few visit that poisonous heap and live to tell of it."

"Oh no, Archmage, I know better than that," he said. Though his tone was light, inside he was boiling. He was through being tested by DeRogna. Had they not come all this way with her through miserable conditions? Why poke, why prod . . . "A benefactor paid for our services, and we did as we were asked. What we did and how we did it, what he wanted and what we delivered, are none of your concern. I wager you know that we succeeded, thus your jaunt over to the Run to hire us."

DeRogna appraised him for a moment, then slowly smiled. "Whatever you accomplished there was a far cry from roughing up green mercenaries in the Tangles," she commented. "And just as I suspected, you've come a long way. But I knew it would happen thus. Did I not mark it at the Academy? You have the stench of the hopelessly ambitious around you."

"Stench?" Lucien chuckled. "If fortune seeks to find me, I gladly accept. Stench, as you say, and all."

Finished with her tea, she folded her hands and stood, breezing by him and toward the door. Clearly, their time together was over. "Ah. Well. You only say that now because you are young and scarred only by tragedies not of your own making. But greatness inevitably requires action, and actions beget mistakes. Your Tombtakers are so far untouched, but that will change. You were lucky in Molaesmyr, in the Run, and with the Jagentoths. Don't forget that had I not intervened, you would be a pile of forgotten ashes. So when our business here in Aeor is concluded, we will revisit this conversation and see then how well you like fortune."

Lucien's brow furrowed, his chest going cold. "Is that a threat?"

"Merely pragmatism." She grinned, heedless of the sudden darkness clouding his face. "You may go."

"We *will* revisit this conversation, Archmage." He put his teacup down a bit harshly, the saucer rattling, then stalked to the door.

She waited until he was almost gone to say, "If I allow it."

If I allow it. He was glad to be away from her; she didn't need to see the snarl on his lips. *Uptight, devious, delusional bitch . . .*

"Good talk?" Cree was waiting for him, her eyes bright and gold in the firelight.

"I'm going to sleep," Lucien muttered. His cheeks were burning despite the freezing cold. "The sooner we wake, the sooner we press on, and the sooner we're free of Vess Fucking DeRogna."

"A BIT OF PITTER-PATTER, a smattering of rain," sang Zoran in time to the swing of his pickaxe. So far, the ice barrier proved unyielding, but he was a determined fellow. "Drives the farmer mental, drives the man insane . . ."

"Must you?" Otis whined, his back to Zoran while keeping the watch.

"I must if you want this wall broken anytime soon," he barked back. "Helps me concentrate, keep the rhythm," he said between hacks. "A bit of pitter-patter, a smattering of rain . . ."

Strange shadows flickered at the end of every corridor, a trick of the light, most times, but they knew better than to drop their guard for even a moment. Lucien had mistakenly assumed that, though the ruined city might be dangerous, it would be at least passively traversable. He was quickly disabused of that notion, as the maps DeRogna had secured showed passages where none existed, cave-ins and floods turning most corridors into dead ends. From their camp outside the ruins to this very blockage had taken just over two days of intermittent travel. The going was slow and treacherous, with previous adventurers having left their share of shattered corpses and abandoned camps, and the unsteady nature of the crash site itself destabilizing even the ground. Twice, Lucien had almost been lost down a sinkhole. He felt like they were crawling rather than walking, clawing their way through, fighting for every inch in a place hell-bent on repelling them.

When they first breached the crater through the northwest tunnel, the true value and wonder of Aeor instantly made itself known. His imagination, as it turned out, was not up to the task of conjuring such things. Pockets of blue light glowed in the distance, suggestions of life—perhaps the lanterns of adventurers, though to Lucien they seemed like the little flickers of lost life, mere ghostly echoes. At the bottom of the nearest steep descent lay a toppled arch, mostly intact, an oddly inviting piece of disembodied architecture that seemed to promise the valuables and dangers DeRogna had made clear awaited.

Much had been completely pulverized in the cataclysm, but now that they were picking their way into the ruins, he could tell that the blue lights were some sort of protective force. They were glowing caps, perfectly round, their smooth surface emanating a transfixing hum.

"What's the blue?" he asked, pointing.

"Stasis bubbles," answered DeRogna. She came to his side, observing the city with a small, secret smile. "The people and objects within are perfectly preserved from the impact. Just imagine what one might find inside. The insights, the technology . . ."

The neighborhoods of the city—wards, DeRogna called them—progressed deeper and deeper into the wide crater. Only pieces of Aeor were accessible, and at the whims of the ice shelves drifting slowly across the island of Foren. Waterfalls poured into the crater, flooding important thoroughfares, making an even greater mess of an already dizzying maze of annihilated buildings. Though DeRogna's maps proved unreliable at best, they at least directed the Tombtakers to a specific ward three miles deep into the crater, accessible only after climbing steeply down, and then breaching a large, arched corridor heaped with rubble.

Once those stones were cleared, they were met with yet another obstacle. At the first fork of a somewhat intact hall, DeRogna consulted her maps and chose the way blocked by a solid shield of ice. Zoran and Brevyn were subsequently put to work. The walls around them were dark blue, painted, but with such a bright pigment that it gave the appearance of radiant sapphire. Down the other fork, the wind whistled. Lucien had worried about whom they might encounter in the ruins, but the unbroken, pervasive silence was somehow worse, the combined absence of so many dead making the stillness palpable.

It was playing havoc with his mind.

"Can't you point your fingers at it and hurl a fireball?" Lucien asked, watching both Zoran and Brevyn remove more and more layers as they strained against their axes. Shards of ice skittered across the floor, bumping his heels.

Vess DeRogna, still cloaked in heavy green-and-black wool, walked solemnly to the brilliant-blue wall beside the ice barrier. She ran her hand over a shield painted there, moons and trees crowned with an unsettling tiara with eyes in the place of gems. There was lettering beneath, badly worn away, but she traced what letters were left with her forefinger.

"The city's great magical thinkers congregated here. Their experiments are not entirely lost to us, as you've seen . . ." And they had indeed. Every stasis bubble they passed was creepier than the last. DeRogna had offered scant commentary along the way, though the quick movements of her eyes told Lucien that was due to secrecy, not ignorance. She probably thought them too dull to understand what they were looking at. "Any errant magic would trip ancient mechanisms, or worse, trigger a landslide. I wouldn't want to bring the whole of the ward down on our heads."

"Here! We're through!" Brevyn called, setting down her pickaxe. She used the white sleeve of her tunic to brush away the detritus, revealing a narrow hole burrowing through the ice.

"I'll take it." Zoran nudged her aside, then drove his pickaxe into the gap with a thunderous shout that echoed down the corridors, filling the empty maze with sound. He pushed his right boot against the barrier, bracing, then turned and grasped the axe handle with both hands, tucking it under his elbow and using it to leverage open a hole eight or so inches across. Chunks of ice exploded outward, and Lucien shielded his eyes.

With the center of the wall collapsed, the rest came away easily. Otis launched themself into the narrow passage, sliding through easily. Tyffial brushed by the others, crawling on hands and knees. Once on the other side, she waved and dusted off her coat.

"Just like Caes Mosor, right, Lucien?" called Tyffial, giggling.

"Ha! Considerably fewer hags," he replied.

"Aye," Brevyn muttered in his ear as they watched Vess DeRogna crawl through. "Just have to deal with the one on this little adventure." She sighed and wiped her forehead with her sleeve.

"Is it just DeRogna getting to you or something else?"

"This place is . . . wrong." Brevyn leaned against him for a moment, catching her breath from the work. "Even in the open spaces it feels like it's closing in on us."

"The mage will have her relic soon, then we can leave this place behind for good."

"Even if it's a gold mine?"

"There are other places to delve," he replied. "Ones that won't make me want to tear my own skin off."

Once the archmage was on the other side, Zoran and Brevyn went back to work, breaking down the ice barrier until the hall was clear. They gathered their gear, pressing forward into a rotunda whose high, domed ceiling had been cracked open like an egg. Water poured in from a fall miles above, though some iridescent bubble kept the flow from filling the chamber. Green and blue lights flickered through the water, and as Lucien progressed into the rotunda, he marveled, mouth open, staring up at the magic protecting them, feeling as if they were standing at the bottom of the sea.

At the center of the chamber, they spread out around a stasis bubble placed up a series of shallow steps, the scene within far more placid than others they had stumbled across. An ancient resident of Aeor was frozen there, sitting on the ground cross-legged, their garb simple and almost monklike, rough spun fabric with a black mantle, a few designs in red embroidery decorating a linen belt snug around their waist. It was an elf, slender, with smooth brown skin and their white hair knotted at the nape of their neck. They were in contemplation of something cupped in their palms, too small to be seen without breaching the bubble.

"Are they not beautiful?" whispered Jurrell.

"Wistful," suggested Otis.

"They look so sad," added Tyffial.

"No, no, not sad," said Vess DeRogna, approaching the tableau. "Enthralled." Then she cast her eyes around the rotunda, searching for something. She must have discovered it, for she gave the first true smile Lucien had ever witnessed on her and murmured, "Light. I shall require far more light . . ."

The archmage left behind the stasis bubble, making a circle around the edge of the rotunda, consulting a small journal and one of her maps. He glanced over her shoulder, watching her fingertips graze across minuscule sites labeled A12, A22, A30, A41, and so on. Now that they had reached their apparent destination, DeRogna was taking her time about it. Lucien's belly snarled with hunger, but they were hours off from making camp. This room, more so than the other places in the ruins they had traveled through, had not been picked clean by scavengers. Soaring, colorful murals covered the internal walls and pillars, shelves laden with broken jars and shattered pottery catching his eye. He pulled off his gloves and wandered over to one of the shelves, taking a shard of ancient glass and holding it up to the light. The watery green glow bathing them from above caught a flaw in the glass, the blemish focusing the light into a wink and then a beam of reflection.

Lucien focused his eyes past the shard, watching where the coy dot of light hit. The mural there, he realized, was different from the pattern covering the rest of the rotunda. When he went to inspect it, wiping the dust away, he beheld a ring of nine red ovals, with a dazzling starburst in the middle, and that decorated with a single open eye. *Enlightenment.*

The mural had been framed within a painted arch, with two small circular depressions at about waist height. Lucien frowned, dropping the piece of glass, and placing his palms on the sunken areas he gently applied pressure, shifting his weight forward until he heard an ever-so-soft *click.*

What had been a slice of wall became a door, the mechanism releasing and pulling it back, revealing a dark passage beyond.

"There's something back here," he called absently, already stepping through. The others didn't hear him, busy helping DeRogna with her project. He glanced over his right shoulder, watching as she directed the other Tombtakers to position themselves at various blue-and-gold lanterns throughout the room and stand ready with torches while she feverishly consulted her journal. The hidden room ahead exhaled toward him, an electric breath from a long-abandoned place, somehow warm and solicitous.

And like a fool, he accepted the invitation.

So close now, so close! I could burst, I could burst, we are going to be found!

Hush now, Mirumus, you will frighten it away.

CHAPTER 18

In the corner of the hidden room, a skeletal figure sat upright in an angular gold chair. Though he was but bones and dusty beard, his remains had not yet collapsed. He was different from the others. They had found mummified ancients and those preserved in the stasis bubbles, but anything else would have long ago been blown away by wind, pulverized the moment the city fell.

But here was a fellow who had come before, presumably after the cataclysm, but long enough ago that he had time to decompose. He sat as if wiling the hours away studying, diligent, illuminated by an orange crystal on the desk in front of him, a gem roughly the size of an egg, but jagged and pitted. It served as Lucien's only light to see by, but it showed enough—the dead man's pauperized flesh clinging to the bone, marred with bizarre markings, his pointed red cap and the robe that now swallowed his diminished form. It showed the skeleton's dry hands upturned on the edge of the desk by a dark, loosely bound journal. Sheaves of parchment spilled into the dead man's lap, revealing journal pages in a chaotic assortment of languages.

Lucien drew nearer, leaning over the man's shoulder, reading by the sickly glow of the orange gem.

What is it to dream and, having plunged into those endless fertile fields of imagination, wake to find those conjurings made manifest? Real.

A breath tickled his neck. Lucien whipped around, but he was alone. Alone with the dead. He reached for the journal and the loose papers, careful not to disturb the corpse too much. The smooth black leather binding the journal was improbably warm to the touch. The papers shuffled, and he struggled to contain it all, stumbling backward and slamming the book shut. A scrap of paper escaped and spiraled to the floor. He picked it up, trying to jam it back into the journal, but not without first reading the script.

> I have searched and searched and searched, collected, and studied, begged for answers from one corner of this land to the other, combed the libraries of wiser men, and all to make sense of what I know in my heart is senseless. The order of it . . . The order . . . Why must it be put in order? Perhaps that is where I have gone all wrong, all wrong! The order. Dawn comes and I see it clearly now: There is no more wisdom in order than in chaos.
>
> I will relent.
> No.
> I will submit.

A lurid red eye was painted behind the words, not an eye with a pupil and iris, but solid, like a thumbprint in blood. Lucien cradled the book to his chest, immediately protective of it. The man before him had died in its keeping, so it must be precious enough to warrant study, study that perhaps took a lifetime.

Lucien fished out the scrap of parchment again, flattening it on the black cover. He looked at the red eye once more and found that it looked back.

It blinked. *No.* Did it?

Lucien closed his eyes tightly, reminding himself that they had been down in that silent, winding tomb for days. It would be enough to drive any reasonable person mad. But he took the journal with him, pocketing the glowing orange stone, and taking the dead man's pointed cap with him.

He returned to the rotunda, holding out the hat to Cree. "Look at this ridiculous little hat! Isn't it marvelous?"

Across the chamber, Vess DeRogna's head snapped toward him. "Silence. We are about to light the lanterns."

And so they were, each of them positioned at a different blue-and-gold orb, torches at the ready. He put the stupid hat on his own head and sat down with his back against the wall, irked. She didn't need to shush him like a child.

She is weak. She is nothing.

Lucien frowned, certain that wasn't his own internal voice speaking. But then, who or what was his internal voice? He only knew that, quite suddenly, it had changed. It didn't sound like him, or the him that rattled around in his brain.

"Be prepared!" DeRogna called, her voice taking on an imperious, almost theatrical quality. A few paces behind him, manning a lantern, Otis made a soft fart noise with their tongue.

Lucien suppressed a snicker, watching as the archmage lifted her torch high, wordlessly instructing the others to do the same. With the journal he had found clutched to his chest, Lucien observed as the impromptu ritual took place. DeRogna's torch met its target first, but Zoran, Jurrell, Tyffial, Otis, Cree, and Brevyn lit theirs, too, the blue-and-gold enamel and glass covering the globes filling the rotunda with a flash of sunset. Warm and cool light flickered in equal measure, a dazzling kaleidoscope that made the room jump to life.

Then came a quiet sizzling sound that grew in intensity like a swarm of bees moving down the tunnel toward them. He saw Cree wince, the noise almost unbearable, and then, when Lucien felt the urge to drop the journal and cover his ears, the chaos ended, the room abruptly silent. The stasis bubble faded, exposing the ancient elf to closer examination.

And theft.

DeRogna took her torch with her, striding to the center of the chamber, peeling the elf's fingers away from their chest gently, with the tenderness of a lover. Whatever magic protected that ancient also had preserved them, and within several heartbeats, they began to disappear, turning to dust, but not before the archmage had her prize. She pulled a talisman free from the vanishing hands. Lucien felt the chamber rumble and jerk sharply as soon as DeRogna touched the amulet.

He leapt to his feet, shouting an incoherent warning as a slab of rock plummeted to the ground, smashing the disintegrating elf, missing DeRogna by a hair. "Packs! Torches! Now! Everyone out!"

Otis was already flying across the chamber, cloak outstretched like wings behind them.

The magical bubble holding the waterfall at bay above them was holding for the moment, but Lucien didn't want to be there if and when that changed. They would be drowned swiftly or dashed to pieces against the tunnel by the force of the water. Jurrell grabbed a stunned DeRogna by the wrist, yanking her away from the plinth and toward the passage they had cleared. More of the ceiling shook and began to detach, smaller chunks falling, debris and dust cascading down, filling the rotunda with a chalky gray haze.

Otis disappeared down the tunnel, Tyffial following, with Jurrell hauling the archmage away from the chamber as it came down around their ears. Cree hesitated at the mouth of the passage with wild eyes, gesturing for the rest to hurry up and run. Zoran trundled by her, but Brevyn waited until Lucien had crossed the rotunda, dodging the new sinkholes appearing in the floor. The lanterns dropped, clanging, rolling, just another hazard to avoid.

"Come on! Move!" Brevyn screamed, the panic in her eyes telling him everything he needed to know about what was happening behind him.

As Lucien reached the exit, Brevyn hooked him under the shoulder, guiding him up over a tumble of smashed stones and into the cold, dark corridor.

"The hall is collapsing!" Cree's voice echoed down the passage.

Brevyn took his hand, and they ran, the light of the torches at the opposite end growing brighter. A wedge of stone from the cracked ceiling dropped, catching Lucien on the toe. He flailed and fell hard on his stomach, the journal slipping out of his arms. Brevyn kept hold of him, nearly dislocating his shoulder as she forced him back to his feet.

You cannot leave us!

No, no, so close, so close now . . .

Lucien cried out in pain, a chorus of angry voices shattering his mind.

Go back for us! You need us as we need you . . .

"The j-journal," he muttered, limping as fast as he could, tucked under Brevyn's shoulder. "We have to . . . I have to . . ."

"It's lost," she hissed, shaking her head. "It's lost, Lu, stay with me."

The torches were so bright now. They spilled out of the hall, past the remnants of the icy barrier, safe and sound on the other side.

"No," Lucien wheezed, at once turning back and leaning against the archway. "That journal . . . I'm going back for it."

"Are you mad? It's junk!" Cree shouted. "We need to clear out, this whole wing could go!"

Lucien set his jaw, growling, freeing himself from Brevyn's grasp and hurling himself toward the corridor. Only he didn't move. He never was as strong as her. Brevyn pushed him away, hard enough to catapult him past the others, and turned to retrieve the journal herself, marching down into the darkened corridor as the stones beneath their feet trembled, threatening to give way.

"This bloody thing better hold the secrets of the universe," she yelled.

The strangest thought occurred to him as Brevyn appeared again with the black leather tome.

Get it back, she's going to keep it for herself!

"Enough! We've tarried too long already!" Tyffial shrieked, tearing at her hood.

"I'm here, I'm here," Brevyn said, out of breath. He could just make out her eyes in the corridor. Lucien snatched Cree's torch, holding it out to see better as Brevyn returned.

Nothing but a pale trickle of dust from the ceiling presaged calamity. Brevyn saw it, too, and gasped as the wall to her left dislodged entirely, the foundation below it groaning as if in pain, the massive stone slab falling slowly and then all at once. Lucien watched her try to outrun it, watched her leap with both arms outstretched, but it wasn't enough.

The wall slammed her to the ground, pinning her legs. Destroying them. If it weren't for the supply pack on her back and the sturdy tent poles inside, the slab would have severed her cleanly in half. Lucien saw the shock in her eyes fade rapidly to disappointment. The shaking shamble of ruins around them settled, as if satisfied now that it had taken one of them, made them pay for their pilfering in blood. The others tried to beckon him away, but the rumbling had stopped, and he wasn't leaving without somehow finding the courage to say goodbye. He could comfort himself with lies and tell himself they could pry up that slab and get her out, save her, but he knew.

He knew.

Lucien glanced up at the ceiling of the passage as he crawled into it to lie with her, but only dust fell now. He pushed away her hood and hat and smoothed back her yellow hair. Brevyn coughed, horribly, until the cough became a ragged laugh. Her hands heaved out together in one motion, pushing the journal against his chest. It touched skin thanks to his damned billowing shirt, the one she never stopped teasing him about.

"I'm so sorry," he told her, wiping at the blood that trickled freely from her mouth. "This is all so pointless and unfair, and it shouldn't be you. It shouldn't be you. I'm sorry."

"Don't be," she managed. He could hear how much effort it took her. She smiled and her arm gave a single spasm. Lucien tucked it back down on the ground, folding his hand over hers. "Remember? To venture forth," she whispered, and he kissed her forehead. "That is the mandate of the soul."

CHAPTER 19

It was a cold, silent march to camp.

Lucien couldn't stop shaking, both arms hooked over his chest, keeping the journal Brevyn had died for flat to his stomach. He should have left it to rot. He should have left the damned thing behind, but instead Brevyn was gone, and it was all his fault. They retraced their steps back through Aeor until dark, finding the evidence of their last camp, Jurrell and Tyffial wordlessly getting to work on digging out the same patch of snow for the campfire. Lucien had the disembodied sense of repeating time, as if they could start the day over again and have it all play out differently. Next time, he wouldn't bother with that secret room, and once DeRogna had her talisman, they would flee the rotunda and everyone would make it out alive.

But he wasn't afforded the impossible luxury of a do-over, and so instead he sat stiff and stunned on a fallen statue, eyes seeing but not interpreting the deep scar of the crater.

Zoran lingered for a while but then disappeared with a grunt, convinced he could somehow shift the slab and get Brevyn out for a dignified burial, but he returned empty-handed, and short one blanket, which he had used to cover her. It wasn't until he began unloading his pack that they realized their predicament.

"We're short half the tent," he said, glaring down at the items he had laid out in the snow. The others shifted nervously and looked to Lucien.

An idea presented itself, and Lucien stood, tucking the journal under one arm, and flexing his hands until they stopped trembling.

"Let me handle it," he said.

"Mate, the poles she had are ruined, they won't—"

"I know, I'll handle it."

DeRogna was the last person he wanted to deal with, but she was also the obvious solution to their problem. The archmage stood apart, as usual, surveying Aeor with her knuckles perched on her waist. She breathed deeply, as if trying to inhale the place itself and take it into her body.

Next to her, he said, "You're going to have to share the Aviary. Brevyn"—he stumbled over her name—"was carrying the other half of our shelter, and it's getting colder by the minute."

"No," she said simply. "I won't be doing that."

Lucien swallowed a curse. "Then you can luxuriate right out in the open, mage. We need the supplies from your tent to make our own. Refuse and your escort to Balenpost freezes overnight."

Her lips pursed, but she nodded. "Very well. I expect you will not let envy become an issue among your band. Any whiff of mutiny and I will begin docking pay."

Lucien snorted. "We suffered a loss for you, remember that."

Cree moved so swiftly, so nimbly, that Lucien didn't hear her approaching until she was right up in DeRogna's face, pointing.

"Is she being amenable?" Cree asked, speaking to Lucien but glowering at the mage.

DeRogna craned her neck back, nose wrinkling. She was wearing the talisman from the ruins around her neck. Cree switched from pointing at DeRogna's face, to pointing at that.

"That's it?" Cree sighed. "That's all we came for? Brevyn died for that?"

Lucien grabbed her by the shoulders, urging her away from the archmage. He wanted to explode, too, wanted to scream and hear it echo for days in the ruins, but without their heads screwed on straight there would be more casualties.

"Do not disparage what you cannot understand," DeRogna murmured. Her eyes flashed and she turned to Lucien with a pitying frown. "Blaming me for this misadventure is pointless, Deeproots. 'Twas not I who lost a possession in the collapsing tunnel."

"I should let her scratch your eyes out," Lucien snarled.

The mage was unruffled. Her eyes traveled to the journal tucked under his arm. "What could possibly be so important that it was worth risking your lover's life?"

Lucien ground his jaw.

"Ah yes." DeRogna laughed. "I know about your dalliances. I also know you think me cold and unfeeling, but that quickness to judge is a weakness. Do whatever you like with the camping supplies, Tavelle, and mourn your dead, and harden your heart if you must. It will only serve for the journey back to Balenpost."

Cree pulled Lucien back toward the others, sensing that it was now his temper in danger of fraying. When they were out of earshot, he felt his control snap.

"You know, I said we would get her in and out of the ruins, I never promised we would take her back to Balenpost."

Otis, Jurrell, Tyffial, and Zoran perked up at that, ringed around the low-burning fire and waiting for instructions. Abandoning the hunk of toppled wall they had been using as a bench, Otis wandered closer. "Are you suggesting . . ."

She is weak, that odd, unfamiliar voice thrilled through his head again. **She is nothing.**

Not nothing, perhaps, but once they crossed the River Inferno, they had little need of her. Cree gripped his arm.

"Lucien, wait, do not be hasty," she whispered, flattening her ears. "Before, I spoke to the archmage in anger—"

"No, you spoke true," he replied. "We won't go home empty-handed, I promise you that."

He dreamed of her face.

Every time I lose someone it's like a door or a window shutting in a house. One by one, it all goes dark.

The first time Lucien saw her, Brevyn had been a lighthouse in a storm. His face was thrashed, shrapnel from the exploding trap embedded in his cheeks, forehead, chin . . . Cree had struggled to get him back to Auntie Mama's, half carrying a bleeding, panicking Lucien to the one place they might receive aid. And Brevyn had been there, visiting, Auntie Mama's favorite child. Golden. Strong. She laughed at the sight of him.

Laughed! Then she laid him on a table among cups and forks and a partially demolished roast, and opened her own veins, stewarding the magic to heal him.

"Should I leave a scar?" she had asked. "Maybe over the nose? I hear it's popular, very roguish."

She healed all but one, leaving a single bump on his cheekbone. It was barely noticeable, just a small reminder from Brevyn that Lucien wasn't as perfect as he thought he was. When he could breathe normally again, he thanked her, and the way she smiled and shrugged, as if it were no big deal, as if she hadn't just casually saved his life, forged a chain between them. In his mind, he saw the links form clearly until they were tethered together, inexorable. Destined.

He was coming to hate that word.

Lucien woke, unrested, in the cobbled-together shelter patchworked from two piles of supplies. Otis's curly head lay on Lucien's thigh, their chest rising and falling steadily as they snored. All in a pile, it was warm, but Lucien already felt the day's chill creeping up his toes. They would tackle the River Inferno that day, and he knew what waited on the other side. He knew what had to happen.

Zoran stirred next to him, sitting up and hugging his knees, unleashing a loud, growling yawn. He turned his bald head, noticing Lucien's open eyes, and grimaced.

"Why do you sleep with that thing?" he asked, nodding to the black journal behind Lucien's head. "It's fucking weird, mate."

"Brevyn died saving it for me," Lucien said. It was the simplest explanation. "The least I can do is keep it close."

That satisfied Zoran, and he kicked off the others who had cuddled up to him, Tyffial and Jurrell in particular, who were always attached to each other in the tent. Lucien pretended not to hear their whispering and kissing when they thought everyone was asleep.

Outside the tent, while the others gradually came awake, Lucien poked at the smoking firepit with a stick, encouraging some air into the coals. Cree perched on a blanket spread across a dug-out patch to the south, facing the lava flow snaking across the white fields. It wasn't until Lucien caught Zoran eyeing him again that he realized he had brought the journal with him, keeping it under his left arm.

The half-giant didn't say anything more about it and knelt to fish out a cooking pot for porridge.

To the east, a band of pale-pink light separated the crisp white of the ice and the dirge gray of the cloudy sky. The mountains and their ruins sloped steeply behind them, the ground tilted as if trying to shake them off, urging them downhill to the river. Unmasked without the tent, DeRogna's Aviary door shone like a beacon, the sunrise sparking against the glass, sending shards of reflection across the snow.

Zoran fixed his attention on the Aviary, a sour expression marring his already sour face. "Can't wait to see her face when she realizes we're fucking off without her."

"This could get messy today."

The half-giant sniffed. "About time, if you ask me."

"We could scrap the plan . . ."

"Why? If we squeeze her now, we get more coin out of her."

"And make a powerful enemy."

Zoran smiled. "A merc has enemies like a horse has flies, it's just natural."

Their second traversal over the River Inferno proved less eventful. Lucien found himself hoping DeRogna would slide into the lava and make the decision to betray her moot. He chalked up his sudden bloodlust to losing Brevyn; it was normal to want revenge, and perhaps it was unfair, but DeRogna was an available target. She was also haughty, conceited, selfish, and generally grating. When Lucien had broached the topic in their tiny, cramped tent, the rest of the Tombtakers, except Cree, had seemed eager for the chance to teach her a lesson.

Cree's change of heart concerned him, but not enough to make caution more appealing.

Lucien could feel the others observing him closely as they began to march away from the River Inferno. They were hungry for a cue, and when they were about a mile south, he obliged them.

"Stop for a moment," he called, putting up his hand. Exhausted, the crew ground slowly to a halt, watchful. "Circle up."

That was what they were waiting for. Otis dropped back, then Zoran, the others spreading out until they stood in a loose ring around DeRogna. She folded her hands in front of her waist, unmoving, taking stock of their treachery with predictably cynical grace.

"All this because I denied you my private home?" She sighed. "Petty."

Lucien took a few steps toward her, planting himself in her way.

"This is the part where we extort you for more gold." He grinned.

"Of course it is." It was midday, shadows long, the sun fat and golden above them, and they were out in the clear open. DeRogna's pale-gray eyes searched his face. "And what are the terms of this delightful little betrayal?"

"Payment here and now, DeRogna, but I'm afraid our price has gone up. I think two hundred gold should suffice, and considering that's an awful lot to carry, a promissory written in your hand will suffice," Lucien explained.

She remained still. "I see. And what good will that do when I tell my steward and the treasure holders in Rexxentrum that you have broken our contract?"

Behind her, Otis licked their lips, eyes darting.

"You're a woman who can appreciate precise language," Lucien replied calmly. "I promised we would get you in and out of the ruins safely with your relic, which we did, and that means our end of the contract was upheld." He spun in a circle with his arms outstretched. "Do you see any ruins here? I don't."

She started to say something but quickly changed her mind. "I knew this was in you."

"Did you? Then you should've prepared accordingly."

"You're assuming I didn't."

"And you're assuming I give a shit. Promissory. Now. Try to stiff us, DeRogna, and the action begins. Try something when you return to the city, and we tell every bounty hunter, occult lunatic, and relic collector in Wildemount about that talisman of yours. Or maybe we just inform your friends in the Cobalt Soul . . ."

The archmage paused, then lowered her shoulders, swinging the light pack off her shoulder and digging for something inside. Zoran grunted, raising his maul.

"Calm yourself, goon, I am simply retrieving parchment and quill."

Zoran kept his weapon at the ready anyway.

"Since you have become such an obnoxious pedant, you will understand that I must also take the journal you found in the ruins," she said, doing as she promised and retrieving pen and paper. Lucien twitched. "We did discuss that I was to be the sole beneficiary of items taken from Aeor; subsequently, I will have that journal you discovered. Give me that, and we part here without bloodshed, only bitterness."

"Brevyn died saving that thing!" Tyffial shrieked. "You can't have it. I mean, get serious, it's a crusty old journal, DeRogna, you're only asking out of spite. By the gods, let him have it as a remembrance of his friend!"

Lucien felt heat against his back. The journal, through his heavy pack, warmed as if brought to life by the argument. He didn't so much hear it whisper as the words passed through hide and straps and cloth and into him, crossing into his bloodstream.

We are yours. You are ours. What you possess, let no one withdraw. We are the scab of your body; pick us and bleed your organs, release your own vital self.

"You're not taking it," Lucien told her. "You can't, remember? It's not magical, and you yourself said we could help ourselves to mundane treasures."

DeRogna raised a single sharp brow of inquiry.

"'Tis mine."

"Indeed, I understand that it is currently in your possession."

"No, no, no. You don't understand, not in this instance."

Lucien unsheathed his scimitars, liking the slick, clean sound of their freedom. Vess DeRogna heaved a weighty sigh and began scribbling on the parchment while her gaze remained pointedly on Lucien.

"Interesting," was all she mustered.

Lucien wanted to take it as a victory over her, but there was something sly in the way she said it, a promise, perhaps, or a threat, that set his teeth on edge. Her eyes lingered on him, though he sensed she was looking through him, searching for, or sensing, the journal's presence. When she had finished writing, she offered the paper to him and he took it, verifying that the correct payment and information had been indicated.

The archmage returned her pack to her shoulder and, strangely, smiled. "Keep that journal close, Lucien, you have paid a dear price for it."

"You're the one what's paid through the nose," Zoran reminded her.

"Today," she replied, then looked away, bored. "And worry not, I will survive well enough on my own. I will be watching with interest, Lucien, to see if you do the same."

And so, the work begins.
 I hear it in your voice, Elatis, a delicious little thrill. You truly relish it.
 Why should I not? Why should I not relish that which shall remake the world?

CHAPTER 20

A day's travel north of Balenpost, Lucien stopped the Tombtakers near a frozen lake. It was shaped like a kidney, iced over, smooth, and as perfect as blue glass. There had been a lake very like it west of the Labenda Swamp near Berleben. During their years training under Sarenne, Karem, and Elias, Brevyn would take him and Cree there to swim, washing away the sweat and blood of a hard day's sparring.

"What's the holdup?" Otis asked, joining him at the lake's edge.

"I want to stop here for a moment," he replied. "To say a word for Brevyn."

Zoran ambled up to them, dropping his studded hammer in the snow and shrugging the framed pack off his shoulders. They had an hour or so before dusk, when the cold winds grew sharpened claws and tore at any exposed flesh.

"Does anyone want to speak?" Jurrell asked, holding Tyffial's hand as they gathered in a semicircle and faced north.

Lucien tried to gather the words, but everything got lodged in his throat. It was Zoran who stepped forward and knelt, hands clasped over his knee as he cleared his throat. "Matron of Death, Ebon Queen of Ravens, destiny claimed Brevyn Oakbender, and we do not question her path; we ask only that you hear our great cry of grief. Pity not our friend, who never knew fear or doubt, who fought arm in arm with any ready soul, but guide us that we may celebrate her life and walk in her example."

Five pairs of eyes stared at him blankly. The hard surface of the lake only amplified the stunned silence.

"What?" Zoran grunted, standing. "I'm a spiritual man."

"Thank you," Lucien told him. "That was . . . just right."

Heads were bowed, more prayers offered wordlessly, and then the Tombtakers broke to make camp. Only Cree remained by his side. Lucien lifted his head, feeling the hot sting of tears burning down frozen cheeks.

"Cree . . . I can't stop thinking about her rotting in those ruins, in the cursed place that killed her," Lucien murmured. "It's in me like a splinter; when I try to remove it, it just burrows deeper." He dropped his head and looked sideways at her. "When does it end?"

"You must give it time, Lucien, it's been but days." Cree stepped closer and rubbed the center of his back. "My mother mourned my father until she passed on, too. When she would take me to his gravestone, she would draw me close and beg me to heed these words: *You never make sense of death, child, you just get older.*" Her hand went limp. "Whatever you want, you won't get it, you just go on like there isn't more woe lurking around the next corner."

Lucien wiped his face dry, staring at the ice.

"You've never mentioned your father," he said.

Cree flopped her head to the side helplessly. "Gods love him, he had a sensitive soul susceptible to vices, drink and gambling in particular, and they took hold of him and turned his face away from everything good, everything that wanted to save him." She gave a dry laugh. "Every night he went to the card tables and dug our graves a bit deeper. I was the only one who crawled out of that sinkhole alive."

He waited by the lake awhile longer, until Cree eventually let him be and left to join the others. The fire crackled. The tent was built. Ale cups clinked. Laughter washed over him as day passed to evening, and a gray shadow fell over the frozen lands. When he could no longer feel his face or his hands, Lucien turned toward the fire, shuffling through the snow to their camp.

NOBODY BOTHERED HIM ABOUT SKIPPING a meal or time at the fire. Lucien craved the solitude, digging through his pack for the journal stuffed at the bottom. They had nearly killed themselves traveling quickly enough to stay ahead of DeRogna, and there hadn't been time on the road to study the odd tome, but now it could serve as a welcome distraction.

The leather was warm again as he laid it out on the blankets and furs. He cracked the disintegrating spine, and the pages greeted him like an old friend. Lucien settled in for a long read, but to his disappointment found that the opening pages were pure gibberish. He flipped and flipped and discovered that on the back of the first section there was an illustration, another bright, lurid red eye, filled in solid crimson. Again and again, he was drawn back to look at it, and after what felt like a moment but could have been any amount of time, it shifted ever so slightly, as if peering at something just over his shoulder.

Lucien slammed the journal shut. Then, hand shaking, he pulled back the cover again, finding that the opening passages were now completely, unbelievably, legible. He yanked the lantern closer, sweating.

> Now put down here are the words of ███████████████,
> Grand Archivist of the Dev-Yat Mahiyi Colleges in ████████
> in the year ██████. What follows are my best attempts to decipher
> fragments retrieved from the wastes of Foren, relics I know in my
> bones came from Aeor, grand city of mages, center of all enlightened
> thinking, and the greatest loss of our age. Calamity is too small a word
> for what was taken. I believe, however, that with enough persistence
> and diligence, much of what was lost can once more be found.

Many of the archivist's details were scratched out and with such a violent hand that the quill nib had broken the integrity of the parchment, little fibrous tufts poking up from the manuscript. Lucien read, feverishly, lying down flat, his nose nearly touching the journal.

> Thieves and scavengers sometimes return to ████████████ from
> far and wide, hawking their pilferings, some whispering of a vast city
> beneath the ice fields of Eiselcross. Initially, I thought this all nonsense
> and boasting, but upon acquiring several of these relics I begin to
> ruminate on their stories. Foren seems the most likely location to me,

as the scathing River Inferno there might handily dissuade the casual adventurer. Such an impediment would keep any ruins protected, and the ice may serve to preserve and perhaps even mummify the ancients of Aeor. If the bones of this theoretical place have not been picked clean, then I may yet prove that the items I have cataloged indeed belong to the mages of Aeor.

Enchantress Lornië tells me I am mad, and that I am wasting my time. What does she know? Her thinking has always been small. Let her experiment on her beasts and birds while bolder souls uncover the true extent of magic. In the end, she will have a talking dog and I will have the secrets of eternity.

The remainder of that page was illegible, defaced with a thick, black ink blotch. Lucien sought a clearer page, dismayed but not particularly shocked by how much had been destroyed. The journal had moldered in a tomb city for hundreds of years; of course it was going to sustain damage.

Certainly (and unlike our disgraceful hierarchy) the Convocation of Aeor prioritized the careers of forward-thinking mages, for I have found three separate tablets describing exorbitant funds being granted to someone called Fastidan, who, though seemingly at odds with the Convocation members, nonetheless won their respect. These sums were given over several years, suggesting that the mage's research was complex and ongoing. It is hard to reconcile these numbers. The figures offered do not match our records of currency used by the peoples of Aeor.

The next page had been scratched through to illegibility, and then:

A breakthrough! Just as I suspected, the tallies on the recovered tablets could not symbolize currency. They instead describe the number of slaves Fastidan put to work excavating, polishing, and constructing "the crests." I have no inkling of what these crests might be, or their use, and further do not trust my own translations of that particular word, nor the translation of "slaves" though that is my best approximation. It is worrisome to consider that a brilliant mind such as Fastidan's might resort to enslaving folk for the construction of magical devices, but perhaps future acquisitions will clear up this confusion.

In the name of pure professionalism, I have asked Enchantress Lornië to review my translation work, and she so far agrees with my assessments. Improbably, her narrow-minded piddle of a thesis was approved, and the ███████████ are advocating for her immediate promotion, upon which she will formally outrank me among the ███████████. Intolerable! She predictably (and jealously) continues to disparage my work and even had the gall and gumption to imply that Fastidan was a sick tyrant. Ridiculous slander.

"These are the words of a small-minded fustilarian!" I admit I screamed this at her. It was not my finest hour. Enchantress Lornië has forgiven me, but something in her eyes suggests otherwise.

Lucien's head jerked back, and he gasped, plunged abruptly into total darkness. The lantern had burned out. He shook his head and reached to close the journal, finding that the others were now slumbering around him.

He had no memory of their arrival.

And then, he dreamed.

Lucien sat on the lip of a fountain. The stones that made it seethed, he thought, moving like a hardened skin, filling with slumberous breaths. He felt it rise and fall below him, a lazy bellows that tricked his gut into the sharp wrench of seasickness. Over his shoulder, he heard a distinct hum. Glancing, he found an immense gate hovering there, a floating circle etched with runes. His mind bent toward it, pulled by some unseen power within it, and by the hypnotic sound emanating from its core.

All around him, red flowers bloomed. When he reached to pick one, it shied away with a hiss. He blinked, stunned. When he opened his eyes again, a handful of children had gathered. Their faces were chalky, dough-soft, not fit right to the skull. He wanted to look away, but they came toward him, pawing.

"Give it," the nearest child said. They wore shapeless smocks and had smooth, egglike heads. In the pits of their big black eyes, he sensed a hungry ache. "Give it," the child whined again. They descended on him, tearing at his clothes and skin, begging and pleading until Lucien roared with confusion, throwing them off.

He gathered himself and looked down in his hand, feeling something there. When he opened his fingers, a little sweet waited on his palm. It was a heart, candy-striped, fragrant like strawberries. A child snatched the treat out of his hand, and as soon as it was gone, another appeared. He offered more and more, doling out sweets until the children were laughing and cooing, rolling on their backs at his feet.

Lucien smiled, feeling he had done well.

Then a child rose from the back, pushing the others aside, coming to stand right before him. Small, sticky hands were placed on his knees, a giggle came, and Lucien felt his stomach turn again.

"Give us the world," the child demanded. His voice became all sound, and swallowed Lucien whole. "Give it."

CHAPTER 21

*At last, at last, I have shown Enchantress Lornië the true depths of my
genius. The High Archivist Enchanter Morillo has at last approved my
request for an expedition to the far north. The Frigid Depths will be
mine to explore and claim. Fastidan assured me this would happen,
and he is most pleased, for now my loyalty and persistence are
rewarded. The marks upon my body are still somewhat disorienting,
but I trust that will pass. To imagine it! I, ▄▄▄▄▄▄▄▄▄▄▄▄,
humble son of a pig farmer, entrusted with a cadre of students and
excavators to discover the lost secrets of Eiselcross.*

*I will find it, Fastidan! I will find it. The crests shall be collected,
your will shall be done. There will be so much to catalog and preserve.
One hopes to come away with a more complete understanding of
Aeorian politics, the Convocation, and, of course, the transgression
that called down the wrath of the gods! My name will forever be
remembered in the halls of ▄▄▄▄▄▄▄▄▄▄.*

The Tombtakers stopped only briefly in Balenpost to resupply,
choosing not to spend a single night there, wary that DeRogna
might pick up their trail. They went on directly to the crossing
instead, resting a night in Palebank Village while Otis recovered from a

nasty bout of seasickness. From there, with only their promissory note and little actual gold, they could not afford to be teleported anywhere sunny. Their dwindling coin at least paid for a cart and two horses, carrying them south across the Crystalsands Tundra. They attached themselves to a train of hardened merchants who welcomed the added protection of mercenaries, and even offered a decent tip when they again reached the familiar sprawling trees of the Savalirwood.

They avoided the main thoroughfares of North Clover, aware that the Run would not be safe with an embittered Vess DeRogna on the loose. It was miraculous, Lucien thought, that they weren't dead already. Miraculous and suspicious. Once clear of the city, they made their way southeast to Yardel, a tiny stonemasons' village north of Grimgolir. Nestled in the foothills of the Dunrock Mountains, it provided high ground for easy surveillance of the single road running north–south along the outskirts. It had been Jurrell's childhood home, a small enclave of elves settling there for a jewelers' venture until a failed crop in the region left them in the grips of starvation, and her family left for Nogvurot, seeking better circumstances.

In a place like Yardel, even a modest amount of coin bought them a cabin. It had a roof and beds, and that was enough for Lucien. The moment he lay down on the coarse feather mattress, he descended into dreamless sleep, and woke, according to Cree, an entire day later. He was glad not to dream of the sticky children again. They terrified him.

How much time had passed since they left Balenpost, he could not rightly say.

"Feeling better?" Otis asked as Lucien wandered into the common room of the cabin. It was a single story with a well-concealed cellar. The front doors and windows, though small, gave a clear view of the path winding up to the home, and two bedrooms off the main room offered enough space for them all to bunk. Lucien preferred sleeping in the cellar, finding the damp, dark cold there soothing.

"Much." Lucien sat down at the dining table with Otis, who had disassembled his crossbow for maintenance. The cabin had a novel construction, with a chunky stone hearth rising from the very center of the room, open on both sides, so that folk could congregate warmly all around it.

Zoran sang to himself in his deep baritone in the corner, sorting through a crate of scrap armor he had purchased for a lark in town. Cree, Jurrell, and Tyffial were nowhere to be seen.

"Where are the others?" Lucien asked.

"They've fucked off down to Grimgolir to see about the promissory," Otis replied, fluffing a bit of brown curly hair out of their eyes. "Wouldn't expect them back before tomorrow."

"They didn't ask me about it first?"

Otis shrugged. "Did they need to? You were dead to the world. Unless you fancy giving up a life of crime for the quaint agrarian fantasy or a stonecutter's toil, we're going to need gold, and lots of it. Can't stay on the run from DeRogna without funds." She nodded to a plate of frosted rolls on the table. "Help yourself. Jurrell says it's the same baker from when she were little, best buns in the region."

"Thought you held that title, Zo." Lucien decided not to worry too much about Cree and the others being absent and bit into one of the soft, heavenly, doughy rolls.

"What?" he barked, looking up from his singing and his sorting.

"Go on." Lucien snorted, a bit of frosting sticking to his nose.

Zoran turned sharply away and began his quiet, rumbling song again. "For the dead yellow king, a throng came and sang on the longest day of rain," he chanted. "He would not rise again, long, long may he reign . . ."

The tune began again, and Lucien tucked into his second pastry, rolling up his sleeves to keep them from getting covered in crumbs and frosting. Otis dropped a screw, their large, oval eyes bugging as they lashed out, snatching Lucien's right hand.

"What are you doing?" he asked around a mouthful of roll.

"What am *I* doing? What are *you* doing? Getting tattooed now without telling any of us? Cheeky. Odd design, though. Say, when did you find the time? You've been sleeping practically since we arrived."

"Song of my soul, my voice is dead," Zoran sang. "Die thou, unsung, as tears unshed shall dry and die in our Penumbra . . ."

Lucien blinked, noticing for the first time the full red eye marked on the back of his right hand. It matched exactly the design from the mage's journal illustrations. He ripped his hand away, shooting up so fast the chair tumbled away behind him.

"I need to go," he muttered. "I need to . . . Tell Cree to come and find me the moment she returns."

"Are you daft? That could be days! You must eat, Lucien, you must take care of yourself. I know with Brevyn and all—"

"I have to go."

Lucien fled back to the cellar, his breath coming in short, sick bursts. When he was belowground, he searched the meager furnishings in the cave-like cellar for any instruments that might have allowed him to create the tattoo on his hand. But there was no red ink, no needle, no hammer, and no sign of cleanup or bloodshed. He made his way back to his desk, where the journal waited, opened to the page with the glaring red eye. Trembling, he held his hand over the illustration, discovering that the tattoo was the exact dimensions of the one depicted in the mage's journal. Sweat poured down his temples. Stomach swirling, he carefully ran his right forefinger around the edge of the mark. The edges were the tiniest bit raised, though the inner meat of the eye was smooth, smoother even than his natural skin.

It seemed to glow faintly, brightly distinct, standing in such contrast to his violet-colored flesh that it seemed almost beautiful. *Welcome.* Lucien slapped his own face. That was idiotic. This thing wasn't welcome, it was an interloper, a violation. His gaze strayed to the book. Not just a violation, but an omen, the crossing of a boundary he didn't understand but innately feared. *How.* How could the picture have jumped from the journal to his body?

He swiveled, facing the desk properly, tucking his knees under it and lighting several candles, illuminating the journal. Hadn't the mage mentioned something about strange marks on his body? This must be some side effect of interacting with the journal, and logically the answer to how to remove it or why it had come might lay within its pages.

Enchantress Lornië has given me some of her trained ravens for the journey. She claims they are not ordinary ravens, but those imbued with her special research, and they are smarter and faster than others of their kind. That she will not set aside her own lamentably juvenile work to join the expedition comes as a great disappointment. She would be useful, even just as a drudge for digging, as I've often admired her muscular hands. But her vision has always been narrow, her obsession with paltry domestics regrettably small and female. She says the raven will help us keep in touch, as spells can only transmit very short messages, and she knows I will want to share the full breadth of my findings; this demonstrates a promising leap in insight for her, and I am proud.

The mage rambled on for several more pages about his colleague, and Lucien skimmed it, flipping pages, rabid to find more about the mark that had appeared on his body. He at last found traces of the mage's journey to Eiselcross, and he was struck by the remarkable echo across time—they had taken a similar path, and used spells cleverly to cross the River Inferno, discovering that proximity to Aeor began to negatively impact their spellwork.

Goldeth lost a hand today. As is his usual way, he attempted to warm us all by lighting a bundle of sticks with a simple manipulation of the fireblast spell. The result was catastrophic, and I may never forget the smell of burning flesh pouring through the camp. It is in my robes now, and horrid. He will continue his work on the expedition, but in a diminished capacity. We are hopeful that infection will not take him. Goldeth is an adept caster, a judicious researcher, and a sober, serious sort, so I do not believe this maiming was due to error. I sense but cannot prove a bizarre warping of the weave, a hiccup, so to speak, in the laws of magic. As we strike north, these hiccups only become more frequent and more severe. For now, I have directed the members of our expedition to use spells only in dire situations requiring self-defense, as our supplies are limited, and we cannot afford more injuries.

And later:

It is precisely as I expected: Some leagues north of the River Inferno, we discovered an immense ripple of frost, brittle and different from the surrounding ice fields. I listened to but dared not trust the voices that guided me to this place, promising answers, promising knowledge beyond knowledge.

Aeor is here. There were complaints when I suggested that we must breach the frost and descend into the ruins, for we are not well equipped for such an endeavor, but I will not give up now. Perhaps brashly, I accused Goldeth, Menzias, and Felinor of cowardice, but I refuse to apologize for it. The voices foretold this, too, that the pursuit of the infinite would require a certain moral flexibility not for the faint of heart. But oh, I do not feel faint now! Not when we have found such wonders, such incredible labyrinths of mysteries to be solved!

A series of sketches followed, many of them vaguely familiar to Lucien, dredging up memories of traversing Aeor's cold, confusing halls. The mage's descriptions of the ruin went on and on, painfully detailed, though Lucien could understand why—this was a major find, and the man might have thought they would be the first and last adventurers to record their experience of the place. Many had probably come before, Lucien thought, and considerably more would come after.

He shivered and looked at his hand and wished that he had never agreed to DeRogna's proposition. The reading had made his eyes burn, and he felt a rare bout of sleepiness. He laid his head down, just for a moment, but that was enough. He dreamed of the children again. This time, the sweets they wanted never materialized. They clawed him to ribbons.

Lucien snapped awake what felt like an eternity later, finding the candle on his desk had not burned down at all. He resumed the work. Turning a page in the journal once more, he recoiled. The script was interrupted by another illustration, this one of a silhouette, a lone, slender figure, their features blank, though it was clear they wore a dragging robe. Their arms were barely outstretched, as if they were levitating. The mage's pen had scribbled all around the outline of the person, as if an attempt to stamp the shape of them onto the page. A single red eye stared out from the center of the white face, but when Lucien blinked, the eye pulsated, growing outward like a bead of blood, then slid from the page, leaving no trail. He never found where it went.

After the picture came a scrap of parchment stuffed into the binding, the quality of the paper different, older, the pulp chunkier, with small flecks of what looked like crushed leaves. The penmanship was also different, leading Lucien to conclude that this was something the mage had found in the ruins and taken for himself.

The philosophers abandoned us. The cursed, plotting dreamers took their whole Ward with them. Curse them. May they rot in

There was no more. Behind the stolen scrap, the mage continued chronicling.

Goldeth has returned to the surface with his infected wound, probably to die. I have written to Enchantress Lornië with one of her ravens and asked that she watch for his return. In this same letter, I have reiterated her foolishness, for she will be absent for the most influential magical archaeological find of our era. I did not inform her of Felinor's disappearance, for I myself do not yet know how to interpret it. We have made camp in the Praesidis Ward, for it provides the most comprehensive shelter. While we had the energy for it, we searched the ruins in which we made our camp, and I have determined it was once the home of an illustrious Aeorian family. A mural in the main hall depicts them at luxurious rest, a mother, father, and three beautiful daughters. Chipping away at the ice, I discovered an artist's inscription reading FAMILY MAXIMUS ON THE EVE OF SOLSTICE: GLORY TO GORUS AND VITALIO MAXIMUS, WEALTH AND LONG LIFE TO THEIR OFFSPRING, MORBO, SILIO, AND BOLO. I have included a sketch, for I know Enchantress Lornië is enchanted by such prosaic trifles. The find was a brief joy, for in the night, we were woken by a mournful howl. It chilled me to the core, but Felinor agreed to investigate the noise. He has not returned. It is only Menzias and I now, and it is very quiet, giving the shadows that lurk behind us more power. I refuse to bend to fear, though daily I feel its toll. Menzias hardly eats, and my hair has begun to shed in clumps.

Tomorrow, we press deeper into the Ars Ward. Watching the raven fly away with my message, I felt a wave of sorrow. I should have told Enchantress Lornië more, and been more honest, but she must not know that, in truth, it is all going very badly here. The red marks are everywhere now, my hands, my chest, my shoulders, my neck . . . And they are changing me. The children hunt me in my dreams, and more marks appear. There has been a shift that I cannot explain, only this: Sometimes when I look at Menzias, I can hear fragments of his thoughts. This morning, I heard him speak clearly in my own head, though his mouth did not move.

"Why did I follow this crazy old fool?" I heard it clear as a bell.

When I examined his face, his guilt was obvious—he was indeed questioning the whole ordeal. There are marks on him now, too.

What is happening to me? Why me, Fastidan? Where does it lead?

The red marks are everywhere now, my hands, my chest, my shoulders, my neck . . . And they are changing me.

Lucien read it three times, his stomach tightening with each reread. *Everywhere?* Everywhere. Maybe it wouldn't happen to him. Maybe it would stop.

Maybe, maybe, maybe.

The mage had even dreamed of those wretched children. Peculiar. And sinister. He tried to shove the book away, but found he was compelled to continue. It was better, he reasoned, to know his fate than to run headlong into the darkness.

CHAPTER 22

This is the fruit of a once barren tree. Now we come to it. Now I see it clearly. Cognouza. That which was promised. The marks upon my body that I once mistrusted I now see as proof of the promise—all that the nine philosophers worked to achieve, I am one of their masterpieces.

The Astral Sea, that was their goal. The texts describing this were not penned by the philosophers themselves, but by doubting imbeciles like Lornië, too attached to the conventions of this realm to see that so much more lies beyond. The philosophers were wise, they predicted the disastrous outcomes of the Calamity, and their elegant solution was not submission or defeat, but to avoid annihilation altogether. A grand exodus. They were shunned. Shunned. Unbelievable! No, it is completely believable. They did not accept the concept of inevitability, in fact, they challenged the bones of reality as we understand it. Matter. Matter could be molded and shifted at will, dreams made manifest, no limitation but that of one's own imagination.

The possibilities are, needless to say, tempting. The mind as architect, unrestrained. It is almost painful to conceive of such freedom, and yet I must possess it. Fastidan would not lie. Everything I have found pertaining to the Cognouza Ward, their ward, has been proven true.

Why then, would their theories prove false?

Much has changed, but I must not fear the change. We returned to our campsite to eat and rest, for Menzias still requires such things, only to find someone or something had left a gift for us. It was the head of Felinor, his scalp and eyes removed. What remained of his tongue had been pulled out ghoulishly, as if to mock us. Menzias wept, but I will not be threatened away from this place, this womb that did not birth me, but birthed that which calls me home.

He dreamed
He dreamed
He dreamed of a red basin, a collapsed and hollow place
And from that misshapen bowl came a blank white face
It had no hair to comb
Possessed no mouth to lie
Its one and only feature was a single crimson eye
"The world is yours," it somehow said. "We gladly give it thee."
"How will I take it? What will it cost?"
"There are no answers for thee."
"How will I take it? What will it cost?"
"Pain and pain and pain. A dear price for a man,
A pittance to a King
And nothing to a God, cosmically ordained."
"Am I God or King?" he asked.
"Long may you reign."

"Lucien. *Lucien.*"

"What?" He snapped awake. He hunched protectively over the journal, shielding it from whatever prying eyes had come. His neck ached, stiff, as he slowly turned to discover Cree hovering behind the desk.

"We have a problem," she said. Her yellow eyes were haunted.

"What sort of problem?" Lucien barked. "Why am I to solve it?"

"It's DeRogna's promissory. It's . . . gone."

"What do you mean *gone*? Who took it?"

"Nobody. It vanished into thin air. She must have hexed it."

Matter. According to the philosophers, matter was fickle. Matter could be changed. Remade.

Lucien shut his eyes tightly and waved her off. He just wanted to return to his studying; it called, buzzed, like a fly wedging its way insistently down his ear canal. "I'll . . . I'll see to it. I'll fix it."

Cree planted herself stubbornly. "How? Did you even hear what I said? The gold is gone. We're in deep, deep shit here, Lucien!" She reached for the journal to close it, but Lucien snarled, slapping her hand away.

"Do you want a dagger in your throat? Is that what you want?" he shouted, then collapsed onto the desk. "Just . . . let me think. By the gods, leave me in peace. The answers are here, Cree, here in this journal. The answers to our problems, to our misfortunes, it can all be redone. We have never been victors, but that will change. Things will be different when I have the full picture."

"And when will that be?" she asked gently. Cautiously. Jurrell appeared behind her carrying a breakfast tray. The elf laid it out on his desk, but Lucien's stomach clenched at the smell.

"You have to eat," said Cree. "You're wasting away down here."

"I'm fine," he muttered. "The work is just taxing. It requires my full attention."

"Lucien . . ." Cree hesitated, and Jurrell wandered back toward the stairs, leaving the breakfast tray behind for him. The catfolk crouched, touching his wrist. "Forget DeRogna and the gold for a moment, we're simply worried about you. Whatever is going on . . . you're not yourself, mm? You haven't left the cellar for two days. You don't sleep, you don't eat—this thing is going to kill you."

Lucien shook his head weakly.

"When I came downstairs last night, you were sitting up in your bed, completely still as if asleep, but your eyes were open. I couldn't rouse you." Cree scrunched up her face in anguish. "You are *frightening* me, Lucien."

"There is no need to be frightened," he promised her. "You just don't understand."

"Then help me understand."

Lucien almost rebuffed her, but then remembered that there had been nine philosophers of Cognouza all working together, not just one. If he wanted to retread the steps of the unknown mage and achieve what he couldn't, he would fail if he tried alone. That was the mage's mistake, he realized, growing giddy: He pushed his expedition team and friends away, failing because it was a task too insurmountable for a single soul.

"Here," he said, offering the journal to her.

Cree hesitated with her hand poised just above the pages for a ponderous moment. She whetted her lips, then turned the journal toward her. Lucien felt his stomach lurch. Her yellow eyes skimmed the topmost page, a twitch starting above her right eyebrow. Her ears pinned back, making her earrings jangle.

"There were nine philosophers of Cognouza," he told her, speaking slowly while she perused at her leisure. "They wanted to protect their ward from the collapse and found a way to project themselves into the Astral Sea to avoid the Calamity. There, they could do anything they imagined, shape the world to be what they wanted. If only I could speak to them directly, I could do so much for us. There's not enough here to know everything, but I know this journal, this promise, will change everything for us."

Cree exhaled hard through her nose and pushed the journal back. "That isn't possible, Lucien. The man who wrote that journal was probably mad."

"Then explain this," he replied, showing her the red eyes blazing from the top of his right hand and now the palm. When he concentrated, reaching out with his mind, he heard her thoughts echo in his mind before they left her lips. "Lucien . . . Gods . . . there are more of those things on you. More of the eyes."

"H-How did you know I was going to say that?" she whispered.

Lucien worked his head back and forth, smoothing out the kink in his neck. He smiled at her, calmly, and turned back to his desk. "It's the philosophers, Cree. It's Cognouza. They're changing me, changing me for the better."

CHAPTER 23

Lucien read long into the night. The more he thought about DeRogna stiffing them, the more it boiled his blood. A searing headache blossomed at the base of his skull, his vision blurring. *Every time I lose someone it's like a door or a window shutting in a house. One by one, it all goes dark.* Their fortune was gone. Another darkened door. He heeded Cree's words of warning and eventually lay down on his mattress to sleep. It was a hollow sleep, his mind somehow jumpy and alert even as he felt powerless to direct his thoughts.

Yet *something* directed his thoughts. The visions that came, though disjointed and bizarre, struck him as organized. Children laughing, a glaring red eye, a sudden rush of movement, and then a sphere hurtled out of the darkness. Eyes burned on a ring around the sphere, and when they flared too bright, in their collapse and death came a collection of glyphs. He was being led to some conclusion, the exact details of which still eluded him.

Laughter, eyes, circle. He had to make sense of it.

When he rose, ignorant of whether it was day or night and with the image of a red circle burned behind his eyelids, he returned to his desk to find a piece of artwork there. It was a rudimentary charcoal drawing of a crooked house, just like Auntie Mama's, with eight windows and one door. Figures stood in the windows and door, and he recognized his mother, father, brother, Auntie Mama, and in the doorway, Brevyn. Their mouths were all turned down in exaggerated frowns.

Underneath, in a handwriting he didn't recognize, were the words: WHO ARE THEY.

Lucien sat down hard in the chair, bewildered. Of course he knew who they were. Had one of the other Tombtakers left this here to unsettle him? He lifted his hands to run them through his hair, and found his fingers covered in charcoal smudges. Low, agitated voices bled through the floorboards. Someone above the cellar paced. They were going to need gold, and soon, and poverty would not be a problem for them, not ever again, if he could finish what the nine philosophers and the unknown mage had begun.

Tearing up the strange picture, he reached for the journal. When his fingers made contact, his posture relaxed, the tension in his body released, a muzzy warmth flooding his chest as he returned to the words. The words, coaxing and enveloping, like sliding into a sun-warmed daybed, the sheets still a tangle from a morning visit to a lover's embrace.

My objectives are clear: Once the threshold crests are recovered, the Astral Sea can be reached, and from there, Cognouza returned. This will be no easy task, as the crests are tremendously large, and I may not alone possess the means to transport them. They might be moved with magic, but the instability of these ruins makes me question such an approach.

I must ruminate on it more.

Enchantress Lornië has written to condemn my studies outright. She has taken great offense at my letters and claims that she will go to High Archivist Enchanter Morillo and the Council and seek an official denunciation. Such an act would strike my name and my research from the ▬▬▬▬▬▬▬ *records, leaving this world once more in blighted ignorance.*

I confess, I burst into tears upon reading her threats. My life's work undone by a cowardly Luddite. It is clear, now more than ever, that I must succeed, for if Enchantress Lornië moves against me, I will return from the Astral Sea with the power to unmake her treachery. In fact, I can unmake her, as well, and mold her into a monstrosity more befitting her twisted, ugly insides.

*We return to the Ars Ward this evening in search of a crest.
Menzias assures me he has not forsaken the research, but I sense
doubt in him. His work is still exemplary; indeed, he has at last
finished fully deciphering the schematics for a device resembling a
gate. Six runes encompass the circular gate, their meaning still
unknown to us, though one displays an eye much like those denoting
the philosophers. Perhaps the rods must be inserted such that the eye
rune becomes the focal point. Conjecture! But oh, it is rather diverting
to imagine breaking the lock on an ancient prison. Moreover, I have
dreamed of this gate, glimpsed it in colorful fragments, a gift from the
Somnovem.*

*Menzias, predictably, does not share my excitement. I fear he is
not strong enough for what is to come. Few would be. Few are.*

A significant portion of pages were missing, torn out and lost, re-
suming with:

*So, it comes to this. Treachery, treachery, treachery! Indeed, I rightly
smelled it upon Menzias, but too late did I understand the depths of
his weakness. I am imprisoned, and all hope is lost. Upon reaching a
high rotunda, well preserved, we discovered a stasis bubble containing
an ancient Aeorian citizen. The philosophers screamed in my mind at
the sight of them, and I exclaimed to Menzias that we must find a
way to discharge the bubble and study this person. He led me to a
small room off the rotunda, certain that he had found an inscription
relevant to the work. While I attempted to verify this, he locked me
inside, dooming me, dooming the work.*

*I heard the bastard painting something on the other side, likely a
warning. Now I sit in the encroaching darkness with nothing but an
enchanted rock and my failing hopes for company. I will try everything
to get out, I will not surrender to this setback, but I fear I will never
behold Cognouza.*

*Cognouza, lost to me! Fastidan! Ira! Vigilan! Why now silent?
Why do you abandon me? Luctus! Elatis! Culpasi! Please, I beg, I beg
for your wisdom and your sight. Timorei! Mirumus! Gaudius! I weep.
I weep to hear you.*

*Cognouza, wait for me. If eternity relents, if there is mercy, I will
find you.*

Lucien sat back in his chair, short of breath. That had been the corpse of the unknown mage in the secret chamber, locked there for hundreds of years with nothing but the journal and his disappointments. Lucien had stolen his hat. And it was no wonder nobody had ever discovered the nine philosophers or Cognouza—Menzias and Enchantress Lornië would have obliterated all mention of the mage and his research.

They had not done enough.

When Lucien turned the page, he found that in isolation and hopelessness, the mage's mind had begun rapidly to deteriorate. Fragments, designs, rantings in languages Lucien had no ability to translate. For sixteen consecutive pages, there was nothing but the word: TRANSMUTE. There were elaborate schematics for what Lucien realized was a contraption meant to free him from the secret room, a sort of makeshift lever made from his wooden staff and found stones, tied together with his own hair, and glued into place with mouse droppings.

The gibberish and diagrams ended abruptly about twenty pages after the last coherent journal entry. The mage's penmanship, unsteady, was at least legible.

I hear their voices once more and dream of the gate. The Nine, the Somnovem, have called. I am called. I go forward to meet them, to become one with Cognouza. The city awaits me in glorious oblivion. Here behold the final words of the Nonagon before his inevitable ascension:

Lucien did not recognize the language of what followed, but he knew a spell when he saw one: the line breaks, the length, and the diagrams beside it demonstrating the necessary materials, focuses, and gestures. He leapt out of his chair, invigorated. The unknown mage had become something called the Nonagon and left behind the spells that empowered him to project into the Astral Sea. Whatever this gate was, Lucien had visions and dreams of it, too—laughter, eyes, circle. What if the sphere surrounded by eyes and then glyphs pointed to a gate? Perhaps it was a real thing somewhere within the ruins of Aeor, but he didn't know enough. He needed more. They had found the man's corpse, but not his soul. He had already left long ago to join the philosophers in Cognouza, somewhere in the Astral Sea. Lucien marked the page, knowing it was the trail of breadcrumbs he had been searching for. All that remained was to find someone versed enough in obscure magic and learning to translate the spell and perform it for him.

One such person immediately sprang to mind.

It pained him to part with the journal, but he pushed himself slowly up and away from the desk. His body ached, but his purpose was clear. Upstairs, he found that the Tombtakers had gathered near the central hearth, their conversation ending the moment he appeared. There was a stranger among them, a dwarf dusted with the gray snow of the stonemasons' camps. His back was to the door, the Tombtakers receiving him in a semicircle. The dwarf scoffed at Lucien's arrival.

"Who's this rangy mutt, then?" the dwarf grunted. He was rather tall for dwarven folk, dressed in a simple leather apron deeply scored by tools. His graying brown hair was tied back in several diminishing knots, strings of white beads strung between his beard and those loops of hair.

Lucien said nothing, watching a panicked Cree absorb his presence.

"Well, boy?" The dwarf strode up to him, bumping his chest against Lucien's belt buckle.

"Not exactly a boy," said Lucien, almost breezy. "Rather, I feel *boy* and *girl* come and go, they change, you see, like the refrains of a song you learn again each day."

"Lucien! You're . . . We . . ." Cree guided Lucien back a step.

Zoran apparently shared none of her hesitations. "'Bout time. This is Gergran Beldehr. Needs an armed escort for a haul of stone up to the Breach."

Lucien nodded, saying calmly, "I thought we agreed to avoid that area for a spell."

"Why are you whispering?" Otis rasped. Jurrell kicked his ankle.

"Coin is coin," Zoran added with a shrug. "We need work."

"And just any old job will do?" Lucien laughed, but he saw a dark curtain of rage fall over Zoran's face. The half-giant pulled himself up to his full height, nostrils flaring.

"You have a better idea?" Zoran growled.

"I . . . can come back at a better time," Gergran stammered, backing away toward the door.

"No," said Lucien. "Stay a moment."

He felt what was about to happen before the idea fully formed in his mind. Someone else, a being outside of him yet somehow connected, made the choice for him. A flicker of electricity roared through his body, though he moved not at all, and then he felt the eyes marking his body flare, a ghost of light breathing greater brightness and life into them.

A whisper floated through his brain, gaining in power. It belonged to a masculine being, lightly accented, with an almost mischievous rhythm. This stranger is trouble. Don't you sense it? He means you and yours ill. There is a dark omen about him, and his intentions are plain.

Yes, Lucien thought, *I see it, too.*

He will lure you into an ambush on the road. There will be no survivors.

Lucien took six steady steps toward the dwarf and placed his hand on the stranger's shoulder. He felt the eyes across his body surge again.

"Tell me, Gergran Beldehr, why do you wish us harm?"

"Lucien—" Cree began in a warning tone.

The dwarf began instantly to sweat. His eyes bounced among the Tombtakers, desperate for an intervention. But none of the others came to his aid, though they did stand at the ready, attentive. Lucien gripped the dwarf's shoulder harder, fingers digging in.

"Why did you plan the ambush along the Graydowns Road? What do you stand to gain from our demise?"

"I—I . . . I . . ." The dwarf wiped at the sweat on his forehead, then stumbled toward the door, leaving without another word, beard beads clacking.

Tyffial stalked to the door after the dwarf, mouth hanging open. "That bastard was going to rob us?!"

"Aye, Tyffial, well sussed, you absolute thumb," muttered Otis, dropping wearily into a chair at the dining table. "Neat parlor trick, Lucien. How'd you do it?"

That same sinuous voice visited him, nudging.

Tell them, Nonagon. Tell them everything.

TRANSMUTE

TRANSMUTE

TRANSMUTE

CHAPTER 24

The Tombtakers gathered around him like his flock, like his children. He pulled his shirt over his head, revealing the other eyes, all nine of them, those he had seen with his own eyes and those he simply knew had arrived.

"You're covered in them," Jurrell whispered, hiding her mouth with both hands.

"There are nine," Lucien replied. He rested back against the lip of stones surrounding the hearth. "One for each of the nine philosophers of the Somnovem."

Silence.

"Oh," Otis finally sighed. "So, you've really gone full crazy boots. Got it. Do we take his ass out behind the barn now or later? I say now."

"With friends like these . . ." Lucien mused, unafraid.

Otis flew off their chair, shoving an accusatory finger in Lucien's bare chest. They were careful not to poke one of the red eyes. "'Friends'? You've got it all screwy, mate. You've been locked in the cellar for nearly a week going madder by the minute, then you chase off our one shot to make some money, so 'friends' is a bit of a loaded word right now, believe it or not!"

"That job was a death trap," Lucien reminded them. "I saved your lives."

"Should we grovel, then?" Otis shook their head. "You made a lucky guess, that's all."

"Cree believes me."

All eyes turned to the catfolk, who had been standing against the table with her arms crossed over her chest. Her ears went straight up.

"How do you know that?" asked Tyffial, squinting at him.

"Because I can peruse her thoughts," he said. "And see through her eyes."

"And the Somnombulem lets you do that?" asked Jurrell.

"The Somnovem," Lucien corrected gently. He smiled, beatific, and gestured for Cree to come to him. "See for yourself."

He took Cree by the hand, plucking off the fingerless glove on her left hand. On the back, leaping out from her black fur, was one of the red eyes, a match to the one on Lucien's right hand.

Cree hissed, pushing away from him, and cradling her hand to her stomach as if cruelly burned. "H-How . . ."

"If you'll all listen," Lucien said, stretching out his arms in welcome. "I'll tell you everything. It begins with a cadre of brilliant minds, the great disruptors and visionaries of a doomed society."

There were many questions, of course, when he had finished telling them the tale, but he could see enlightenment creeping into their eyes. He tried to make it clear that the philosophers were similar to them in many ways—fringe thinkers, those who were exiled, shunned, and unfairly rejected all for the sin of seeing behind the curtain. Power, he declared, pooled at the top of a narrow mountain, rarely spilling over or trickling down.

Dusk fell outside, purpling the sky. Otis was the last to ask his questions, and the most skeptical. That made sense to Lucien. Otis had served a once powerful family in Trostenwald. Scandal and corruption had brought them low, poisoning anyone associated with them, including Otis and his mother, true innocents who had done the family's bidding out of loyalty. Social regard turned to harsh judgment, a secure position evaporating into indigence, and all through no fault of Otis or his mother.

It was hard to let go of The Dream That Could Have Been and accept The Nightmare That Was Now.

"If you can get us this power of Cognouza—and that's a big if—how do you reckon we start?" asked the halfling. Zoran had brought out the ale, which also helped in softening their minds.

"There is a spell I've discovered in this mage's tome, a ritual that will allow me to speak directly with the city." That was largely speculation, but the growing chorus of voices chiming in with his thoughts did not refute his theories. "Cognouza is eager to meet with the Nonagon, and when they are finally reunited, the shaping magic perfected by the Somnovem will pass to me."

Otis arched a brow. "And you're sure about this?"

Doubt is a poison that corrupts slowly, a voice whispered. *Draw it out at once.*

"Aye," Lucien replied. "I am certain, and I will know so much more when I speak with the Somnovem directly."

"Then how do we begin?" Jurrell asked, sitting on the floor beside Tyffial. After Cree, Jurrell had been the most willing to entertain his plan to empower them all through the Aeorian philosophers' promises.

"Aye, we'll be starved soon," Zoran added. He stood at the very back, leaning on his axe like a walking staff. "We're down to our last gold."

"You have to think bigger than gold," Lucien replied. "The philosophers will allow us to shape matter as if it were clay. Any dream, anything the imagination can conjure . . ."

Zoran's eyes went blank, and Lucien wondered if the big fellow was having trouble conceptualizing such a reality. It was, admittedly, a lot to take in.

"Sadly, the required ritual is beyond my ability," Lucien told them. "The language is not one I understand, and the materials are costly, but I believe Vess DeRogna could—"

"Vess DeRogna!" Otis screeched. "Vess DeRogna wouldn't offer us a sip of water in the desert! She'll suss out what we're up to, won't she? She would never let us—"

"*Let* us?" Lucien thundered, growing impatient. Otis shrank. "*Let* us. I am no longer concerned with what the powerful will let us do in this world. No, I am only concerned with what we ourselves want to take from this world. What we demand. What *we* deserve." His voice softened, and he sat back down, gesturing lightly to his chest. "I am the Nonagon. The Somnovem have chosen me as their instrument—not a king, not a warlord, not a politician, but me, one of the Tombtakers. Your friend."

Cree spoke, gradually, as if afraid to lure out his temper again. "Lucien, that does not change the fact that Vess DeRogna despises us, and for good reason."

"She is also obsessed with the mysteries of Aeor and her own advancement," Lucien replied. "She will be easily duped into helping us. We will tell her whatever fiction we wish and dispatch her without fuss once I reach Cognouza and the Somnovem imbue me with their knowledge. We only need her for the ritual, but after that?" He shrugged and pursed his lips.

The implication pleased the Tombtakers.

He opened his arms to those gathered again, speaking with the smooth confidence of a man at last stepping into the shoes destiny had shaped for him. "Let me handle DeRogna. In the meantime, we ride north. The dark magic of the Savalirwood will serve perfectly for our purpose."

They slept beneath the stars just north of Yardel, on a hill crowned with a ruined church. Lucien retreated from the warm glow of the campfire, sitting apart in the long grass, staring up at the moon, the dull ring given to him by Vess DeRogna cupped in his right hand, placed just over the red eye marked there.

He activated the Whisper Ring, sending a simple message to the lady mage. "We need to talk."

Her response came swiftly, her sure, arrogant voice filling his mind. It burned like a headache. "Ah, then you've noticed my little deception."

"Indeed we have." Lucien laughed, sending the message.

"You're in a remarkably good mood for a doomed man."

Lucien skipped the banter. He was impatient for eternity. "I have something you want, and I'm willing to trade for it."

This time, her response took longer. He blinked up at the stars and then closed his eyes, the cool night air and chirp of frogs and crickets lulling him into a meditative numbness. She would agree to his terms and the plan would go off without a hitch, because everyone all his life had been telling him this moment was coming. Cree, Brevyn, even DeRogna herself had insisted he was meant to walk a path of such import. He would succeed where the unknown mage had failed—he would not reach for Cognouza on his own.

"Do you mean the journal?"

Lucien smiled. Bait dropped and taken.

"I do."

"And what do you want for it?" she asked. "Two hundred gold?"

He grimaced but kept his anger in check. For the moment. "I found a spell in the tome. I need you to perform it for me, then the journal is yours."

Another pause. Another hesitation.

One of the Somnovem must have sensed his flicker of fear and doubt.

Let it feed you, Nonagon. Victory lies on the other side of fear.

It was Timorei speaking. Lucien was beginning to tease their voices and demeanors apart. Timorei possessed a high, quavering voice, discordant like a too-tight lute string.

Let the fear rise around you. Submerse yourself.

DeRogna might refuse. She was a clever woman, after all, and she would naturally expect a trap. She might not show her face at all but send someone or someones strong enough to end the Tombtakers once and for all. But no, she had pride, too; she would want to claim that satisfaction and distinction for herself.

"What manner of spell?" she finally asked.

"A costly one." A smile slid across his face. "A jacinth without flaw, and a silver bar carved in the shape of an eye."

"And the tome is mine when all is done?" DeRogna's voice filled his brain again.

"The tome is yours and we part as strangers."

"No, Lucien, you and I will ever be enemies."

He shrugged, though she couldn't see it. "The Savalirwood. A fortnight from now."

There was no answer. Lucien tucked the ring back into his coat pocket, satisfied that DeRogna would be too curious, vain, and vengeful to resist. She would no doubt come with ill intent, but that was all right. The Tombtakers could keep her under control until the spell was completed, and then it would be far too late for Lady DeRogna to do anything but succumb.

CHAPTER 25

The evening of the ritual, Lucien meditated beneath the gold and purple trees of Renart's Clearing. He had played there once as a boy with Aldreda and Elric, before Elric was lost to them and scooped out, and made into a hollow-eyed puppet. Their parents had been furious, and hided Elric raw for not setting a better example. Lucien remembered smearing a chewed cud of feverfew and chamomile into the cuts and bruises on his brother's back while he and Aldreda pretended not to hear their brother's sobs, and their parents practiced a lively duet outside the caravan.

Lucien no longer slept, but the Somnovem continued giving him visions like dreams, and so as he sat perfectly still in the clearing, he felt the strong drag behind his eyes that meant he was no longer conscious. Someone else was in control, and thus he dreamed: Once upon a time, there was a happy family. (He recognized the sweet, musical voice of Elatis, one of the few Somnovem who seemed interested only in matters of joy and possibility.) Mother and Father loved their three children dearly, and they all lived in a green wooden house with tall windows and strong doors. Mother taught the young of a fine, rich family, and Father carved instruments for the kingdom's musicians. They never went hungry, and they never quarreled, and their lives were golden for all their days.

When the story ended, Lucien woke, drawing in a deep breath

scented with the wild grasses and flowers exploding through the clearing. There was only a light, late-winter snowfall, and it dusted the tops of the new flowers like a coating of baker's flour.

Once upon a time. He stood, slowly, as if rising to process through his own wide kingdom. It would come true, for time was as malleable as matter, another material to be shaped and carved by the Nonagon who would reach Cognouza. He would see Elric and Aldreda again, not as they had become, but as they were meant to be.

Brevyn, too, could be his again.

No. *No.* Lucien shook off that thought, striding back toward the Tombtakers, who had gathered at the edge of the clearing on a patchy blanket, eating a feast bought with the last of their dwindling coin. He didn't allow himself to think about Brevyn anymore. It hurt too much, was too near, and drew him sharply off course. If he wasn't careful, his meditative dreams veered into nightmares, and down a black hall he saw her crawling along the floor, moaning, dragging her entrails and spine like a hideous tail.

Zoran was singing for them, perhaps already a little drunk. It was one of his favored tunes from the Menagerie Coast. "Song of my soul, my voice is dead, die thou, unsung, as tears unshed shall dry and die in our Cognouza . . ."

Lucien looked at each of them in turn, satisfied that soon, whatever they wanted done, whatever they wanted fixed, would become reality. *That old mage didn't have the tenacity for this work, but I do. It consumed him, but I will be its master.*

"What's the first thing you'll do when we reshape the world?" asked Tyffial wistfully over Zoran's song, cuddled up against Jurrell, her long black hair cascading down the other elf's shoulder. Her cheek was pressed against the new red eye burning on Jurrell's skin.

What could be better than a shared dream? Elatis asked, sweeping lightly through Lucien's mind like a path of glitter.

"Gonna make my cock two feet long," Zoran roared, slapping Otis on the back. The halfling nearly choked on the heel of bread they were gnawing.

"Even fewer lasses will fuck you then," Otis joked back.

"If that's possible," Cree added.

"I want my whole body to be made of diamonds," Jurrell said, preening Tyffial's hair. "And I'll go back to Yardel, make the fields there blossom until they burst. Nobody there will ever starve again."

Cree sat up straighter, dropping a piece of cheese she had sliced. "Hush. Someone approaches."

Indeed, the shrubs to the west rattled and shimmered, then parted to reveal Vess DeRogna in all her green woolen glory.

"Join us!" Lucien called to her without standing. The others glared. "Welcome her as a friend," he told them in an undertone. "Let our last moments as these sparse mortals be as gracious hosts and good company."

Tyffial raised a cup to that, sloshing wine on herself. "To a better world," she toasted.

"To us," Otis corrected.

DeRogna approached, carefully, a small velvet satchel clutched in her hands. Her eyes swept the party, the food, the drink, and she gave an almost imperceptible sigh. Her judgment didn't bother Lucien. Her opinions generally were no longer his concern. She now served one function and one function only.

He felt the eyes across his body flare, Timorei's quavering voice trembling through his mind once more. *She is not to be trusted! Beware, Nonagon, beware . . .*

Lucien shook off the warning. Tyffial poured herself more wine, then dunked a huge portion of bread into it. They were all ravenous, bolting down what amounted to their only possessions save the armor on their backs and their weapons. There was no turning back now, not when their need was so dire.

"Greetings, Lady DeRogna," Lucien said politely. He grinned, broadly, and withdrew the mage's black tome from his pack. He pulled out a sheet of paper on which he had transcribed the various snippets of the projection spell, then offered it to her. DeRogna's mouth curled in a tight smile at the sight of it, though she hesitated to take the parchment, noticing the eyes on his hands, and the one just visible creeping up along his neck.

"You find us somewhat altered," he said, sharing Cree's wine. "Come, sit, I want to make a toast."

"Altered," she repeated, kneeling primly at the furthest edge of the blanket. While Lucien cleared his throat and put his cup in the air, DeRogna sat quietly perusing the spell, brows arched. Even as she knelt,

Lucien climbed to his feet, impatient to begin. The faster they got things started, he reasoned, the less time DeRogna had to create mischief.

He raised his chipped wooden cup to each of them in turn—Cree, Otis, Zoran, Jurrell, and Tyffial, excluding DeRogna, for she was not even observing his speech, but remained absorbed in her own examination of the spell. Lucien longed to remember them all like that, under the shade of a tall tree, full of wine and bread and potential.

Beware, Timorei whispered. *Beware.*

"Friends, we gather here in the cursed grace of the Savalirwood with a shared purpose—to claim a stake and make, at last, our long-deserved fortune. Chance brought us together, strife and adventure made our bonds strong, but now we do as all adventurers must—we stride into the darkness, no light, no torch, no lantern, only our belief to guide us." He felt a shiver in his soul, a premonition of greatness. Cree, DeRogna, and Brevyn had seen it in him all along, a garden of rich black soil begging for the right seeds. Now the Somnovem would sow what had always yearned to prosper. "We do as adventurers must," he added, voice cracking. "We venture forth, for that is the mandate of the soul."

LUCIEN REMEMBERED THE RITUAL LIKE this: He waited in the clearing with arms outstretched, bathed in a rare patch of sunlight piercing the dense canopy of the Savalirwood. With jacinth, carved silver, and the projection spell in hand, DeRogna faced him, her eyes narrowed, the hood of her wool coat pulled low over her forehead. The Tombtakers surrounded them, weapons drawn, eyes trained half on the mage, and half on Lucien.

It had taken no threats to coax DeRogna into the center of the clearing, though she complained about the lack of civility in the weapons aimed in her direction.

"Fool me once," Cree had purred, showing DeRogna her claws.

DeRogna settled down once she was given permission to verify the spell against the notes Lucien had found in the journal. After a moment or two alone with the tome, she assured them that she understood the task, and joined Lucien in the middle of the clearing.

A slicing wind blew in a circle, enfolding them, as DeRogna began to murmur the spell. Her words grew in strength and conviction as she repeated the litany, chanting it, the language strange and serpentine, foreign to all their ears but hers. Whatever it was, it crawled inside Lucien, drawn into him like roots sucking water. He felt the eye markings on his body, the gift of the Somnovem, alight, burning, searing until he cried out and forced himself not to drop to his knees.

Hya-sek, thuu-raath, somtoresh sek-thraa . . .

The chant circled back, began again, DeRogna jerking forward as a beam of purple light exploded from her chest, linking her and Lucien together. A fell, fetid black mist rose from the ground, obscuring the Tombtakers from his sight. He heard Cree shout something behind him, but the mist narrowed his senses to the purple column forged between him and the archmage.

Distantly, he heard his name, though it sounded like his sister had called out to him.

A concentrated heat began where the beam hit his chest, hotter and crueler, until he shrieked in agony. He felt sure his flesh would melt clean away from his skeleton. Were his insides boiling? Was that what he felt? Why did he not hear the voice of the Somnovem? Where was Cognouza?

He heard Cree again, this time her voice cutting through the veil of mist.

"Lucien! Something isn't right!"

Then he dropped his gaze, and saw DeRogna's coy, knowing smile, and the world went abruptly dark. He knew he was dead before his heart stopped beating, panic icing through the relentless sear of DeRogna's magic. Something inside cracked, splintered, as his soul was ripped into pieces.

"No!" he cried. "I won't be made hollow! I won't be empty! Not like this! Not like—"

But the spell was cast, his soul was fractured, and Lucien Tavelle fell among the wildflowers, red eyes open and unseeing, the sunlight dimming as he died.

INTERLUDE

Now

Through the darkness a young woman comes striding. She sits on a stool? A crate? Anyway, she sits. Her skin is the color of the ocean and moves like it, too. You never know quite where to look, but she does, and she looks you up and down. She takes your measure.

"Once upon a time," she says, then her milk-white eyes pop open in surprise and she giggles. You want to stay forever with her, in her odd, forever-moving sensuality. "No, twice upon a time. Now we can begin. Begin again, I mean."

She takes a deck of cards from a pocket within her black silk gown. When the cards are dealt, you see four distinct patterns—four jesters riding gryphons and clinking cups; a halfling facing down a blue bull; three shadows linking arms and dancing around a bed; a woman sitting up in bed, her hands clasped over her face in grief, a purple-eyed demon peering in the window behind her.

"I knew you would see it," the woman dealing cards says. "Everything old is new and everything new is old. Are we finished here?"

She stands and leaves, and there is only darkness once more. There's a kind of peace, like when everyone has left their seats in a theater, and you're just there to be with the empty stage and fallen curtain. When she is gone and you are well alone again, you hear a child's voice, and it comes from every direction. You don't like it, but you have no choice, do you? You're here now, so shut up and listen.

The child-that-comes-from-everywhere says:

And in the veins
The familiar ice runs cold
An arrow pierced by a moon that
Bleeds red and gold

Empty. Free. Obsessed . . .
Death-obsessed, but free.

No! Don't trust it
Never trust it!

Or do
Do
Drink and fuck, strip and sing songs!
Be free in the chaos of this world
It's very rarely steered me wrong.
And in another time and place
I'd be in another time and place.

Where I'm from, stranger, there is a song that goes:

For the dead yellow king,
A throng came and sang
On the longest day of rain
He would rise again
Long, long may he reign.

A slithering in the void
Hands searching—searching
Always out of reach
Maddening
Maddening, and out of reach

One, he grabs!
Two, he grabs!
They vanish in his grasp.

Alone again, alone.
The slithering comes once more
Faster
Faster
Shards of stars pelt across the mind
Puncturing holes in that ignorant void
Every tear, a promise
A stroke of paint
A dash across the canvas filling, filling
Until . . .
THE PURPOSE. THE PROMISE. THE VISION.
OPEN YOUR EYES NOW.

And a whispered command
silken
and so alluring: Wake up.

The child's voice is gone, thank the gods. What a creepy little shit. The woman with ocean skin and white eyes has come back, just for a moment, but that's all right, you like her. She sits on the stool? Crate. The crate, she sits on the crate again and says, "Thrice upon a time. Can you believe it?"

Fuck, that weird kid is back. Why do they swear so much? Their creepy fucking voice is everywhere. I'm sorry, but you can't escape it. Just bear with us, it's almost over. I promise. The child giggles and goes quiet. For a long, blissful time they are quiet, and then:

A sudden blade
in to the hilt,
this blade
it twists and twists!

and

the

light

pours

CHAPTER 26

836 PD

Dirt. Dirt in his mouth and in his hair and in the cracks of his skin. He howled and ate yet more dirt, and clawed and clawed, fighting invisible earth in a nonexistent grave. Someone pushed him down as he tried to rise. He cracked a single eye and shrieked, the light too much, too much, like a dagger in the eye socket.

"You might have brushed him off proper before trying the spell!" he heard a deep voice grumble.

Someone. His mind raced. *Who, who, who?*

"DeRogna!" he coughed, heaving himself upright but keeping his eyes shut. "Vess DeRogna! Where is she?"

"Never mind that now," said a rasping, accented voice. Familiar. A soft, furred hand brushed his forehead, then a warm, wet cloth was wiped across his face.

"Fucking hell, he's been alive all of five seconds and already he's after revenge . . ."

WHO ARE THEY?

Darkness once more. Darkness and silken promises.

Time stops and starts, indistinguishable among the unbroken dreams.

Then:

Three pairs of hands held him to the floor, and he stopped struggling, breathing heavily. The warm cloth on his face felt good, but he couldn't slow the erratic hammering of his heart, pounding like an angry fist against his rib cage.

"The light," he whispered, almost forlorn, his hands curled up on his forehead like dead spiders. "Please, the light. It's too much."

Heavy footsteps trundled away, then a window slammed shut, a curtain was pulled tight. Whoever was washing his face used the rag to tug gently at his eyelids until at last he peered into the welcome darkness, a pair of catlike yellow eyes staring back.

"It worked," she breathed. "He's here with us. Alive. Lucien?" So that was his name. Information returned in a trickle. Yes, his name was Lucien. He was from Shadycreek Run, then lived in the Marrow Valley, training and hunting, then the Tombtakers became his life and then . . .

DeRogna. Vess DeRogna.

Lucien rubbed at his eyes. "I don't . . . It's hard to remember." He noticed trailing designs all over his body, vines and leaves, tattoos that weaved over his hands and then disappeared into the sleeves of his stained, ivory shirt. "And this . . . I don't remember this."

"You've been dead for two years," the yellow-eyed catfolk explained. "But you sort of . . . went on a walkabout during that time, only you weren't yourself, you were someone else."

"That doesn't make any sense," he moaned.

"It will come back," she assured him. "At least, I think it will . . ."

"Maybe if I knock him upside the head it will help." A gray-skinned, bald half-giant settled into view, crouching behind the catfolk.

"Doubtful." There was a halfling, too, with a funny, nasal voice and a mop of curly brown hair. An elf stood behind them all, arms crossed, hip jutted out, a long tumble of black hair spilling over her right shoulder.

"Do you remember us?" asked the black-furred creature. "My name is Cree. We've been friends since we were children in the Run. Do you remember Shadycreek Run? That's where we are now."

The trickle of information deepened, becoming a steady river. And it hurt. His head throbbed. The halfling fetched him a cup of water and he drank it down greedily, then gestured for more. "If I was dead and my body intact, why didn't you bring me back then? Why wait?"

Cree clenched her jaw. "It . . . it is complicated, Lucien. We tried to resurrect you, but nothing worked. Your soul was weakened somehow, or broken. Another part of you had control of it until they died, and then we went and found your body, and brought you here to see if we could rouse the right version."

"Agh," Lucien growled. "My head hurts."

"Mine, too," said the black-haired elf. "We were as scattered as you—Cree went off to work for The Gentleman, Zoran took a job for the Myriad stuffing hot pokers in folk's eyes, and we ran a card den with Otis in Nogvurot until the law caught up with us." She looked down at her boots, her shoulders drooping. An improbably bright, expensive jewel twinkled on a plain string around her neck. "They took Jurrell, Lucien. She's gone."

A horse rode by outside, the hooves as loud and clear as if they were trotting across his skull. So many names he still didn't remember, so many things he'd missed. He lay back down, crumpling in a heap.

"Rest," said Cree, wiping his face with the rag again. "It will all come back to you with time."

Lucien was easily persuaded and retired to rest. Did he dream? He . . . saw. He couldn't remember the last time he had slept normally, with the usual flurry of anxieties and thoughts before being dragged under by some internal force. Sleep had always fascinated him; how did the body know when? Why were some nights smoother and more restful than others? Maybe this was a sign, he thought wistfully as he was pulled under, that death had changed him. Had it wiped the slate clean? Was he different now, more himself and less the man possessed by visions and a summons from folk he had never really met belonging to a place he had never seen?

Yet he did not dream. Did he? He could manipulate his own body in the image that visited. The room was large and open, with mismatched portraits displayed on the wall and a big roaring fire behind him. The name and place came to him instantly: Auntie Mama's crooked house. He sat at the table near the hearth, his palms flat on the wood, a ticking in the back of his head as if he were waiting. The door opened, and he feared who might walk through. The faces of his past were still a jumble.

Reality was still a jumble. Who and what and how all of it was real still made his head spin.

He did not understand the shapeless figure who hurried inside. The creature's shape never resolved, shifting like a floating silhouette made of black sand. It raced across the room toward him, startling Lucien half out of his chair.

"Oh!" It laughed, and it was high and trilling, like a flute running a scale. Its arms took on greater weight, a blobby, four-fingered appendage extruding digits. "Oh, you thought you were free! That's pretty cute. That's hilarious, actually. No," it said, taking Lucien's right hand and flipping it, the palm facing upward, the red eye glaring outward. "No, you're the Nonagon. That's forever. That lasts well beyond death, my friend."

Lucien jerked his hand back. This thing didn't feel like a friend.

"Don't be like that," the creature chided. A red slit split the glob where its head would be like a mad glint of a smile. "We're friends, Nonagon. You know me. I've been in your head a hundred hundred times. Don't you know me? Don't you remember? The dreams? Our dreams? You're breaking my heart here."

The creature sighed.

Lucien shook his head, the wave of guilt hitting him, the wave of recognition cresting immediately after. "Culpasi," he whispered. "I remember."

"Yes! Friends! You remember now. Good, that's good. Phew!" Culpasi, one of the nine philosophers of the Somnovem, or at least the projection of him, clutched his own chest with both hands. "Thought we were going to have to start this whole ordeal over again. So if you remember, then you know what must be done. There's a charlatan out there, an impostor, and she thinks she's the Nonagon. Can you imagine? Stupid idiot. We can't let that continue, can we? We can't let her keep the tome . . . I mean—I mean," he stammered, dissolving into tearful laughter. "That's just untenable! Can't have it."

The tome. The tome!

Lucien's mouth dropped open. "That's right, she took it."

"You wouldn't let us down," Culpasi said, lowering his head. Four white dots appeared on his head like eyes. "Cognouza, my friend. Cognouza. That's where you reign. This is not where you belong, but there are answers beneath the ice."

Lucien shot awake, sitting upright in bed and tossing the thin blanket aside, gripped by a consuming dread. He knew it was night by the quality of the silence outside. There was nothing to hear but the sounds of distant music and the bullfrogs that clustered in the alleyway puddles. The questions burning through his mind overlapped, dozens of voices weaving in and out of one another, impossible to discern.

"The journal," he murmured. "Where is it? Where is my journal . . ."

The seething morass of voices in his head went silent, leaving only one to keep him company in the dark.

She has it. Vess DeRogna, the betrayer.

"Who are you?" he asked aloud. There was still so much about himself he didn't understand and couldn't remember. Lucien looked around. He was alone in a cramped bedroom that smelled strongly of unwashed hair and greasy blankets. "How are you speaking to me?"

We are the Somnovem, you are the Nonagon.

Nonagon. Lucien clutched his head, willing the words to make sense. The red eyes marked across his body tingled and then blazed. The jolt of sensation brought fear and then clarity. The journal . . . the Nonagon . . . Yes, he remembered now. He had been chosen by the nine philosophers to reach the lost city of Cognouza in the Astral Sea and take their power for himself. His death had come at the hands of DeRogna when he tried to project himself to Cognouza and at last meet the Somnovem; instead of honoring their bargain, she had ripped his soul apart and taken the journal for herself. Payback for the treachery they had visited upon her in the ice fields of Foren.

Foren, where he had lost . . .

Lucien squeezed his eyes shut, tears melting down his face. The door to the bedchamber opened, and Cree poked her head inside, her yellow eyes faintly visible in the darkness. She joined him while he wiped the dampness from his face with the back of his hand.

"It hurts to remember," he muttered, hoarse.

Cree sat on the edge of the mattress, a safe distance away. "We should remember our past and remember it honestly. Even if it hurts. Has it all come back?"

"Some," he replied. "Most. Brevyn . . ."

Out of the corner of his eye he saw her wince. "Before your death, you asked us not to speak of her."

"Right," he said. "That's probably for the best, then."

Cree said nothing, gazing toward a window with the curtain drawn.

"I need to recover that journal," he told her. "The one DeRogna stole."

She coughed out a laugh. "And how do you plan to do that?"

"I don't quite know, not yet, anyway," he replied. "But I've had a dream, or perhaps a vision, and the Somnovem want me to return to

Eiselcross. There's something there we need, something in the ruins of the ice fields."

Cree dropped her head into her hands. "I was afraid you would say that. Lucien, we've no money . . ."

"That gem around the elf's neck would fetch a pretty price."

"Lucien, that belonged to Tyffial's beloved, you can't ask her to sell it. Besides, it's a royal gem, we would be caught in half a moment if we tried to fence it."

He looked into her yellow eyes, gathering the threads of doubt he saw there, studying them. This was not what he wanted to do, but what he had to. He drew on the eyes connecting them before thinking and speaking with the same mind. He watched Cree's eyes shift from gold to red, her expression softening as the Nonagon became their shared identity.

"Otis can fence anything," they said together.

Lucien let go, her gaze blank before she shook her head and squinted, confused.

"You're right," he said with a grim smile. "Otis can fence anything, so we'll have him get rid of Tyffial's jewel, and that will get us to Eiselcross and beyond."

"I . . . understand. Aye, Otis can do it." Her words came out disjointed.

"We shall be long gone before anyone is the wiser," Lucien assured her.

And so it was done, and his rest was over. It did not take long for Otis to secure an interested buyer, for the Run was full of wealthy criminals eager to thumb their noses at the Dwendalian rulers. The jewel probably ended up on the end of someone's codpiece. And the gold from the sale, though they took a heavy hit on the price from the heat it would cause, allowed them to bring the gear and horses to Palebank Village and once more charter a ship leaving for the frozen lands of Foren.

This time, they avoided Balenpost, Lucien concerned that someone might recognize them from the last expedition. Instead, they veered north from the landing, paying a whaler handsomely for passage to Syrinlya, a cluster of yurts and tents serving as a base camp for those venturing on to Aeor. The Tombtakers arranged a yurt of their own, keeping the lowest profile they could among the largely dwarven encampment. On their first full morning in Syrinlya, Lucien invited Cree out to the edge of the village, and they stood together in the snow, watching gray-bottomed, threatening clouds gather over the mountains to the northwest.

"Just to soothe my mind," Cree broached through chattering teeth. "How did you convince Tyffial to give up her necklace?"

Lucien shifted. He shifted, and he lied. "I didn't want to force a sacrifice she wasn't ready to make," he replied. "But ultimately, she accepted the bigger picture. I told her she could build a temple to Jurrell made of sapphires and pearls when we reach Cognouza."

In truth, Tyffial had scoffed at his suggestion that she hand over the jewel. When he reached into her mind to convince her otherwise, he felt a cold, dark slithering in his gut. The tattoos were a change, but he was different now in other ways, ways he couldn't put a finger on. After Tyffial "agreed" to hand over the amulet, Lucien made her forget the whole thing, and the jewel itself.

He comforted himself that he had magnanimously not touched any of her other fond memories of Jurrell.

"I'm glad," Cree replied, smiling at something in the distance. "This is all so much to take in, and of course sacrifices have to be made, but keeping the group strong is—"

"Sh-hh." He put up one hand, tilting his head to the side. Turning, he felt another presence, cloaked, but indelibly there. Watchful. Prying. He waited until the feeling dissipated to whisper, "Someone was scrying on us."

"What? How do you know?"

"The eyes," he said. "The eyes could see them. Quickly, back to the camp. I need to concentrate; someone could be trying to find us. It could be her."

Her.

When they returned to the yurt, Tyffial, Otis, and Zoran were absent. It was a cramped, three-room dome with a central firepit that leaked smoke up to a vent with a lifted cap, letting the choking stink of the smoke out. He trotted to the back room, flinging off his boots and crawling into the bed. Cree followed a moment later, handing him a watered-down tumbler of wine before leaving his side to stoke the fire and urge the flames higher, lighting the yurt.

Look, a voice whispered. *Look with your true eyes.*

Lucien drained the wine and handed the empty cup to Cree, then took the pillow and mashed it against the stout leather headboard, sitting back against it, upright, his legs stretched out in front of him. The room around them dimmed, the sounds of the encampment growing farther away as he sank back from his immediate perceptions, stretching outward with the Nine Eyes given to him by the Somnovem. He felt a strain in every muscle, a tension just behind the bridge of his nose, a feeling gathering like a sudden change in pressure. Against his eyelids he saw a shadow world, a place of suggestions and whispers, half-formed thoughts, and interrupted dreams. It flattened like a map, continents and mountains rising, spires of cities joining the topography as the shadows became mottled with blues and greens and reds. Somewhere in a distant tower, he sensed a woman's unease, and carefully, he pulled himself toward that flicker of distress.

Though he concentrated and directed his thoughts through the Eyes of Nine, he sensed only that vague suggestion of emotion. It wasn't enough. Something was blocking his ability to scry upon her and spy. He opened his eyes and swore under his breath.

Cree shifted toward him in the darkness. Her claws clacked together nervously as she cleared her throat, his burning red eyes flying to her.

"You can't reach her?" Cree asked.

"Some sort of magic is blocking me, damn it all."

"I might have an idea about that."

Lucien's shoulders sagged. He hadn't expected to be so calmed by her willingness to help, but then he had been shouldering the burdens of the group by himself. Any aid, however small, was a relief. He nodded, letting her continue.

"Those who are scrying on us—you—they must be able to do so because they traveled with you. They could have something of yours." Lucien glared and Cree hurried on. "Not *you* you, but Mollymauk Tealeaf. They knew you by that name when . . . well—and don't get pissed—when DeRogna broke your soul, but your body was still waltzing around without you. And they know me, too. We wouldn't want to meet them in battle, they're a dangerous lot, but they could prove useful to us now."

"I assume you're getting to the point," Lucien growled. His relief was gone, replaced with impatience.

"The Mighty Nein are trying to locate you—"

"The what?" he interrupted.

"The Mighty Nein, that's what they call themselves."

"Are there nine of them?"

"N-No . . ."

Lucien nodded stiffly. "Ridiculous name."

"I said they were dangerous, I never said they were smart. Even so, they're mercenaries. Mercenaries for hire. If there are rumors of you up and about, then they'd be keen to find you, but DeRogna would be keen, too. Follow me now?" She grinned.

"She's hired them," he murmured. He had to hand it to Cree; it was a brilliant theory.

Cree began to speak more quickly, excited. She had been skulking in the middle of the chamber, but now she hurried up to him and dropped down to her knees. "One of them was pestering me about you for ages. They're going to keep spying and searching, but we can spy back."

"Do it," he commanded softly.

With deft hands, Cree spilled out the contents of the satchel on her belt. She sifted through the items—a comb, a few rings, an earring that had belonged to Brevyn, and a few vials that seemed to be full of blood. Cree snatched up the vials and held them in her hands, sitting back on her haunches. Her eyes fluttered shut, a hypnotizing, looping spell dropping from her lips as she reached out magically, seeking those who had sought them.

Behind her closed black eyelids, Lucien saw her eyes moving back and forth rapidly.

"What is it?" he asked, leaning forward. His palms were slick with sweat. "What do you see?"

"A map," Cree said in a flat, numb voice. "They're consulting a map."

"Can you make out any of the details? Hear anything?"

"A shape like mountains," she replied, again flatly. "Post . . . Balenpost."

"Eiselcross," Lucien murmured. "She's traveling to Balenpost. She's returning to Aeor."

So DeRogna wasn't far. She was following them, no doubt to seek out the gate of his visions. He couldn't let her get there first.

Cree's eyes snapped open, the vials tumbling out of her grasp and onto the floor. She shook her head, then stared at him in the darkness for a tense moment. *This is when she gives up on me,* he thought. *This is when she decides it's too much.* She glanced down at her hands, nodding. It occurred to him that as the Nonagon, he could take the choice away from her and make her go south to intercept DeRogna. Their link gave him power, power he was loath to use.

"Then like the Tombtakers before them, she's hired the Mighty Nein for an expedition to Aeor."

Lucien wanted to draw her into a hug, but he came to his senses. "She thinks me dead. She underestimated the Nonagon, and it will be her downfall." With purpose and direction renewed, Lucien felt relieved once more. Anger, rage, desire, he could control; hopelessness he could not. Now they had a lead and his good mood returned. He reached for Cree's face and cradled her jaw in his palm for a moment.

"You're brilliant," he said. "What would I do without you?"

"Flail around in the darkness?"

Lucien smirked. "You always take care of us, and sometimes I wonder why."

"It's always been us," she said. "Brev would come back and haunt me if I let her down." Cree took his hand and squeezed it, and for a moment they were silent. They almost never spoke of her, and like a summoning of her ghost, the room filled with an unnamable chill. "I think she would want me to finally do this, seeing as how she never got around to it."

Cree pushed away from her heels, kneeling high, and nicked her own palm with a distended claw. The blood bubbled up, and she gathered it, the smear changing into a bead of brightest silver, guided by her magic. She thumbed that bead over his cheekbone, chasing away the last, forgotten scar there. A little peppering of freckles followed, like pockets of fireweed growing back after a forest blaze.

"Everything we do is awash in blood." He sighed. "I have something for you, too."

"You don't need to repay me."

"But I want to. Blood of mine for blood of yours," Lucien told her. He didn't like to play favorites among the Tombtakers, but Cree had been his right hand since childhood. She had never given up on him, not even when he was dead and buried. He leaned over the edge of the bed and flicked open the toggle on his traveler's knapsack. At the very bottom, he groped around for a disk of soft metal and, finding it, brought it out for Cree to see. It was a perfect spiral of metals, with a crystalline oval at the center.

"Silver and gold." She gasped. Then her head craned back. "But Tyffial's jewel—"

"I had to keep this," Lucien said, waving her off. "It's the witch's amulet, melted down and reforged. I had it done in the Run and kept it for . . . for now. For you." It was a special medallion, wrought by a silversmith Brevyn had suggested, an old friend of her father's. A tiny latch in the top was almost impossible to notice. Lucien opened the latch with his fingernail, then offered his palm to Cree. "Slice it."

She hesitated but did as he asked. The deep scratch burned. Lucien made a fist, squeezing until blood dripped from the bottom of his hand and into the amulet. As it filled, the oval crystal turned crimson. When it was full, Lucien popped the latch down and handed the necklace to Cree, who ducked her head, allowing him to place it around her neck.

"Keep it close," he urged her, the eyes along his body glowing bright. "It holds the blood of the Nonagon."

CHAPTER 27

Lucien stared up at the tower from the confines of his furred hood, holding his hands out to warm them idly by the bonfire raging outside the central fortress's walls.

"Never thought we'd see this bloody place again," said Zoran, slinging his weighty hammer over his shoulder and pacing. He, too, wore a hood—they all did—cloaked and covered head-to-foot to disguise their identities and their distinct red tattoos. A dark-gray scarf dangled out from Lucien's hood, and he took his hands away from the fire, worrying the ends of the scarf for a moment, his eyes never straying from a specific window. Balenpost was the same snowy, dull shit heap it had been the last time, filled to the gills with bored soldiers and antsy adventurers. There was more grousing, perhaps, as troubles in Icehaven hampered the flow of supplies to the outpost.

Day by day, it was becoming easier to live in this skin again. He had taught himself not to fret over the new tattoos that weren't to his taste and found a measure of comfort when Cree presented him with his old scimitars. They felt right at home in his hands.

"What are we waiting for?" Otis grumbled, their face swallowed and nearly invisible among all the leather and spotted white fur.

"A sign," said Lucien, soft. Thoughtful. He took a tiny wedge of wood from his pocket and stuck it between his teeth, chewing.

A quiet crunch of snow behind him was the only indication that

Cree had returned from her errand. Tyffial sat on a bench near the bon-fire, quite plainly eavesdropping on the soldiers beside her as she sharp-ened her impressively long sword.

"Loose lips all over this place," Cree purred, sidling up to Lucien. "Embarrassingly lax."

"Good for us," he said.

"Bad for them," Cree agreed. "It's definitely her."

"You're sure?"

"Mm. I saw her face plain as day in the hall," said Cree. She fidgeted, shifting her weight from side to side. "What our scry suggested, my eyes confirmed."

"Go on." Lucien sighed. "I can tell there's more."

"She's hired mercenaries just as I—we—predicted . . ."

"Spit it out," he barked, doing exactly that with his toothpick.

"And we were right," Cree told him, grim. "Her Ladyship has hired the Mighty Nein. Given your—their—history, will it be a problem?"

"My dearest Cree, of course not," Lucien replied, forcing a confident grin. "That was but an aberration, an uninvited guest. I am obviously all myself now."

Nonagon first, he insisted. Lucien second. He wasn't entertaining a third option.

Blistered, bashed, broken. Cold, cracked corpses.

The voices bubbled up like magma between the gaps in his control. He held them at bay but knew it wouldn't last for long—those voices yearned for blood, and for the return of the journal, rightful property of the Nonagon.

"How will you get to her?" asked Cree. "Her chamber is likely to be locked and guarded."

Lucien continued smiling up at the window. "DeRogna and I share a special bond now. I'll simply walk up to the door and knock and see if she's keen for a little chat. Keep an eye on those mercenaries she hired; make certain they don't go anywhere near her rooms. It would be a pity if they intervened, for I have a terribly important appointment to keep."

CREE HAD PERHAPS UNDERREPORTED THE crude nature of the fort's security; Otis had only to skulk in the main barracks hall for an hour during evening mealtime to hear exact information on when and how the shift change would take place. DeRogna's visit was unscheduled and sudden, and thus men had been pulled from other details around the outpost to accommodate the lady's demands. Her own hired mercenaries had even failed to keep watch outside her door, allowing Lucien a ten-minute window to slip past the guards in the central tower, hurrying up the stairs and past a snoozing sentry on the second-floor landing. The stairs spiraled up the main column, with each landing widening out to include an arched corridor leading to chambers for officers and important guests.

DeRogna had been placed midway up the tower on the third level, away from the distracting chatter and bawdy ribaldry of the main floor's large meeting and dining chamber. A breathless excitement carried him swiftly up the stairs; the journal was so close now, so ready, he could sense its proximity. It called to him like a lost lamb, bleating in the wilderness, eager for the safety of his possession.

Outside the heavy, fortified wood-and-iron door of DeRogna's chamber, he found an empty chair and two tall candelabras. The candles had dwindled to stubs, anemic flames left long unattended. He put his ear to the door, hearing the scratch of a quill and a single, muffled voice. His pulse leapt. He yanked his hands away from the wood, afraid that his own blood would punch through his skin and alert her. The scratching beyond the door stopped.

To reach her through the eyes was a simple thing—they were close now, and he had her exact location. Lucien closed his eyes and felt the swirl of voices that had become a constant hum under his thoughts shriek with impatience.

"Is . . . someone there?" she called.

It was the voice of a frightened little girl.

Good.

Lucien waited, every passing heartbeat an agonizing eternity. Revenge made appetent lunatics of even the most studied ascetics. The voices hungered. The voices screamed.

Three separate bolts were drawn on the door, the hinges creaked, and Lucien came face-to-face with the murderess who had shattered his soul.

"Greetings, Lady DeRogna," Lucien growled, wedging his foot and shoulder in the door as she tried to slam it. "How kind of you to answer my call."

"N-No," she stammered, eyes blown wide with fear. He sensed the glamour covering her marks. It enraged him. His hand lashed out, ripping the eye-shaped talisman off her neck. It had been hiding beneath her cloak and gown, but he knew it was there, knew she couldn't resist carrying yet another piece of the philosophers and Cognouza. "You're dead."

"It would appear not."

DeRogna stumbled back into the chamber while Lucien thrust the amulet into his coat pocket. She was not defenseless, calling a ball of flame to her hands. It grew and crackled, but she could not release it before Lucien called to the eyes marked on her body. They simmered as his simmered, and the fire in her hands went out as she shrieked in pain, falling to her knees. Lucien crossed the space between them, lifting her back to her feet by her throat, tearing the bracelets from her wrists with his other hand. As he did, the glamour hiding the eyes on her body lifted, revealing that she had as many of the staring crimson marks as he.

"The true inheritor of Cognouza would never conceal such gifts. Now walk there," he snarled, pointing. "The Nonagon commands it."

"I . . . can resist you," she hissed. "I will not be commanded by the likes of you."

Lucien showed her his teeth. "And what am I?"

DeRogna clutched her head, fighting his influence with admirable temerity. It was not enough. The Somnovem had chosen him, and while he was not theirs, he was their willing conspirator. He saw it clearly, then, as he gripped her mind with the vise of the Nonagon's domination, the psychic onslaught piercing her brain, unraveling the already loose grip she had on her thoughts.

"This is why you failed," he told her coldly, watching her cross, inch by inch, to the center of the room. "You sought to control the will of the philosophers. They cannot be controlled, only persuaded."

"You are a pawn," she whispered, her eyes dawning red. She mustered one last act of resistance, a blast of energy rippling out from her palms, sending the window exploding outward. Lucien braced, knocked back a few paces. "They will use you, fool. They must be resisted lest they take you over completely! Only the amulet protected me from turning into their unwitting thrall!"

His eyes roamed from her rumpled cloak and mussed graying hair to the black journal, opened on the desk to the left of the window. Other tomes were piled there, but they were inconsequential next to the true prize. Through the growing power of the eyes, he anchored her to the rug in the middle of the chamber, then he went to the journal and took it, feeling a rush of warmth pour over him as he held it close to his side.

"They will destroy you," DeRogna seethed, clawing at her own face. "It is a torment, their poison. There is so little of me left, so little! A pittance! Just a corner of sunlight in a world gone dark!"

"Ah, but you're wrong. You are the poison, DeRogna," he replied. "You are the betrayer. You can't see what they offer, and that ignorance is your doom."

The archmage collapsed, shielding herself from him. "And now you will kill me, and their vile influence will spread. May the gods spare Exandria the coming of Cognouza."

Lucien went still, frozen not by DeRogna's words, but by a third presence. The Somnovem came to him in dreams, but was he asleep now? Turning only his head, he saw another black, shapeless figure floating and watching him near the door. He closed his eyes tightly. *No . . . no.* Their disembodied forms were too unnerving. And too inelegant. The Somnovem had been philosophers, the wisest of their age, even if now they were little more than a fractured chorus of whining children. They deserved better, he thought. And so, before he opened his eyes again, he gave this philosopher form. He could only guess at their true appearances and bodies, so he invented on the fly. She was . . . elven, tall, heavyset, wearing gold-rimmed spectacles and an embroidered gray robe much like Culpasi's. The more he imagined, the easier it became. Her moon face and messy mop of short-cropped black hair belied a roiling intensity just beneath the surface of her pearlescent skin, he decided. Red fractal designs decorated the hood and sleeves of her robe, bleeding seamlessly onto her skin. She adjusted her spectacles, lips pursed in thought.

"Why have you not destroyed her utterly?" she asked.

Lucien frowned. "If you gave me but a moment, I could be keen to finish the task."

"Shouldn't it take longer than a moment?" She wandered in a wide, indirect arc to DeRogna, considering the mage as she trembled on the ground. "She defied the Somnovem. Delayed Cognouza. Delayed our arrival."

"A knife to the throat will do the job," Lucien insisted. He had never understood the allure of torture. The pain of another did not delight him, and taking a life was sometimes a regrettable necessity, not a task to relish. But the elf was not convinced, watching him with mild exasperation, as if he were a student repeatedly giving the wrong answer to an obvious question. "Ira," he whispered. "The hound who bays for blood."

"Two years," she spat. Her hand hovered over DeRogna's head. "Two years were taken from you, but more important, taken from this world. Think bigger, Nonagon. You are not the only one suffering. We await you in Cognouza, but Exandria waits for liberation."

He sighed and nodded. "I do realize that! Do ye not see us here? Are we not back to complete the job? We are going as quickly as we can!" Lucien paced, glaring at the wretched creature on the ground, shivering and helpless. "She didn't know, did she? She didn't understand what Cognouza was capable of . . ."

"You . . . You are already lost to it," DeRogna wheezed.

"Be silent!" Lucien thundered. There he was, trying to spare her torture, and all she could do was mock him.

"What does it matter if she knew or not? Her ignorance was time wasted, and time, time is precious. What do you suppose we philosophers would have done to have more time to save our city? Save all the people of Aeor? I would have chewed off each of my fingers and toes and kissed them into the mouth of my enemy to have more time." Ira sliced her hand through the air, just above the frizz of DeRogna's hair. "She tried to stop the work. She nearly stopped the work. Becoming the False Nonagon gained us little. You were the true inheritor all along."

Lucien hung his head. "The true inheritor," he repeated.

"She's a fading imprint, not who we chose but who we were forced to accept as pale imitation." Ira left DeRogna behind, swooping in to place her hands on Lucien's shoulders. Her eyes were silver-gray, the irises ringed in crimson. "We are the Somnovem, Nonagon, and we are inevitable. Liberate this worm of her sanity before you liberate her of her life."

CHAPTER 28

When it was done and the blood wept freely from every hole in DeRogna's head, Lucien felt only a grim satisfaction that he had outlasted her. The archmage had always supposed herself better than him, but now the record had been set straight with finality.

Ira no longer appeared to him, becoming a strange, hovering shape with a flash of a red orb before vanishing the moment the life left DeRogna's eyes. The dead archmage was sprawled across the bed behind him while he strode to her desk, searching for anything useful. None of the books she had traveled with appealed, and so he placed the mage's journal on the table and perused it quickly, finding that DeRogna had inserted new sheaves of paper throughout with her own observations and notes. The threshold crests mentioned here and there by the unknown writer had become her clear focus.

. . . the only solution is technological—astral projection is too unreliable and too impermanent a method of transportation. The correct alignment and installation of the threshold crests should allow me to reach Cognouza through a gate within Aeor itself, creating a stable means of conveyance to and from the missing ward.

I must expand my search, A2 and A5 south of the River Inferno look particularly promising.

DeRogna had included sketches of these crests, which appeared more like enormous crystals, along with a crude map with predictions on where they might be found within the ruins. He summoned a distant memory of their first expedition to the ruins and seeing sites marked ALPHA-2 and ALPHA-5. These were circled on her newest version of the map. Lucien swept her desk one last time, taking anything that could be bartered for coin, as well as a bundle of scrolls to pick through later. It was folly to linger any longer.

He picked up one of the bangles he had ripped from DeRogna's wrist and held it up to the light, watching it sparkle. The nape of his neck prickled, then the eye mark on his shoulder blazed.

Lucien froze. Someone was watching. This time when he looked back, he saw the trespasser clearly through her scrying window—a little blue devilkin with curious violet eyes. One of the Mighty Nein, no doubt, poking around where they didn't belong. He was noticing a worrisome pattern.

"Oh, well, lookie here. A return visitor." He chuckled. "Now, don't get running, you've curiosity to sate, right? I take it you're the one who's been peeking recently. I have to thank you, for without your scent, I wouldn't have been able to follow her." Lucien calmly stuffed the bangle in his pack. "Now, don't be alarmed. I see many things with mine eyes. Been trying to watch this one's path awhile now until you found me. Saw the threads and we made a detour. Shame really, all that knowledge and so little understanding. Ah!"

At last, he took up the journal and folded it all together neatly, tucking it under one arm and smiling down at it before turning back to the devilkin. "But you see now things are set right. Once more, I have what she took from me." Darkness had fallen outside, a thick snowfall obscuring the stars.

These fools will actually try to stop me, he thought. *Now the race begins.*

He stepped toward the open window, pausing to look back one final time. "To alpha and alpha, we trek till homeward bound we be." He laughed again. "Maybe we'll see you there."

ANNOYINGLY, HE SAW THEM THERE.

Seven little flies, buzz, buzz, buzz. Either the mercenaries calling themselves the Mighty Nein had tracked them or DeRogna had already equipped them with a map for the expedition she would not join. A5 proved fruitful, indeed. They had encountered a number of vultures among the glowing blue corridors of the ruin, adventurers picking a fresh corpse clean. It had angered him at first, seeing a bunch of profiteers scratching at the relics and coffers of the rotunda, eager for whatever scraps they could haul back to the mainland and sell. But his rage turned swiftly to bemusement—they didn't know how close they were to stealing an item of incredible value.

The threshold crest. It was large, larger than Lucien had expected, a polished, flashing gem, two feet across, dangling from a facet in the rotunda ceiling. The hall itself had been the main research facility for one of the Somnovem, Elatis. He could feel her giddiness spreading through his own fingers and toes as soon as they stepped foot in the chamber. In the time when Elatis was alive, it was called the Dawn Crucible, where Aeorian citizens volunteered to have their dreams studied and recorded.

The Dawn Crucible, the Crucible of Dreams . . . Elatis seemed to walk beside him every step of the way. He wondered if the other Tombtakers could sense her, but if they did, none of them commented upon it. Lucien could have spent hours wandering the rotunda, where the philosopher's own writings and research might still dwell. The whole site of A5 was a wonder—a long, plunging corridor down through the ice, the halls suffused with a dreamy blue glow, arcane energy surging through every stone and tile.

But it was not to be a leisurely delve, for the Tombtakers first dispatched the fool adventurers bumbling around in the rotunda and were immediately after interrupted by the Mighty Nein. It became instantly clear to him that DeRogna had left them in the dark about her true purpose in returning to Aeor—everything they knew of Cognouza and the Somnovem had been gleaned from fragments of information, from DeRogna's vague instructions, or from his own lips.

Cree had already informed him, generally, of what to expect from the Mighty Nein. There was a tall, scarred, green-skinned half-orc called Fjord, as silent and standoffish as their own Zoran. An agent of the Cobalt Soul walked among them, too: Beauregard, a grunting human woman with piercing blue eyes, carrying a staff. Even at rest, she exuded a hostile, impatient air. The horned, blue infernal of the group, Jester, a slip of a thing with a gnat's voice and demeanor, was the one who insisted on spying upon them with her magic. The mage of their cohort was a nondescript human man, soft-spoken, bearded, wrapped in a striped scarf and calling himself Caleb. There was also a halfling in a pink, frothy frock and antlered earmuffs—Cree did not know this one's name—as strange a sight as any Lucien had encountered in the ruins of Aeor. No less strange was the magenta-haired feygiant healer, Caduceus Clay, with pale-gray fur and an elaborately embellished robe. His ears were long and slightly flipped, pierced, his nose elongated and flat like that of a stag. A scruff of coarser pink fur lined his sharp jaw. He carried a crystal-topped staff and shield, his frame as willowy thin as his weapon of choice, his demeanor unnervingly calm, a frustratingly blank page of a fellow.

And finally, a sturdy, silent, beguiling woman called Yasha traveled with them. Something about her, either her eyes or her silhouette, made his brain burn with confusion.

Lucien closed his eyes as the snow continued to fall around him. They had emerged from A5 unscathed, with the unbelievably heavy and unwieldy threshold crest strapped to Zoran's back. He was slow-moving with it, and as soon as they cleared the ruins, they marched to a low rise of hills, settling behind them to make camp. A thin line of gray smoke marked their position. Lucien turned away from it, snowflakes settling on his eyelashes and horns, and in his hair. The cold had ceased to bother him. The wind tugged at his thick leather coat, but he stood firm, eyes fixed on the swirl of snow over the ice fields. Somewhere out there, the Mighty Nein were stalking them.

He tried to take pity. After all, they had seemed stunned at the sight of him. It must be difficult to see their friend's body alive, inhabited by a person they did not know or like. It was that shock, he decided, that had spared them all a confrontation. For the moment, anyway.

If Cree spoke true, the Mighty Nein had a reputation, and they would not give up. They did not pursue him for Cognouza, they pursued him for the love of their lost friend.

And what would you do if Brevyn somehow traveled in their party? he asked himself. He knew he would match their tenacity.

Lucien reached into his coat pocket, withdrawing a tiny sprig of greenery. In the ruin, the muscular woman with long white hair had given him a gift. Lucien twirled the four-leaf clover between his fingers, watching the delicate leaves turn wet with snow.

You gave me this four-leaf clover one time. And you told me that hopefully that would bring me luck, and that life would be a little bit better, so—and it was, thanks to you. So, I know you're not in there anymore, but we really did care about you. But we'll be following behind you, be safe.

There was something about her, an unnatural familiarity, that frightened him. Her gruff way, her searching, haunted eyes, the strength available only to a woman who had walked in a world that underestimated her at every turn, a world that punched and punched from every direction, often connecting but never finishing the job. The little broken details. The resilience. The persistent, awkward kindness.

He felt the eyes on his body flare with alarm. Lucien ignored it and ignored the desire to crush the gift under his boot.*

* *Wake up.*

The Somnovem, he thought, driving him back to his purpose. No . . . The voice wasn't quite right. Yet it lingered. An echo. An echo that left behind a fog.

Wake the fuck up, you bloody loon. Snap out of it already. Hello? Hello? Is anyone in there? Hope you're not all full up on crazy, because I'm here, too. That's right, I'm here, you can't get rid of me, not really. I'm you, too.

Lucien flattened his hand over the four-leaf clover. The voice . . . Perhaps the Somnovem were changing tactics. Playing with him. They were, after all, feckless and wild.

Lucien brushed it aside.

CHAPTER 29

"Nonagon . . ."

Nonagon.

"Is this the path? Are you sure?"

You're slipping.

Ahead of them, through the blustering flakes and bitter wind, Lucien's many eyes perceived a dome in the snow. Within the dome, the Mighty Nein rested, sure that they had outwitted them, outpaced them, and confounded them.

Me, confounded me.

Us, you mean. Confounded us.

"Nonagon? Lucien!"

His head jerked to the side. Cree waited behind him, hunched against the biting scratch of the frozen winds. A moment ago, her voice had sounded a thousand miles away. Stranger, it had sounded mixed with that of the Somnovem. There were too many voices now, and he found it harder and harder to tease them apart.

You're slipping.[*]

---

[*] That fucking voice. What was it? Why did it make his brain pulse and pulse . . .

I'm you. Y O U. You from after but also before. Hello? HELLO.

"You're gone," he told the wind. "You're a cured disease. Eradicated."

Eradicated, am I? So, why are you going to hunt them down? Aye, I know us. We never could leave well enough alone.

"Are you sure you want to do this?" Cree asked, coming to his side. "Don't you think we should wait until dark? Ambush them?"

The voices in his head roared with approval. Cree had scried on the Mighty Nein again and seen that they had managed to recover a threshold crest, and taking theirs would expedite things nicely.

"Blood!" cried Ira.

"Shock!" added Mirumus.

On and on. The Somnovem agreed heartily with Cree. But Lucien shook his head, sniffling, his nose red and persistently running. He wiped his face with his sleeve and nodded toward the magical dome in the snow. The new sun sparkled, catching on the places where the snowfall could not conceal the shield. Inside, the Mighty Nein stirred. More important, the threshold crest they had scooped out from under the Tombtakers waited.

"They were gracious enough to let us go without incident before," Lucien pointed out. "Perhaps they will be obliging once more. Have I not told you already? The first Nonagon failed because he attempted this work alone. The more we gather to walk the path, the less resistance we face."

"Is this . . . Is this the other one influencing you?" she asked.

He whirled on her. "Is it *what?*"

"Otis has noticed it, too," said Cree. She shrank. "You are the Nonagon, we follow you, we speak with one voice, move with one purpose, but something has changed since we saw the Mighty Nein in those ruins."

Lucien had never had the urge to strike her in earnest, and yet. And yet.

Where had that come from? He stepped back, ashamed. It wasn't his own desires pushing him toward violence, it was the maddening bloat of voices stuffing up his mind. What would he be if even Cree feared him? Cree, who had followed him faithfully, fought by his side, even helped bring him back to life . . .

"We need the crest," Lucien told her coldly. "First, we ask nicely. After that . . ."

Cree nodded. "I'll tell the others."

"If they argue, tell me. There can be no dissent—no doubt—where we're going."

Cree reported nothing to him after they broke camp and the others were roused, though Lucien's eyes informed him of everything he needed to know. He sensed a weariness in Otis, who was looking increasingly gaunt, thinned from the constant marching and sparse food. The packs they carried felt heavier each day, for Zoran could not be expected to haul around the threshold crest and the frame for a shelter. And so they split the duties up, each of them carrying a portion of the tent, food, blankets, and cookware. It would be a cumbersome load even on warm, flat terrain, and in the ice and snow it wore the body down like a sword over a whetstone.

That morning, as they mustered to approach the Mighty Nein's camp, Lucien doled out a bit more yak jerky, hoping to rally spirits. Tyffial took her portion with a dead-eyed stare, her once lustrous black hair snarled and limp, plaited over her shoulders like the arms of some lank furry beast. Zoran had developed a permanent stoop from the weight of the crest, one shoulder resting higher than the other.

"Ah," Lucien drawled, watching first the tall, magenta-haired man emerge from the Mighty Nein's conjured magical dome. The man seemed shocked by the blast of snow that greeted him from the unruly skies. "I was wondering when you'd awaken."

"I've been awake," came the man's frustratingly placid response. "I just was—I was busy. This is nice."

"Well," Lucien said, momentarily caught off guard by the man's serenity. He'd been hoping for a bit more awe. Lucien snapped his fingers, and the other Tombtakers shifted into view.

The bargaining from there went about as well as expected. Perhaps slightly better than anticipated. For all their weaponry, magical ability, and bluster, the Mighty Nein did not meet Lucien with open hostility. The hostility, Lucien knew, ran just below the surface, a rancor in the vein. Even after he dispelled their cozy magical dome with the flash of a glaring red eye, the party of adventurers did not retaliate. The calm man, Caduceus Clay, sleep-addled and muss-haired, along with the green half-orc Fjord, were the most eager to parlay. Their curiosity made them easy to manipulate, as did their desire to see their friend Mollymauk Tealeaf, somehow returned.

They would sooner draw blood from a stone.

It was all, to Lucien, a bit boring and banal, but it was necessary for the work. They went around and around in circles, testing one another. Their suspicion was not unwarranted, of course, for Lucien would take the threshold crest however he needed to, but their attempt at civility mattered.

It meant they need not die—not if, in the end, they saw things his way. The Nonagon's way. Through the eyes, Lucien sensed the relief of the other Tombtakers—a grueling pace through the ice fields of Foren had left them exhausted and ill equipped for an all-out brawl with an evenly matched foe.

Evenly matched in martial strength, perhaps, but not in wits, for the half-orc speaking on behalf of the party seemed allergic to arriving at the point. By degrees, Lucien's patience ran out. The work must be done. In the back of his mind, the Somnovem hummed like a hive.

This is folly, a waste. They are not your friends. They are not worthy to don the eyes.

Vigilan, ever paranoid, would not keep quiet. The philosophers had entrusted Lucien with the bringing of Cognouza, and so they would have to accept his methods. He would not do the work alone, he could not. The Tombtakers must survive, for without assistance, Lucien could not haul the weight of multiple threshold crests to the necessary—and currently quite distant—ward of Aeor. Lucien snarled in his mind to silence Vigilan, returning his focus to the circular conversation he realized he was still having with Fjord.

"Indeed. So what is the trade then? You will give us the stone, and we tell you what it is we're after." Lucien felt it a fair enough offer, especially considering the Mighty Nein had not put forward one of their own.

"No," said Fjord, shifting back and forth in the knee-deep snow. "I don't think so."

He possessed a bold voice, strong and deep, the tone of it leaving little room for negotiation. Lucien's good-natured smile dwindled. Their magical shield was dispelled, the other members of the Mighty Nein huddled in the white heaped dunes behind Fjord.

"I don't think that has the right weight to it, does it?" continued the half-orc. "I think it's more like we come with you, and you inform us, as much as you're comfortable, a little bit about what you're after and what you expect to happen. See, the thing about having one piece of a puzzle is yes, you could go find another, but it just might not fit right. So you really do need our piece of the puzzle. And I sure would like to know what the whole picture looks like, or at least get a hint."

"Very well." Lucien sighed. Behind him, Otis's teeth could be heard chattering as they waited for direction. Cree cleared her throat, eager to be gone. "Well then, you look a bit tired, and I think we can use a bit of rest. Finish up, have some breakfast, then I guess we'll be on our way together." Lucien turned to go, pausing briefly to add, "I think we've got quite a bit to talk about on the road ahead."

When at last all had gathered their nerve for the day's travels, the combined parties ventured north. As they hiked, Lucien felt Cree's eyes ever upon him. Questioning. Wondering. Waiting. They walked together for a while, and that was pleasant, for the buzzing in his head from the Somnovem quieted down when she was near, the philosophers perhaps intuiting that her loyalty and sense of purpose were like a balm.

"Stop your staring," he told her in an undertone, trudging. "I'm quite all right."

"The bags under your eyes could carry the threshold crest," she muttered.

"Aye, I no longer have a need for sleep," Lucien replied. "There is consciousness with you, and unconsciousness with the Somnovem. There is little else."

"Now there is the Mighty Nein," she reminded him.

Lucien sniffed. "And they are no concern of mine, until they raise a sword to us or wish to see the wisdom of the Nonagon—then we renegotiate terms."

"Don't you see how this all ends?" she pressed. "They aren't part of our vision, our world . . . I don't trust them, and neither should you."

"I trust what the eyes see and what the eyes have touched," he replied. "No more and no less."

Along the route, he heard the Mighty Nein making their expected overtures. Lucien had at last learned the name of the halfling among them. She called herself Veth, and attempted to speak with Otis, misguidedly assuming that their shared halfling blood would bond them.

"Hello! Hello, young lady. What's your name?" asked the earmuffed

Veth, who spoke in a high, singsong voice, swinging her arms as she pranced through the snow.

"Otis," they answered, with their usual charm.

"Oh!" Veth cried. "You're Otis!"

"Ah."

"I'm Veth," said the other halfling. "Nice to meet you."

"Nice to meet you as well."

The befrocked Veth plowed on with the usual pleasantries. "What village did you come from?"

"Oh! Well, I grew up in Trostenwald originally, but the place is a fucking dump."

"Yeah." Veth sighed. "We've been there. It *is* a dump."

Lucien smirked and the eyes flashed; perhaps they would reach an accord after all. The path led, after several hours and a regrettable encounter with a despicable fog, to a familiar sight. The Tombtakers and Mighty Nein, temporarily allies, traversed the River Inferno, but not without incident, banding together to defend against the fire elementals that took issue with their crossing. On the other side, they paused, preparing to recover for the evening and make camp. The burning red scar of the river seethed in the distance behind them, the roaring tumble of rocks submitting to the melting heat of the lava a constant noise under the sounds of unhitching packs and groans as limbs and backs were stretched.

"The River Inferno," Lucien called over the surge of the lava, breaking away from the others to marvel at it. "It cuts straight down the island, dividing east and west, and keeping us from our goal. But no impediment is uncrossable. It is here that the river is narrowest, just shy of a mile." He began to walk slowly toward the edge of the blazing-hot river, Cree not far behind.

"Maybe we'll get lucky, and she'll just walk in," she muttered under her breath.

"Gold melts, too," Lucien replied. "We need only tolerate her awhile longer, Cree. Chin up."

"She hates us, Lucien, can't you see it in her eyes?" Cree asked, her voice numb, almost hollow. "The disdain? The disgust? We're beneath her."

"We're nothing of the sort, Cree, not so long as she needs us."

"And after that?"

"This place is a graveyard; it's making you paranoid."

Cree scrunched her eyes shut, then shook her head. "Wait . . . And after that? After that . . . Who are you talking about? Whose gold?"

"Vess DeRogna, she's right over—" Lucien said, then stopped. He glanced away from the river, down at his own hands, flexing them. The red eye stamped against his right palm shimmered and seemed to wink. What was this madness? Were they going in circles? In a sudden panic, he spun, finding that the Mighty Nein were there assembled and discussing what to do next, the Tombtakers a few paces away.

"Are you all right?" whispered Cree, stricken. "Are *we* all right? We've already . . . We're already on the other side. The elementals attacked, just like before, only this time I used one of DeRogna's spell scrolls to cross."

"It's like the time before," Lucien breathed. "Time . . . Here we are again. It's like we're walking in a great spiral, invisible until you come back to the same bloody spot."

"We need to rest," she insisted. "Only . . . we're tired, is all. We're just tired."

Vigilan's voice obliterated his next thought.

You're slipping.

---

* *I'll fucking say. Can't believe I'm agreeing with an ancient, nutty philosopher in our head, but stranger things, eh? What does it feel like to be back with the old squad? Anything coming up? Yasha looks nice. The white hair suits her. Ya know, when we worked together for the Fletching and Moondrop Traveling Carnival of Curiosities she was the bouncer. Scared the shit out of every trinket-dicked man who came to see us, they didn't know if they wanted to scream and run away or fuck her. She's special like that. Contains multitudes. Kinda like us. Badum-tss. Have you looked at that clover she gave you lately?*

Lucien had turned away from the River Inferno, his eyes straight ahead, piercing through the distant silhouette of Yasha, who spoke in hushed tones with Beau.

"You're not welcome here," Lucien told the voice. He refused to acknowledge who and what it was. The eyes flashed. A warning. "I don't feel anything when I look at your old friends."

I wouldn't be here if you weren't feeling something. There's a crack in the cobbles, Lucien. Peekaboo, I see you.

You're slipping.

Slipping.

Transmute the Nein before they delay Cognouza.
The work must continue.
Give it.
GIVE IT TO US.

Transmute

Transmute

Transmute

CHAPTER 30

Lucien's neck throbbed as he stood in the disturbed, partially shoveled snow and stared at the bizarre door that had sprung up where the Mighty Nein had put down their camp. Their mage, Caleb Widogast, had conjured the thing for their comfort and—quite rudely, in Lucien's opinion—failed to invite the Tombtakers to join them to escape the brutal cold. It might have been nice to all sit together in the safety and comfort of a real home after barely surviving the onslaught of fire elementals. Of course, the Mighty Nein assumed he was ignorant of the tower, the spell supposedly rendering the shelter invisible, but they didn't understand the power and reach of the Eyes of Nine.

They didn't understand, but they soon would.

He approached the portal granting passage to the tower, raised his hand, and politely knocked.

Caleb, worn and bedraggled from the trek, appeared, scarf loose around his neck, a sour note to his voice as he primly asked, "How can I help you?"

Lucien shrugged, casual. "I was just curious as to where this strange portal led."

"This is my house," the mage barked back, brow furrowed. "We are going to have a comfortable night before trudging through the bleak frozen north tomorrow."

"Ah." Lucien grinned. "Didn't mention you had a home before."

Caleb crossed his arms over his sweater. "Have you told us everything?"

"No, but you've told me so little."

"Well!" The mage sighed, exasperated. "I have a tower that I carry around in my pocket and only we fit in here. Thank you. We'll see you in the morning!"

Lucien imagined the sound of a door slamming in his face, which only made the whole thing ruder. He would never have supposed them all friends, and he certainly did not trust them, but the thought of them all warm and cozy in the tower, scheming away, set his blood simmering. He wouldn't have it. Further, the Somnovem, buzzing as if the hive had been jabbed by a hot poker, wouldn't have it, either.

The eye on Lucien's palm glowed brightly, redder than the bands of mahogany signaling the setting sun. At once, the tower disappeared, dumping Yasha, Beauregard, Caleb, Jester, Caduceus, Fjord, and Veth unceremoniously on their arses in the hardened snow. Well. If they were going to fight together, then they would also freeze together. It might have been a minor trespass, just a misunderstanding of the hazy boundaries set by a hazier alliance, but the slight, the impoliteness, crawled up Lucien's spine like a bug. He remembered huddling against Zoran, battling for sleep against the half-giant's farts and musk, while *Lady* Vess DeRogna chugged wine and gobbled bonbons in her insufferable glass birdhouse.

The mage took the greatest offense. Understandable, given it was his conjuration the eye had ended.

In the face of his frustration, Lucien hedged. "I'm careful," he told Caleb. "Especially around practitioners of magic. Have a bit of a history. Especially those that walked alongside such individuals. Pardon me if I mistrust certain aspects of the arcane that, I don't know, might be hanging out in the unspoken wings of our arrangement. So, I'm careful. I'm not offering for you to leave, but if you were, it would be annoying. What you have isn't so precious. It's just convenient."

Other crests could be located and retrieved, but that would only delay Cognouza, and setbacks were to be avoided, if at all possible.

"Let's save some time," the mage replied, voice low and fierce. "Here's what I propose: I'm very curious. I love books and learning. Show me your book." Lucien recoiled. The man hurried on, slicing the air with his hand. "Don't *give* it to me. *Show* it to us. Let us look at it together—look at it together and try to ascertain what it is you have been unable to. You can stop us from leaving at any time, it seems. Share a little bit more of your knowledge. Enjoy a bed tomorrow night. What do you have to lose? We can't leave. We've tried twice."

It was best to let Caleb think he was winning the argument. In truth, Lucien could not wait to expose them to the philosophers and watch as they, too, learned the great truth of Cognouza. After that, it would only be a matter of time before the eyes appeared on their bodies and they shared the indelible, beautiful link.

"I'll think on it," he said.

"When?" The brawler, Beauregard, approached, swathed in blue wool and fur. She was still brushing away snow from her coat. "Like tonight?"

"Aye. Tonight, while I rest."

They are impatient to know the Nine. That is good.

Lucien returned to the Tombtakers' camp, finding a worn depression in the snowbank near Cree and sitting in it, legs outstretched, waiting for the Mighty Nein to collect their possessions and their pride and join.

"Oh, have they deigned to sit with the poors?" Tyffial asked, rolling her eyes as one by one the adventurers arrived.

"Stow it for now, eh?" Lucien told her. "Remember the visions."

Through the eyes, he had showed them wonder. He spared them the terror and fear and pain that he knew were to come, too. Unmaking the world and doing what the philosophers failed to do would be no simple task. He needed them to know what awaited on the other side of all that uncertainty. Soon, the Tombtakers would occupy spires, castles with walls like mountains, an endless stream of smiling servants presenting wine, feasts, dance, song . . . whatever their hearts craved, they would have.

Zoran, he knew, despite all his blustering, would perch himself on an island and lie in the shade, watching the merchant ships of his mighty fleet come and go. There would be songs sung about him, of course. Tyffial would have Jurrell back, and their heaps of jewels would make even queens blush, though in this world, there need not be kings or queens or rulers of any known kind. Otis would see the land cured of all sickness and disease, and live forever, healthy as a little ox.

And Cree, well, Cree did not so much imagine as remember—she remembered a funny, old, crooked house in the Run with three friends coming and going. But this time, the cellar was always full, the pantry ever stocked, and they made a family as grand and powerful as any of the houses of the Tribes. She could keep nothing from him now, not with the eyes connecting them, though he sensed her sheepishness and fear, fear that he would grow angry at Brevyn lurking in her thoughts.

The visions Lucien saw in their hearts and shared with them were unbelievable at first, too grand, too impossible. Lucien would gesture to the eye tattoos marking them, connecting them, and ask how he could gift them such dreams if this wasn't the singular thread of the gods' own tapestries. Tyffial believed soonest and hardest, and he knew that loss spurred her caving in.

Lucien's own dreams would frighten them, so he shielded them from the philosophers' madness they would need to untangle before the exultant reward. He hated thinking it, but they were, not unlike the Somnovem, practically children. Everyone, it seemed, needed his guidance.

"We don't strike unless we must," he told Tyffial.

"I so hope we must," she murmured. "Insufferable twats."

"Take pity on them, dear," he said. "They haven't seen what you have. Through the Nine, your eyes have been opened. They're dwelling in darkness."

"Cognouza." She closed her eyes and breathed in deeply through her nose. A small, private smile flitted across her face, as she no doubt imagined all that would come when they held the power of dreams in their hands. "Soon."

"Soon," the Tombtakers echoed, eyes red, in unison, and in one hearty voice.

The Mighty Nein trickled over, some in pairs, others venturing over alone. The little blue infernal raced out ahead, a sapphire blur across the snow as she landed with a thump in front of Lucien, violet eyes vivid and mischievous. "Do you want me to read your tarot cards?" she asked.

Around the side of the fire, Cree's ears flattened. She stared at Lucien intently, giving a tiny shake of the head. He grinned.

"Certainly."

The horned girl, Jester, waved the pack of cards in front of his face. "Really?" She gasped with delight, then narrowed her eyes. "You know, I learned this from Molly. Does that change your opinion of it?"

"No. I'm just curious."

"Okay!" Jester squealed.

"Why do I get the sense this is a hobby rather than an art?" he heard Otis mutter to Zoran. Zoran shrugged, only half paying attention, busy with a bit of whittling. He hummed softly to himself with the bottoms of his boots pressed near to the campfire.

Lucien pulled three cards from the offered deck, as instructed. He was amused that they had drawn a crowd. The Mighty Nein circled them, watching intently as the cards and their images were revealed.

"This is the card of your past," Jester explained, pointing. "This card is History and the Dream!"

The painting showed a hulking creature—black, horned, and twisted—obliterating a city. The irony of the imagery did not escape Lucien, but he was not eager to give her anything of his past. He simply nodded, unblinking, waiting for her to proceed.

"This card," she continued, giddy. "Ooh, this is your present! Ooh, two dragons fight each other in a figure eight. The one facing you is red."

Cree cleared her throat, trying to draw his attention, but he ignored her once more.

"Hmm," Lucien replied, thoughtful.

"Flipping your last card," Jester said, doing so for him. "This is your future! Oh, um, well, facing you is Death. B-But that's not necessarily a bad thing, Lucien, you know," she hurried on. It was almost touching that she meant to console him. "Some people think that Death means a rebirth. Something must end for something new to begin."

A spike of white light lanced through his forehead. Lucien stayed perfectly still. The eye over his heart, unseen, flowered with pain.

You're slipping.

Vigilan, he thought, frozen in place. *Not now. Have mercy, philosopher of the Nine. Let me think! Let me think . . .*

Yes, now. Now when you are at the very precipice—you were lost to us once; slide further, and you are lost to us forever. How can you hazard the risk, when Cognouza is so close?

Despite his efforts, his hand jumped, leaping twice off the ground. There was a weight on his chest, like someone had laid him flat on his back and pressed their knee into his sternum. Sadness. So much sadness. A warm, welcome light hovering just where the pain in his chest was greatest. His eyes weren't closed, but it felt like they were, and in the darkness, he saw a woman's face.

Brevyn. Then it . . . changed. She was someone else, and hers was a quieter strength, a mark down her lip, her hair dark and wild, wings spread out from her back. Her pain was his and it crushed him. It was a miracle only his hand moved. He heard her whisper, "It happened again."

A scream split his brain in two, then a flash of sapphire lightning in the distance. He saw it now over the River Inferno to the south, the coming of a raging storm.

"How do you feel?" Jester's voice tore him away from the scream and the storm. When he looked again, there was no trace of lightning, just the sun disappearing under a skirt of soft gray clouds.

"Thank you," Lucien murmured. "That was interesting. Always been . . . oddly curious from a distance about such strange . . . hobbies. Thank you for indulging in the offer."

You're slipping. Fear not Death! Reach Cognouza, bring it home, and dream a deathless world for all to share.

Jester smiled, and even Lucien could admit it was like being punched in the face by a swarm of butterflies. Utterly charming. She tucked a piece of blue hair behind her delicate ear. "Of course!"

He stood, carefully, and pushed through the gaggle of adventurers, taking great pains not to look at them, not to look at one face in particular. Gathering himself, he walked past Cree, gesturing wordlessly for her to follow. Otis hopped up, then Tyffial, and finally Zoran, and without consulting one another, they fell to constructing their shelter. It was hard work as the temperature plummeted, all of them fatigued from the chaos of the River Inferno and its damned guardians.

A long rest was in order. Only . . .

Only.

Lucien stood for a long moment, a tent pole in his hands, watching the river of fire snake south, wondering if another strike of blue lightning would come and split him open again.

CHAPTER 31

*ou're slipping.*

This woman you keep dreaming about, what's her name?

Lucien stared resolutely up at the stars that drifted in and out of view behind tufts of cottony clouds. He would have preferred any of the other pushy voices that frequently overrode his own coming out to converse, but instead he felt the sewage leaking through the cracks of his restraint, fetid waste surging up from the very depths of his mind. But the garbage spoke true: More and more, when he gazed into the distance and let reality fall away (his approximation of rest), Brevyn's face appeared. But he did not want to encourage the interloper, and so he ignored the babbling.

He might have anticipated his coming, as the tarot reading had proved . . . trying. But he would survive it; he would persevere. Cognouza was close, Aeor itself but two days north. Soon, soon, soon.

That blue lightning you imagined? It's Yasha. You've seen her wings? She has angel blood; she shines from the inside out. You'd like her if you gave her a chance. Your hand didn't twitch, Lucien, mine did.

"That certainly is one theory."

You're afraid, aren't you? Afraid you'll fail. Afraid you'll die with nothing to show for all this misery. Afraid you'll lose your body to me again. Or maybe the Mighty Nein will just kill you and put a stop to it. They've faced far worse than you.

He flinched. He didn't want to talk about who owned what body; it made him squirm. "Brevyn," Lucien blurted, choosing what felt safe. "The woman's name is Brevyn."

I like her tattoos. The butterfly? Much better than ours.

"Ours were a gift, you fucking ingrate," Lucien hissed. "A gift that will give and give until it gives me the world."

I've seen your visions of Cognouza. How can you want that? A black city, a living, thinking city, all too eager to jam its tentacles into your brain and flap your mouth for you . . . That's what you want? You're smarter than that. I sure as shit was smarter than that. At least, I'm pretty sure I was.

"What do you expect? That I'll turn back? Give up? Return this body to you?" Lucien snarled. His voice did not break the silence of the camp, for this was an argument waged only in his mind.

I am sorry, Lucien, but I can't let you do this. I can't let you unmake and destroy this world Yasha walks through. She's suffered enough without you and your buddies turning everything upside down. I'll do whatever I can to stop you.

The corners of Lucien's lips turned slowly up. The clouds gathered, obliterating the stars. "You had your chance. This body is mine, the eyes are mine, and in two days' time, Cognouza, at last, will be mine, too. No more darkened doors and windows, just a warm welcome of endless, peaceful light."

You're completely gone. You're mad.

"No." Lucien smiled in earnest. "The Somnovem are quite mad, but me? My eyes are open. I will guide them, show them, and when we reach Cognouza you will see."

I'll see, he says. What will I see? More important, what will you see? By the Betrayers, do you even know what to expect when you get to this Cognouza place? Tea and a biscuit? Tea and a biscuit but standing on your head because it's a bloody mad circus in the Astral Sea?

The Mighty Nein had gone to sleep in a pile beneath their precious domed bubble. Snow gathered on it, frosting the lightly radiant surface. Zoran and Tyffial had taken the watch and discovered something, though the chaos did not stray near camp as they chased off whatever wild beast had come sniffing around. The coals of their campfire smoked, little more than embers. In the tent they had erected, Cree tossed and turned among her blankets.

"Once upon a time," he said, eyes open and staring across at the dome gathering snow. "There was a happy family, and they were that way for a little while. Something tore them apart from the inside out. Have you ever bitten into a fruit and found it wormy inside? That's how it was. There was a worm inside all along, but nobody knew, nobody could tell. Oh aye, the apple looked shiny and red, tempting enough, but there was a hideous blight spoiling its insides. There was a happy family, and then it was gone."

So, what? You think Cognouza can bring your family back?

Lucien smirked, chuckling. "No, little mistake, that wouldn't require much imagination, would it? I want to change it all. I'm already inside the fruit. I've found a way to reach the good, fleshy bits. I'll have everything before anyone goes to take a bite."

CHAPTER 32

More eyes, more eyes, more eyes! Oh, but when they see it—when they know—it will be such a wonderful surprise!

Lucien ignored the breathless chatter of Mirumus, his voice coming upon him like a hail of glass, pelting the brain, his whole skull rattling with their excitement. Sometimes a single word from the Nine would crack open his head, a sudden shout from a tangle of memory, a desperate, half-forgotten cry for *something*. Day had broken, though sunlight and darkness were distinctions now lost to him; there was no sleep and no true rest, only the meditation and waking dreams, visions of what was to come.

Zoran and Tyffial broke down their camp, singing snatches of the same Menagerie Coast tune, while Cree and Otis stirred a cauldron of potent, liquored gruel. It was the only thing Zoran knew how to cook, and he could only cook a heap of it. The halfling among the Mighty Nein had called it chowder; sometimes Zoran referred to it as *that shit*. Chewy, fruity, somehow gristly yet also savory, the *brew*, as Otis tended to call it, was their customary breakfast.

The Mighty Nein had been foolish enough to try it the night before, and even pretended to enjoy it, a sign of cooperation that somewhat cheered Lucien. He wasn't certain if the two groups were experiencing camaraderie, but he recognized that an overture from him now would not seem out of place.

The offering of brew had been an experimental offer, and his decision to approach their camp that bright, cold morning was the next natural step. Cree watched him dig in his pack for a moment and then produce the mage's journal. The binding had completely softened, the pages inside free and wild, only held in place because Lucien had wrapped a narrow leather thong around the covers, sandwiching the information in place. Cree's yellow eyes danced between him and the other camp.

"What are you doing?" she asked, crouched over the cauldron, stirring the brew. Her ladle gradually came to a stop.

"Making friends?" Otis suggested with a snort. His thick head of curly brown hair was hidden under a furred cap. "Could bring some brew. Always perks you up in the mornin'."

"Actually, I thought I might let them have a peek at this," Lucien replied. He was giddy with excitement at the prospect, though he couldn't discern whether that was his own feeling or the influence of the Somnovem.

"The journal? Are you certain?" asked Cree.

"I am." Lucien tapped the eye mark on the side of his neck, one that had been embellished with feathers and paisley to resemble a peacock during the interloper's brief time with his body. "I'd feel better knowing we were traveling with those who see as we do."

"Seems a waste," Otis groused. He shifted his weight from foot to foot, then took a wooden bowl from the fireside and scooped it into the cauldron.

"Like them or not, they are well traveled and intelligent. I could use that—*we* could use that. Some among them might be able to make sense of the later pages," Lucien explained, ignoring a hurt glance from Cree. Even after studying the tome for as long as he had, there remained mysteries within. He felt himself the focus, the lens through which the Somnovem's brilliance would be guided, yet these were nine minds against his one. If any surprises lurked within the mad mage's work, Lucien wanted to know. Cognouza neared, and he would enter it empowered with knowledge. "We're nearing the end, my friends, and the end never comes easy. Before we march into battle, so to speak, I for one would like the odds stacked in our favor."

"Let 'im go," Zoran growled, interrupting his own song. "The Nonagon killed for that thing; he won't let it wander into the wrong hands now."

"Why thank you, Zoran. Well put." And with that, Lucien set out for the other camp, crossing the distance with a spring in his step. As he approached the Mighty Nein, it was impossible not to notice the difference between their camp and his. It reminded him of the first expedition the Tombtakers had embarked upon to Aeor, sleeping in a pile of bodies, Tyffial and Jurrell sneaking off to touch each other and then returning with theatrically innocent expressions that nobody believed, and the strewn evidence of whittling, drinking, cooking, reading, merrymaking . . . he even noticed tiny cat footprints in the snow.

Now the Tombtakers' camp sat mostly silent. Zoran and Tyffial had begun dismantling the makeshift tent while Otis scooped snow into the cauldron to clean out the remnants of breakfast brew. He could feel Cree's eyes burning into his back as he approached the other adventurers.

Lucien was greeted by the Mighty Nein with furtive glances, questioning stares, and predictable suspicion. They fell silent as he drew near, but he slapped on a smile.

"Before we finish breakfast, since we had a bit of a conversation the other day . . ." He shrugged and laughed to himself. "Sure, I'd be curious." He waved the bound journal around. "I assume someone wants to give it a shot?"

He heard the blue infernal Jester lean over and softly whisper to the halfling, "It's like he doesn't have Nonagon face today, he has Lucien face. Maybe even Molly face!"

"Sh-hh." The halfling shook her head.

But Caleb's blue eyes flew open, and he stood, quickly, though he reined himself in admirably to allow a cool, "Absolutely."

"He's the one that understands that sort of stuff," said Jester, still seated.

"I certainly hope so," Lucien murmured. "Here."

The human mage produced a leather mat from his pack and rolled it out, taking the journal with extreme care and laying it out on the barrier. It was the kind of reverence that Lucien appreciated. A promising start. Beau joined him, kneeling at the mage's side as they both hovered over the book. Her expression, by contrast, was not one of awe or reverence but skepticism. It rankled Lucien, and he watched her closely, leery. A flash of arcane energy emerged from Caleb's hands, glittering white runes rising from his palms and dissipating into his forehead as he imbued himself with the ability to read the journal, which was written in a somewhat obscure language.

As they read, Beau reached for a parchment and quill, and furiously began jotting notes without glancing at her own hands as they dashed across the page.

Lucien wasn't interested in that. He remained fixated on their eyes, their faces, detecting the interest, surprise, confusion . . . Most fascinating of all, he observed that they became naturally lost in the text, ignorant of what others were saying and doing around them, completely numb to the passage of time. Those not reading grew fidgety and anxious, waiting for a verdict on something that could not rightly or succinctly be judged.

Caleb flipped the pages, arriving at the unknown mage's utter descent. His stunned expression matched perfectly the flummoxing diagrams, fractals, and meaningless scribbles that filled the lengthy remainder of the journal.

"I think that's enough reading for now." Lucien stooped down and swept up the pages, rebinding them and holding the journal to his chest. It was warm. "So. What'd you think?"

"Whet my appetite, why don't you? They seem a lot like the Cerberus Assembly of their time, but better or worse. Depending how you look at it." The mage sat back on his haunches, rubbing his bearded chin for a spell. When he spoke, it was directly to the brawler at his side. "Well, it's very much . . . We're talking so much about dreams, this is—this is dreams on paper."

Dreams on paper! The voices in his head—or one voice in particular—lit up like a lantern festival at dusk. It was Mirumus. He recognized their giddy, breathless chatter. *What a pleasant surprise! I like this one! What it will be to see through his eyes! To have him see through ours! Dreams! Drams! Dram-flam-flim-flam! GIVE IT TO ME. GIVE.*

"Yeah," Beau said softly. Her piercing blue eyes wandered to the journal pressed against Lucien's chest.

"This is your friends talking to the writer, in their way," added Caleb, still stroking his beard. *His friends. The Somnovem.* "And you are able to read or make something of this?"

"Not at first. But if you make sense of any of it, please do let me know," he said lightly. The mage swayed a little as he knelt, then pinched the bridge of his nose. Lucien knew the feeling. "Well! Think on it a bit. We've got a bit of travel. If perhaps you've got an idea, do come let me know."

Cree glared at him as he rejoined them. Her eyes did not relent as he stuffed the journal in his pack and shoved a few pewter plates in beside the book to help distribute the load.

"What?" he muttered, glaring right back at her over the top of the cinch.

"Anything to show for that?" she asked crisply.

Lucien sighed and pushed his bag down roughly, then stood while the rest of the Tombtakers hauled their things onto their backs and waited for the Mighty Nein. When they were ready, the group trickled over, and Lucien was waiting for them. He could still feel Cree's eyes boring into the back of his head. Annoying. Before the Mighty Nein could reach their broken camp, Lucien reached through the eyes, finding Cree by using the Nonagon's invisible chains. Her eyes snapped open, glowing red, and with Lucien controlling her mouth, she gave a broad, toothy smile.

"That's better," they said in unison.

Lucien dropped the thread of control, and Cree hissed, shaking her head. "I thought you hated puppets," she sneered, and turned away to trudge through the snow. Lucien stared at her footprints, numb. That was a barb aimed at another man, a stranger. Otis passed her as she left to sulk and glanced up at Lucien, hitching his bag higher.

"What's got her tail in a twist, then?"

"She doesn't agree with my methods."

"But you're the Nonagon."

"Aye, and I helped her remember it. Ah!" Lucien pasted on a grin for the Mighty Nein and opened his arms wide. "As requested, to build trust in the bridge that's been so asked of us, I've shown you something very private and personal to me. As a response, just show me that you still have it."

The threshold crest.

Fjord stared coolly, then reached into a nondescript bag hanging from his belt, holding up an orange crystal, the amber shining in his hands as he turned it this way and that. He tilted the bag toward the Tombtakers, showing the seemingly endless contents of their magical bag.

"Cute, isn't it?" trilled Jester, making a shimmying *ta-dah* motion.

"Quite clever," Lucien agreed, bowing to them both. The half-orc handed him the amber, and Lucien studied it.

"Wave to Vess!" added Beau with a crooked grin.

And indeed, within the bag he noticed a tangle of graying brown hair. DeRogna's head.

Lucien snorted. "Two keepsakes in one? Well!" He turned and pointed to Zoran, who was still being slowly crushed by the immense pack strapped to his back. "It's a much easier way to travel! Shame you don't have these fancy things, eh?"

Zoran looked almost crestfallen. "Can you make more of those?"

Caleb answered, "I can't, but there's more room in it, if you'd like to have us carry anything for you?"

It wasn't even the least bit sly. Lucien rolled his eyes. "Why shouldn't I just take this right now from you?"

"Because you like us!" said Jester.

At the back of the group, the pink-haired Caduceus shifted and leaned on his crystalline staff. "Would be a poor sign of trust."

"If you hold on to it, you won't get to stay in my tower tonight," warned the mage.

The half-orc waggled his black eyebrows. "It is so warm in there."

"And there's lots of good food," Jester assured them.

Lucien was not concerned with warmth or good food, but he did hear Otis groan softly with frustration. She was close to losing a toe from frostbite. Otis would lose all ten toes if she had to, for what mattered was Cognouza, and before that, the threshold crests that would allow them to reach it and return it to this plane.

"As we said, when we arrive, we get the crest. We made a deal."

Fjord reached out his palm to Lucien, who returned the crystal. "We did."

The crest was near, their destination but a day's trek away. Cognouza, the city where dreams were clay. He could sense it blackening the horizon, hidden to his sight, but not for long. Better still, Caleb and Beauregard had seen into the journal. Soon the eyes would appear upon them, and visions of Cognouza would open their minds to the work that must be done.

No longer would they stand in the Nonagon's way.

CHAPTER 33

Only miles north of their last camp, the storm descended. It was an unnatural fog, obscuring as night, the air itself jagged with frost. Even without snow it was impossible to properly navigate the hills. They pushed and pushed, but there was no fighting what had no armor or flesh to strike. The wind tore at their clothes and carried their voices away, the march continuing until at last they stumbled upon familiar tracks. If they kept on, Otis wouldn't be the only one losing appendages to frostbite.

Cree nearly collapsed against him as what little light remained began to diminish. Her teeth chattered, her black fur turned gray from the sheeting ice. "J-Just like the River Inferno before," she whispered. "Spirals, spirals, spirals, bloody circles. We're going in circles."

"We camp for the night!" Lucien called, and nobody protested.

Cree sagged as he helped her back to her feet. "Thank you, Nonagon."

He nodded but otherwise stayed silent. Her outburst that morning still rankled, the frustrating weather doing nothing to improve his mood. They were too close now; petty infighting and dissent would only slow them down, just like the freak, bastard ice fog.

Ice crusted in his beard, Caleb knelt in the snow, huddling against the wind, setting out his ingredients to conjure the pocket dimension the Mighty Nein used for shelter during their travels. Lucien could only imagine what it looked like in full, for he spied only a single door.

The inside of the magical tower was striking—colorful and cheekily overstuffed with furniture, art, tapestries, and a profusion of cats. Otis sneezed the moment she stepped foot inside, drawing a confused glance from Cree.

"What?" the halfling muttered, rubbing her nose. "You're just the one, there's probably seventy fucking cats in here. There's more dander than air."

"They're not real cats, you muddle butt." Tyffial sighed.

"My nose thinks they are!"

Dozens of furry servants rushed through the tower, appearing from archways that led to a dizzying labyrinth of rooms and halls. Caleb promised food and lodging and graciously showed the Tombtakers to a series of rooms just for them while the Mighty Nein dispersed to find their usual apartments.

The immediate warmth of the tower was enough to pause Lucien's irritation at being led to what was a shrine to their lost friend, Mollymauk Tealeaf. Even the stained-glass windows depicted scenes of the Mighty Nein locked in battle or celebration with him. Stripes of red, gold, and green fabric swooped down from the central lamp, giving the impression of a circus tent's candy-striped interior.

Not for the first time, Lucien silently mused that subtlety was not the mage's forte. Points, however, for boldness and boundless imagination. Which . . . Lucien paused, finding that one of the windows did not display the interloper, but Cognouza itself. The Somnovem must have already sent the mage visions of the city.

Lucien grinned.

"You've seen more than you let on."

Visions. He wondered if they were as spiraling and strange as his own.

"Dare to dream," Caleb replied coolly. "You can all sleep in here."

As he spoke, a pair of bunk beds appeared, enough for four. Lucien cocked an eyebrow, but his question was answered before he could vocalize it, the mage leading him through a set of double doors that opened onto an even more ludicrously manipulative ode to the Mighty Nein's dead friend. Lucien was about to good-naturedly tell Caleb that it would suffice but that he should also absolutely go fuck himself when Tyffial piped up.

"Is there a meal included as well?" she asked, eyes wide and hungry.

"*Ja.*" The mage nodded and swept back out toward the corridor.

"Make yourself comfortable and, in about an hour, exit your chambers. Go higher up until you reach the room with all the cats in it."

Otis moaned softly in agony.

"Very well," Lucien replied. The Tombtakers shared a look, with Cree adding, "We'll be there shortly."

The mage sensed accurately that he was being dismissed. He wasn't quite out the door when Cree muttered, "Just like DeRogna's birdhouse. Fucking rich kids."

Cree sidled up to Lucien, reaching out to touch his shoulder, but Lucien stormed away, concealing himself in the circus tent bedroom and slamming the door. He couldn't believe he was expected to sleep in this absurd place. Even the walls were patterned a deep pinkish red, swirls of yellow, white, orange, and purple forming phoenixes, moons, and sunbursts, the same material emblazoned on the re-creations of their friend in the stained-glass windows.

The plush, quilted blanket spread across the gold, enameled bed was the exact lilac color of Lucien's skin, the tassels along the edges crimson and black. A rustic painting of a four-leaf clover hung above the bed, noticeably crooked, as if Lucien was meant to touch it and put it back in place. Instead, he shucked his clothing and ran a bath, sinking into the delightfully scalding water, and only then noticing that the design of the tub mimicked two horns interlocking.

"The mage is consistent, I'll give him that,"* Lucien murmured, closing his eyes for what felt like the first time in months.

---

* *Snazzy digs. Really sets a mood. Any strong feelings about the décor?*
Lucien peeled one eye open, knowing there would not be anyone there. The interloper had returned. Bothersome. Lucien snorted and closed his eyes again. "It's horrid. Most carnival barkers dress that way because they must, not because they actually want to."
You're just jealous. I have friends and style.
"Had," Lucien growled. "Now you have nothing. You're a flea biting a giant."
I'd rather be a flea than a naked loon arguing with himself.
He sighed. "I've been naked with plenty of men, though none so vexatious as you."
Sounds like you fucked boring people, but that tracks.
Lucien smirked, sinking lower into the bathwater. "Your Caleb and Beauregard have perused the journal. Did you know that?"
I said they were my friends, I never said they were wise.
"Indeed, well, it's only a matter of time now," Lucien told him. "You've lost."

A lot of dead dummies have underestimated the Mighty Nein before. You're no different. Even if you try to pull them into your spooky little cult, it won't matter. They've only given you this much grace because they want to believe you're me. They'll find a way to best you, they'll kill you before you ever reach Cognouza, but not if you stop this now. Admit who you are. Admit that part of me still exists in your soul.

"But that would be lying."

I'm your only way out of this.

"No," Lucien said, absently brushing the eye marked across his chest. "Cognouza is my way out. My way forward. Dreams will be reality, shaped by my will, and when that day comes, you will no longer be a figment or a fragment, you'll just be"—he snapped his fingers—"gone."

And the best parts of us along with me.

Lucien flinched.

They only tolerate you for one reason, you dope. Your "friends" can't even do that anymore. You're slipping.

His eyes flashed open, water churning as he sat up straight in the tub. "Do not put the words of the Somnovem in your mouth, aberration!"

For a moment there was silence, cold and empty. Then: *How do you know those are their words? How do you even know what's real anymore? What the truth is? What's yours?*

CHAPTER 34

I t seemed the evening would begin and end in absurdity. Lucien had made the mistake of expressing interest in the various rooms composing Widogast's tower, which prompted Jester to insist on a tour. A tour! An ordinary thing! But of course, there were no ordinary things when it came to the Mighty Nein, which meant taking the tour as a cat. Jester, helpfully (sort of), used a bit of spellwork to transform them both into felines, and then took him on a winding escapade through the Cat Only tunnels running the length and breadth of the tower. It was dusty, frustrating, and ultimately meaningless. He learned absolutely nothing of value from her but came away with an admittedly comprehensive understanding of the tower's architecture and the bizarre inner workings of Jester's mind. Which brought them to the next absurdity, after the tower was put away and the journey resumed, for first there was the feline tunnel tour and now there was a bloody *dragon*; Lucien was beginning to think they would never make the far reaches of Aeor.

We never promised the path to Cognouza would be easy.

And so it wasn't. The dragon descended, ivory wings beating, wide, scarred snout sniffing and testing the air. They had hardly gone two miles from their last stopping place. Lucien heard one of the Mighty Nein whisper a name, Gelidon, and it became clear that this was not their first run-in with the beast. They had no choice but to defend themselves, and to work together to survive the dragon's fury. She circled in the air in brief spurts, snow flying, shards of ice slicing through the air, seemingly at the command of the creature's wings.

There was not a coward among the Mighty Nein, and Lucien could admire the tenacity with which they fought; Beauregard hurled herself into battle with no hesitation and no thought for her own well-being. He tried not to think of Brevyn, who had always acted with similar abandon, and instead observed the Mighty Nein closely. Their tactics. Their tendencies.

It was, as their dead friend predicted, likely that it eventually would come to blows. Lucien hoped that Caleb and Beauregard might be swayed to their side, drawn to the Somnovem's power by what they had seen in the journal and witnessed in visions after, but they would not join him without the others protesting. He watched as first Beauregard and then Zoran leapt upon the dragon's back, each of them taking a nasty beating for the effort, their distraction giving the others time to strike at the beast's legs and neck.

The ground shook with each pounding step the dragon took, and she tossed her great head, throwing off her attackers. Once more, the beast braced against the slick, icy ground and leapt into the air, blood pouring from breaks in her scaly hide. Holes had been torn in her leathery wings, Veth's and Otis's crossbow bolts feathering her front left leg and cheek. The dragon shied, working her wings, blasting them all with a freezing wind before deciding she had tolerated enough and flying away. The beast might have been victorious against the Mighty Nein, but a dozen skilled warriors and blood hunters of the Orders had given her pause.

Blood soaked the snow, theirs and the dragon's.

Cree wandered between them, clutching the amulet around her neck. It was still filled with Lucien's blood, a sign of their bond. With her magic, she healed cuts and bruises, mending them well enough to make a short march to safety plausible. A gentle snow began to fall as the afternoon light faded, puffy flakes covering the chaos of the battle, gradually obscuring the craterous zone of char and gore. Zoran limped along beside Lucien on the trek, leaning heavily against the shaft of his maul. All of them had taken a beating, delaying Cognouza once more.

They slowly gathered when the darkness became impenetrable and the winds turned razor-sharp, and, as if it were now a given, the mage conjured his tower, and once more they retired to rest. Once more, they dined on heaping platters of elk, steamed vegetables, pastries, and wine.

Conversation, though, was restricted to heaving grunts and sighs as everyone filled empty, desperate bellies, hands shaking with exhaustion.

Lucien rose and excused himself before dessert could be brought in by Caleb's dutiful fleet of felines. The Tombtakers followed, Otis snatching an extra sausage pasty on the way out. Their early retirement was not remarked upon, and he sensed the Mighty Nein were just as eager to find their beds and shake off the terror and toil of facing Gelidon.

No more than three feet into their assigned apartments, Otis slammed the door shut behind them, trotting to the center rug and gesturing for everyone to come close.

"What's the matter?" asked Lucien.

"Nothing, Nonagon! Nothing! Behold . . ." Otis reached into the deep pocket of their oiled leather coat, withdrawing first the pasty, which they chucked aside, and after a return trip, they produced a small, familiar satchel.

The Mighty Nein's endless, magic bag.

Lucien instinctively clamped his hand over it. Otis stared up into his face, eyes round and searching, like a child desperate for praise.

"How?" he breathed.

"When the green one was distracted with the dragon and whatnot, I just palmed it, ya know, like this," Otis replied, demonstrating by swiping their hand near Lucien's belt.

"What have you done?" Cree hissed, appearing at Lucien's elbow. "How will we explain this?"

"We won't! Why should we? Cocky fuckers." Otis cackled, then their face fell. "What do you think, Nonagon?"

"Perfect, Otis. Perfectly done."

Otis beamed. "Aye, aye, they told me to do it."

Lucien paused before asking, "The Nine? How exactly?"

"The voices!" Otis glanced behind their back, then whispered, "The Somnovem. They spoke to me. Most of it was gibberish, couldn't understand a fucking word, but then! Then! Flashes. Just . . . pictures, weird and blobby, but there was a green shape floating in a white field, and then someone screamed: TAKE! TAKE IT!"

That certainly sounded like them.

"So I just figured, shit! Right! Knick it off the green one when he's not looking!"

Lucien tried not to guffaw, for stealth was now paramount. He strode to the door. "Good, that's good, but we must leave. At once. Find what strength you can. We march to Aeor this night."

There was no arguing, for how could there be? They could not stay in the mage's tower while in possession of their most precious stolen items. Lucien led them swiftly and quietly from their rooms, and they floated down to the tower's nine-sided foyer before slipping out into the frozen night. Lucien mourned the tower's warmth at once but knew the time was right. The Mighty Nein would need time to recuperate and rest, and Lucien might not get another prime opportunity to abscond with the crest.

"Can I whack this in there?" asked Zoran, patting the glowing threshold crest strapped to his back and then the magical bag on Lucien's hip.

"No," Lucien muttered. Zoran glared. He had to remind himself that he was still dealing with his compatriots, but it was becoming easier to slip into every character required of him—the unflinching leader for the Tombtakers, the bearer of tremendous power as Nonagon, and an unflappable rogue for the Mighty Nein. "We should not put them in one place. The Mighty Nein will notice the theft, and they will come for what was stolen."

"Let 'em," barked Otis. Tyffial grunted in agreement. They lagged behind Lucien, who raced up the hillside to the northwest, sent by a determination hotter than any mage's tower hearth could provide. "We can handle 'em, Nonagon, no problem."

He remained intensely silent. *Time, time, time. It is time.* Snow gathered in heavier clumps on his eyelashes. He lifted his feet high for every step, listening to the rhythmic *slroosh-slroosh* of the snow crunching under his boots. They were in it now. In it. There would be no stopping until they reached Aeor, for he had seen the Mighty Nein face the dragon and he did not relish the thought of testing their mettle.

I will crawl on bloodied stumps to Cognouza. If that is what it takes. If that is what is required . . .

That theory would soon be tested, for Tyffial alerted them to shapes in the darkness above, releasing a high whistle and unsheathing her longsword. "Above us! Birds! Owls! They've come for the bag!"

Each of them froze in place, ambushed, a sudden spell shimmering down around them. The eye on Lucien's chest flared to life—even without armor or weapons, he was never defenseless. Each gift offered by the

Somnovem imbued him with deadly power, and he dipped into the well of that power now, projecting a shield outward that would nullify any spell cast within its confines. Still, the Mighty Nein came, diving at them hard, magicked into massive, magnificent birds. The moment they neared Lucien's nullifying shield, an owl careened out of the sky. Fjord dipped low on another winged mount, the owl's sharp talons lashing out, tearing the threshold crest free of Zoran's back. The half-giant toppled into the snow, then shook it off, standing and yanking the maul around and into his grasp, blood spurting from where the bird had scratched. That blood now supplied the pointed end of his maul with a growing sheen of cursed sorcery.

Otis shrieked, picked up completely by one of the diving birds. They thrashed, breaking free, then dropped into a snowbank when they were found not to have the stolen magical bag. Lucien smiled. No, it was in his possession, and he would be far more difficult to capture.

Cree hesitated at his side, still shaking off a stunning spell. It was no matter, for now the Mighty Nein had been foolish enough to draw near, discovering that their magic was useless against Lucien at close range. He watched them struggle, one by one, all of them powerless as their hands waved, conjuring nothing, conjuring air.

Rage turned to bemusement as Beauregard knocked Cree aside, charged up to Lucien, and—face contorted in a snarl—unleashed a series of blows against his chest with her wrapped, callused fists. Her fists knocked the wind out of him, but he didn't crumple. He was growing ever more tired of her meddling.

"Were your beds not comfy enough?" Beau sneered.

She was a menace. Lucien roared and grabbed for her, then bent down and took her by the neck, lifting her into the air, the eyes across his body igniting like flares in the darkness. She scratched and clawed at his arms, but her strength was evaporating. Where were the snide remarks now?

The terror in her pale-blue eyes ought to be satisfying, yet . . .

Yet.

There was a flash of something on the edge of his vision—no, in his mind. Just a flicker, a nuisance, a brief instant of disgust or regret. He almost dropped her but held firm and called to the blood racing through Beauregard's veins, commanding it, drawing on it, crimson erupting from her mouth, ears, and eyes. The blood poured over his fingers and wrist, hot enough to steam in the breath-stealing cold.

"Is this really how you want this to go?" Lucien asked, and with his other hand, he withdrew a scimitar from its sheath, crosswise across his body, letting the blade score the skin of his stomach and paint the edge with his own blood, glowing tongues of magic licking up the metal.

Otis crawled to safety beside him, dropping to their knees and loading their crossbow.

Through the swirl of chaos and snow, the half-orc called to him, his voice roughened with anger. The bird he was astride banked, shying away from Lucien's range. "Now who's taking things from whom? I assume if you need the rest of this, we should all settle down and discuss what our options are as we near the end of our journey, wouldn't you agree?"

"Take the crest if you like; there's more where that came from," Lucien replied. "We'll just kill your friends and take a little more time than we anticipated."

The woman in his grasp bucked, dodging a blow as Zoran advanced with his maul, ready to finish her off. She twisted, avoiding the first hit but taking the second hard in the stomach. She convulsed, coughing up another wad of blood. The life drained from her eyes. Lucien stared at her face, caught, for an instant, by another paralyzing wave of confusion and regret.

Beau . . . Beau . . . Live, damn it, don't give up. Don't give in.

It was his own voice pleading. No . . . the aberration.

Lucien stumbled back, Beau wrenched from his hand by a shimmering white owl that burst from the starlit wash of the sky and screamed down toward him, pulling Beauregard free of his clutches. He could only assume it was the woman Yasha, for she was not among them in her usual form. That was fine, there were others to address—like the pink one and the human mage.

Lucien advanced on Caduceus and Caleb, who had been tumbled in the snow, dropping out of the sky as Lucien's nullification ended Caduceus's transformation. An annoying miasma of colorful light burst in Lucien's peripheral vision—some pitiful spell from one of the Mighty Nein meant to distract, he assumed—and he ignored it, focused on Caduceus and Caleb. Both men rose to their knees, but Lucien was upon them. He wrapped both hands firmly around Caduceus's head and squeezed. Tyffial prowled, her sword dripping blood sliced from her own tongue. She giggled, watching as blood spurted from the feygiant's wide-open eyes, dark stains spreading across his gray fur.

"It's just business, friend," Lucien growled. "My apologies, but you didn't have to follow."

The *thunk-thunk-thunk* of Otis firing sounded off behind them, perhaps a warning of the Mighty Nein re-forming. Zoran roared with each swing of his maul as he dared those still hovering in the air to come near and have a taste of his wrath. Lucien glared at Caduceus and Caleb as they attempted to scuttle away, until he felt a sharp, stabbing pain in his back—Fjord, the meddlesome half-orc, had managed to surprise him. Without turning around, Lucien lashed out with his scimitar, and as the blade struck true, a red pulse flashed. Lucien felt a vicious thrill as power roared through him, using his blood magic to brand the man's chest.

Lucien had no time to revel in it, his attention drawn away as Zoran stepped in to take his place and deal with the half-orc. That would keep Fjord busy. He risked closing his eyes, just briefly, taking a deep breath. Cognouza had been delayed for too long. It was time to end this.

Sneering, he advanced swiftly on Caleb, who was in the middle of conjuring up what promised to be a powerful spell, and brought his scimitars down across the man's neck . . . but the blades flashed right through him, and the image of Caleb disappeared. Maddening.

His forehead tightened, burning with pain, as if something in there was scratching to get out. It calmed as soon as Caleb turned out to be little more than a clever mirage. He shook off the distraction, alarmed by another wave of chaos from the battlefield. Behind him, he could hear the distant shouts of the Tombtakers and the panicked yells of the Mighty Nein, the explosion of spells and sizzle of countering spells being cast once, twice, thrice—but Lucien could only fixate on his own fury, roiling under his skin, and the odd sensation of giddiness and delight from the Somnovem as he turned to glare at those who would try to stop him.

Lucien stalked back into the fray, blood dripping from his blades and wrath ready on his tongue, but before he could enact his justice, he heard a shout and the beating of wings.

"Look out! It's back!" shrieked Tyffial, reeling and retreating to where Cree stood, the blood healer doing her best to protect the Tombtakers with healing wards. "Shit! Shit! Shit!"

He looked beyond where the Mighty Nein were mustering to where the white dragon Gelidon reappeared. She had waited until her enemies were locked in battle to return, swooping past the many creatures the

Mighty Nein had transformed into in their haste to escape, and landing in the bloodied space where Caleb and Caduceus had just been, spreading her wings and splitting the night air with a hideous shriek. Lucien staggered back and huddled with the Tombtakers, covering his ears against the deafening roar. The Mighty Nein scrambled to capitalize on the chaos, fleeing, one of them transforming into a galloping mammoth mid-run, ferrying the others away.

"Otis! Fire! Otis! They're getting away with the crest!" Lucien shouted, and the halfling struggled to reload, hyperventilating, packing the crossbow with a bolt and sending it after the mammoth.

Lucien steeled himself, eye tattoos pulsing, and drew his black scimitars once more, darting forward to protect the others, slicing at the dragon's right foreleg. His blades cut straight through, finding nothing, passing through thin air. *Just like the fucking mage.*

The Mighty Nein were gone, vanishing into the night. The half-orc had been out of range of his nullification, conjuring a perfect mirror image of Gelidon to distract them. Lucien tossed his scimitars pointsdown into the snow, enraged. Cree stumbled over to join the rest of the Tombtakers, the warmth of her healing spells shimmering across his stomach, closing the wound there.

"After them," Lucien whispered.

"Can we not rest a moment?" Tyffial sighed, sheathing her sword.

"No," said Lucien testily. "We cannot."

They marched, Cree mending their wounds silently, Zoran lightened now that the Mighty Nein had stolen his hefty pack, which carried their threshold crest, several magical intuit charges, and a good portion of their camping equipment and supplies. Lucien charged ahead, quickly doing the math, realizing they would have just enough food to reach the great depths of Aeor, but nothing for a return trip.

There will be no return. Only Cognouza. Only the dreams of my dreams.

The Mighty Nein's trail was not tricky to follow. As he trudged, the vista of mountains and ice before him dropped away. A darkness thicker than night enveloped him. He slowed his steps but did not stop, watching as the nine philosophers encircled him. The Somnovem. They wore their gray embroidered hoods, their faces cast in shadow but still noticeably shifting in unnatural ways. It took a beat for his mind to conjure faces for each of them, human masks obscuring their true, hideous, shapeless nature.

He didn't care if the Tombtakers were within earshot.

Lucien raged.

"How good of you to visit," he sneered, spitting. "Want to apprise me of any further mischief? Very clever, using Otis to circumvent talking to me. They've a malleable enough lump of dough in their skull. Everything was under control, you meddlesome fools, until you sought to undermine me! Have I done something to deserve this? Have I not dedicated every sinew of my being to the task?"

Froth gathered at the corners of his mouth.

Under her hood, Mirumus's narrow chin warped as she grinned. Their faces were becoming more human, more settled, but the familiarity did nothing to assuage Lucien's anger. "You've been ignoring our advice, and I thought it a lovely surprise."

"You have not sacrificed everything," Luctus told him softly. Her face was shiny with tears. "There is more yet to give."

"To the work," they all said in unison. "To the work. The work continues."

"You question our methods?" Fastidan asked. He had a golden beard shot through with gray and stood taller than the others. "You question us?"

Luctus burst into tears, covering her face.

"Look what you've done." Culpasi gasped, pointing to Luctus as she shook in her grief, her long black hair cascading over her hands. She wiped at her face with the lank strands. "Luctus, Luctus, the work will continue!"

"We await you in Cognouza!" cried Elatis, shaking with excitement. Her very white teeth stood out from the darkness. They began to talk over one another, desperate to be heard. Some chastised him, others heaped praise.

"Cry not, Luctus, cry not, our ascension is at hand!"

"Two years wasted! We are eager for progress. GIVE IT TO US."

"Who are you to question our methods?"

Lucien clutched his head, the sound rising and rising, a maddening cacophony, pain dancing across the top of his skull as he dropped into the snow on his knees. When the torture became too great, he screamed, tearing his hands away. "You're mewling children screaming in the dark! What are you without me? Without the Nonagon? Lost! That's what you are! Crawling infants crying for your mother! A voice without a mouth!"

His shrieks echoed across the mountains to the east, bouncing back to mock him. The Somnovem were gone, leaving him alone with a blistering headache in the cold.

"Hello?" he called, quiet and searching. "H-Hello?"

Nobody answered.

Until.*

---

* *Looks like it's going well, boss. Crushing it.*

Lucien slapped the side of his head, hard. "Begone, flea, gnat, fly, begone!"

Oh, but you're such pleasant company just now! And all alone, too. Don't you want company?

"How did they tolerate you, I wonder, let alone mourn your death," Lucien snarled, climbing to his feet and brushing off his trousers. The Tombtakers were slowly gaining, and Lucien continued, following the trail of mammoth prints stamped into the trodden ice. A thin trickle of blood ran alongside the tracks. "They should have thrown a party; what a relief it will be, to be rid of you for good."

He ignored the throb in his head and the fatigue in his legs, brushing the purple hair out of his face with soiled fingers.

Wash the blood of my friends off your hands, you degenerate freak.

"They didn't have to follow."

Does it ever get old? Lying to yourself like this?

"Cognouza is not a lie," Lucien replied fiercely. Either his eyes were deceiving him, or they were closing in on the Mighty Nein. Shapes, figures, moved along the horizon. "Even your friends have seen the visions of it—a world of dreams was promised, and that's what I've earned."

Killing for a dream—are you too dense to see the irony?

Lucien shook his head. "Giving everything for a dream that you can hold is the only way to go on. You would know that if you had lived the life I did. You have the luxury of amnesia, I do not."

So tell me, then. Help me understand.

"Not interested," he replied, sniffling through the cold. "Waste of time. I nearly killed your friends. Any chance at an understanding has passed."

Otis betrayed them, not you.

"A distinction without a difference." He laughed and hitched his pack higher, picking up the pace. "Even you can't stand me, mm? So where does that leave the others?"

That's not how we are, Lucien. We love broken things the most.

"Maybe you do," Lucien growled. "But I've picked up the pieces long enough. The dream of Cognouza will make all things whole again, starting with me."

You're a wounded soul, Lucien. Fractured. Any world you create will bear those scars, too.

"Well then, if that be true, let the world hurt as I hurt." In his mind, he saw the cozy crooked house in Shadycreek Run, all the windows going dark in the haze of a sunset's gloom.

Another finds us, finds their way home!

Welcome.

          Welcome.

                    Welcome.

We dream with you. Dreams are the first step!
  We can make dreams into anything. Into everything.

                    Together.

CHAPTER 35

Lucien held his breath, sliding the knife's edge along the base of the hexagonal device, wiggling until he felt a crisp, satisfying click. The intuit charge came free once he rotated it slightly, guiding it out of the grooves in the storage container. At last, he exhaled and wrapped the dormant bomb in a scrap of leather, placing it inside the magical, endless bag they'd stolen.

"That's the last of them," Lucien called, stepping away from the shelves stacked neatly in the cavernous storage vault. It was no easy feat, finding intact intuit charges in the ruins. Most had detonated during the cataclysm, when Aeor plunged from the sky and hit the ice wastes of Foren. They had their supply of charges, and the threshold crest, the true prize, beckoned. The Mighty Nein may have escaped with their original crest, but Lucien didn't need them, and so the Tombtakers had forged onward, deeper into Aeor and toward Cognouza.

Zoran, his burden stolen, now carried Otis's pack, and the two of them appeared in the archway leading from the vault to the Anylon Ring.

"Another one here," said Otis, holding up a clean, untripped charge. They had picked clean the outer halls along the edge of the Praesidis Ward, but soon they would have to venture deeper. Their goal lay within the farthest, most dangerous reaches of the city, and it would take days yet to reach the Immensus Gate.

Lucien joined them in the doorway, brushing a layer of dust from his coat.

"Our luck is changing, then," Lucien said, grinning.

"Aye, time for a celebration." Otis followed Zoran out into the Anylon Ring, digging in the half-giant's pack as they went. They fished out a piece of leathery jerky and tried to bite off a chunk. Tyffial appeared from the shadows and slapped the jerky out of their hand, taking her own ravenous bite.

"That might as well be precious gold," she growled. Her cheeks had gotten hollower, though all of them were sallow with hunger.

"You've already had your share today!" Otis snatched the bit of food back, holding it protectively against their chest. "You can pry this from my cold, dead hands."

"Maybe I will!" Tyffial lunged for the halfling, wrestling the jerky out of their grasp again and snapping off more for herself. "I'm twice your size, Otis, you'll manage."

Lucien stepped between them before the halfling could fetch out their crossbow. He held out his hand, palm-up, and stared until the elf sighed and smacked the jerky down in his waiting grasp. Her eyes were bloodshot, and clumps of her black hair had started to fall out.

"Just a few more days," Lucien promised her. "We're nearly there."

"How many days? How many?" she rasped.

"Go if you like, but you'll find nothing but misfortune," Lucien replied, calmly stowing the food back in Zoran's pack. "The Mighty Nein are here somewhere and hunting us."

Tyffial snarled, scrunching her nose. "Truly? They're here? Revenge—"

"Is not our priority," Lucien reminded her. He was exhausted. It was like corralling feral hogs—sleep deprivation and lack of sustenance had turned them into dim-witted little demons, squabbling over everything and anything. "And yes, they are here. I can feel them poking around, scrying. We deal with them if and when they intervene, but our interests lie elsewhere. We have put off Cognouza for too long." He squeezed her lightly on the shoulder through her leather armor. Her metal cuirass was scratched and stained, badly in need of polishing. "You will want for nothing where we are going."

"By the by, boss, you never did say how long," Otis grumbled, glaring as Lucien detached from them and began leading them down the vaulted, round Anylon Ring. They had dug their way in at the southern edge of the corridor, working from Vess DeRogna's additional notes and maps in the journal.

"If we press north from here, through that passage," Lucien explained, pointing and consulting only from memory, for he had burned the images of the journal and the maps into his mind, "it should take us less than a day to cross the Praesidis Ward, another long day to traverse the Genesis Ward, and a half day's journey from there to reach our final goal."

Otis nodded vigorously and rubbed at the deep-purple smudges beneath their eyes, invigorated by the specificity. "And the Immensus Gate. Do you suppose it will be grand?"

"It's machinery of the ancients," Lucien said with a laugh. "It is sure to impress."

Cree appeared in the tall, blue, metallic archway that led to the Praesidis Ward, having scouted ahead for any signs of scavengers, ruin-dwellers, or the Mighty Nein. Otis and Zoran began to discuss which of them would get to trigger the intuit charges, the target of which they had not been told, though the mere idea of exploding the bombs filled them with giddy excitement. Lucien let them wind each other up, his gaze fixed on Cree. What he had not told them—could not tell them—was that the Somnovem had gone silent in his mind. They were punishing him for his outburst, and perhaps for his insolence.

The silence, at first disorienting and terrible, had ultimately given him time to think. Much-needed time. Plans were in motion, amorphous but increasingly distinct, though he dare not think a whole thought, convinced that the Somnovem had not abandoned him and still lurked, waiting to pounce on his next impertinent thought.

WHEN THEY REACHED CREE AND the archway to the next ward, Lucien slowed, letting Otis, Tyffial, and Zoran go ahead. He observed them carefully, for though he could control them through the eyes if necessary, he preferred their loyalty to the cause. Rather, to him.

"What took you so long?" Lucien asked her in an undertone as they meandered at the back of the pack.

Cree drew back the hood on her deep-red cloak, jangling the gold rings in her ears, and scrubbed her face with her hands. She was tired, too, but concealed it better than the others.

"There are Dynasty trackers prowling, but I've got their scent. They'll likely ambush us the moment we step foot in the ward," Cree reported. "Did you find the charges?"

"We did. How far did you push into the ward?" he asked.

"Far enough to scout a good position to defend against the Kryn trackers and any mischief they have planned."

The eye on the palm of his right hand burned, and he grimaced, not from the discomfort but from what it suggested. "You're keeping something from me, Cree."

"Nonagon . . ."

"You should know by now that lying to me isn't a wise choice. It's not even a choice, really. I see all. Have I not protected you? Have I not led you to the very precipice of greatness?"

She nodded, then glanced over her shoulder, jumpy. "I . . . saw something."

"What?" he rasped.

"Last we camped, I dreamed, or at least I think I did, and the Somnovem showed me something, only . . . I don't know how to interpret it." Her golden eyes widened. "The others," she murmured. "The others were dead. Otis, Tyffial, Zoran . . . they were torn to pieces by birds with red eyes."

She was shaking so badly that Lucien reached for her, placing his hand firmly on her shoulder until she stilled.

"We're all going to die in here, aren't we?"

"No," Lucien told her. "But the cost will be terrible, Cree."

She tried to wrench away from him.

"Wait. *Wait*. Cree? Listen to me, Cree. I need you to listen." Lucien took her by the shoulders once more and pulled her until he could gaze down into her face. "They're only showing you what you already know."

Tears gathered in her eyes, but she quickly blinked them away. "You and me . . ."

"Yes," Lucien prompted. "Yes, you and me. It's always been you and me." He let go of her shoulder and brushed the amulet around her neck, the little vial holding his blood. "It's always been you and me, Cree, and it always will be."

"I think I understand," she whispered. Then she flinched and finally jerked free of his grasp.

"There's more," he said.

"I found the secret entrance like you asked, and scouted it, the one Vess showed us." She hesitated.

"And?"

Cree closed her eyes and blasted out a heaving sigh. "I went to check on her, all right? I wanted to see if . . . if she was still there."

Lucien grimaced. "We're not to speak of her, I made that clear."

"And I disobeyed you," Cree hissed, eyes flashing. "I backtracked and searched, and I found her. She's still there. Scavengers have . . . but you know, most of her is still there. This horrid cold slows everything down and so there was, well, more of her than I expected."

"That's enough."

"I pulled the blanket back a little and sat and held her hand," Cree charged on. "It was so, so cold."

He glanced away, a surge of anger passing through his clenched fists. "I said that's enough . . ."

"I can't know for certain, but I felt like she was happy that we were close, that we had come back, and that she wasn't alone in the ice anymore—"

Lucien silenced her through the eyes, taking control, Cree's mouth hanging open, tense, as she tried to fight it off. They walked like that for a while, and Lucien told himself it was Cree who had shattered a promise, not him.

"You won't speak of her again," he muttered, and that was that.

LUCIEN PLACED HIS BOOT SQUARELY on the dark elf's chest and withdrew his scimitar, then let the body slump to the floor. He crouched over the corpse and paused to admire the man's curious armor with the thick, chitinous plates emblematic of the dark elven Kryn Dynasty. The Dynasty trackers had done, ostensibly, what they did best: track. The ambush, however, was clumsy. Trackers tracked, but Tombtakers killed.

"Those bastards are traveling with the Kryn now?" Zoran muttered, looming over Lucien's right shoulder. Zoran had sustained a few wounds in the skirmish, and casually broke off an arrow that had been stuck in his shoulder. While he and Lucien glared down at the dead, Cree finished seeing to her own bandages and turned her attention to Zoran's injuries.

"They travel in motley circles." Lucien sighed.

Zoran spat on the insect-like armor encasing the Kryn soldier.

"Then they'll die in motley circles, too."

"You reckon there are more patrols looking for us in the ruins?" asked Otis, joining them. He had escaped the battle with no visible abrasions. The Kryn, with their little daggers and bows, were no match for the dark and deep magic fueling Lucien, running through them all, a thread of zealous power that the tracker could neither anticipate nor defend against. Lucien had barely registered the looks of horror on their faces, just visible behind the thick black caps on their heads, as he enshrined the Tombtakers within his nullification field and all the red eyes marked into their skin shined bright with shared purpose.

"It's always best to move with caution here," Lucien replied, standing. He wiped off his blades and shoved them back in their sheaths. "Aeor is full of surprises."

THE CORRIDOR SNAKING DEEPER INTO the Praesidis Ward dipped downward, sloping, leading them toward a blast in a foundational wall. Through the crack, they discovered a darkened pit, with a room visible above. Blue lanterns glowed up the walls of that upper reach, thick metal plates bolted to the walls sending eerie reflections and dancing lights across the chamber. The way ahead was dark, well below the glimmer of the lanterns and metal, but Lucien's red marks flared to life, guiding him toward the edge of the dank, frozen pit.

"There," he said, nodding toward a steep tumble of debris and dirt that led up to the metallic chamber on the other side of the pit. "We're going the right way now. If DeRogna's sketches are correct, and thus far they have been, then we're just north of Central Deliberations. I'm afraid we'll need to climb down."

"Why not that way?" growled Zoran. The road they had been on blasted through to the other side of the pit, disappearing into a completely black cavern.

"The halls of the ward will give us a direct path," he explained. "You're hungry and tired, aye? Think of this as a shortcut."

"And then we rest?" Tyffial asked, a flicker of light coming to her eyes.

He nodded. "There should be a defensible rotunda just outside Deliberations."

"Nonagon," Cree said suddenly, darting out ahead of them and holding out her hands. "Let me go first."

"Would you bloody hurry it up?" Otis sighed, impatient. "I want off my bloody feet. Boots are pinching something fierce . . ."

Lucien was silent, watching Cree's golden eyes fill with panic.

"Just one sweep—"

"Fuck that." Zoran pushed past her, Otis trotting alongside the bald half-giant. Tyffial followed, asking Zoran if he could sing something rousing for them all. Cree hung back to pin Lucien with a pleading look while Zoran secured the lines that would take them down into the collapsed area. He sang as he worked.

"You were to scout ahead," he told her coldly.

"And I did! Only swiftly, you know, and aye, I may have detoured, but—"

"This is why you must follow my instructions to the letter," Lucien sneered.

"I do." Cree shrank. "I will."

Zoran's hammer clanged as he anchored the last of the leads into the stone at the edge of the precipice. There were only three ropes to take, and Lucien gestured flippantly, letting Otis, Tyffial, and Zoran swing out and begin the descent. Lucien waited for his chance to take up the rope, but Cree took his elbow, leading him back into the shadows.

"I'm sorry," Cree said. "I'll do better."

"You know what we've come to do, Cree. We're so close."

"You've never led me astray before," she added with a frantic nod. "The glint, I've followed it—followed you—and I've no regrets."

"Good," Lucien said, softening. "I'm . . . that's good to hear."

The warning came, but too late. Timorei's high, quavering voice shot through Lucien's mind with only a single word: Death.

Zoran, Tyffial, and Otis were halfway down the ropes when the attack came. The slick black stone of the pit lit up with a flash, a warning, then an instant later a strangled cry came from where Zoran dangled. He froze, his mouth twisting into a grimace of pain as some magic sheared across his mind, tearing him easily from the ropes, flinging the half-giant like a ragdoll into the glistening pit below. Something was hidden in the dark, a trap, a bomb, some deadly device rigged to destroy them. Destroy his plans. Tyffial shrieked, calling out, a strangled cry of confusion ripped from her throat before she too flew like cannon-shot from the smooth surface of the descent wall. Otis followed her, both of them hurtling end over end, plunging with shocking speed to the unforgiving stone.

Lucien had exactly an instant to react, and he shouted for Cree, yanking her into the sheltered path back the way they had come, away from the trapped pit. The magic that assailed them thundered through their skulls like the booming, mocking laughter of some unseen villain, and though Lucien heard it, he did not feel the pain that ripped through the minds of the others. Even now, the Somnovem protected him. The pain brought Cree straight to her knees and Lucien dropped with her. As Cree grabbed her ears against the mind-splitting roar of the psychic assault, Lucien realized that the attack came from their own equipment—the intuit charges stolen by the Mighty Nein. The charges he had his own plans for.

When the noise had calmed, Lucien stumbled to the edge of the pit. He saw the empty ropes. He saw the oddly still and eerie pit, and his friends, mangled, bleeding, and stunned.

They were dying.

Slowly, they began to move, a chorus of moaning and whimpering rising from the three Tombtakers prone on the ground. Tyffial held her side, blood pouring from a gash where she had fallen on a jagged spike of stone. Blood trickled from her pointed ears. Her legs were stiff, useless. She couldn't move. Trapped by pain. Trapped like . . .

No, no, no.

This is all so pointless and unfair, and it shouldn't be you. It shouldn't be you. I'm sorry.

Cree yanked on his coat sleeve. "It was a trap, Nonagon. We can't linger, we need to keep moving . . ."

But he was frozen, staring.

We could have warned you. Timorei, the bastard. *We could have saved them. Who is the helpless child now?*

A tiny shower of pebbles rained down from the cracked open room across the carnage, shadows popping up along the metallic blue glow of the walls.

The Mighty Nein had come.

CHAPTER 36

Lucien stared long and hard at Cree as they descended the ropes. It was all coming undone.

It couldn't. He wouldn't allow this. One way or another, he had to unfuck it.

It was always going to be us, he thought, telling himself to forget the look on Cree's face, forget it *now,* telling himself that any pain was bearable if the reward was great enough. He couldn't blame this hopeless implosion of thoughts on the Somnovem. His mind was breaking.

Maybe it was already gone.

And if it was gone, maybe that was for the best.

He let Cree's face slip his mind. *Let it all go,* he thought, and then: *You can bring them back when this world is remade.*

First, unfuck it.

"Well." Lucien sighed, breathing with someone else's breath, a breezier man, a soul in another man's body. He had been acting all his life, hadn't he? This was no different. After all, he was the Nonagon, and Lucien no longer. He swaggered over to his fallen Tombtakers, writhing on the stone floor; there was nothing immediate that he could do for them. *Let it all go.* "That's a real dickish thing to do."

The crimson eye on Lucien's chest flickered, the air in front of him warping from the magical nullification field. Not even a precaution, a necessity, as a blast of arcane energy ricocheted away. The Mighty Nein and an elf he did not recognize mustered in a half circle on the other side of the cracked rotunda. Lucien knelt and with a grunt of effort dislodged Tyffial's bag beneath her useless leg, then he found Zoran's pack. With his right foot, he shoved Tyffial's pack toward Cree. They were outdone, ambushed, and the only solution was to take what they could salvage and press on without the others.

It all had to go. Every emotion. Every inopportune thought.

Otis, Tyffial, and Zoran were lost, he knew it, but Cree had been trying to yank Otis to his feet, even as the halfling lay dazed and convulsing, unconscious. His hand was frozen, locked in a position that reached for Cree, three fingers on his right hand bent in the wrong direction from the high fall.

Beauregard leapt into the air above them, blue robes swirling, a device flung from her hand detonating over their heads. Dazzling motes of light skittered across the pit, floating like lightning bugs in the summer dusk. As Beau descended, Jester sent another bolt of energy at them, catching Lucien in the chest. He staggered back, bag drooping from his hand. Whatever Beau had discharged gave away their position, allowing Jester the lucky shot.

It was always Beau. Always. Grating, arrogant, smirking.

Let it all go. Even revenge. Even against her.

As he recovered and shifted toward Cree and she toward him, the half-orc grabbed the hat on his head and blasted forward, spurred by magic, gaining his feet, and letting loose a barbaric shout as he unsheathed his longsword, the blade swooping back and up over his head. He plunged the weapon down into Zoran's neck. The half-giant's torso jerked, then fell still.

Let it all go.

"This really fucks up my plans a bit." Lucien grunted, heaving the bag onto his shoulder and sidestepping Otis. He glanced toward the tunnel blasted through the pit, the one Zoran had mentioned earlier. "But well played. I cannot lie, well played. Cree, take care of this."

Cree spun, swirling her dark-red cape over herself and Lucien, concealing them both. There were shouts of confusion and outrage as they huddled beneath the fabric, the magic within its weave buzzing, snapping to life.

"Yes." Lucien sighed from beneath the cloak. "I guess there's only one thing left to do."

They vanished. Not far. Cree trembled as the cloak transported them, exhausting the power within the fabric and leaving them not half a mile down the passage punched through Central Deliberations. Lucien pulled her along, heedless of her bloodied, mangled shoulder. She winced with every step, holding the immensely heavy pack over her left shoulder, limping, leaning hard against Lucien for support.

A light appeared at the end of the passage, and he dragged her toward it, then whirled and stuck his hand into the magic bag, swiftly producing an intuit charge.

"Nonagon, wait—"

But he set the charge, clicking the two halves of the device in opposite directions. There was a telling whir from within, and then he rolled the bomb down the shaft, a cloud of dust and rock spewing as the charge blew and they barely managed to lunge to safety.

Lucien coughed and wiped the dust from his eyes, crawling to where Cree had fallen onto her side. His hands shook with rage. He couldn't let them know, couldn't let them see . . .

He froze, all Nine Eyes marked upon him crackling. Through the network they provided, he searched for the irritating brawler, Beauregard, and the mage, Caleb. He could reach their minds and speak to them through the eyes, and so he did, calming himself long enough to say:

"I'm not going to lie, that was inspired, well thought out. More than I expected." He took a deep, centering breath and rolled onto his back, glaring up at the ceiling. "You're brave. But you've also shown to be more of a thorn in my side than I ever gave you credit for. That's not going to fly. But I'm excited for you to see my handiwork soon enough." The passage behind them rumbled again, a secondary collapse triggering in the tunnel. There was no way the Mighty Nein couldn't hear it. "Just putting a bit of space between us. You understand. I've got important work to do. But please, come along. Hate for no one to see the product of our hard work."

The work continues.

The work, the work, the work.

In the constellation of minds visible through the Eyes of Nine, Lucien watched two more blink out of existence. He, Cree, and the two members of the Mighty Nein continued to pulse softly in that network. The rest?

He shook his head. "Gone."

"They'll take their heads," Cree spat. "Like they took DeRogna's."

"Let them."

"*Let them?*" Cree struggled to her knees, gaping at him. "You cannot be serious."

Lucien shut his eyes briefly, then swallowed.

"You were with me when we outsmarted The Red Debt, and you were with me when we joined the Orders, when we slayed the witch, and when we breached Aeor. All those jobs, all those times we might have died or given up, but we've kept strong. Together. We've always known, haven't we? We've always known it would be like this," he murmured. His lower lip quivered. In truth, he thought the power of their purpose would render them all invincible.

"Like my vision," she murmured.

"Yes, like your vision. I wanted to protect you from the pain of that truth, and the Somnovem . . . I'm not sure it was wise for them to tell you," Lucien told her, watching her golden eyes soften. "I'm beginning to see it clearly: The others were always destined to take us this far and only this far. They gave themselves to the mission. They brought us to Cognouza."

"Then we can't fail them," she whispered. A tear streaked down her black fur, and Lucien wiped it away. She clutched his hand. "I miss them already."

"Aye, me too," he lied. It was a relief to be free of the complaining, the doubt, the voices he did not want to shepherd and control but must. "But the work continues."

"I could have scouted that room," said Cree, wilting. "I could have saved them."

"Through mine eyes I saw their fate," he insisted, gathering himself, gathering the cumbersome bag Zoran had carried. "I see ours, too, and it does not end in this chamber."

"No," Cree said slowly. She stood, too, and passed a healing spell across her shoulder, the flesh knitting, pink and bright until fur darkened it. "No, the work continues. You and me."

"You and me."

The work continued.

From the passage blown through Central Deliberations, they swung north, climbing, slowly, a pyramid of broken stones that carried them to a higher level of the Aeorian compound. The Genesis Ward had risen like a shining blue boil from the flesh of the earth, shoved up and out of the lower wreck of the city. The climb was hard, harder burdened by the possessions of the others. Food, at least, they had. Cree stopped frequently to eat, and Lucien let her have as much as she desired. He no longer had need of water or food or sleep, aware of a growing hollowness within. The hunger didn't feel like gnawing and burbling, but heat, as if some unseen alchemy transformed him gradually from the inside out.

At the highest point of the ward, where the metallic silver and blue walls had been split cleanly, as if by a cleaver from the gods, they discovered a sheer drop into a crater below.

"Find the ropes," he told her. "That's our destination."

Lucien stood surveying the terrain below while Cree fussed with the spelunking ropes. A presence joined him at the lip of the Genesis Ward, where the world fell away, and the city collapsed in again on itself. He turned slightly, though knew what he would find.

Gaudius. The hood of his gray robe was pushed back, revealing close-cropped black hair with fractal designs shaved into the sides and back. Lucien had assigned him a welcoming face, ever plastered with a smile, bright-hazel eyes, and a formidable nose all set against lustrous black skin. Lucien did not know whether to be heartened or dismayed that the figures of the philosophers no longer seemed to bleed beyond their edges, solidified now in his waking visions the closer he got to his goal. At least seeing them this clearly made it easier to imagine besting them, one by one. By far the most inviting of the Somnovem, Gaudius rocked back and forth on his heels like a child, drumming his fingers together as he joined Lucien in observing their destination.

"The records you will find below detail our expulsion from 'polite' society, whatever that means," Gaudius told him. He giggled. "The weak will always fear the strong. The Nine were destined to make Aeor a place of eternal life and glory, enemy to suffering, enemy to death. For our vision, for our creativity, we were banished, locked away in Cognouza, kept from our loved ones, prisoners in our own home."

Lucien felt no pity for him or the others. "We all make sacrifices."

Gaudius made a soft sound of agreement. "Mm. The lock will break. The will of the Somnovem cannot be contained by a prison or by time."

"Indeed, well, soon that will all change, the will of the Somnovem unleashed."

Gaudius clapped his hands, twirling.

My will, you insouciant fool, mine.

"The ropes are ready," said Cree. Gaudius vanished.

"Good," Lucien replied coolly. He took one of the orange crystals from within the Mighty Nein's bag and dropped it, watching the light cascade down into the yawning void below. At last, it bounced, twinkling gently, marking the floor. "That's the last of the Genesis Ward there," he said, pointing. "According to the lost mage's notes, the Immensus Gate cannot be repaired without parts from the Repair Terminal."

Lucien lashed Zoran's heavy pack to his back and swung out over the rope, watching Cree slide away, vanishing into the swallowing darkness beneath them.*

---

* *Shit, you're cold. Your friends are dead, you could at least pause to mourn them.*

Lucien grunted, reaching the bottom of the rope, bathed in the orange glow of the amber crystal at his feet. It was the coldest place he had been in the ruins. A sheen of frost glittered across the stone floor. Cree wandered ahead, gazing up at a series of increasingly taller arches looming over the path forward. "Cold? I'm not the one cutting people's heads off and carrying them around in bags."

You could at least treat the one friend you have left a bit better. You could stop lying to yourself and her.

"Cree is not a friend; she's a vessel, as am I." Lucien pushed the hair out of his face, jaw set, teeth clenched. There was something just on the other side of the heat that had been gathering in him steadily for days, an exhaustion so immense, so overwhelming, that it would destroy him if he paused to even consider it. His skin was just skin, the pressure crushing against it devastating, a paper roof holding out a torrential storm.

"Can't you see?" he growled. "It's all that remains! THIS IS ALL I HAVE." The eyes on his body lit up. "Fuck! Just! Leave me in peace, you wretched prick."

There was only a momentary reprieve. He sensed the voice hovering. Waiting. He dared not give it a name. Names had power.

Whoever convinced you that you're too pretty to fail should do us all a favor and drop dead.

"Well, you'll be pleased to know that wish was granted years ago."

You don't dream of her anymore.

"No, I only dream of them now."

Oof. Downgrade.

Lucien snorted, then hated himself for it. "She was beautiful, wasn't she?"

Thought we weren't allowed to talk about her or think about her.

"We're not, you just never shut up in general, about anything. You're always trying to trick me, it's exhausting, arguing with my own bloody mind."

No sooner had they begun to push into the flooded levels of the broken Genesis Ward than he felt the Mighty Nein scrying on them again, the relentless ants, this time through Cree. She informed him at once, and he brushed it off.

He waited some hours, until Beauregard and Caleb slept. When he was certain they could be reached through the eyes and their dreams, he found them, a purring voice in the repeating labyrinths of their dreams.

"Your friends are peeking. You are wily bastards, continuing to stick in my sides like a thorn in my drawers. Clever, but not enough that I have to respect it. I'm not here to kill you. Yet. I'm here to open a door, to take my reign. Long may it be. You're welcome to watch, if you can keep up. There's so much beyond this door. So much . . ."

Fair. In my defense, I was a Circus Man, tricks are sort of the whole thing. You know, you could go to her, the friend you lost, maybe sit with her for a while. It might bring you back to us.

Lucien shook his head. "No. I told you: I don't want to come back to *us*. There's nothing left." In the darkness, his nine red eyes glowed brilliantly. "This is all I am now, who I am. If anything, I'm bringing your friends—that surly brawler and the mage—on a journey with me. If there's to be an us, let it be that one."

CHAPTER 37

They worked in silence, Cree twisting a silver orb chased with gold into place on the left rigged post. Orange and blue light—hanging lamps and scattered amber crystals—suffused the chamber with a warm-to-cold gradient. Lucien trapped his tongue between his teeth, straining, using a pair of iron tongs from their pack to replace a blown spring on the right post.

There was a peace and a symmetry to it that momentarily calmed Lucien's thoughts.

The Immensus Gate hummed with intriguing power, a vibration that increased as each worn and lost part on the gate was replaced. The gate stood on a raised plinth still damp and pocked with puddles. When they had arrived, the entire chamber had been flooded, the gate attuned to a realm of endless ocean. Once they reached the second half of the Genesis Ward, submerged but not destroyed, they made their way to the Repair Terminal, recovering the focus rods and replacement parts for the gate mentioned by the journal. They also made a brief stop in the adjoining archives and records room, where they located a more complete map of the city and, more important, a route that showed the once bustling avenue that bisected all of Aeor. The Cognouza Ward had once been joined to this main artery, but after the Somnovem proved too unstable and powerful to control, the Immensus Gate was erected to cut off access, trapping the Somnovem and hundreds of citizens inside.

For over a thousand years, the prison had held. Lucien replaced another spring, listening to the hum of the gate intensify.

"You're quiet today," Cree said, glancing at him across the arched opening of the gate. A sizzling crack ran horizontally across the ten-foot-wide ring of the gate. A constant trickle of steam and water emerged from the seam. "The calm before the storm?"

"Aye. Something like that."

"Do you remember that fiend we fought outside Berleben? Gods, but that thing had a stench. I thought it was going to feast on my entrails, and Brevyn couldn't get a clear shot, then you found us and got it to chase you just long enough for me to cast and bind it," she said, laughing, and wiped at her brow. "I think that was the day Brev fell for you."

He tried to access the memory, but all he could conjure were the blurry faces of a younger Cree and Brevyn, one on each side of him, haloed in the luminous shine of an enchanted swamp, a few scraggly trees behind offering shade. "Bloody good timing!" Cree had shrieked, and she and Brevyn kissed him on the face. His cheeks burned where the kisses had landed.

"Hmm," he murmured, distracted. "I remember it differently."

"But now it's just the two of us," she added quietly, almost to herself. The glow and buzz of the gate swelled again. "Just like how it started. You know, I thought you were mad when you agreed to go with Brevyn to the valley and hunt monsters. The Orders will never take us, I said. But they did, and they taught us, and now we're here."

Lucien shrugged absently. "Few more steps in between, but sure."

"You don't think it's incredible?"

"I think it's inevitable."

Cree finished screwing a runed compartment into the left post where the circular portion of the gate was its widest, then she stepped back, not to admire her work, but to look at him. After a moment, she said thoughtfully, "You said you saw the fate of the others . . . does that mean it's me and you together at the end? Is this how you saw it in your visions?"

"It is all how I saw it," Lucien assured her. "This is what the Somnovem promised: you and me standing at the end."

"Just like with Azrahari," she said wryly. "And all because of your glint."

He paused, and as expected, Cree knew what he would ask.

"It's gone, by the way. I don't see it upon you anymore." She sounded neither happy nor sad, and expressed it as simple fact.

Lucien frowned. "I'm the Nonagon. I've no need for luck now."

"I would have followed you anyway, Lu—Nonagon. Glint or no glint."

"It's you and me, Cree. It's always been you and me and it always will be."

Cree said nothing, though he swore he saw a resigned smile tugging at her lips. Then she turned back to the packs strewn across the sodden stone floor. A small, broken crystal had tumbled free of the Mighty Nein's bag. Lucien gathered it before Cree could shove it back in the satchel. He held it up and watched it turn her into six different versions, rainbows slicing through the middle, making her a lovely prism. That was all wrong; there was only one Cree, the steadfast one. He slipped the crystal into his pocket while Cree rummaged, gathering two intuit charges and cradling them in her left arm. They had found a slew of the charges in a semi-sealed equipment room outside of the gate, and then had to fight off a feline creature with many eyes and razor-sharp teeth to collect those charges. Both of them had been injured in the scrap, and Cree had been too weak to fully mend them. Lucien's forearm still burned where the beast had raked its claws across his coat.

"I'm going to set more charges," she said, wandering off. "Just in case."

"Not a bad idea, I sense our friends nearing; they're likely to come by any moment to see our project in action."

Indeed, the Mighty Nein arrived, and sooner than Lucien had anticipated. But fortunately, he had already finalized preparations for the gate, double-checked that their threshold crests were still present and accounted for in their packs, and withdrew the two focus rods that would switch the locking mechanism on the gate. Once these were placed correctly, if the lost mage's conjectures were accurate, the eye rune displayed above the gate would glow, clearing the path to Cognouza, thwarting the ancient prison locks.

The adventurers attempted deception, of course, and even managed to nullify several of the intuit charges lying in wait to pay back the stunt that had cost him Otis, Tyffial, and Zoran. Still more were primed to blow, linked by magic to his mind. He had only to consider the charges for an instant, and they would explode. Footsteps crept along the damp tunnel leading to the gate. Cree scampered up to his side, positioning herself breathlessly at the left post of the gate.

"Breathe," he told her. "Our journey begins."

"It's been a long one already," she huffed.

"But nothing compared with what awaits us." Lucien tore off a bit of his shirt and began idly to polish the gate while Cree stood on the other side making final calibrations. He patently ignored Beauregard, who had arrived at the end of the tunnel, wading closer. As the ramp steepened, the water grew shallower, revealing more of her legs. The other adventurers were dispersed in the water running alongside the ramp that led to the gate, and still others were concealed by what they probably considered sly magics.

The eyes revealed all.

He could feel them burning now in heightened anticipation. The voices of the Somnovem crested in his mind like a rising tide, drowning out his own brief flickers of anxiety. Their voices were his—gleeful, ready, celebrating in anticipation of the freedom and the homecoming.

"I think that's far enough," he said, when she was several paces from the top of the ramp and their packs. "For I've my thoughts on turnabout should you take another step."

She paused, and he could feel the eyes reaching for her. Hungry.

"You may have to just twiddle the finger. I know how you figured these little scramblers work, seeing as how you murdered most of our crew with them, so you know that if I think so much as a greener color shade, you all go. And you bleed from every memory."

Slowly he heard the water around the ramp swish and bubble, sensing the clearer presence of the other person most marked by the eyes. Caleb pulled himself onto the ramp, water sluicing from his coat as he stood beside Beau.

"Sorry we're late," said Beauregard.

"I'd say you're quite quick in some ways. I'm impressed." Unseen, Lucien smiled.

Beau took a tiny step forward. "How long have you been here setting up the party by yourself?"

Cree grumbled from the shadows, perhaps obscured by her magical cloak.

"Not terribly long," said Lucien. "Maybe about a better part of an hour. But we had to set up some precautions, since you tend to follow and nip at our heels, and, well, you taught us a few tricks along the way."

Caleb lowered his hands, sighing. "Isn't this the part where you kick back and tell us all your clever plans?"

"Sure. Step in a bit."

The mage did as he was told. Obedience. That was good. The eyes flared.

"I've not been a poor host," he said, turning at last. He felt the eyes react to their presence, as if thrilled by the sight of others bearing the marks. "I lent you my personal reading." He chuckled. "And taking what I was owed, I borrowed a few things with intent to return them, though some of these pretties intrigue me." Lucien cupped his hands together, then smoothly performed a subtle sleight of hand, producing a fragment of round crystal taken from the bag. He sensed the object's power, and filed it away as something to be dealt with at a later time. When he parted his hands, the crystal was gone. "We defended ourselves when assailed and even then I invited you to come see what we've been working on. Letting bygones be what they are and still, you treat us with such animosity. Shame. Manners are important and the last thing to go when an age runs dry. I do still very much want to show you what I've been working on, but I feel like you've shown me how hard it can be to trust. So I need you to earn it."

Cree stumbled toward him, pushing off from the left post of the gate. "Why don't we just kill them, Lucien? Stop the games!"*

Her voice shimmered through his mind. *Think of Zoran, of Otis, Tyffial . . . What did they die for?*

Lucien put his hand up, his eyes never leaving the mage and brawler. "Sh-hh. Because try as I might, a part of me still *likes* them."

Needs them, was perhaps more apt. They bore the marks of the philosophers, and while his claim to Cognouza was greatest of all, they might at least share a fragment of his understanding.

---

* *Bit anticlimactic, don't you think? Womp-womp. I mean, you could kill them with those thought bombs, of course you could, or you could prove to them you were right all along.*

"If they oppose me in Cognouza, their deaths will not be clean."

That's a risk I'm willing to take. Not yet, just . . . Not yet.

"Very well, then their blood is on your hands."

Ours. Our hands.

Beau chose to respond, reaching out to him through the eyes. An even more promising sign. "You should listen to the woman," she told him psychically.

He shrugged, but it turned, unexpectedly, into a shiver. Had the Somnovem failed to warn him that proximity and the spreading influence of the eyes might affect his resolve? No, it was only figment. There was nothing to fear.

Cognouza was only one step further.

Caleb flashed his blue eyes, holding out his hands, inviting Lucien forward. Warmly, the mage said: "Well, tell us more, Circus Man."*

At his side, Lucien's hand twitched.

* *You're slipping.*

You're slipping

You

Slipped

Let go

Let it all go

You're slipping.

Lucien froze. In time, in . . . his mind. Everything went still and black in a flash, immediate reality somehow unreachable, existing outside of a blurred bubble, as if he had blinked and been transported into a snow globe.

Several paces away, a figure stood, watching.

"It's too late for all of this," Lucien sneered. He had no idea if he was speaking aloud or to the vision clouding his mind. "I'm going through."

The figure approached him steadily, their features sharpening on every step, until a lavender-skinned devilkin with curling black horns, a wild mane of purple hair, and twinkling red eyes stared back, a mirror come to life. Lucien froze. He had never been physically faced with . . . himself.

The image reached for him, running a single finger over the visible tattoos on Lucien's right forearm. Then the interloper smiled a far-off smile, as if grinning at a distant memory.

Proud of these.

"Not me," Lucien insisted. "You corrupted the Somnovem's gift."

The mirror image plowed on as if he hadn't heard Lucien at all.

This was right after getting the tattoos finished—you're welcome by the way—and the pain was unbearable, so we went out to find some mead to take the edge off. I remember Yasha was so drunk, just annihilated, and she kept poking me in the arm, and mind you she's nothing but muscle so these pokes are landing like punches. So I kept yelping, "Ouch!" but then she'd forget and five seconds later she'd be at it again. Anyway, as she's drunkenly staring at my arm, she says in her very stoic way: The peacock. He's perfect. The boy peacocks are all pretty and covered in colors, and that's what you are, a ball of color. And then she poked me again and it was awful, and I told her I wasn't exactly a boy, that I felt boy and girl come and go, and change—

"Like the refrains of a song you learn again each day," they spoke in unison.

Fuck.

"Fuck."

You don't have to do this. You don't have to be this.

Lucien recoiled, watching the bubble around them fade and reality return. "All this time in my head and you still can't see—this is what I want to be."

I know you want to change things, Lucien, and you can, but it takes hard work.

"Nothing about this has been easy, and the hard work is at an end. Our chats have been . . . edifying. Goodbye, Tealeaf. You won't survive where I'm going."

CHAPTER 38

There was nowhere left to go but onward. Into the welcome unknown. Lucien flourished his coat and swiveled, positioning himself just before the Immensus Gate. The fissure running through it, still spitting mist and water, looked like a mouth ready to snap wide open. Beauregard and Caleb hesitated, exchanging a glance as Lucien hovered before the doorway.

"Long ago, there was a group of people who had an idea to get away from oppressive minds and pursue their dreams. And when destruction came, not of their making, they were ready. Or so they thought, as they shunted their people across the planes to safety in the Astral Plane, where they knew they could make their dreams a reality." And here, Beauregard and Caleb shared a troubled look. Lucien ignored them, barreling on. "Unfortunately, what they didn't account for was this terrible psychic storm that awaited them, that racked every mind and spirit and shattered them until they became one with their own city. Death would have been a sweet mercy, but instead thousands of people and the Somnovem that guided them were broken, and over time slowly re-formed, powerful, the instinct of their dreams driving them, in a place where they could will their dreams to be, were their will not so fragmented. They needed help. But it was hard to push through the hunger. For now, the city was alive, and things that live need to eat."

He paused for breath, and in doing so felt a wave of terror wash over him, terror and need.

STARVED STARVED STARVED.

GIVE IT TO US NOW.

The Somnovem shrieked and clawed and urged him to hurry.

They could wait awhile longer. This was his moment, not theirs.

"I was lucky to be a mind free, went to speak to it, and there's so much that they could do, but they just lack the guidance. It's a waste of potential. But I think I can show them. And . . . maybe if you decide to be more friend than foe, when all is done, I could make your dreams come true as well."

Lucien gently palmed the first rod they had installed in the gate, twisting it. The cleaved gate behind him bubbled and spit, water beginning to rush in around his feet. The water foamed, washing across his boots and Cree's.

"This door can go many places," he said, nodding to Cree.

She gathered one of the runed rods on the ground, darting around Lucien to breathlessly swap out the old one and push the lever into place. The gate groaned and heaved, some internal mechanism waking up after over a thousand years of slumber.

Beauregard grimaced. "Assuming you want us to go on a little field trip?"

"Well, I'm certainly going on one. I guess it's a shame to work so hard, and, I don't know, not to have anyone who really understands it, who's right there to see it. But I've seen potential in at least a couple of you. You're already walking the right path."

Caleb took a trembling step forward. "And you plan to go and stay there or bring something back and make this world better than how you found it?"

They had been bestowed the gift of the eyes and yet they still knew so little. "Yes."

"And you want us to be an audience?" asked the mage haltingly.

"I'd love an audience, but I'd like for you all to earn your ticket. Come join the show."

Cree cranked the lever one notch further, the eye symbol above the gate, right at its apex, bursting with crimson light.

Lucien threw back his head, filled with the rush of anticipation, and sighed, then inhaled deeply and took a bow. On his way up, he grabbed the lever from Cree, jamming it, the lock irreversibly destroyed. A pulse of sound and energy radiated outward, the seam in the center of the gate widening, revealing a vast starscape beyond. Infinite beauty. Infinite possibility. Purple and silver streamers drifted through the aether, the sudden absence of sound and void leaking from the gate and deadening the air around them. Lucien felt a sudden pressure in his head, sucking against his ears.

A city floated delicately into view, hovering, the foundations torn and ragged, trailing roots and comet tails of stones and bricks. A dizzying array of towers sprang from the broken hunk of city, spires of darkest blue and brightest silver, others of patterned crimson and crystalline white. The nearest, widest tower grew taller even as Lucien beheld it, a crack below a high window opening until a crimson eye bulged outward, surveying what might approach, before closing and disappearing into the outer wall.

The water rose. Lucien hurriedly gathered the wet sack with the threshold crests and the last of their intuit charges, and took Cree by the wrist, dragging her, at last, to Cognouza.

welcome

welcome

welcome

welcome

welcome

welcome   welcome

welcome

guests

minds

kin

so rare

welcome

welcome

welcome us home.

you know the terror of the end   mortal ones

the nothing, the acceptance of fate

or even oblivion. we—we cannot end.

No
at all costs
          oblivion must be
destroyed

we will endure.

CHAPTER 39

So this . . . this was Cognouza.

Lucien's flesh crackled with electricity. The power was total, exhilarating, but terrifying, too, as if he had lived all his life underwater, struggling and clawing, and now he had broken the surface to drink greedily of the air. More and more and more. He needed to see more, feel more, do more. They had entered a vastness, a void, strange red stars twinkling an incalculable distance away. A blossoming jewel of a city winked like a comely girl, coyly concealed by a sheer, high wall of towers.

Lucien held Cree close to his side as they floated in the perfect stillness of space. She clutched him back. "It's incredible, Nonagon. It's just like you promised. I had . . . doubts. I admit, sometimes I had doubts, but it's real, and we're here. It's all real!"

"And our reward is at hand, which I promised, too," he assured her. He had never been so sure of anything in his entire life. He put his left hand out in front of them, imagining a sixth finger there. Before their eyes, that finger grew. He chuckled and imagined it receding, and the finger disappeared. Imagination as reality. Incredible. He unleashed a hideous laugh, finding that the endless nature of this reality was almost too much to bear. They floated toward the city in the distance, moved simply by willing it to happen.

"The voices," Cree hissed, burying her head against his shoulder. "Is this what it's like for you all the time?"

Lucien had hardly noticed the change, but yes, there were a thousand vying screams all around them, coming and going, loud enough to feel like a shock wave upon the skin. He couldn't say whether he had learned to shut them out or if he was simply immune to the noise. When he let it in, it was overwhelming, a throbbing, hot pain at the base of the skull that spread upward and out, wrapping around one's head like a sonic vise.

"Concentrate on my voice and your own thoughts," he told her. "There is one last task to be done, Cree, do you remember?"

Her chest rose and fell sharply as she tried to calm herself and ignore the onslaught of shrieking, pleading voices. He watched her eyes travel to the city and fix on it. The towers undulated as if flesh, beckoning. "The crests . . . they must be placed correctly before the city can be brought to Exandria."

Lucien nodded and untangled their limbs, holding her at arm's length. "Aye, exactly. Now, take the first crest to the heart of the city. Follow the signs for the Praesidis Junction, and I will guide you from there. Once the crest is in place, we meet at the Aether Crux, understood?"

"I . . ." She bit down hard on her lower lip then nodded once. "We're close, aye? Say that we are almost done."

"We made it, Cree," Lucien whispered. Her yellow eyes brightened. "Like I promised: you and me until the very end."

"If it all goes wrong . . . if they catch us . . ."

"It won't. They can't. We're far beyond them now."

"But if it does!"

"I'll bring you back," Lucien promised. "Not bigger or stronger, but just as you are. Now, chin up, the throne lies empty, all that remains to be done is to climb the stairs, claim this land for us, and begin my reign."

"Then your will be done."

"My will be done."

Cree swirled away from him, her dark-red cloak fanning out behind her. As he watched, it seemed to grow longer and longer, spreading like royal velvet wings. She drifted gracefully down to the western edge of the city, to where a ragged, winding road dropped away suddenly into a yawning maw of a pit.

The Mighty Nein would not tarry, he knew, and so he fled east, gliding below the front-most tower with its immense, prowling eye. He shied away from it. What he had planned must not be divined too early.

The Somnovem were searching for him, desperate to gather and bend him to their scheme. No doubt they would attempt to use the eye-marked members of the Mighty Nein against Lucien once they realized his intent.

Nonagon, Nonagon, Nonagon...

They hunted. They searched. Scrambling little voices, prying and seeking. But Lucien had been living with their chatters for years and learned, by painful degrees, to numb himself to it. He had meant what he said—they were useless, mewling babies, and such wild, unfocused power could not be relied upon. Only he could be relied upon—his own wits, his own unmatched determination.

He felt a ripple shake the city as he touched down on the ground. A sob rose from the very cobbles, a searching, high cry repeating: HELP US, HELP US, HELP US.

The message was not for him. Lucien grimaced, running out of time. The western half of the city comprised densely packed towers, clustered like a bundle of kindling, some so close together that there were no alleys, just claustrophobic cracks wide enough to traverse with one's belly pressed to the wall.

Lucien had seen the city only in visions and dreams, and then it had already shifted, grown more fleshy hills and listing towers since the last time he beheld it. Yet he persisted down the same straight path, veering due east, passing through a courtyard of perfectly straight red trees and ivory statues. The statue figures knelt, hands clutching empty faces. A fountain spurting black water bubbled in the center of the courtyard.

The Somnovem hunted. Prowled. Fat, glistening red eyes slid by above his head, floating patrols, the irises spinning chaotically, urgently seeking the Nonagon. As they appeared, Lucien imagined himself not as nothing, but as the interloper. Tealeaf. It was easier, more foolproof, than picturing nothing, which held no substance and no imagery. The Somnovem were not interested in Mollymauk Tealeaf, they were interested solely in the Nonagon.*

---

* *Risky biscuits, don't you think? You're already on the verge. Already slipping.*

"Impressed? I knew you would be good for something."

You're a clever bastard, I'll give you that.

"Sit back and enjoy the show."

At the eastern edge of the courtyard stood a sign reading: GARDEN OF ERRANCY.

Lucien left the courtyard behind, entering the garden, racing with unnatural speed to a cluster of rosebushes, the orange blossoms weeping what looked and smelled like human bile. He dropped the sack carrying a glowing blue shard of threshold crest and buried it deep in the bushes, beyond anyone's notice.

A voice echoed around him, searching, wanting, but it was different from the others. Crisper. Lucien focused on it, finding Cree calling out to him.

"Nonagon!" she cried. "Nonagon . . ." Then, more softly, rasping, coughing, "Lucien."

Her voice grew weaker, her presence, her soul marked with the beacons of the Nine Eyes, dimmed. She was dying. Lucien stood, brushing dirt from his trousers while she sputtered, psychically pleading from across the city. The Mighty Nein had found her.

She's lost to me now.

He wouldn't be able to save her in this moment, but he would bring her back, every hair, every claw, every whisker in its rightful place. What manner of king failed his subjects? Her loyalty would be repaid in his new world. Lucien turned away from the weeping bush, staring at the tower directly ahead, beyond the statues and black fountain. The windows there were darkened except for one, a single, resolute candle glowing on the sill.

"Did you place the crest?" he asked Cree, the eyes on his body fluorescing.

"Y-Yes, but—"

"You're certain? It's in place?"

"Yes!"

Exhaling shakily, he passed a hand over his face. Her voice quavered, and had she the life left in her, she would have shed tears. "You and me," she cried. "You and me standing at the end . . . that was our destiny. You told me, it was meant to be you and me!"

"And so, it is," he told her. The others were probably listening. He didn't care. "The end has passed, Cree. I stand now at the threshold. Reborn." In his mind, she shuddered and went silent. The eyes showed him her final stand: The Mighty Nein fell upon her in a dark and fleshy hall pocked with pillars. They surprised her with the first shot, a magic bolt sending her immediately off balance. Cognouza itself tried to repel them, tried to protect her, sensing Lucien's need of her. Yasha charged, slashing at Cree with her longsword while green fire erupted from the half-orc's hands, eldritch fire searing down the tunnel. Blood. Blood and flesh, the blood and flesh of the city and of Cree. Her life force ebbed as Beau joined the fray, peppering her with blows . . .

Cree curled herself inside her magic cloak, desperate to escape. The magic failed, sabotaged by Caleb. She tried to run, but the Mighty Nein were relentless, and she hopelessly outnumbered. Yasha advanced, cutting off her escape, thrusting her longsword into Cree's belly, her soft, broken body draped forward over the blade.

It was too soon for her to go.

"You've done well. But I need you to hold them off a little longer. I'm not done. I'm not ready yet. Become a vessel for the pattern and show them the way."*

He needed her still, but he needed her to change. Yasha shoved Cree off her sword with her boot, sending her sprawling, limp, to the wet, puddled ground. Callous. He vowed to remember it. Better still, Cree might take her revenge.

Yes, he needed her still. And so he imagined her anew: a creature, an unstoppable force, spreading, growing, flesh and matter free of what their reality had demanded. Her rib cage broke through the skin, unfurled, beautiful, almost, viscera and muscle cascading into a star. He splattered her across the floor, let her expand, arms and new tentacles lurching upward, claws spinning like a whir of murderous blades. The red eyes on her new body burned bright. Her bones cracked and splintered and embedded themselves in the fleshly arms, every part of her a weapon.

She was already going to die, he insisted, this just made her that much more potent. He broke her open and remade her, shoved her toward the Mighty Nein, and in the back of his throat, he tasted smoke and ash. Lucien knew she couldn't hold out against them for much longer. He turned his attention back to the tower before him. The candle

---

* *That's cold. Even for you.*

"Still convinced I can change?"

No, but you keep letting the Mighty Nein get away, mm? You haven't killed my friends.

"Yet."

flame in the tower window bent sideways, twice, the light flickering, fighting, before it went out. Then it was all dark. Lucien imagined the pathway to his goal, silencing, irrevocably, the channel running between him and Cree. The sky above him lit up with searing red lines, fractals sketching themselves across the stars, burning brighter and brighter and then flaming out.

The path he needed appeared before him, a straight, shadowy tunnel piercing into the ground. Cobbles flew, trees shook, and Lucien ducked into the passageway, hurrying toward the heart of Cognouza. The Aether Crux. The pitch-black tunnel stretched on for what seemed like a hundred miles, but there were no limitations to his speed, and so he dove through it, eyes filling with tears as the wind whipped at him. The Somnovem were digging, nipping at his heels, their sight sharper and sharper as he neared the Aether Crux, where their nine minds met to converse and debate and exist as one.

At last, the way forward leveled out, dumping him onto a soft, undulating floor. Tiny fissures and lines ran through the bluish-white substance beneath his feet, zinging lights traveling along the strings, drawing his eye to a pillar in the center of the chamber, where nine bulbous red orbs hung. Wet sinew bound the eyes together, clustering them like a deformed tumor, each shot through with veins and lit from within by blistering orange light. As they pulsed, he could see the irises spinning wildly within.

Here. The Nonagon. Here. At last, at last!

The irises found him in unison, fixing on his position, the giddy, childlike laughter of Gaudius filling his head. He hadn't missed it, the way he had felt a jolt of bereavement when they abandoned him before in the wake of their tantrum. *Tantrum* once more became an apt word, for the voices lashed out, hungrier, angrier, needier . . .

Children. Spoiled, rotten children.

Lucien clucked his tongue as he unloaded the sack slung over his shoulder. The intuit charges sprang free, guided by his imagination to hang around him, a dangerous constellation. A red pulse of light blasted through the chamber with each bomb that orbited him.

Is it not what we promised?

Nonagon, you come at last! But you are displeased . . .

Exandria awaits us. The glory of Aeor rises once more!

He released the final of the ten charges, then retraced his steps to the tunnel leading away. Settling against the wall, he willed his mind to quiet and imagined himself nothing more than the same repulsive flesh as the chamber's walls. Across from him, the cluster of eyes—the Somnovem themselves—stared, the distraction finished, as they were forced to keep track of both his movements and those of the Mighty Nein. They had bet on the Nein—the irony not escaping him—and now the adventurers arrived, coming as he did, through a passage they simply imagined into existence.

He watched them tumble out into the room and discover the Aether Crux, enjoying their expressions of mounting horror at what they had found. The Somnovem spoke as one, each individual voice layered on top of the other, begging the Mighty Nein and the purple-skinned, white-haired elf that accompanied them to locate the Nonagon.

He was here, but he has vanished from our sight.

Where?

WHERE

He seeks to end us, kill us, but you must not allow it! Bring him to us, bring him . . .

Lucien pushed away from the wall, making himself known.

"Well, I'm glad you came," he said, priming the intuit charges with a single, happy thought. "The invitation was there, and you've all proven exactly as useful as I hoped."

We are the Somnovem. We are consciousness evolved through high emergence. We thank you for coming. We welcome our children who see with our eyes. You walk the path of the Nonagon. And though through, you will become one. We will not grant your every desire. We will teach you how to manifest them.

Dreams are the mind testing its limits. Reaching out and expanding the will. Consciousness is boundless with awakened will. A soul is consciousness. The soul should not be trapped in a short-lived vessel and collected by treacherous idols as a trophy. Dreams are the minds discovering potential, and together, we, the Somnovem, have become Dream. Every mind, every soul, deserves to know this joy, this endless understanding of purpose and meaning. We are a proto-realm, a new plane of existence about to be born, the next step in the evolution of life and the enduring spirit.

We are just the spark. It would be meaningless to hoard our understanding. It is the right of every living being to know our joy. It is their inevitable reward for the trials and toil of running the divine maze under the alien minds of false gods. They deserve to be with us and we will not deny everyone their destiny.

We are the Somnovem Omega.

CHAPTER 40

The Mighty Nein turned to face him, seemingly untouched by their battle with Cree. Had her sacrifice been for nothing? It seemed impossible, for they should have encountered untold dangers in this strange realm. But that was immaterial. They had come, as he knew they would, and the curtain was rising, revealing the stage and his throne upon it.

He watched Beau raise her fists, and Jester, with her darling horns and puffy white coat, covered her mouth, a burst of pink butterflies flying from her hands as she did.

Lucien gestured to the bulging eyes behind them. "These people, this city—tragic in its fall, yes, but glorious in its discoveries. The Somnovem had studied and prepared enough to harness their terrible fate, but in doing so, they were reborn greater than they could have ever anticipated. The power of a thousand minds, dreams, imaginations, and wills made one, founded in the aether of manifestation. A miracle. Unstoppable. Yet—rudderless, fractured, wild, jealous, impotent."

He could almost perceive the thoughtful steam rising from their heads as they each tried to think their way out of the trap, or remember the right thing, or somehow outrun the beast that was already gnawing at their necks.

"I once saw them as gods, beings so far beyond my ability to understand. And they chose me to be their herald. But when I died, when I scattered, when they put me back together, I was given a view behind the curtain, and I saw the fallacy. I'd given everything for genius souls, now mewling toddlers, bickering over the power of creation. Someone needed to be the parent. When children have been acting out, making a mess of their potential, for this long even, a responsible caretaker must show discipline, enact punishment, and take the reins with force. So I invite you to stay for the show, but I think you'd prefer to run."

And so they did—adorably, he thought—for it would only prolong their lives a little longer. They raced by him on their way to the tunnel leading up and out, the Somnovem's screams of betrayal following. The ground beneath him gave a jolt, the impish little infernal casting some quaking spell at him on the way out.

Lucien laughed as the Mighty Nein vanished down the tunnel. The charges blew, cracks splintering across the floor becoming gashes becoming gaps wide enough for a man to slip through. The city sank, and Lucien along with it.

Lights flashed in front of his closed eyes. After a time, he realized he had slipped out of consciousness. Gone. Screams echoed in the distance, pulsing, rhythmic, each beat bringing the noise closer. When it reached him, it fused with his heartbeat. He had no concept of how far he might have fallen, though he had sustained several grievous cuts across his abdomen and arms. Blood wept from him freely, pooling on the fleshy ground. His clothes had been shredded. Someone was on the ground beside him. Lucien frowned, reaching for the body and rolling it.

Brevyn.

She was just as she had been in life—tall, muscular, her sunflower-yellow hair pillowed all around her. As he watched, her eyelids flickered and then opened. Grinning, she poked him in the nose.

"Creepy. Why are you watching me sleep?"

Lucien blinked, confused. Words came to him, unbidden, a memory replaying itself now in this land of total dreams. "Just admiring you. I always am. You're easy to admire, you know."

"I know."

"I never did ask," he said quietly, brushing his palm across her bare chest, where the fresh tattoo glistened. "Why the butterfly?"

"All the usual bullshit—transformation, change, something dumb and ugly turning into something wonderful," she said with a light shrug. "Do you like it?"

He did. He came back to himself, realizing that he hadn't told her what he wanted to in that moment—that he was terribly afraid, afraid that he had been something tender and colorful and lovely to behold and was becoming something else.

"You're brilliant," he had told her, taking her into his arms. "Vivid, strange, an exclamation mark in the middle of a whisper."

Brevyn clung to him. When he gently let her go, he was holding a frozen corpse, or half of one, brittle, the exposed bits of stomach hard as stale sausage. He heaved and closed his eyes, stumbling away. Was he dreaming? He must be. No, he could be. Anything was possible in this place. He decided it had been a dream, and when he opened his eyes again, he stood in that same pale, fleshy spot, surrounded by what seemed like velvet-soft black petals, as if he were enclosed in a towering tulip.

The Somnovem, he realized, had grown quiet. The petals released gradually, revealing the Aether Crux in shambles around him. The nine egglike eyes laid in a heap, a collapsed sack. Slowly, Lucien lifted into the air. The eyes upon his body flared and tingled and burned, then vanished. One by one, they became bumps, detaching, the skin tearing and remaking itself, the pain incredible, illuminating, as sharp and exhilarating as a whole new idea. The eyes moved, traveled across his skin, shifting and gathering along his back. He drew in a deep breath, hunched, and then the eyes grew outward once more, longer this time, muscular stalks that hovered up and out, cartilaginous as wings.

The floor glowed softly beneath his feet.

"Command us," came the first voice. Fastidan. Lucien smiled. So. *So.*

It was all as he wanted, all as he designed. No more voices in his head, only separate entities to command. There were, however, loose ends in his domain. They had served their purpose, and if they cooperated, they could fuse with this new, intriguing form of his.

They should be so lucky.

"Unexpected," he murmured, his voice the city's voice, his heartbeat the city's heartbeat. He stretched out his arms, watching the cuts slowly begin to mend. He flexed the muscles in his back, testing the feel of the eyestalks. "But still, I needed a little time to heal. I've always wanted to be a butterfly, anyway. Come."

THEY FOUND HIM ON A rising hill at the center of Cognouza. The ground shifted at his command, lifting the land like a swelling tide. The towers of the city were as soft as the undulating ground, bending toward him, enfolding him, protecting him as if concerned for his modesty while he finished his rest and adapted to his new form. The pulsing red sacks of the Somnovem hung behind him like the red moon Ruidus itself.

He heard the Mighty Nein and their elf companion approaching, and the chrysalis of obliging towers released, the city regaining its shape as Lucien was revealed. Lifting in the air, he floated to receive the trespassers, eager to be beheld and known and admired. For who could not admire this new, bizarre form? So perfect. So earned.

They had come through an imagined tunnel of their own, one that he allowed, for now his will was the will of Cognouza. At last, his dreams were material and his hands the ready shapers. The Mighty Nein gathered, glancing at one another, the horror plain on their faces as Lucien reached out to meet them, the eyestalks hovering and peering over his shoulder, curious as could be.

"We welcome you. I welcome you. This is incredible. I'd always wondered, but this is . . ." Lucien breathed deeply. "This is something."

Beauregard gaped at him, for once, her smugness all forgotten. "What's it like?"

"Oh." Lucien sighed.

He gave them all a taste, filling their minds with just a fraction of the power and sight now available to him. Colors beyond comprehension. The combined knowledge of a cosmos yet to be fully explored. The heat and radiance of a thousand stars. Blood burst from their noses.

"I wish I could share it, but there's . . . Well, you'd need to be with us. You have to be with the pattern."

The blue infernal stumbled forward, shaking. "The pattern?" asked Jester.

The half-orc took a more direct approach. He pushed Jester out of the way, leveling a finger at Lucien. "You've left us alive. You said you wanted an audience. We're here now, it doesn't seem like many more are. What was it all for?"

That seemed like an oversight he wouldn't make. Lucien frowned. "I left you alive. Why did I leave you alive?"

Silence. Then, ever so softly, Jester tiptoed around Fjord, whispering, "molly?"

Beau sighed and wiped the blood away from her mouth. "If there's no one to watch your ascension . . ."

But Lucien wasn't paying attention to her; his eyes stayed firmly on Jester.

"Hmm?" he grunted.

"Molly?" she suggested again, louder this time.

Caleb joined her, placing his hand on her far shorter shoulder. "Mollymauk Tealeaf."

Distractions. These were just petty distractions. It could be rectified. The eyes on his back twisted to perceive Caleb.

"No, child. I needed witnesses, yes. To hear my birth cry."

He raised his arms and Cognouza trembled, then heaved, the ground rolling and rolling in a nauseating pattern until at last the very air seemed to inhale itself and release, a wail echoing across the towers.

Jester covered her ears, tiptoeing one step farther. Tentatively, in a tiny voice, she began to sing: "For the dead yellow king, a throng came and sang on the longest day of rain. He would not rise again, long, long may he reign . . ."*

Beauregard joined in, out of tune, but willing.

"Toya . . ." Jester trailed off. "Do you remember her? She had the kindest face . . ."

Lucien twitched, one eyestalk drooping before he composed himself again. Enough distractions. They would become part of the pattern, they would be absorbed, or they would perish. The order hardly mattered. "Well, I do believe now it's time to take the city back to where it all began."

Caleb shook his head vigorously, visibly perspiring. "Oh, but surely—"

Lucien stretched his arms wide again and sighed. "Where the pattern can reach all the minds."

---

* *Toya's song . . . I remember it from the circus. She said it was a favorite from the Menagerie Coast.*
silence, abomination

"Th-There'll be time for that later," the mage stammered, shoving Jester behind him.

"Do you still intend to leave the world better than you found it?" asked Beauregard. He had a dim memory of discussing their dreams and intentions while encamped near the River Inferno. That was another time. Another lifetime.

Well, do you? She's got a point. This doesn't look like charity to me.

how? how have you escaped your confinement?

You're slipping, old boy. Circus Man.

Lucien growled, the eyes upon his back wriggling uncontrollably. "Where's the other crest? I can't feel it. What have you done?" Cree . . . They destroyed her and removed the crest. He should have foreseen as much. Cognouza would never reach Exandria, but the Immensus Gate had been opened, the Somnovem breached and controlled, and now the realm of dreams was his to rule. He flitted from mind to mind, prodding each of the Mighty Nein in turn. "Well then, through dreams it'll be, then. Whom do you care about? Whom shall I reach out to in their night's slumber? And show them the pattern until they come and bring me what I need? Your husband?"

The eyes focused on the halfling, Veth, still wearing her antlers and earmuffs even in the twisted nightmare of Cognouza.

"What?" she squeaked.

"Your boy? Maybe they can make the trek up, too, and bring me the other crest I need."

Veth reached for Yasha's hand. Yasha gathered the halfling close as Veth blurted, "No, no, I don't think they will. They don't steal from nice people!"

Lucien nodded, unconcerned with their obstinance. These were the quibbles of ants. They were droplets in the deluge. Powerless. "One by one, they will all begin to see as you have. They'll begin their own paths to becoming my Nonagon. I am the Neo-Somnovem, and in time another Nonagon shall rise."

After all, there were still several crests littered throughout Aeor. All was not lost.

Beauregard slid next to Veth and Yasha, grabbing the angel-blooded woman by the arm and yanking. "Why don't you ask *the charm* about it? The charm is here."

Yasha's face flamed but she lifted her chin high.

That's her. The charm. Do you remember? The circus, the lights, the way Yasha's rare smile just lights up the whole fucking night? I know you remember her. She's like your Brevyn, Circus Man. She and I might only have been friends, but I think you have a type.

they will be one with the pattern

Lucien let the ground drop away, rising to the tops of Cognouza's towers, taking the trespassers with him. They were not coming willingly. If only they could see it, know it, feel in their hearts the power and wisdom of the pattern, infinite and peaceful in its eternal repetition. Well. He had given everything for this moment, and now it was his to claim. They would join the pattern, join with him. It was time for integration to commence.

CHAPTER 41

The Nine Eyes were eager to serve the Neo-Somnovem, and Lucien reached for them each in turn. They hung behind him in their heart-beating sacks, flickering with internal lightning, brightening the sky as Cognouza slipped away below them. The stars were their battlefield, and it was almost all too easy.

They could struggle and fight, and hurl their magic, surround him, encroach, swing fists and swords and whatever they wished, but the realm of Cognouza responded to Lucien's every thought. The Somnovem proved useful soldiers, controlling what he could not, filling his enemies' heads with visions of delight or guilt or terror as needed. No longer did they prey upon his thoughts; they existed only to be wielded.

Yet as one stumbled, another rose. Relentless.

Yeah, they're like that. Sometimes irritating, but I'm loving it just now.

be silent

Fat chance, friend. You're fighting the Mighty Nein, and you're fighting me, too.

all will join the pattern, you included

Beauregard somersaulted toward him, flying through the sky, aiming a flurry of punches at his right side. The pain was negligible, but she came armed with words, too. "Don't you still want to see Gustav, now that you've paid off his debt?"

Unbidden, the image of a lanky half-elf in a ludicrous top hat flashed across his mind. Pain seared up his back. Yet again unbidden, he thought fondly of the circus barker, who had always been in anguish over his terrible debts. But now that burden was lifted and . . . and . . .

Lucien slashed with his hands, gnashing his teeth. Those were the memories of a weak fleshling, not the Neo-Somnovem.

The blue infernal girl decided to give it a try, too, prodding him, waving to get his attention. Lucien gave it to her, rocketing across the sky, landing nose-to-nose with her. She shrieked and leaned back, scrunching up her face. "You see? It's—it's—fuck. It's just like the tarot reading said, Molly! You had to die. You had to die to be reborn!"

She's right, this is awfully coincidental . . . But then, you don't believe in coincidences, do you, Chosen One?

Lucien laughed in her face. "Oh, little girl, don't you know those cards are stacked every time? Simple storytelling. Make you hear what you think you want to hear."

Fjord was swift to follow, soaring toward them and slashing with his broadsword, struggling to balance as he lashed out at Lucien. "We're all circus people. We all have our issues."

Circus Man

Circus Man

Circus Man!

The eyestalks pinwheeled, unfocused. There were too many, surrounding him, bombarding him . . . Perhaps he could just concentrate and banish the interloper shrieking at him from within. Lucien clawed at his own chest, raking it open, blood foaming and pouring down his naked chest.

"Somnovem!" he thundered. "Elatis! Ira!"

The sack of eyes behind him lit up, their attention falling on the angel blood, who navigated the sky deftly with her ivory, feathered wings.

Why are you choosing her? Why Yasha?

Lucien roared. Elatis in her red, gooey sack flickered and flashed, Yasha hesitating, shaking her head, invaded by the voices of the Somnovem. Bent to their will. She whirled and let out a cry of rage, seeking out Beauregard amid the chaos. That would do nicely, Lucien decided. Let them fight among one another for a spell.

It did not last long, for almost as quickly as he commanded the eyes to control Yasha, another of the Mighty Nein had dispelled the illusion.

They could not be stopped.

You're slipping.

Lucien spun, erratic, trembling with frustration. This was his realm of dreams, not his tomb, whatever the blighted little blue infernal claimed. Cards and carnivals and meaningless chatter . . . He had suffered their resistance long enough. The pattern waited. The pattern called.

Molly! He had lost track of where the voices were coming from. They were all around now, encroaching, enclosing . . . *Molly! We miss you! Molly! Molly, I've never forgiven myself for not being there when you died. I wish I could have saved you. I wish I could've done something . . .*

On and on. On and on and on. It could not be tolerated.

Too much? Why? Because nobody will miss you when you're gone?

Lucien threw his arms wide, the Somnovem sacks suddenly free falling, hurled toward the city waiting below. "I think I've been doing this on my own a little bit too much. Now that I've flexed this a bit, let's borrow the full power of the city around me."

He dove down, streaking across the sky like a boulder loosed from a catapult. The city braced for his coming, then opened to greet him, a portal in the ground swallowing him, granting blessed relief. The voices, the taunting . . . He just needed to think. To be silent. To let his imagination truly stretch and unfurl. It was obvious to him now: He was simply thinking too small.

They won't stop, you know. They will never stop fighting you. It can all be over.

Lucien curled up in a ball in the darkness. The Somnovem drew close, enfolding him. He felt their nearness, their fear, their disdain. They loathed him now, of course, for he had foiled their plans and punished them, and made them his nine weapons. But they were part of Cognouza and Cognouza was now part of him. He shivered, bones rattling, teeth clattering, and slid into a deep, brief sleep.

He dreamed only of himself.

When the Mighty Nein returned, tunneling into the sanctum created by the city, he was more than ready to begin again. Brevyn, Otis, Zoran, Jurrell, Tyffial, and *Cree* . . . they had all died for this chance at paradise. They were not nothing, they were simply not as much as him.

I am Cognouza, he thought, renewed. Reinvigorated. *I am the hand that puppets the nightmare, that spins the web of dreams. I am the Neo-Somnovem, and my Nonagon waits to rise.* Empty. He felt empty. And then, when the interlopers arrived, he felt new.

The Somnovem released him. *Unleashed* him. There was a deep, strange pull in his belly. Red walls covered him, contained him, and then gradually were shed. When he rose, he found he had grown, no longer the size of a normal creature, but expansive as the city itself. He spun upward and the eyestalks vanished, instead unfurling wings with the span of city blocks. Lucien lifted his hands, sharp with claws, his teeth painful in his mouth as they too grew and grew, dripping from a malformed, melting jaw. Ropey tentacles of flesh clung to the stones of Cognouza, sinuous fibers glittering with eyeballs like beads anchored him to the foundation even as he sprang from it.

This vast chamber, once the Aether Crux, was now the empty womb that birthed him.

I gotta say, I preferred you the other way. Yeesh.

This rebirth, it seemed, had not rid him of the poison seeping through his mind.

The Mighty Nein launched upon him, fighting what they could not possibly defeat. Cognouza reached for them, for the fresh meat of their bodies, dragging them down into the churning, bubbling cauldron of meat beneath their boots.

"My city is hungry!" he shrieked. "We are ravenous to expand!"

The Somnovem eyes drifted apart, separating and floating, still responding to his commands, targeting his attackers, racking them with visions of guilt and loss. Fastidan gathered strength, hovering over Lucien's deformed shoulder, sending a blistering beam of wither and blight to scorch the skin of those who dared slash at city made flesh.

Why do they fight like this? Hellions. Incredible. And they lift each other up, and they do all of this together.

Together.

Tealeaf echoed whatever blather the Mighty Nein hurled at him. They would find no sympathy, no reprieve . . . But he felt a strange twisting with each mention of Mollymauk's name. As he had grown and spread, so too did the troublesome little fragment inside him. As Lucien's body melted into the foundations of Cognouza and filled in the cracks, so too did Mollymauk's power inhabit the gaps in his mind.

Don't forget. Don't you fucking dare forget the people who died to bring you here. What would Brevyn say, if she could see you like this? If she could see what you did to Cree. Do you think she would be proud? Every vision you've had of her, everything I've seen, I know she would be ashamed. You're unrecognizable.

Worse, you're a puppet of something you don't even understand.

Lucien tensed, wings trembling, as a vision of Brevyn flashed in front of his eyes. She was reaching for him, crushed, *dying*. Without the interloper's prompting, he imagined his sister, Aldreda, and the look of horror that would darken her lovely face if she could see him in this form. No, no, this was trickery. Deceit. They would revel in his newfound power, they would relent and join the pattern, they would . . .

They would . . .

The Mighty Nein were scattered before him. Caleb flourished a spell toward Lucien's chest, the beam smoldering and turning bits of his exposed rib cage to ash. "Mollymauk! Molly! I am begging you, hunger for control is insatiable. It will never be enough. Let it go."

"He's gone," Lucien hissed, seething into the mage's mind. It had to be true. For Lucien to live, Molly had to be annihilated. "Let him go. Let it all go. Go, go, go, go."

Veth threw herself at the stones twisted around the tendons of Lucien's lower half. He lashed out with his clawed wings, knocking her aside, her body tumbling away. At once, the city slopped sinew over her, beginning to take her, absorbing her into the pattern. The angel blood swooped down to protect the fallen halfling, spreading out her own white wings and tearing brutally at the flesh dragging the girl down. The mage fell next, the elf crying out as if he had been the one struck down. As with Veth, the elf grabbed for Caleb, trying to keep the city from taking him.

My friends are smart, Circus Man. Watch out.

Lucien twisted, wings flexed, realizing that the clever thorn in his side, Beauregard, had mustered the others to use their own imaginations against him. They conjured snakes as tall as the towers of Cognouza, godlike cobras lashing out to sting him. What was real in his mind was real in theirs, too, for this was the land where ideas were matter, and the snake tore into his wing, yanking him hard to the side. The appendage ignited, burned by a sudden conjuration from the infernal, Jester.

Lucien slashed and clawed, catching Jester and scooping her up, throwing her into the air like a rag doll before impaling her on the end of his sharpened, clawed wing. He threw her down, more meat for the ravenous city. In his momentary pride, he did not see Yasha screaming toward him, shot like an arrow, slashing with her sword and slicing a deep gash across his midsection. Then she was gone, joining Jester, protecting her.

"You're killing her, you're killing her, you love her, you're killing her!" Caleb flung himself forward, crawling, beating the ground. Lucien snarled. Caleb's hits tickled. His words, however, tore.

Who dreams like this? Mollymauk Tealeaf's voice quaked in his mind. His skull split, a crack splintering up the back of it. He reeled, vision blurring for an instant. The city repaired him, slopping fleshy goo over the broken bone of his head.

Once upon a time, there was a happy family . . .

In the dream they would be whole again. In Cognouza, it would all be fixed. He looked down at the towering ruin his body had become. He told himself it wasn't too far gone, then pulled his shoulders back and clawed raw wounds down his monstrous face, smiling all the while, his teeth becoming fangs becoming tusks.

Once upon a time . . .

It echoed and echoed through his broken head. He glimpsed Jester struggling onto her side, with her last breath casting a spell to heal and mend her friends. Such care. Such tenacity.

This is who they are. They will use their own bodies to shield one another. A squeeze of the hand, a kiss on the forehead . . .

A kiss on the forehead, Lucien's last touch given to Brevyn. Another kiss came to him like a tricky word just on the tip of his tongue, elusive yet tantalizing, though the sentiment felt real enough—a friend in crisis emerging to a kiss on the forehead. A tender banishment. Caleb. Softness and light. Clammy skin under rough lips. Molly's nose brushing Caleb's hair . . .

Those memories were gone. All of it was lost to him now.

Kindness is never lost or forgotten.

Blood spouted from Lucien's lips, the tears down his cheeks joining with the ragged hole of his mouth. Beauregard sprang to the base of the tower, laying into his stomach, pummeling him with fists glowing red with empowered flames. She had wrapped something purple around her hand, a familiar, gaudy pattern now spattered with blood. Mollymauk's belt.

"Long may he reign!" she screamed, spit flying from her lips as she struck.

"Now!" he heard one of them say, though he was too twisted around, too distracted to know which. The foundations beneath him and inside of him quaked, then began to shake apart. He reached for nothing with his hands, the city collapsing beneath him, tearing him asunder as the sinews growing into the stones gave.

The towers around them began to sink, disappearing beneath the ground, toppling, breaking in half as the remaining Eyes of Nine flared and then dropped like anchors out of the sky, exploding into pockets of fire. Jester, her face crusted with gore, her legs tremulous and failing, reared up, finding the strength for one last spell.

Take us home, Jester. Are you tired, Lucien? You look tired.

So tired, he thought, and then: *And here, so quickly, my reign is over. Unless . . .*

"I know you're in there, Molly," Jester cried, her voice, somehow strong, echoed against the crumbling towers. "We love you so much and we want you back. Lucien doesn't deserve you."

I don't, he thought.

Unless . . .

Unless.

When a hand reaches out to you in accord, you take it.

Yes, Lucien thought, *I'll take it.*

The bright blast of a spell punched into his chest, a rain of blood and sparks exploding from the wound. Lucien pushed his hands into the opening, pulling against the flesh and bones, eager, at last, for the pain to stop. There was a flicker of laughter somewhere in the distance, and a smile he wanted to curl up inside of, and a promise of a long sleep at the end of a longer journey. This was the realm of dreams, after all, and anything was possible.

And so, they pulled themselves apart, knuckles grazing as they did, and in the city of a hundred thousand maybes, it was over.

For a time.

The woman with skin like the ocean and twin moons for eyes greets you with a demure smile. She parts a curtain you thought was the sky and sits before you once more. The way she observes you, it makes you feel safe, like everything might just be all right. Her smile is the smile of your mother or father, your grandmother, your older sister, whoever rubbed your back when you were little and you couldn't sleep.

Her black silk gown shifts and settles, and she shuffles a deck of colorful oracle cards. They look familiar. She fans out the full deck and offers them to you.

"Go ahead," she prods. "Pick one. Don't be shy."

You do, sliding one card free, facedown.

The woman with deep-blue skin takes the card and places it faceup on her palm, showing you. It's a woman with streaming white and black hair, a face like vindication, wild wings spreading from her strong figure. A pennant hanging from a trumpet streams behind her. She reminds you of the one with angel blood, Yasha.

"The Love card," the woman murmurs. "Do you know what that means? It's okay if you don't." After a moment, the card begins to tremble, a single, delicate, green tendril sprouting, unfurling upward. "Here we go: Once upon a time, twice upon a time." She pauses and giggles. "*Thrice* upon a time, f—"

Her white brow furrows. "Hang on. What comes after thrice? Does anyone know?" She glances around for help, but no one answers. "Isn't that the strangest thing? There is nothing after thrice in the sequence, it just ends there. But that doesn't seem right, does it? Or fair. Well. I think we shall just have to make it up."

As you watch, the brave little sprout grows and grows, stretching.

"One might call that a miracle," she whispers. "Perhaps fourth time's the charm."

EPILOGUE

Empty. He was empty. But not for long. Two hands shook, unlikely as that may seem, and something new was born. His skin was lavender, and his eyes were stunningly red, and his name was Kingsley Tealeaf.

Long may he reign.

ACKNOWLEDGMENTS

There are some rather obvious folks to thank for this one, namely the brilliant minds behind the achievement that is Critical Role. The creativity, humor, and humanity of the cast were a constant inspiration, and I'm fortunate to be playing in their sandbox. Specifically, I want to thank Matt Mercer and Taliesin Jaffe for being so generous with their characters, and for allowing me the space to get weird. I'd also love to thank Dani Carr, Niki Chi, Shaunette DeTie, and Adrienne Cho, although we need to have a conversation about Dog Jokes.

Thanks to Elizabeth Schaefer for getting me started and on the right path. Sarah Peed, what can I say? You were the guiding light on this project. You are such a talent, such a joy, and your patience and enthusiasm made this a blast even on the hard days.

Kate McKean is the agent supreme, and I'm forever indebted to her for believing in my voice and my work. Thanks also to Trevor Smith for keeping the machine running smoothly, and to my dogs for understanding when I couldn't go on the walk.

I'd also like to acknowledge the following books for the heaps of inspiration they provided: *House of Leaves* by Mark Z. Danielewski and *The King in Yellow* by Robert W. Chambers.

MADELEINE ROUX is the *New York Times* bestselling author of the Asylum series, which has sold in eleven countries around the world. She is also the author of the House of Furies series, *Salvaged, Traveler: The Shining Blade,* and the Allison Hewitt Is Trapped series, and she has contributed to anthologies including *Resist, Scary Out There,* and *Star Wars: From a Certain Point of View.*

madeleine-roux.com
Twitter: @Authoroux
Instagram: @authoroux

CRITICAL ROLE is one of the fastest-growing independent media companies in the world, starting as a roleplaying game between friends and evolving into a new kind of organization dedicated to storytelling, community, and imagination. As Critical Role continues to expand the unique universe it has created, with complex stories set in an ever-evolving world, it also continues to create more ways to experience the brand, including books on the *New York Times* Best Sellers list, comic books and graphic novels, collectibles, tabletop and roleplaying games, podcasts, live events, and an animated series, *The Legend of Vox Machina,* airing exclusively on Amazon Prime Video. Additionally, Critical Role has launched two major initiatives: an official 501(c)(3) nonprofit, the Critical Role Foundation, and a tabletop game publishing company, Darrington Press. With an original cast of award-winning veteran voice actors who are also co-founders of the company, including Matthew Mercer, Ashley Johnson, Marisha Ray, Taliesin Jaffe, Travis Willingham, Sam Riegel, Laura Bailey, and Liam O'Brien, Critical Role is committed to ensuring anyone can discover its stories, characters, and community.

critrole.com